**Jeremy Dyson** was born and raised in Leeds. He is the author of the highly acclaimed short story collection *Never Trust a Rabbit*, which was nominated for the Macmillan Silver Pen Award.

Jeremy Dyson is co-writer of the television series *Funland* and the BAFTA award-winning *The League of Gentlemen*. He lives in London.

Praise for *What Happens Now*

'A beautiful sense of pathos hangs over the whole novel ... Dyson's one of those rare authors who can write from the heart while still creating something deceptively clever and complex' *Independent on Sunday*

'Written with genuine verve and insight, this is a surprisingly moving exploration of how ordinary lives come to be controlled and defined by fear' *Daily Mail*

'Jeremy Dyson's original novel probes the perils of an overactive imagination. It's as mordant and original as you would expect from *The League of Gentlemen*'s co-writer' *Observer*

'Darkly addictive. Dyson has created an unputdownable story that twists and turns its way to a satisfying ending' *Sunday Business Post*

'Intriguing, funny debut ... The dialogue is great, as is the characterisation' *Daily Mirror*

'A compelling novel about faith, fear and the power of the imagination, a gripping read about two frightened people, haunted by ghosts from their past' *Word*

'Poignant ... nostalgic ... engrossing' *GQ*

'A memorable tale of love, pain and redemption' *The List*

*Also by Jeremy Dyson*

NEVER TRUST A RABBIT

# WHAT HAPPENS NOW

Jeremy Dyson

ABACUS

First published in Great Britain as a paperback original in 2006 by Abacus
This edition published in 2007

Copyright © Jeremy Dyson 2006

The moral right of the author has been asserted.

A CIP catalogue record for this book
is available from the British Library.

ISBN: 978-0-349-11815-4

Typeset in Caslon by M Rules
Printed and bound in Great Britain by
Clays Ltd, St Ives plc

Abacus
An imprint of
Little, Brown Book Group
Brettenham House
Lancaster Place
London WC2E 7EN

A Member of the Hachette Livre Group of Companies

www.littlebrown.co.uk

*for Nicky*

# PART ONE

So we beat on, boats against the current, borne back ceaselessly into the past.

F. Scott Fitzgerald, *The Great Gatsby*

# Chapter One

When Alistair Black was eight years old this happened.

It was a Tuesday morning, cold out, the leaves brown and yellow, orange as bright as a street light where the sun shone through them. Daddy was in the garage, warming up the car. A thick cloud of exhaust puffed out across the tarmac. Eventually the pale blue Triumph Toledo rolled backwards and paused for Alistair to jump in. He knew it was a Toledo. It featured in his British Cars Top Trumps. Everyone was playing Top Trumps at lunchtime and Alistair was excited because he had a new set – Spiders and Scorpions. The dark blue vinyl of the car seat was cold against his bare legs where his raincoat had rolled up around them. Daddy was quiet this morning. There hadn't been any breakfast talk, but then there hadn't been any breakfast. Mummy had given him honey sandwiches to eat when he got to school. Most days Daddy shaved as he drove, but this morning as Alistair was cleaning his teeth he heard the low buzz of razor coming from Mummy and Daddy's bedroom. Usually Daddy would talk to the car radio, arguing with the people on the news. Today he was silent.

The car slowed as it hit the first bad bit of traffic. There was always a jam here. The road was a dual carriageway, one side divided from the other by a big stone wall. Every so often there was a break in the stone for cars to turn. On the other side of the road was a higher wall made of the same dark greeny-brown stone. There were bright green benches spaced regularly against it. Sometimes when walking back from synagogue on a Saturday morning Daddy would let Alistair jump up and run along them.

The car rolled slowly forward in the traffic. A song came on the radio that Alistair knew. It was called 'Girls, Girls, Girls' and it was in the charts at the moment. He'd seen it on *Top of the Pops*. He liked it when they played pop songs on Radio 2, rather than old songs. There was a click from the front followed by the soft tick-tock of the indicator. Quite suddenly, with surprising speed, Daddy turned the steering wheel and the car left the queue of traffic, lurching off to the right through one of the gaps in the stone wall.

'Daddy?' Alistair said. This wasn't the way to school. School was straight on over the roundabout and past the Fine Fare supermarket. 'Daddy,' he called out again, 'where are we going?' Maybe Daddy had forgotten his briefcase – but no, there it was, as black as a gravestone on the seat next to him. 'Daddy!' Something was terribly wrong. The car swung out with a little screech onto the other side of the road. They were now going back the way they had come. There was less traffic in this direction and they seemed to be moving very fast. 'Daddy, where are we going?' Daddy wasn't answering him. It was as if Daddy wasn't there. His eyes weren't visible in the driving mirror, only the top of his forehead with its big brown mole poking out beneath the thinning hair. Alistair sat forward in his seat and reached for Daddy through the gap in the two front seats.

'Sit back down, Alistair!' His huge arm sleeved in brown sheepskin pushed Alistair back into the car seat. 'Sit back and stay back,' said Daddy. Alistair turned helplessly and faced the window. There was the water tower outside, its massive moss-covered drum black against the clouds.

4

'Where are we going?' asked Alistair, 'where are we going?' But inside he knew where they were going. And when, after only a couple more minutes, the indicator again made its gentle tick-tock he began to cry.

Here was the white scumble-walled building that he knew so well. It looked like a house, nestled as it was between the other semis on Harrogate Road. It had a garden and a drive and a hedge and a gate. But the upstairs windows were all opaque and mottled – as if there were too many bathrooms. One was dotted with stickers and topped with a circular extractor fan. That was the room waiting for Alistair.

Daddy had parked just outside the blue and white gate. He slammed the car door with purpose and strode round to the pavement. Alistair's howls filled the inside of the car. Desperately he pushed down the plastic peg of the car lock before Daddy could open the door.

'Alistair!' The menace was clear in his glass-muffled voice. Alistair reached out for the lock in the front. Daddy rattled the door, then without saying anything else put his car key in the lock. Alistair tried to hold down the lock peg but the opposing force was stronger. The door flew open.

'Out of the car!'

'Daddy, no.'

'Out of the car!' Alistair didn't care that Daddy was shouting. His chest burned with crying and fear. 'Do you want me to drag you out?' Daddy would have to drag him out. Alistair's hand gripped the edge of the car door. His fingers coiled around the black rubber that rimmed the metal. Daddy prised them free. He pulled Alistair back from the car and slammed the door. A young woman with a pushchair looked at them briefly then turned away, moving on with a brisk squeak from her buggy.

Up the path then, with Daddy dragging a bawling

Alistair. Through the door made of ridged glass almost being carried under Daddy's arm like a bag. And then, once inside, the smell. Sweet and high like a public toilet but underneath something sharper like lemons or bleach. And somehow, underneath that, the stink of the mask. Alistair tried to slow his sobs so he could speak.

'Please, Daddy, no, please.' But Daddy wasn't listening. That was why it was Daddy doing this. It couldn't have been Mummy. In the end, Mummy would always listen. Daddy just carried on doing whatever he was doing. Alistair wanted to fight, to plant himself into the ground, to turn himself into a tree and grow roots, except even if that happened, Daddy was too strong. Daddy would have wrenched him out of the floor and hauled him up the stairs as he was hauling him now. There was a thick piece of orange rope hanging along the wall, threaded through brass loops fastened to the brickwork. Alistair reached out for the rope with both hands, but Daddy saw this and pulled him so the rope was out of reach. Alistair was looking down now, at the creamy lino stairs slipping past one by one until they ended altogether and the landing arrived. There was a slight shush in the air, like escaping gas, and there were two doors both with the same ridged glass as the front door – one for the grown-ups and one, with Tom, Jerry and Spike the dog painted on it, for the children. The three animals grinned widely, all of them displaying gleaming white teeth.

'Ooh! What a noise,' said Mr Ross, who was waiting inside.

'Such a big noise, for a little boy,' said Aunty Phyll, who wasn't really Alistair's aunty but was a friend of Mummy and Daddy's. 'Come on. There's no need for such a fuss.' The big orange chair was facing Alistair. It was plastic like a car seat, but with little lines imprinted on it, like the lines on your hand. Alistair was limp, still crying but the cries were quieter now, more of a low rolling moan. It didn't take much force from Daddy to get him into the chair. He didn't know what to say or to do. He had stopped fighting. He was flowing with his moans, not thinking about what was coming.

'Into the space chair, little space man. That's it.' Mr Ross pressed a button and the chair clicked and whirred, rising and unfolding like a mechanical toy. Its back sank away and Alistair was now lying down flat, staring up at the huge disc of the light with a peeling Goofy sticker fixed in one corner. 'Now then, you remember the elephant's trunk, don't you?' said Mr Ross. 'Would you like to put him on again?' And there was no chance to speak because here was the mask. Daddy was holding his shoulders. Was it the gas that smelt of sickly rubber, or was it the mask? It roared cold in his face and as he breathed the roar went to his ears.

'It's just magic air,' said Aunty Phyll and her blue skirt and brown tights went away from him, as did the room, shrinking down to a dot and him in blackness still there, but not. He could hear them talking somewhere small and away from him. He could not hear words, just the distant honk of their voices. He waited for the world to come back.

Somehow over the years the whole event, the faux school run covering the secret dental appointment, became a family anecdote, rather than a forgotten trauma – at least for Mum and Dad. There was more than one gathering where Alistair overheard the tale retold as an amusing incident – 'He was so scared of the dentist's that Neville had to pretend he was taking him to school – it was really the only way to get him there. Otherwise he'd grab hold of the furniture and you couldn't get him out of the house' – this last sentence delivered with a neighing laugh as if it were a punchline. Alistair was fifteen now, yet every single morning between that one and this he could not be in the car with Dad on Harrogate Road without feeling a quiver in

7

his stomach as they rolled towards that exit in the dark stone wall. There was always an accompanying expectation that the car might swerve abruptly to the right and Alistair would be delivered once again to the waiting mask. Then the hissing, sickly gas would uncreate him, taking him away from everything he needed: away from the world, away from his mind, his life. Each morning he would not feel safe until the exit was passed and the lead-blackened water tower was receding in the rear-view mirror.

There was a dentist in Travulia. There were two, in fact – Mr Drevel and Lavinia Tanktop – but Mr Drevel was the only one Alistair had given a voice so far. Mr Drevel had come easily. A deep Scottish burr combined with a slight lisp. It was always easy to find the voice when Alistair could picture the character. Mr Drevel wore his white coat over a faded blue suit that was large and loose, similar to those favoured by most of Alistair's teachers at school. He was kind to his patients and hence popular with the citizens of Travulia, who were only too happy to submit to his treatment. Alistair had completed a tape of an encounter between Mr Drevel and Jacquie Shoulder, who edited the *Travulia Telegraph*. Jacquie had been putting off a visit for far too long. Mr Drevel gently admonished her then proceeded to treat the ailing tooth so skilfully that Jacquie barely felt a thing. She left the surgery exclaiming that she would never again postpone any treatment out of fear. Alistair had found a new way of doing female voices – since his own voice had broken last year it had become harder to make the female characters convincing. He was using Dad's old cassette recorder now, which had a completely different layout to the little portable he'd used before. It was a big brown oblong the size of a large shoebox. All its controls were laid out flat on its uppermost surface. The cassette went straight into a depression in the machine's centre and it was this feature that had facilitated Alistair's discovery. By pressing down on one of the capstans that turned the tape, he could make it slow down while it was recording. Then, when the tape was played back at normal speed, whatever voice Alistair had been performing would come out high-pitched and squeaky. This was useless at first – none of Travulia's citizens were supposed to sound like a cartoon mouse – but Alistair found with practice that he could modulate the effect. By just applying slight pressure to the rotating cylinder and speaking slowly without lowering the pitch of his voice he could produce a remarkably authentic result. With some experimentation he found that many of the existing female Travulians flowered into a new and authentic life: Carol Kay talked convincingly to her ballet pupils; Grandma Platypus meditated on preparing the Friday night chicken; Mrs Skrutt complained about the Pakis next door – all became so delightfully real that Alistair forgot he was listening to his own voice.

Alistair was putting the finishing touches to the cover of Henry Hudson's first Bar Mitzvah lesson. I'll just finish this and then I'll make some tea, he thought. Dad was downstairs, probably asleep in front of the chattering television. Mum was in bed, not sleeping, but reading her 'mad books', as Dad called them. Alistair would go to bed just before 10.30 – not because he was tired, or that he was made to, but because there was a programme on Radio 2 with Les Dawson that he loved. His favourite thing was to lie under the duvet with his silver clock radio. The clock had an LCD which lit up when the radio was on. The dull grey of the screen became a buttery yellow, illuminating the underside of the bedding. There Alistair lay, curled up and cosy in his softly lit grotto. This was his world and the best thing was fading out from it into sleep, so gently that he didn't notice the passage. He carefully folded the paper cassette cover so that it fitted around the orange card inlay, then slid the combination into the scuffed plastic box. He took a moment to admire the finished item. 'Henry Hudson – 24 Riverrock Road', it said in neat block capitals. Then beneath that, in smaller letters, 'Bar Mitzvah Lesson Number One – also featuring Reverend Evans'. Henry was an easy character to get – the adolescent warble of his voice was not so far from Alistair's own. Reverend Evans was somewhat harder. The guttural foreign croak that Alistair had imagined actually hurt his throat if he had to sustain it for any length of time. He stood up and went over to the white-painted shelves that filled the alcove in the corner of his room. He'd need the chair to reach Riverrock Road. He climbed up and set about making a space for the new tape, which required moving a number of others from the end of the shelf in front of him to the one below. Originally, when the population of Travulia had grown enough to require storage, Alistair had settled upon a simple alphabetical arrangement. But as he'd continued, and it occurred to him that each tape had been given a location, the idea of organizing the archive around location felt much better. It made Travulia seem more real. Alistair had never drawn a map because Travulia was growing all the time, but he could imagine a day when the boundaries had been established and such a plan could be produced. Then he might devise a storage system that echoed the shape of that town plan and the tapes could be placed where their characters' houses actually were. And then he would be able to see at a glance who the most interesting characters were because the place where they lived would be the highest pile of tapes. Alistair got down from the chair and walked to the light switch by the door. He turned and looked at the white shelves and their neatly stacked 317 tapes. Then he turned the light off and left the room.

The flickering glow under Mum's door suggested she was still awake. It had only just gone nine. Alistair gently pushed open the door and looked around its edge. Mum was stretched out on the bed sitting up on a wedge of pillows. She wore her dressing gown – the blue and white one like a willow-pattern plate. She had a magazine open in front of her but she wasn't reading it. Next to the magazine was a small spiral-bound notepad. In her hand was a pencil. Alistair went to sit next to her on the bed. He folded his legs underneath his bottom, settling himself at her side.

'I thought you were with your dad.' Her dressing gown smelled of one of her perfumes, like fruit mixed with soap.

'Uh uh.' There were a number of figures on the pad written firmly in pencil. Those at the top of the page were recognizable as dates. Over the lines beneath, the dates were unravelled into individual numbers, broken up with plus signs. Alistair followed the logic of the maths and saw that Mum had made sums of the dates, adding one number to the next to arrive at a total, the two digits of which were then added together to leave a single number – a seven. Mum had gone over it several times with the pencil, making it stand out from the other numbers on the page. She looked over her shoulder and saw Alistair studying the addition.

'Do you want to help?'

Alistair nodded.

'All right. But don't tell your father. You know what he thinks.'

He sat up straight, enjoying the conspiracy.

'Get the Ephemeris for me, would you, doll.'

Alistair hopped off the bed and went to the bookshelf tucked beneath the window. It was packed tight with randomly piled volumes – a few women's magazines like *She* and *Good Housekeeping*, but mainly copies of *Prediction Monthly* and Mum's related books. These titles were advertised on *Prediction*'s back pages. She would send off for them and they would arrive some weeks later amateurishly wrapped in cardboard and brown paper. *Biorhythms – The Key to Life*, *Your Stars: Your Destiny*, *Egyptian Astrology – The Wisdom of the Ancients*. He knew which one was the Ephemeris. It was a fat book packed with tables of dates and symbols. He sometimes leafed through it trying to understand what it could possibly mean. Many of Mum's books were fun. He particularly liked the biorhythms – following the wavy lines along their graphs from his birthday into the future, seeing what his state of mind or emotional life, whatever that was, might be like in 1983 or 1992. Unimaginably distant dates. He liked the suggestion that he would still be here then. The future ended in 1999, however; the biorhythms weren't tracked into the next century. 'I think I'll be happy if I just get to thirty-three,' he would sometimes hear himself thinking, 'that seems like quite a lot of life to be allowed.' Unlike the biorhythms, the Ephemeris remained impenetrable. He carried it back to the bed wondering if Mum's use of it might help reveal its purpose or meaning.

'Each birthday has a number, each sun sign has a number.' Mum gestured with her pencil to the page in the magazine. There was a chart, which gave each sun sign a number. 'Let's do yours.' She turned over a clean sheet on the notepad and wrote:

11.3.66

then separated out the numbers so they became:

1 + 1 + 3 + 6 + 6

12

and added them together, her lips moving slightly as she did the maths. Pressing down firmly with the pencil she wrote:

17

and smiled. 'Seventeen's good. One and seven makes eight.' Then she leafed through the Ephemeris. 'Now we need your rising sign.' She stretched out her legs as she adjusted her position on the bed. Her shins and calves were shiny, like the inside of a shell. She flicked through the heavy book, pausing occasionally to examine a page and determine where she was. Eventually she stopped and ran her finger down a page, pausing at one of the dense tables. 'Sagittarius,' she said, switching her attention to another graph in the magazine article, 'equals seven.' This number she wrote carefully under the existing 8 and then drew a line beneath both. She totalled the numbers to 15 under that, then added 1 and 5 into 6. 'Six,' she said smiling warmly at Alistair. 'You're a six.'

'What's a six?'

She turned another page in the magazine. '"Consider yourself fortunate. You will pass through life with a carefree disposition and the ability to greet all that comes your way as a challenge or an opportunity. Courage, precision and accuracy of perception are your distinguishing characteristics. You know how to be spontaneous and trust life while honouring those around you."' She reached over and ran her hand through his hair. 'You're such a doll.'

'I'm going to see if Dad's awake – make him some tea. Do you want some tea?'

'No, sweetie, no tea.' She turned back to her magazines.

Before he went down to the kitchen he found himself touring the other upstairs rooms, something he liked to do particularly when he needed to poo, as he did now. In addition to Mum and Dad's there was his bedroom, the bathroom and the spare room, which he wandered into without turning on the light. He pushed the door to, allowing a slice of light from the landing to remain at its edge. In the dimness he could just make out the single bed with its pink candlewick bedspread and the shelves above it where all the prayerbooks were kept. The Haggadot containing the Passover story, the books for New Year and Yom Kippur, the Chumash from which he'd learned his Bar Mitzvah piece, the Hebrew inside it as hard to understand as the dense tables in Mum's Ephemeris – harder in a way, since he'd only ever been taught what sounds the words made without ever being told their meaning. He moved over to the window and pressed his head against it, looking out into the darkness of the garden. The hedge was a slab of green and grey, slightly lighter than the lawn, cut off by the mess of trees and bushes that stood between it and his old climbing frame. He stood there for a moment enjoying the combination of the coolness of the window on his forehead and the fullness in his bowel, feeling deliciously safe as he stared into the blackness outside. Would I want to live in Travulia, Alistair sometimes found himself thinking. The answer was always the same: Why would I want to live in Travulia when I can live here?

Alistair went downstairs and pressed his ear against the brown grainy door of the living room. When Dad was asleep you could hear him snoring. It was always best to check, since if you woke him up with a start he could be very grumpy and would shout his loud barking shout. Sometimes, it wasn't hard to imagine Dad as a bear or something else with big teeth. Alistair listened carefully.

'. . . the USSR has described the military manoeuvres near the Polish border as "normal" while in a defiant message the Kremlin dismissed Solidarity resolution as . . .' The chatter of the *News at Ten* but no snore. He pushed open the

14

door. Dad was sat up unusually alert for this time of night, concentrating on the TV.

'Dad . . .' He didn't immediately look up from the TV. 'Dad . . .'

'Shh. I'm watching this.' Alistair turned to look at the television. There was an orange map of a small Poland sitting next to a big USSR.

'Do you want some tea, Dad?' Alistair waited a moment before heading for the kitchen.

'Uh-huh,' said Dad, his gaze fixed on the screen.

Dad had piled the dinner plates by the sink but they hadn't been washed up yet. He liked to do it last thing before bedtime. If Alistair was still awake the pleasing chink of cutlery and crockery from downstairs would often help him sleep. Alistair opened the cupboard and pulled out the mugs then bent down and reached for the blue metal tray next to the cooker while he waited for the kettle to boil. He found the biscuit tin with its dazzling mosaic of tiny flowers and placed it on the tray. He put a small amount of milk in each mug and placed them next to the tin, leaving an appropriate space for the teapot. He thought about the weekend to come. He could get up late tomorrow, listen to the radio in bed, go to town with Mum in the afternoon, have lunch with her at the Danish Kitchen, an open sandwich on brown nutty bread, a chocolate milkshake in a cone-shaped glass. Then be absorbed by Travulia in the evening, for as many hours as he wanted, the cushion of Sunday still to come. The kettle clicked off and he reached for the tea bags.

The adverts had come on. Dad got up and turned over to BBC2 where Dave Allen was dressed as a werewolf, howling at the moon. Alistair placed the tray carefully on the dining-room table and poured the tea. Dad sat back down and turned round to look at him.

15

'Alistair.' There was a little pause, then, 'How are things at school?'

'What?' Alistair was surprised by the question.

'Is everything all right at school?' Dad was looking at him expectantly, waiting for an answer.

'Yes.' He knew he sounded as if he was concealing something, even though he wasn't. He began trying to work out what was behind the question.

'I had a phone call this afternoon. From Mr Hindmarsh.' Alistair felt his heart beating. Dad's eyes remained fixed on him.

'Mr Hindmarsh.' Alistair was beginning to feel guilty. What had he done? Why would Mr Hindmarsh be ringing Dad?

'Your English teacher, isn't he?'

Alistair nodded. His mind worked to remember if he had done anything wrong in English or if there was homework he had missed or if he had been told off for anything.

'What did he say?' said Alistair, suddenly needing the toilet too much.

'I don't know. I was out of the office when the call came. When I called back he'd left for the day.' There was a moment's silence and when Dad started up again his voice was harsher and faster. 'I thought this had all stopped, Alistair. I thought you were shaping up. After we met with Mr Crozier. I thought I'd made it clear.'

'But I've been doing everything I'm supposed to.'

'Is that enough? Everything you're supposed to?' A deadly pause, and then, 'I know you, Alistair. I know what you're doing up there. Those bloody tapes.' Dad stared at him, searching Alistair's eyes with his own. Alistair tried not to look away. He fastened on to the grey of Dad's irises, their fibrous texture sinewy like torn meat. Finally Dad added, 'Well, we'll see on Monday. There's nothing more to

16

say until then.' Feeling awkward and ashamed now, as if his act of tea-making might appear to have contained an element of buttering-up, Alistair handed Dad his mug. Then he sat down in the brown swivel chair trying to pretend that everything was all right. He turned his attention to Dave Allen, who was brushing his knee, talking to the camera. A cloud had descended, separating Alistair from the Saturday he had just imagined. It felt like trouble and it took the colour from everything, soaking it up until there was only the bare shape of things left. He sipped his tea and tried to think of Travulia and the next tape he might do. A few minutes later he went to the toilet and then to bed, coiling under the cover with the quiet prattle of the radio.

Alistair was almost relieved when Monday morning arrived to put an end to his morbid speculation. He shuffled into the form room and went straight to his locker. The English lesson wasn't until that afternoon.

'What's up with you?' Herby Kirby clattered down next to him on one of the orange plastic chairs.

'Nothing.'

'Nothing,' he mimicked, holding his pencil case to his face, to represent Alistair's supposedly Semitic nose.

'Nothing,' Alistair countered, waving his hands in the air and thickening his lips – a Negro minstrel imitation that was his standard response to any of Herby's Jew references, since Herby was black.

'Where's Prune?' Herby continued, ignoring Alistair.

'Not here.'

'Out the back tossing himself off,' said Herby.

'Out the back bumming someone,' said Alistair.

'Out the back bumming himself,' said Herby. '. . . shhh . . . he's come.' Herby quickly gathered himself and silence spread abruptly through the rest of the class.

It wasn't Prune who entered, however. Instead the door frame was filled with a heavy-set prefect, from the Upper Sixth.

'Black. Is Black here?'

Alistair didn't know the prefect's name but he recognized him as one of Mr Hindmarsh's sixth-form drama group. He'd seen him in the lighting box at the school play.

'Mr Hindmarsh is in the library. I'm to take you there,' said the prefect. He spoke no more as they walked silently down the lower corridor. He was one of those tall, massive boys with a five o'clock shadow spread over the bottom of his face like iron filings. Alistair could never imagine being that old. He searched the boy's face for a glimmer of a clue as to the trouble he was in but the doughy features remained impassive.

It was a surprise to push open the swing doors and find the normally silent space humming with agitated chatter. A group of boys – about half the size of a normal class – sat spread out among the bookshelves. They were not a class, though. Their age ranged from second years through to sixth-formers. They looked up as one at Alistair, standing in the library entrance. Mr Hindmarsh was at the main desk flicking through a file of loose papers. He too glanced up at Alistair. Unusually, he was wearing his black gown. Mr Hindmarsh had wild brown curly hair and a cowboy moustache. He looked very odd in such formal attire.

'Ah. Black.' He moved out from behind the desk, gathering his gown around himself. He was the kind of teacher you liked very much most of the time. Very funny, without ever laughing much himself. He had a temper, though, which could often flair unpredictably, so that while Alistair looked forward to his lessons he never felt he could entirely relax in them. 'Sit down. Sit down with the others.' He gestured to an empty library table at the rear of the room. The bell went in the corridor outside. 'It's all right. It's all right. I've spoken to Mr Nettles,' said Mr Hindmarsh. 'As essential a discipline as woodwork is, you have his leave to be late.' He looked directly at Alistair, a mischievous twinkle in his eye. He kept his hands on the back of the chair as if he was about to sit down in it, but he remained standing. 'Who has seen the television programme *Then and Now*?' He raised his voice, now addressing the whole room.

'Sir,' the assembled boys muttered together. Alistair turned around trying to take them in without being seen to do so. There were faces he recognized: Nigel Tyler from the year above, a third-former who lived near him in the Primley Parks. His fear began to drain away.

'As you are no doubt aware, I'm no fan of . . . children's television.' The last two words were spoken with some disdain. Alistair remembered an exercise where they had to write a piece of criticism of the previous night's TV. As an example, Mr Hindmarsh had read out his own lambasting of *Magpie*. The teacher let go of the chair and began moving around, taking little paces to the left then to the right. 'I will concede, however, that *Then and Now* is – on occasions – an admirable exception. I can at least see why it might have been the recipient of a Royal Television Society award.' Alistair wondered how Mr Hindmarsh had seen *Then and Now* since it was on Tuesday and Thursday afternoons and he invariably stayed late running the Drama Club. But then he remembered that they had started putting it on Sunday afternoons on BBC2 in an hour-long omnibus. 'I take it you watch this programme yourselves?' Again the muttered, collective 'sir' which Alistair too joined in with. 'And why . . . can anyone tell me . . . do they make a point of watching it? Black?'

'Sir?' Alistair suddenly sat upright. He hadn't been expecting to have to do anything. He'd just been settling down into a pleasant easy-lesson daze.

19

'Why do you watch *Then and Now*?'

Alistair thought for a moment. Mr Hindmarsh was staring at him expectantly. Why not reach for the truth? Why did he watch it?

'Kirby, sir.'

'Kirby?'

Alistair heard a muttering behind him. 'Kirby was always going on about it, saying it was really good. So I started watching it.'

'And what is it in particular that keeps you watching?' Mr Hindmarsh was looking at him intently. Alistair searched for an answer.

'You know how most stuff isn't really any good, sir, even though it's supposed to be, or the paper says it is, but really it's boring or obvious or there's just nothing to it.' Alistair expected a witticism at this point, in fact he'd half-consciously constructed his reply to provide Mr Hindmarsh with the opportunity of making one. Mr Hindmarsh, however, just nodded for Alistair to continue. '*Then and Now is* good. It just is. It's just well done and interesting, with interesting stories that keep you watching and you look forward to seeing the next one.'

'Excellently put.' Mr Hindmarsh smiled, turning his attention back to the rest of the room. 'I don't know if you are aware, but the team that make *Then and Now* have managed to persuade some very talented people to work on it in the past. Trevor Griffiths, who has written some very fine plays indeed. Another writer called Frederic Raphael. A director called Alan Parker—'

'Who made *Bugsy Malone*,' said Hovsepian, one of the third-year boys, sounding very pleased with himself.

'Correct. And they've all been tempted to do it for little money . . . probably because they observed the same thing Black observed.' Mr Hindmarsh paused in front of one of the library tables and eased himself onto it. He began to swing his legs back and forth like a child. 'Now then, gentlemen . . . I've been having conversations with a man called Cyril Davenport who is the production assistant on *Then and Now*. Apparently it is part of their policy to cast new young talent in each pair of episodes. According to this Davenport, they like to avoid, as far as is possible, the London theatre schools because the handful of faces they provide are very familiar and, more importantly, as he put it, "They're not very good." Instead, they are constantly scouring the country, speaking to schools whose Drama departments have a good reputation – such as ours' – he patted himself on the head in a comical way – 'and asking if they have any likely candidates.' Alistair was aware of a rising excitement. Was it in Mr Hindmarsh's voice or was it inside him? 'Consequently they are coming to the school to conduct auditions.'

'When?' said Nigel Tyler without putting his hand up.

'Ah . . . now . . . there's the rub.' Mr Hindmarsh smiled mischievously. 'This afternoon.'

There was inevitable consternation in the room, which Mr Hindmarsh successfully parried. When he'd settled everyone down again, he carried on.

'The auditions don't begin until three thirty. There will be time for me to spend some time with each of you preparing. So on your way for now. Here is a timetable for the day.' He held up a piece of photocopy paper. 'Please collect one on your way out. There is a list of things to think about typed at the bottom. I shall be speaking to each of your parents in turn.' Another volley of questions came, which he immediately waved away.

'I want you to return to whatever lesson you are in. As I said, I will speak to you individually throughout the day.' He shook his piece of paper again and held open the library door. 'Come along, come along. I've had to pull enough strings to get this far. Don't undo all my good work by being later than you need be.' He gestured theatrically as if he was directing traffic, shepherding them through the door.

Alistair watched the boys in front of him filing out, some of them chatting excitedly to each other as they went. His heart was thudding in his chest. Mr Hindmarsh had let the door shut. Maybe he had failed to notice that Alistair was still in the room. He was back behind the main desk counting playscripts.

'Sir . . .?' said Alistair, tentatively.

'What is it, Black?' Mr Hindmarsh's head remained bowed, attention fixed on the books.

'I think . . . you've made a mistake, sir?'

'Made a mistake?' Now he looked up, his big blue eyes wide, his mouth open comically.

'Put me down – by accident.' An uneasy pause. 'For this play.'

Mr Hindmarsh closed his mouth.

'On the contrary – I think they'll be very interested in you, Black. I think you may be just what they are looking for.' There was a pause in which Alistair didn't know what to say.

'But I can't do it, sir,' he said, finally speaking.

'Can't do what?'

'Act. I mean act properly. Like that.'

'Oh, you can.'

'But I mean I've never even been in a school play or anything. I don't even go to Drama Club.'

'Although I've asked you to attend.' Mr Hindmarsh tilted his head and raised his eyes in a reproachful way.

'But how . . . how can I . . . I can't do it, sir.'

'Black – I've heard you read aloud. I've seen you perform in class. I've been teaching drama long enough to know you can.' He was silent for a moment. Alistair could hear the dull repetitive thwack of a hammer on wood coming from somewhere outside in the school grounds. He resumed his protest. 'But what about Nigel Tyler or Pete Hardman. Or Herby. I mean Kirby. Kirby's the best actor in our year.' Mr Hindmarsh shuffled uneasily. He quickly recovered his composure.

'As you've seen . . . some of them will be attending the audition. Knowing Nigel Tyler I expect he is rehearsing his piece as we speak.' Mr Hindmarsh leaned forward slightly. Alistair could smell the Nescafé and cigarettes on his breath. 'But I want you to attend, too.' He stood up, gathering his robes about him like laundry. 'You are the kind of boy who needs a boot up his arse to get him going – and this is as nice a boot as I can think of.' He pulled at his gown to straighten it. 'I want you to go to this audition. I will brook no refusal. I shall talk to your father about it. I take it he would have no objection to your being involved?'

Alistair shook his head. His mind was already working, imagining the potential humiliations ahead: forgotten lines, a stammering performance, embarrassment in front of his peers.

'I'll work with you later. You won't be unprepared.' Alistair looked up at him. 'Good,' said Mr Hindmarsh, moving to the door. 'Go on then. Mr Nettles awaits you with his lathe.'

At first Alistair didn't say anything to anyone. He thought about sitting down to watch *Then and Now* on a Tuesday or Thursday. Tuesdays were the 'Then' and Thursdays were the 'Now'. They always took something from history and some modern-day situation that connected to it in some way. Sometimes the links were obvious but sometimes they could be oblique, which is when Alistair enjoyed it most. The last series had ended with a 'Then' about some kids in the French Revolution and a 'Now' about a boy from a council estate who'd got a grant to go to a public school. Alistair tried to imagine himself in one of the episodes. His white face and dark hair and black eyes lost in the middle of the screen. It was, of course, quite ridiculous.

He didn't know how to tell Herby about the audition. He'd assumed from what Mr Hindmarsh had said that Herby hadn't been asked to take part. On morning break they walked down to the newsagent's behind school where the man sold single cigarettes for 5p each.

'You're quiet.' Herby knew that something was wrong. Herby always knew. 'What's up?'

'Nothing.'

'Don't believe you, Jew boy.'

'It's nothing.' More silence. Alistair ran his hand along the boxy green hedge as they passed.

'It's *Then and Now*, isn't it?'

Alistair looked at Herby. He didn't want him to be cross.

'You know?'

'Everyone knows.' The silence kept coming back. Alistair wanted to push it away.

'Did Hindmarsh ask you to do it?' said Alistair. Herby didn't answer. He didn't need to. Herby wouldn't have been asked, simply because Herby was black. 'I won't get it,' he said, pushing at the silence again.

'You will.' Herby's face gave no indication of how he was feeling. He stared ahead as they walked.

'I'm not going to get a part,' said Alistair.

'You'll get it.'

'I won't. I'm not an actor. Not like Tyler or someone.'

'No. You're better than that.'

'Hey!' Alistair shouted, grabbing Herby's arms. They stopped walking. Alistair stood in front of Herby, blocking his way. 'I'm not going to get a part. All right?' Herby looked at him, staring straight into his eyes. Silence hung around them until they arrived at the newsagent's. Herby pulled down a copy of *Mayfair* while the man wasn't looking and turned to a page showing nothing but a close-up of a woman's crotch. Then he carefully placed it – open – on a lower shelf next to *Whizzer and Chips* and *2000AD*. They laughed about it all the way back to school.

In the library, after lunch, Mr Hindmarsh helped Alistair choose a piece for his audition. He'd been reading *The Time Machine* again, which was one of his favourite books. Mr Hindmarsh encouraged him to find a piece of dialogue from the book to read. For Wells' unnamed Time Traveller, Alistair tried a variety of dialects before changing his mind altogether and deciding he wanted to be the narrator – the Time Traveller's best friend. He chose the last passage in the book and settled upon a kind of cultivated Geordie burr. He took it from a student teacher they'd had for Chemistry the year before. The teacher was from Newcastle and his infectious enthusiasm stuck in Alistair's mind.

'Even if nothing comes of this, Black, you will find yourself with a part in my next production – whether you like it or not,' said Mr Hindmarsh as he ushered Alistair from the room.

'Can't I just . . . do that instead? And not bother with this?'

'You can drop that act with me, Black. I can see straight through you.' Mr Hindmarsh's hand hovered over the light switch.

'Sir?'

'I know you've been imagining yourself on that television. Picturing the envy of your peers. Projecting yourself into a glittering, graciously unfurling career.'

'I don't know what you're talking about, sir.'

25

'Don't think I don't know the workings of a boy's mind,' he said as he flicked the lights off, holding the door open for Alistair.

By the time he found himself in the old music room, most of the other candidates were already there. Nigel Tyler sat at the front wearing his colours blazer, his black Adidas bag on one side and parka on the other, so that no one would sit next to him. All his attention was focused on a book backed with brown paper, presumably a play text. Hovsepian from the third year sat a few seats along. A shock of black hair, a grubby-looking blazer and a pair of black trousers which were shiny and worn. He stared into the middle distance, occasionally scratching his head or rummaging in his tatty blue rucksack. Alistair didn't know the boy behind Hovsepian. He recognized him as a sixth-former he'd seen in the school-bus queue. Nobody was paying attention to anybody else. They were as unconnected as patients in a waiting room. The thought of being in a waiting room made Alistair think of the impending casting, standing in front of a group of strangers, stammering as he tried to read the words of his piece. He wished now that Mr Hindmarsh had never considered him for this part, that he was sat safely in a Geography lesson with Herby, laughing about Mr Milligan's stupid glasses and Showaddywaddy haircut. He couldn't get comfortable in his chair and shuffled around. Tyler glanced up from his play text and stared at him briefly before returning his gaze to the page. Alistair wanted to get up and pace around but he wouldn't have dared. Suddenly Mr Hindmarsh's head appeared around the door.

'They're early. Do you want to come up? Leave your bags down here.'

'All of us?' asked Tyler.

'Yes, they want to see all of you together.' Everybody's

chairs scraped backwards and they headed for the door and the empty assembly hall upstairs.

The assembly hall doubled as the school's theatre. It had rows of chairs on rises that could be pushed in and out depending on what the space was going to be used for. This afternoon the rises had been pulled out. Mr Hindmarsh had made an attempt to create a theatrical atmosphere by turning on some of the appropriate lighting. Sitting about three rows back from the improvised stage area were a man and a woman. Alistair found it hard to see them with the theatre lights shining in his face.

Mr Hindmarsh was skipping around with a light step quite different from his usual, ponderous stride.

'Boys – this is Miss Pye, the producer of *Then and Now*,' he said sounding very pleased with himself.

'Gabrielle,' said the smaller of the two figures. Her voice was surprisingly loud.

'And this is Declan—'

'Mr McMenamin,' said the other figure slowly and deliberately.

'– the director,' finished Mr Hindmarsh.

'Yeah, Colin, do you think we could just have the house lights up? And could you kill the spots? Let the kids see us.' He had an Irish accent like the singer from the Boomtown Rats. Alistair wondered who Colin was – and then realized with a shock the director was addressing Mr Hindmarsh by his first name.

The theatre lights went off and the normal lights came on. The director – Declan – also looked like the Boomtown Rats singer. He had messy, curly hair and was wearing a long blue raincoat over tight black jeans and a furry blue jumper. The woman – Gabrielle Pye – was smarter. She didn't have much of a chin and she wore a big pink jumper with one of those massive, loose roll-necks. It made her

27

look like a turkey. They were both younger than Alistair had thought they would be, younger than Mr Hindmarsh. Gabrielle stood up and walked a couple of steps down the rises towards the boys.

'Hello, everybody. Thanks so much for coming along today. I thought I'd begin by taking you through what the process will be, both today and beyond – and then I believe you've prepared some pieces for us to hear – so it would be great to hear them.' She clapped her hands together and continued. 'We are in the process of casting the new series of *Then and Now*, as you probably know. At this stage we're not looking for people to fill specific roles, but rather we're putting together a little repertory company.' Alistair saw over her shoulder that Declan had lit a cigarette. Alistair waited for Mr Hindmarsh to ask him to put it out, but Mr Hindmarsh said nothing. 'It is possible that you may be chosen at this stage but that we don't end up using you in this series. That won't mean that there's anything wrong with your performance per se – simply that we don't have a part that's right for you at this moment in time, OK?' She smiled broadly. 'So, who would like to kick off?' She looked down at the typed sheet in her hand. 'What about . . . Nigel?' Tyler stepped forward.

'And what have you got for us, Nigel?' asked the director, who was now sitting up, alert and attentive.

'Edgar's monologue Act 2 scene 2 from *King Lear*, and Moon's summing up speech from *The Real Inspector Hound* by Tom Stoppard, sir.'

'Please don't call me "sir",' said the director, smiling. '"Declan" is fine. Let's go with the Shakespeare. In your own time.' The producer had returned to her seat next to him and produced a large, black notebook which she rested on her lap. Her pencil hovered over the paper.

Tyler walked a few paces towards her, holding his play

28

text in front of him, and lowered his gaze to the floor as if preparing himself. Then, in a single graceful movement he brought a hand to the side of his head, altered his posture and began to speak.

'I heard myself proclaime'd, and by the happy hollow of a tree, escap'd the hunt . . .' Tyler had that ability – which Alistair found greatly impressive – to speak Shakespeare's lines as if he knew what they meant. His voice, in its precision and its intonation, sounded like a real actor's, something Alistair was unable to imagine of his own. Tyler moved with a confidence and elegance that was alien to Alistair. He couldn't conceive of having that much control over his own limbs or face. Real acting must be about the ability to make a marionette of one's body. Alistair had never been able to find his own strings. He was relieved as he watched Tyler strut assuredly around the parquet floor. The part would go to him and Alistair could return to Travulia, which was, after all, home. It was only as Tyler reached his conclusion, pitying pelting villages, sheep cotes and Tom Turlygod, whatever that meant, that Alistair became aware of another feeling sinking behind his relief, which he had no desire to strive for and name.

Gabrielle finished writing in her pad and clapped delightedly. Taking this as a cue the other boys clapped too, eager to show their enthusiasm. Alistair knew that anyone in school who acted looked up to Tyler and wanted him to like them.

'Excellent, Nigel, excellent. Well done.'

'Do you like that stuff, Nigel?' Declan looked at Tyler as he lit another cigarette, shaking the match out with an extravagant movement before dropping it in his plastic coffee cup.

'Sir? – I mean . . . ?'

'Shakespeare. Do you like him?'

'Very much.'

'Do you watch television?'

'Yes . . .' Tyler seemed guarded, as if he hadn't antici-pated having to answer questions.

'What do you like?'

'I'm sorry.'

'What television do you like watching?'

'Erm . . . drama. *Play for Today*.'

'Anything specific?'

Tyler thought for a moment.

'*Tinker, Tailor, Soldier, Spy*.'

Declan nodded, then with a sudden, unexpected move-ment he jumped to his feet.

'OK. Let's try something different. I know you've all prepared pieces but just put them on one side for a moment.' He reached the floor where the boys stood, his dusty-looking raincoat flapping around him like a costume. 'You and you.' He pointed out Hovsepian and the sixth-former from the bus queue. Alistair guessed that Declan had already dismissed him as a possibility. 'Sorry, I don't know your names.'

'Hovsepian, sir.'

'Dryhurst, sir.'

'First names, please, and no sirs.'

'Alex,' said Hovsepian.

'John,' said Bus Queue Boy.

'Hi, I'm Declan, good to meet you.' He put his cigarette out and shook their hands vigorously. 'I want to try some improv – you've done improvisation exercises before, yeah?' Hovsepian said nothing but Bus Queue Boy nodded his head. 'Just see where you get to. I'll tell you when to stop. No need for self-consciousness. And you two lads' – he pointed at Alistair and Tyler – 'I'd like you to pair up too.' Alistair's stomach clenched. He looked up at Tyler, hoping for a smile or some hint of enjoying a shared experience. Tyler's face showed no more warmth than if they'd been partnered for a PE exercise.

'Now,' Declan continued, 'I want you to take one of the characters you prepared and set up a conversation with your partner's character. You can be anywhere you want where strangers might meet – park bench, stuck lift, railway platform. Oh, and you don't have to tell your partner who you are – let him work it out. Let it be a genuine meeting. OK. Off you go.' Declan moved to the side of the hall and gestured that the producer – Gabrielle – should join him. Alistair looked round for Mr Hindmarsh but couldn't see him anywhere. There was a moment's uncomfortable silence. Alistair tried to ascertain, without being seen to look, what everyone else was going to do. He could tell that they were doing likewise. He had done this kind of exercise before in class, and the others – who were all Drama Club members – were likely to be even more familiar with such activities, but still there was an air of nobody wanting to be seen getting anything wrong. Alistair couldn't help but feel foolish. He was doubly nervous – of being seen to mess up in front of the TV people, and, by not being any good, of messing it up for Tyler. He felt if he opened his mouth only stupid, shit things would come out. He waited for Tyler to begin.

Tyler had begun. He was walking around in a small circle with his hands clutched behind his back, gazing at the ceiling. He moved his eyes around the room allowing them to settle on Alistair, whom he then purposefully walked towards.

'I say, you don't know when the train is due, do you?' said Tyler, towering over him. Startled, Alistair realized he was going to have to reply. He searched for the Geordie accent.

'Sorry?'

'I said, you don't know when the next train is due, do you – back to London,' said Tyler again.

'No, I'm just waiting. To see what comes first.' Alistair winced as he spoke. It didn't mean anything.

'Yes,' said Tyler, who had yet to look Alistair directly in the eye, 'I must be there by six. I've got this play to review.'

'I see,' was all Alistair could manage. He was aware of the noise of the other pair but tried not listen to what they were saying. He knew he needed to concentrate. Maybe for now he could just let Tyler do the talking.

'It's very important I get there on time. I've got to get my review in with the paper. Are you going to London, too?' Tyler was still not looking at Alistair, rather just addressing his remarks vaguely in his direction. And now Alistair was aware that Declan was squatting very close, almost at Alistair's side. His mouth was very dry. He tried to wet it by swallowing. He knew the director was staring at him.

'I'm going back there, yes. I've been away . . .' Alistair tailed off, waiting for Tyler to step in. He didn't want to look round but he could feel Declan at his shoulder, as if the director was touching him. Tyler didn't step in. The silence hurt. Surely Tyler would say something and then Declan would watch him speaking for a bit and move on to the other two. Tyler remained silent.

'It's OK. Just feel your way into it,' said Declan, who remained stubbornly fixed at Alistair's side. Something in the word 'feel' made Alistair remember why he had decided to do the part of the Wells' narrator rather than the Time Traveller himself. It was the sadness on the last page of the book and the picture it painted of the narrator waiting for his old friend to return, knowing that he never would. He began to speak, allowing the softness of the Geordie voice he had in his head to lead him.

'I sometimes just get on a train and go. It doesn't seem to matter where to.'

'Sounds a bit off. My name's Moon. You may have heard of me. Theatre critic.'

'I'm waiting for a friend to come back,' Alistair said. 'He's been away travelling. He set off without really knowing where he was going. Sometimes I think if I do the same it might somehow speed up his return.'

'Hmm.'

'Silly really. Do you believe it's possible to travel through time, Mr Moon?' Alistair managed to look Tyler in the eye. He could see that Tyler didn't know what to do, didn't really know what Alistair was talking about. Alistair decided to take that and use it as something to work with.

'It doesn't matter.' Alistair shook his head. 'I don't think any of his other friends believed him either. I didn't . . . at first.' He had in mind a kind of smile to smile. It felt like the right movement to make with his face. He let the smile come and carried on.

'I think you might be a bit mad, sir. Maybe you should take a seat. Oh look – here's the train. Shall we get on it?' Tyler was trying to take back control of the scene but his words didn't really make sense. They weren't sounding real. Making it sound real, that was always Alistair's guide through Travulia. With that thought he carried on.

'He was frightened of what he'd discovered, Mr Moon. I could see how frightened he was. But he still went. I was terrified he was going to ask me to go with him.' Alistair looked down at the floor. 'I was relieved when he didn't.' He looked up again, staring at Tyler now, finding something wild inside himself. 'But now he's gone – and with each day that passes I fear that that which he was frightened of may have actually taken him. And that if I had gone with him, I might have prevented that from happening.'

'Yes, well, why don't you take a seat, old chap? Take some deep breaths.' Tyler put his hand round Alistair's shoulder and was taking him towards a chair, pulling a comic face. He was looking round at the others in the room, too – trying to turn the scene into a piece of comedy. He pushed Alistair into the chair with surprising force. 'Maybe I should see if there's a doctor about, hmm.' Tyler continued looking around and held a forefinger to the side of his head, circling it round to suggest madness. It seemed that the other pair of boys had halted their improvisation. Alistair was aware of a silence around him.

'Can I show you something, Mr Moon? I keep these on me at all times now.' Alistair reached inside his pocket. He knew it was empty but he felt for the contents that his character demanded. And found them. He carefully withdrew his hand and held it in front of Tyler's face. In the book the narrator had been given two white flowers that the Time Traveller brought back from the future. Alistair saw the two strange white flowers resting on his palm, as described in the novel, felt their delicacy, made the carriage of his hand towards Tyler's face reflect their fragility. 'They're shrivelled and brittle now' – he remembered Wells's description – 'but once they were the strangest, most beautiful things I had ever seen. He gave them to me. One day there will be nothing left of them but dust. But as long as I am here, I will remember how beautiful they once were.' Alistair moved his eye-line from his palm to Tyler's confused face. He thought about what it would be like if Herby died and he never saw him again. He let the feeling rise from his chest, up his throat and a tear coalesced in the corner of his eye. He allowed the silence to continue as if it was part of the scene and then lowered his hand.

Declan stood up and put a hand on Alistair's shoulder.

'Excellent,' was all he said. Alistair saw that everyone else in the room was looking at him, too.

34

# Chapter Two

Alice Zealand stood at the bottom of the steps and made her second attempt to begin an ascent. It didn't matter how difficult it felt. She was going to do this.

How long had Alice been thinking about it. Two months? Three now, surely. The exhibition had been advertised all around the university. Ben had completed his postgrad over a year ago but somehow the Slade had persuaded him to mount this show within their space. Part of their continuing drive to demonstrate to the world (or to the governors of UCL) the enduring high calibre of their students.

So many steps. It reminded her of a stage set she'd once been on, a fictional staircase lost in the fog of her memory, stairs she'd descended and never climbed up again. She looked down at the flyer in her hand. The edge of the paper was damp and thin where she had been clutching it. Some of the print was running, the fine black line bleeding into a grey smear. *Ben MacCawber – Caught Straws. A retrospective: 1993–2001, Slade School of Art.* Above this text a picture she recognized. His only self-portrait. A mezzotint. Delicate white lines scratched into a dark slab. She looked at her palm. It carried an imprint of part of the picture. She rubbed at it with her thumb feeling clumsy and messy. Stuffing the picture into her jeans pocket Alice carried on climbing, hoping the exhibition would be busy enough to hide her presence.

She hadn't seen Ben for over a year. Well over a year. The urge to turn round and head back downstairs was strong. She imagined standing in the evening sun on Gower Street. Heading back home. A cold glass of white wine. Come on, she said to herself, feeling the effort in her thigh muscles, each stair tougher than the last.

Had she made too much of an effort with her hair? She wanted to go to the toilet now and wipe off the make-up she'd so carefully applied. Come on. The noise of a crowd now audible. A low tumble of voices, the clink of glasses, some stuttering music – something contemporary and ambient – Four Tet or Cornelius, she couldn't tell which. Her stomach felt light and raw.

She rounded the last corner, passing a pair of young-looking students sharing a cigarette, and entered the studio – out of the gloom of the stairwell and into painful brightness. A version of Ben's face greeted her, filling her vision, obliterating everything else. An enlarged reproduction of the mezzotint covering the wall ahead of her.

Other people edged around the space. So many pictures and paintings. She'd forgotten how prolific an artist Ben was. There would be a table of drinks somewhere. If she could make it there that would be a start.

Now she was trying to narrow her gaze. She didn't want him to see her. She was behaving like a pre-school child – believing that if she couldn't see him, he wouldn't see her. What on earth was she doing here? The compulsion to turn and pelt back down the stairs was strong. It was as if the room held danger, and walking across it made her vulnerable, an antelope alone on an African plain.

There were the refreshments, some gorgeous nineteen-year-old student handing out the glasses – her tanned midriff, taut as a gymnast's, exposed to the room. Alice felt paunchy and old. She gratefully reached for the glass and forced herself to take a sip rather than gulp it down in one. The wine's cheap sharpness was welcome. The only friend here.

She risked a look around. She couldn't see Ben. Maybe he was absent. It was quite possible he wouldn't have attended. For a moment she thought that might be a good thing. She turned to her left. There on the wall in front of her was another image she remembered, although the work's title 'Cyril Devano' was new. Something about the name gave her an unpleasant jolt of déjà vu. A painting of a middle-aged man with a heavy silver moustache and narrow eyes. He looked weighed down by guilt and weariness. Alice approached the canvas, examining the layers of paint. She remembered watching Ben work, utterly absorbed in his technique, the careful application of paint with diminishing sizes of brush, beginning with the simple architecture of a face, progressing to the detail. Unlike any other artist she had met, Ben made his faces up. He never sketched from life. Instead he worked and fiddled and scratched and revised until he had the face he had set out looking for. Then he would draw it from every conceivable angle until the imagined person had taken on a solidity and a verisimilitude that satisfied him. Until he'd reached that point he was unable to begin the finished composition. It was an extraordinary ability. The final artefacts depicted characters so complex and intriguing it was impossible to imagine that they didn't exist. She moved to the next image, another large canvas of a young woman. She sat in an old armchair, her head cast back, lolling to one side. The woman looked tired and defeated. Alice hadn't seen the painting before. She felt a hand on her shoulder.

She turned. It was Christopher – the artist with whom Ben shared his studio.

'Alice? Alice Zealand?' He looked shocked. As if he had thought she was dead. And here she was, unexpectedly revived in front of him.

'Hello.' She took another mouthful of wine. She couldn't go and get another glass yet. She was hoping the girl by the table would go out for a cigarette or something.

'Does Ben know you're here? I thought you were in Israel?'

'I came back.'

The muscles on Christopher's face shifted abruptly. He smiled. 'He didn't know you were coming?'

'I haven't spoken to him.'

A pause in which Christopher looked around the room. She knew Christopher was gay. She often wondered if he loved Ben. He had been fearfully protective. 'How are you, Alice? Are you all right?' Concern in his voice. No doubt affected.

'I'm fine.' She laughed. She felt the drink warming her face. It would be nice to have a cigarette.

'He's over there. Talking to some arse from the NPG. Still debating whether they'll exhibit him.'

Ben had won the BP award two years ago. And then there'd been a stink when they'd discovered his subjects were fictional. Alice followed the line of Christopher's pointing finger. Her view of Ben was obscured by a white brick pillar. 'This is a big night for him, you know.' There he was again. Admonishing her. It was clear Christopher thought she shouldn't have come. Maybe he was right. She could always leave now. But then Ben would know that she'd been and gone. And that would be worse.

Christopher turned towards her. He shifted a pace to his left. Was he trying to hide her presence from Ben? 'What are you doing now?' He smiled politely. 'Did you finish your Masters? Are you a fully qualified theologist?'

He was trying to make a joke but she could taste the acid. That's right, Christopher. I'm still mad. Mad Alice. Thirty-six years old and still at university. 'I'm nearly finished. I'm finishing it now.' She was finishing it now. It wasn't a lie. Christopher pushed his heavy-framed glasses back up his nose.

'Are you going to say hello? Do you want me to take you over?'

Alice panicked. She drained her glass. For a moment her field of vision was filled with barrelled versions of Ben's paintings. It was hard to distinguish them from the people in the room, distorted too, leaning in towards her.

'He's having a conversation. I won't interrupt. I'm all right, Christopher. I'll look at the exhibition.' She was backing away from him. 'Is much of this new?'

'What?' He was looking at her as if she was dangerous. Perhaps he thought she was going to start shouting. Or get undressed. 'About a third or so. Are you sure you're OK?'

'Fine.' She'd started walking off. 'I just need the toilet.' She knew that would bother him. He tried to smile at her. 'I'm coming back.'

The toilet was bright too, the exposed bricks painted the same matt white as the studio space. She stood in front of the mirror examining her face. She pulled some make-up from her bag. Her cheeks looked blotchy. There were dark patches beneath her eyes. Wrinkles at the apices of her mouth. Old Alice. How could this be? He would have a young girlfriend now. Some twenty-two-year-old with tits like half-apples. She imagined the seduction. The girl asking if he would paint her. Slipping her pants down. Ben would never take advantage. Ben was the kindest man she had ever met. But he was passionate too, and such a passion could be harnessed. She had done it herself.

She was terrified at the thought of a new girlfriend. Convinced now that she would be out there in the room. Maybe the brown-bellied girl handing out the wine. It was all too plausible. She couldn't go back. Someone rapped on the door. Hurriedly Alice turned on the tap. She made a noisy show of sploshing water. She unlocked the door drying her hands. A tall ostrich-like woman with her hair scraped back was waiting outside. Alice didn't smile at her.

For a moment she hovered on the landing, tracing the brickwork with her eyes. The wooden banister rail that echoed the slope of the stairs, levelling out the horizontals and verticals into one smooth line. She could go, or she could stay. It was a stark and simple choice. But if she went, that was it. She would never see Ben again. The stairwell felt like a deep hole. Alice hovering on the edge of a black wonderland. What would it be to make that choice and walk away? To step forward and let gravity take her down? Would she ever hit the bottom? She almost lifted her leg to do it. She didn't. She turned. Back into the drone of the room and the pain of it.

Better to go straight over to him. Better to tell him she was here. And say what, Alice? And say what?

But she was doing it. He was in the same place, lost in his argument, his hands shaping the air in front of his face. She was now directly behind the man from the NPG at whom Ben was still intently staring. She edged to one side. On the pillar beside her was a row of Ben's miniatures. A series of engravings she could remember him preparing. She had watched him labour, nothing else there for him but the smudgy paper and the point of his pencil, the look of concentration exaggerated by the bright light of the desk

40

lamp at his side. Absorbed as he was, oblivious to her, oblivious to anything, she recalled the great wave of protective love she had felt for him. Lost to everything but his own act of creation he had seemed utterly vulnerable and alone.

Ben had seen her. He swayed, rocking back on his heels. His brow furrowed. His hands frozen in front of him, stiffening. His face settled into a look of puzzlement, as if he were seeing something impossible – an Escher drawing, or a ghost. He turned back to his man and spoke. Alice couldn't hear what he had said. And now he was walking towards her. His hair was short again, styled as it had been when she had first seen him alone in the cafeteria at UCL. He looked young, younger than he was. So much younger than her. She tingled. She felt it in the end of her fingers. He still struck her like a bell.

'Alice?'

'I'm sorry.' Her mouth dry already. Why hadn't she got more wine?

'Sorry?'

'Sorry for coming. For just turning up.'

He started laughing. 'What are you doing here?'

She needed to sit down. Was there a chair anywhere? She looked around. Only paintings and people.

'Why are you here?' he said again, his voice precise and measured.

'I saw the posters.' She gestured back towards the door. 'I wanted to see everything.' She knew how ludicrous she sounded. There was no choice. It had to be got over, this part. Like being sick.

'But I didn't know you were back. How long have you been back?'

'February.'

He looked shocked. 'Six months!'

41

'Four months.' As if this was any better.

'Why haven't you called me?'

She didn't know what to say. She wished she knew the answer to that question. 'I'm here.'

'Oh, Alice.'

She thought he was going to reach for her. She tensed. He remained standing where he was, at least a foot between them. The cloud had already descended. The cloud that separated her from what she knew she should feel – what she felt about him when he wasn't there. Standing before him now, she couldn't remember those feelings. They might have been a lie, nothing more than a fantasy she conjured in his absence. Lights on shore seen through fog. Lights that could have been lit to deceive her – to lure her onto perilous rocks rather than the safety of a harbour. Someone else had come to stand near Ben. A short man with grey cropped hair. He seemed to be waiting for Ben to finish, or at least for a gap in the conversation long enough to break in on.

''Scuse me. Sorry.' The man genuflected theatrically towards Alice, then turned back to Ben. 'Marvellous. Marvellous. Marvellous . . .' Alice wondered if she could walk away. She felt lost. She turned to look around the room. All those faces. Each one intricate and plausible and vivid, hinting at a depth of personal drama that she knew existed nowhere. Other than in Ben's imagination. What was he calling on when he brought them to life? A touch on the side of her arm. Ben was alone again.

'You didn't choose the most private place. Assuming you want to talk.' He was looking at her, his brow wrinkled, trying to work her out.

'I know.' She could sense him bristling now, the shock of seeing her already replaced by anger. Stupid Alice. Stupid. Stupid. Stupid. Someone else now grabbing him by the shoulder. A young black woman in a lime-green summer dress.

'Ben!'

Ben turned towards her, leaving Alice alone again. She stood for a moment, feeling heavy and useless, aware of her arms hanging down at her side like an ape's, feeling her thighs pressing together at the top of her legs. Ben kissed the young woman. Alice turned to face the exit. She should just leave now. She started walking.

Then both his hands on her. One clasped on each shoulder. 'No! No. No, Alice. No.'

They sneaked out together. Into the anonymous pub on the corner of Torrington Place. A table next to a chiming fruit machine. The relief of a cigarette and another glass of wine.

'Will you get in trouble?' Adopting the voice of a child. An old defence mechanism.

He shook his head. 'It's my exhibition. I can do what I bloody well like.' The soft Edinburgh accent. Like a wise old teacher. 'You could have written, Alice.' He was staring straight at her now, that hard black-eyed stare. 'You could have called. You could've emailed. Anything. Anything would have been better.'

'I left you a note.' From child to petulant teenager. Ben leaned back on his stool. He reached for one of her cigarettes.

'You don't smoke.'

'You drive me to it.' He lit it, inhaled deeply and immediately coughed. He waved the smoke away extravagantly. '"Got to go to Israel. May be some time." So romantic. I memorized every word.'

'You knew what I was like.'

'Your universal get-out clause.' They stared at each other, eyes locked, another battle taking place on a level that neither of them had access to. 'How do you think I felt?' he

43

said. 'I couldn't write to you. I couldn't speak to you. What was I supposed to do?'

'I know.'

'Is that all you're going to bloody say? "I know. I know."' His voice rose an octave and he wobbled his head from side to side in parody.

'I can't be with you, Ben.'

'So I'd gathered.' He drew on the cigarette this time. She could see him struggling not to splutter. There was disappointment in his eyes. He could never conceal his emotions. 'What did you do out there? Study?'

'Partly.'

'It was nothing to do with the course. I know that.'

'What?'

'I went down to Heythrop College. The week after you went.'

'Why?'

'For Christ's sake. I thought there might be a way of contacting you. I spoke to some old priest.'

'Father Pablo. You spoke to Father Pablo?'

'"She's gone of her own volition, my son. No, I couldn't tell you where she was staying. No, she didn't tell me when she'd be back. I've no idea where she could be."' More adept mimicry. He'd caught the peculiar Spanish lilt precisely. 'He was very helpful. As were the other acquaintances of yours I managed to track down. None of them knew where you were.'

'I needed to go.'

'To get away from me?'

Don't answer that, Alice. Don't fall into that barely covered pit. 'I needed to go.'

'If you'd said where in Israel. "Gone to Jerusalem." "Gone to Tel Aviv." I would have come to look for you. You know that, don't you?' His face was red. He was so angry.

44

But angry was better than what would have happened if she'd stayed. There would have been much more pain if she'd stayed.

'It wasn't about you.' Was this a lie?

'Is that supposed to make me feel better?' A silence between them. Then he started up again. 'Do you know where we'd got to, Alice? Do you know what was about to happen?'

Don't say it. Please don't put it into words.

'I was going to ask you to marry me.' He sat back on the stool puffing ridiculously on his cigarette. She looked at him, blinking. 'And the only conclusion I could reach, did reach . . . was that you knew . . . and that you gave me your answer in advance.'

'I went,' she said, gathering herself, feeling her own anger burning, 'I went . . . because I needed to make sense of things.'

'It's not the going, Alice. It's the manner of going.'

If he'd have been with her that May morning, stuffing her case, unable to see through tears. All I want, she would say to herself, all I want is a normal life. All I want is what everybody else has. But not everybody else did have it, did they? Dad didn't have it. Going was the answer because she couldn't bear inflicting more hurt. She'd hurt people before. She wasn't going to hurt him, not like that. This way he might hate her. This way would be easier for him. Mad Alice doing another mad thing. If Mad Alice stayed with him she'd destroy him. She could feel the urge. Feel what she was capable of. She would not be responsible for destroying that beautiful, beautiful boy with any more of her badness.

'Why did you come here today?' He put out the cigarette, pressing the butt with his thumb until any glow was extinguished. 'It's ridiculous, Alice. Just ridiculous.'

45

'I'll go then.' Angry herself now. Standing up.

'You went some time ago. Didn't you?'

Just incensed. She couldn't even remember what she'd been thinking a moment earlier. He was only seeing one thing. He was seeing a fraction of a corner and calling it a square. Tell him what's in the square. Tell him what fills it. Go on, tell him. Not possible, of course. And she was out of the door, alone again, cold in the evening sun, confused, half there and desolate.

# Chapter Three

The snow had started falling last night. The ground was thick with it now. Alistair pressed his face against the cold glass of the taxi window, feeling the thrum of its engine in the bone of his forehead, watching London roll past. The already unfamiliar landscape was now rendered even stranger, an abstract block-work of complex white shapes. The vehicle had been waiting for Alistair outside his hotel that morning, black and shiny as a hearse. Eventually it pulled up in front of a charmless concrete towerblock.

Alistair made his way inside the building. He was brusquely told to wait where he was by a pinched-faced woman behind the reception desk. He sat down on a brown sofa covered in cigarette burns, clutching the script he had been sent. Pressed against it was a piece of paper with the address of the Bray Hotel on it, so he knew where he was going back to at the end of the day. He looked down at the heavy sheaf of paper in his hand.

```
            BBC rehearsal script
The sending of this document does not constitute
      the offer of any part thereof within
```

In bigger letters beneath that it said:

It had been waiting for him in the hotel reception. Mrs Frieze – Rosalyn – had handed it to him when he had arrived last night. He hadn't read it yet. He was going to but he had fallen asleep. He knew what the play was about. It was to do with Leila Vinteuil. The Vinteuils were a Jewish family in Romania or Bulgaria who hid from the Nazis in a cellar. Leila was fourteen or fifteen. She had a younger brother – Alistair was playing him in the show. And there was another boy down there. An older boy who was her boyfriend or something. He'd seen a film of it. He hadn't liked Leila. There had been a hint of the goody-goody about her. He remembered the Nazis battering down the door at the end. The violence of it. He wondered if there would be Nazis in this *Then and Now*. Dad hadn't wanted him to do it at first. 'The world already knows about that story. Why do they need to know from it again?' he'd said, an uneasy hint of rage in his voice. In the end Mum had persuaded him.

Alistair looked around the foyer. There was a man at the reception in a dark blue raincoat. He looked like Captain Peacock from *Are You Being Served?* Alistair realized with a shock that that was exactly who it was. The pinched-faced woman wasn't being rude to him. She was smiling and calling him Frank. Alistair thought about Herby and Tyler and Hovsepian and everybody else sitting behind their desks at school.

'Alistair Black? Yes . . . no?' A tall young man in a check

48

shirt and woolly tie came over to him. 'Alistair . . . are you?'
he said again. Alistair nodded. The man walked Alistair over
to the desk and scribbled something in the visitors' book.
He pointed to where Alistair should put his signature. Then
they went over to the lift, which was waiting with its doors
open.

'I'm Cyril Davenport. Not everyone's here yet. But
Steven is. Have you met him before?'

Alistair shook his head.

The lift was tiny, a narrow metal cupboard which trem-
bled as it ascended. Cyril looked like he remembered
something and muttered, almost to himself, 'And Alice.
Alice Zealand. Do you know Alice Zealand?'

He shook his head again.

'No, no, of course not,' Cyril said, making a fist of his
hand. He had raw-looking acne which disappeared beneath
the loose collar of his shirt. It looked like it might spread
over his whole body. 'Would you like a cup of tea? Or
coffee? It's from the machine.' He looked apologetic.

'Do they have hot chocolate?'

'Yes, yes, they do. I'll get you one of those. There are biscuits on the table.' The lift came to a halt with a judder.
They were near the top of the building. 'This way. Yes.
OK?' They went along one corridor which turned a right
angle following the edge of the building round a corner,
then through a pair of double doors into an empty room
with chairs placed in eccentric positions. In one corner at
the back there was a small table with a long mirror next to
it – like the kind in a clothes shop. They stopped at another
door, which Cyril pushed open for Alistair. 'We're waiting in
there. I'll get your drink.'

He walked off speedily back across the room leaving
Alistair at the threshold of the open doorway. He didn't
have much choice but to go in.

There was a trestle table in the middle of the room. At irregular intervals around the edge were old-fashioned chairs made of metal tubes and green canvas. In one corner were a girl and an older boy. The girl had dark shoulder-length hair. It could have been dyed black. She wore a long coat, tweedy-looking, that reached down to her feet. Her shoes had thick rubber souls. She was talking to the boy, who on closer inspection looked more like a man. Alistair tried not to stare at the girl.

The boy had golden blond hair. It was swept across his head in a severe side parting. He was dressed like a pop star. He wore a black cavalry shirt, the oblong patch in its middle folded down to reveal a triangle of red satin. Alistair edged into the room. The boy/man looked up and beamed when he saw him.

'Is this our Marcel?' he said with wide blue eyes. Alistair smiled, relieved at his friendliness.

'You're Alistair Black?' asked the girl, who stayed in her chair, feet drawn up to her knees. Sensing that this gave him permission, Alistair turned to look at her.

'Yes,' he said. He looked away again, scared to take her in. The boy/man leapt out of the chair with startling speed and bounded across the room.

'Steve Raw, sir. Pleased to meet you. Very pleased to meet you.' Steve held out his hand for Alistair to shake. He was big. Much taller than Alistair, five foot ten or eleven. His hand grasped Alistair's very firmly and squeezed it tight as he shook it.

'You're not who we thought you were,' said the girl, who had moved her feet to the floor, adopting a more conventional posture.

'What she means is you're not who she thought you were going to be. Alice thought she'd worked with you before.' Alistair wondered what he meant by the word

50

work, then realized Steve was talking about acting. He thought about what he was going to have to do over the next few days.

'I thought I'd worked with an Alistair Black at a National Youth Theatre workshop. But he didn't look like you.' She was scrutinizing Alistair intently. Her eyes were a deep blue and very large. She had lots of make-up on, mascara and eyeliner like Siouxsie Sioux or Poly Styrene. She was much prettier than either.

'Have you ever done NYT, Ally?' asked Steve, who had let go of his hand. Alistair was pleased to hear him use the contraction of his name.

'Nothing like that, no.'

'Well, you haven't missed anything,' said the girl. 'They're all wankers.'

'Except for you, Alice,' said Steve beaming again.

'Of course.'

'Where's everyone else?' asked Alistair, going over to one of the chairs near but not next to Alice and Steve.

'Late. They're always late. Particularly directors,' said Alice scornfully, drawing her knees back up to her chest.

'I think they tell us to get here early,' added Steve. 'They think we won't make it otherwise.'

Alistair felt he should try to keep the conversation going. 'Have you done one of these before?' he asked Steve.

'A *Then and Now*? Uh uh.' He shook his head. 'How about you?'

Alistair shook his head.

'Have you done telly before?' said Alice. For a moment Alistair wondered whether he should lie about it. But he knew that would be ridiculous.

'No. I'm a bit nervous about it.' He tried to smile. Alice rubbed her eyes with one of her fingers. Her nails were painted bright red.

51

'Nervous? Why are you nervous? What's to be nervous about?'

'Well . . . just . . .' He felt the heat rising, knew his face must be reddening.

Alice unfolded her legs again and straightened out her skirt.

'Really, what?' She was looking at him, her eyes wide, her eyebrows arched.

'If he's not done it before,' said Steve.

'He's acted before . . . you've acted before . . . presumably?'

'Yes.' Alistair's throat was tight. He hadn't, though. Not like this. He couldn't possibly admit to that.

At that moment Cyril Davenport arrived, followed by the producer from the audition, Gabrielle Pye. She carried a big rafia shopping bag which was slung over one of her shoulders. She looked harried and tired. Cyril handed Alistair a plastic cup. It was too hot to hold comfortably.

'Biscuits on the table,' he said again. Alistair got up and helped himself to a biscuit. As he turned around to head back to his chair he found himself looking at Alice. She was looking at him. He moved his eyes away sharply. He took a bite from the biscuit but his mouth was too dry to chew it properly.

'Good morning, cast, or half the cast. I don't know where the adults are,' said Gabrielle fussing in her bag. This was immediately followed by another theatrical 'Sorry!' as a middle-aged man came through the door. He had silver hair and was wearing a smart camel-coloured coat.

'Good morning, Jack.'

'Morning, good morning. Morning all,' he said without looking up. He had a leather bag, almost like a woman's handbag, which he placed on the trestle table and immediately began rummaging in. Methodically he pulled items out of it and laid them neatly in a line in front of him. His script, a pair of thick black glasses, a pencil case, a pipe and a box of tobacco. When all these items were there, he carefully unfolded the glasses and placed them on his head. As he did this another woman entered, out of breath.

'Wouldn't let me in the car park. Sorry. Had to walk miles.'

'It's all right, Emese,' said Gabrielle. 'We're not even close to starting. No Declan yet, as might be expected.'

The woman had short dark curly hair and wore a long pink anorak that seemed too big for her. Underneath she had on some kind of loose tracksuit. She sat down and began to take her shoes off.

'Oh really?' Barefoot now she took her coat off and smiled at everyone in the room in a winning way. 'Hello, all.' She pulled a face as if to say knowingly, here we go again. Alistair had sat down next to Steve and Alice. There was already a clear division between 'adults' and 'teenagers'.

'I take it you all got your scripts?' said Gabrielle, waving her own about, which looked old and battered compared to Alistair's. There was a general grunt of confirmation. 'Can I assume you've all read them?' Alistair immediately felt that he was back at school and that he was about to be told off. He felt something poke him in the hip. It was a biro, wielded by Steve. Very quietly, without moving his face much, Steve mouthed, 'Have you?' Moving his own head just as slightly Alistair mimed a 'no'. Steve grinned. 'And does anyone have any initial thoughts – while we're waiting for Mr McMenamin to arrive?'

'Actually, dear, I do,' said Jack, who had settled himself into a seat at the table, now he'd marked his territory with his various possessions.

53

'Sorry, everyone, I've been rude. I haven't done introductions. This is Jack Deal, who is Mr Vinteuil,' said Gabrielle, standing over him. 'Do carry on, Jack.'

'Yes, dear, thank you. I was going to say I think it would be good if we could have some coffee. Before we begin. Wake up and settle down. You can sort that out, can't you?' He smiled winningly.

Gabrielle quivered for a moment as if she was uncertain how to respond. Then she said firmly, 'Of course. Cyril!' She called to Cyril Davenport, who was scraping chairs around in the big room outside. Emese, who had now replaced her normal shoes with a pair of little plimsolls, had gone up and sat herself next to Jack at the table. She placed a hand on his arm.

'Jack, darling. How are you?'

'Hello!' he said, turning to her as if seeing her for the first time. 'My God. They're scraping the bottom of the barrel on this one, aren't they?' They both laughed.

'It's been a long time, you know,' said Emese, raising her eyebrows.

'Don't tell me. I don't want to know.'

'Bolton Octagon. Seventy-one.'

'It wasn't *built* then,' said Jack, looking around as he spoke. Gabrielle had gradually moved away from them as if she didn't want them to notice, and made her way over to the teenagers' corner.

'Was everything in the script clear to you?'

'Pretty much,' said Steve, pressing his leg conspiratorially against Alistair's.

'Alice?'

'There's not really a story as such, is there?' Alice had taken her coat off. She had a buttoned-up black shirt on, and a black skirt. As she bent forward the shirt came open a little between its buttons. Alistair could see honey-coloured skin underneath, above a black bra. 'It's sort of three sections – one after the other.'

'Well, it tells the story of what happened to the Vinteuils compressed into half an hour, if that's what you mean?' This discussion was interrupted before Gabrielle got any frostier by the arrival of Declan. He was holding a crash helmet and wearing a black leather biker's jacket over oil-smeared jeans. Jack turned round and peered at Declan over his glasses.

'The Silver Dream Racer's here,' he said innocently and Emese burst out laughing.

'Good morning, Mr Deal. Nice to see you again,' said Declan unfazed, putting his jacket over a chair.

Cyril Davenport appeared again with a tray full of plastic cups.

'We'll have an urn tomorrow,' he said. 'There was a mix-up.' Without having to be told, everyone had found themselves a place at the table. Alistair just followed Alice and Steve. Steve pulled a chair out for him. The cups were distributed.

Jack had filled his pipe and as he ignited it he said, 'Nobody minds? Good,' and puffed out a cloud of smoke which hung around him like a silver halo. Gradually everyone seemed to gather themselves, the volume of mutter diminishing to a low burble as they settled into their places.

'The thing that strikes me most about Bunny's piece,' Declan said abruptly, 'is its mood. It's a mood piece.' He took a chair and sat on it the wrong way round, his legs spread wide. He took a sip from his coffee and grimaced. 'What I'm after most is an atmosphere. An expression of something universal. This isn't just about Nazis and the Second World War. I want this to be alive for us now.' He looked around the room as he spoke, allowing his gaze to rest with each of them individually. 'It doesn't matter if you're black, white, Hindu, Muslim, whatever. There's something about this girl's plight that we can all understand.' He stood up and leaned forward, his hands gripping the back of the chair. 'So I don't want us to think of this as a piece of history. It isn't history. This is something that's happening all around us, all the time. We can all learn from this story.' Emese was nodding as she turned the pages of the script. Jack was puffing more smoke out across the table. Alistair wandered how Alice was reacting but he didn't want her to catch him looking at her again.

'Now then. Accents,' said Jack, peering over his glasses. 'What's it to be? Do you want my Maurice Chevalier? He *was* French, wasn't he?'

'Maurice Chevalier?' said Emese, as if she was now the other half of Jack's double act.

'No, darling. This fellow. Vinteuil.'

'No accents,' said Declan firmly. 'I know this is a "Then". But we're playing it as if it's now. Not just "now" but "here". I suggest neutral accents.' He moved round to the front of the chair. 'Which doesn't mean neutral characterization. But as far as possible your own voices, please. So if we could go from the top. Gabrielle – will you read stage directions, please.'

'Interior. Cellar. Day,' she began. 'A large gloomy cellar. There are packing crates lined up around the walls . . .'

Alistair suddenly felt very small. Not one of the teenagers, but a child on his own. He didn't see how he was going to be able to do this. He was startled from his thoughts by Jack calling out in a thick French accent. The voice was quite amazing, deep and low, rumbling across the table as if he was speaking through a microphone.

'Will you be quiet, Leila. Zere is nothing to laugh about.' He looked over his glasses across the table as he delivered his lines, searching for Alice.

'Why should I be quiet? It's a beautiful day and we're going on an adventure.'

'Some adventure,' pitched in Emese, whose head was buried in the script.

'We will 'ave to cover up zat for a start. Marcel. Titu! Will you get down here. Titu. Fetch that chair. Help me with this.'

'OK,' said Declan, holding up his hand. 'We'll just stop there for a moment. Jack. The accent.'

'Yes.'

'As I said, I just wanted to hear it in your own voices first.'

'Ah, but I'm saving time, you see, because you'll want it French in the end.'

'Really? Is that so, Jack?'

'I take your point, dear boy, but you do *know* that Vinteuil was French, don't you? The others were all Romanian or whatever but he had moved there from France in 1920 to study at the music academy.' Jack raised one of his eyebrows. 'We surely want to know that this is a stranger in a strange land. It's right that *everyone else* should want to use their own voices. You're aware of the history of the Vinteuil story, aren't you?' Jack relit his pipe, looking very pleased with himself.

Declan crossed his arms and continued. 'OK. We'll carry on and see how it feels. From your last line.'

'Titu,' Jack said over his glasses, 'fetch zat chair. Help me with this.'

'Oh, Papa,' said Alice. 'Why do we have to cover up the light? It looks so pretty.' Alistair was amazed at the change in her voice. It was rich and precise and confident. He began to panic. He had a line coming up.

'We cannot risk being seen, Leila – you know zat. If we are discovered down here we will be arrested.' Jack looked

57

over at Alistair. He must have known Alistair was playing Marcel. Alistair's mouth was now as dry as pumice stone. He read the line flatly, modulated only by the vibrato of his nerves.

'Is that why we had to leave the house so early, Papa?'

Jack held his gaze as he spoke his next. 'I'm afraid so.'

'Poor Marcel,' said Alice in her clear, impressive voice, 'he doesn't like waking up early.' She looked directly at Alistair although she wasn't really seeing him. 'Why don't you unpack and then you can sleep.' Alistair scanned the page. Titu and Mr Vinteuil had an exchange and then he had two more lines, then nothing for three pages. Steve was speaking now. His voice was strong and clear too.

'I don't see why we have to hide like rats in a cellar. We should be above ground. Fighting.' He had something of the command of Nigel Tyler together with a strident confidence of his own. His acting style matched his body.

'You know what your father would have had to say about that. Sometimes the best way to fight is to survive.' Jack's accent was already beginning to sound less absurd and more natural in the drama's circumstances.

'My father was no coward,' said Steve, with genuine aggression.

'I know that,' snapped Jack, and then gentler, 'your father . . .' His voice broke slightly, convincingly, '. . . your father was the bravest man I knew. He was also the cleverest. And he understood that there were other ways to oppose the Nazis than with bayonets and rifles.'

There was a pause as Jack finished delivering his line. Then Alistair realised with horror it was because he was supposed to be speaking.

'Oh, sorry. How long will we have to stay down here, Father?'

'Until ze war is over. Not long I think.'

'But how will we live? What will we eat?' Alistair tried to sound confident. He could feel the artificiality of his voice. Declan looked at Gabrielle, who turned to look back at Declan. She made a little face. It was obvious that neither of them knew Alistair was looking at them. He felt something deflate within. An emptiness in his stomach.

'OK. OK. Pause there.' Declan was on his feet. His index finger was jabbed in his hair and he looped a coil restlessly round its tip. He turned to face the table, addressing everybody. 'Look. I know this is only a read-through. Why would I give notes at this stage?' He looked at each one of them in turn. Alistair felt his gaze approaching like a searchlight. 'We've got three days. Three days. That's precious little time to explore anything.' He was moving now. He paused behind Alistair and Emese. 'It's crazy but that's the schedule. We're limited each day on our hours with these.' He pointed at Alistair, Alice and Steve. 'So . . . I would appreciate it if we treat every pass at this as a full rehearsal. Concentrate. Focus. Perform. OK.' He held his hand up again. 'One other thing. Are we all familiar with the Vinteuil story? Does everyone know what happened to them?'

'I've seen that awful film. The one with Ray Milland and Rochelle Hudson,' Emese offered, putting down her script.

'We'll take it as read that everyone agrees that the film stinks.'

'Vinteuil was a Jewish composer, born in Paris, who left to study under Gheorge Dima at the Academy of Music in Cluj.' Jack had interrupted Declan. He was speaking with unexpected and impressive gravitas. 'He married a Romanian woman called Magda and stayed, raising two children. Leila' – Jack nodded at Alice – 'and Marcel' – he nodded at Alistair. 'When the war came and Cluj was annexed to Hungary, Vinteuil took his family into the wine cellars of his friends, the Stanescus.' He looked around the table before settling pointedly on Declan. 'They stayed down there for several years. Ironically they were discovered by the Nazis only months before the end of the war. They were all deported to Auschwitz.'

'You've done your homework,' said Emese.

'They were deported to Auschwitz,' said Declan gravely, holding Jack's stare. 'Now we don't go that far. In fact, we end with them being hauled from the cellar. OK. Let's go from the top again.'

When they had finished the first read-through Declan made them go back to the beginning and do it again. Once again Alistair felt the inadequacy of his own reading. By the end Declan looked exasperated, muttering to Gabrielle without Alistair being able to make out what he was saying.

'Right.' He had stood up. He stretched his arms over his head. 'I'd like a word with some of you, individually. If everyone else could read through to themselves.' Declan approached the table and squatted down next to Jack. Alistair risked another glance at Alice. She was drawing something on the side of her script with a fountain pen. Alistair sat upright, straining to see what it was: a figure in a soldier's hat. And then Declan was at Alistair's side. He spoke in a low voice:

'OK. Alistair. Did you take in what I said . . . a moment ago?'

Alistair nodded.

'Good. Then stop dicking me around. All right. You need to give this your all. Even at this stage I want to hear how you're going to pitch it. We want some semblance of what the character's feeling. The fear and the desperation. Yep?'

Alistair nodded. His insides felt hollowed out. Declan's instructions were meaningless to him. It was like asking someone who couldn't drive to improve their gear changes. What was he doing there? He wanted to be at home, in his bedroom, in Travulia. Not this. Cyril Davenport appeared in the doorway. He waved to Alistair, gesturing that he should come and join him. He looked up and tried to catch Gabrielle's eye. She saw what was happening and nodded that he should go.

He immediately felt more comfortable away from the table and the actors, grateful for Cyril Davenport's fussiness and apparent incompetence.

'Hmm . . . yes . . . it's your costume fitting. Everyone else was done last week, OK? This is Penny.' There was a woman waiting at the back of the room, next to the long mirror. She had two outfits on a hanger in a big clear plastic bag like something from the dry cleaners. She smiled when she saw Alistair.

'Hello, dear,' she said in a loud whisper, mindful of the drone of the reading coming from the smaller room. She must have been about Mum's age, although she was dressed as if she was younger, in canvas trousers and a pink sweatshirt. 'There's just the two things to try on. A white shirt and trousers and this coat.' She held up the two plastic-sheathed outfits as if to prove she was telling the truth. 'Go on, you can slip your things off. There's no one about.' Alistair did as he was told, feeling raw with embarrassment as he pulled his jeans off, standing in just his pants and a vest. He dearly hoped nobody could see. He hurriedly pulled on the rough shirt and woolly trousers as Penny handed them to him. Cyril sat on one of the chairs in the middle of the room leafing through an exercise book and ticking things off. Penny crouched behind him on her knees fiddling with the hems of the trousers. Eventually she stood up and examined the shirt, making him lift his arms and turn round. 'Go on. That'll do.' Alistair started to unbutton the shirt but she stopped him, saying, 'No, love, you've got to try the overcoat too. She pulled it out of its clear-film shroud and held it out for Alistair to put his arms into. She fastened it around his front then fixed something with a safety pin to one of the lapels. The coat's thick collar scratched the back of his neck. 'Very nice, fits you perfectly. Have a look.' She gestured for him to examine himself in the mirror. Alistair turned to face his reflection. The thick grey coat stopped just above his knees. There was a large yellow star fixed to its front, just over his left nipple. He reached up to feel it. It was made of soft felt. Penny came up behind him and pulled something onto his head. 'I nearly forgot,' she said. It was a small brown cap. She tucked his hair up under it leaving his ears exposed. She looked at his reflection and fiddled slightly with the cap. Alistair stared at himself for a moment. He looked like somebody else, but somebody he knew or somebody he'd seen. Impulsively, he held both his arms, bending them at the elbows, palms flat and outwards as if to say don't shoot. He held the pose for a moment, examining the tableau he had made. 'Perfect,' said Penny grinning broadly.

When Alistair emerged back into the main rehearsal room he found the rest of cast standing in a small circle in the centre. Facing him, between Emese and Alice, there was a gap, wide enough for a person to pass through. Declan sat on a chair to one side, his shoulders hunched forward. Gabrielle was at the back of the room.

'Alistair. I'd like you to make your way into the centre of the circle.' Declan looked at him encouragingly. The only face Alistair could see among the circle was Jack's, who was on the opposite side of the opening. He was looking at the floor but his scowl was visible.

'You don't have to do anything.' Declan held his hand out in front of him. 'Just make your way into the centre of the circle.' Alistair looked at him doubtfully. 'Go on.'

Uncertainly Alistair stepped forward. He walked slowly between Alice and Emese – both of whom had their eyes cast downwards. Alistair stood there in the middle. He turned around not knowing where to face.

'Goldberg!' shouted Emese suddenly, making Alistair swivel, involuntarily.

'Penny-chaser,' said Jack, not as loudly but somehow more forcefully. Again Alistair found he had swung round to face him.

'Christ Killer!' That was Alice. Her face was impassive.

'Sheeny!' shouted Steve. Alistair looked for a flicker of irony on his face, a wink or something that would help puncture the mood that was already building. But Steve seemed serious in his intent.

'Hymie,' said Alice.

'Hooknose,' from Emese.

'Shylock,' said Steve.

'Kike!'

'Hebe!'

'Half-dick!'

'Bagel dog.'

'Cap head.'

'Ikey-mo.'

'Jew boy.'

'Oven-dodger.'

'Four be two.'

'Khazar.'

'Canaanite.'

'Gatemaster.'

'Dial.'

'Yid.'

'OK! Break it.' Declan now, bounding forward enthusiastically. But Alistair was crying. Crying and he didn't want them to see. He pushed his way through them and went over into the corner of the room, then out into the other room where Penny was still gathering her things and Cyril

Davenport sat adding up figures in a book, oblivious to everything around him.

The door swung open and Declan entered. He ambled over. Alistair screwed his face up tight, pushing away the tears. Declan crouched next to him.

'OK there?' Alistair didn't respond. He hung his head, still trying to avoid showing his eyes. 'Pretty intense exercise.' Alistair could hear Declan rummaging in his pocket, the click and rasp of his lighter, the draw on the cigarette. 'You know I used to have this car. A little Mini-Cooper. A bugger to get going – 'specially on cold mornings.' Alistair risked looking up. Declan's face was level with his. The black of his stubble like Desperate Dan's. 'Guy in the flat below had a Rover 2000. Great big thing. Decent bloke. Used to give me a jump-start. And when that Mini got going, man. It was a racer. Outpaced his big old Rover. Or pretty much anything on the road.' He got to his feet patting Alistair on the arm. 'Come through when you're ready. We've taken five.'

Alistair watched Declan slip back into the rehearsal room. He couldn't imagine himself walking back in there. He sat immobilized on the chair. He rubbed his face trying to remove the evidence of tears. The door opened again. He immediately dropped his head. Now it would be Gabrielle. But the heavy rubber-soled shoes he saw approaching told him otherwise.

'I brought you a biscuit.' It was Alice. She smiled at him uncertainly. Alistair found he was on his feet, standing up in her presence, like an Edwardian gentleman. 'He's such a fucking wanker.' She sat on the chair nearest him. 'Like I said. They're all fucking wankers. Directors. Are you all right?' She had turned to face him, taking him in with her wide, inquiring eyes.

'It wasn't . . . I mean normally . . . that exercise . . . I wouldn't have . . .' He found these words coming out unwilled.

'We shouldn't have done it. Jack was right.'

'No . . . I mean . . . I think . . . I . . . it's because I'm Jewish.' Alistair tried to steady his voice. 'I don't think . . . they know.'

'What?' But this was out now too. Alistair was surprised.

'I'm Jewish.' Said like he had a disease. I'm spina bifida. I've got leukaemia.

'You're Jewish!' She looked horrified. 'I'm sorry.' She had put her arm around him. She felt hot against him. 'I'm really sorry. Do they not know? They don't know.' The door swung open again. It was Steve Raw. He stood there for a moment looking at Alice holding Alistair. Alistair was aware of what Steve was taking in, Alice at his side, comforting him. Then Steve's expression changed and he came over.

'Is he all right? Are you all right, sport?'

'He's Jewish.'

'What?'

Alistair found he had pulled away from Alice.

'He's Jewish. They didn't know . . .'

'You're . . . listen . . . hey . . . I'm sorry. Really sorry. You're Jewish?' Steve had come over to Alistair's side. He put his arm around him too. It felt different to when Alice did it. Stiffer. More theatrical.

'I'm telling them. I'm telling them now.' Alice was standing up, inflamed with indignation. She marched off through the double doors, leaving Alistair with Steve.

'Bit of a rough deal that.' He patted Alistair on the shoulder, before removing his arm. 'Listen . . . what are you doing after?'

'After?'

'This afternoon . . . they've only got us till three . . . they're only allowed us till three.'

'Don't know.' Alistair shrugged his shoulders. 'Going back to the hotel.'

'They've got you at the Overlook?' Steve started laughing.

'It's called the Bray. The Bray Hotel.'

'Yeah . . . the Overlook. They put everyone up there,' said Steve, grinning.

'Why not come out with me this afternoon? Go into town. Have a shmy round the shops.' 'Shmy' was a Yiddish word. Steve didn't seem Jewish. How did he know it?

'How will I get back? I'm being picked up.'

'We'll ring 'em. I'll put you in a cab. Come on. You've got to spend your per diems on something.' Alistair looked at Steve uncertainly. 'It'll be a doss.' Alistair shrugged his shoulders again.

'OK.' It would be all right. A taxi would take him straight to the hotel. There was nothing to worry about.

The double doors from the reading room swung open again. Alice swept back in, upright and righteous, accompanied by Gabrielle. Her face was very red. She came straight up to Alistair and gripped his shoulders.

'Are you all right? Is everything all right? You must come with me. Come with me now.' She led him back through the doors and towards the waiting adults.

There followed a stumbling apology from Gabrielle, in front of the rest of the cast. Declan sat soberly at her side. He looked at Alistair as he listened, nodding to what Gabrielle had to say, seemingly approving her use of the words 'sensitivity' and 'respect'. Strangely, Jack looked very pleased. He smiled slightly as he puffed on his pipe, enveloping himself in a cloud of smoke.

There was more discussion about the script and the presentation but Alistair found it hard to follow. His eyes kept drifting to Alice. He still had her smell in his nostrils. She'd

66

left something of her scent on his jumper – a fiery mixture of perfume and a hint of sweat. It made him feel light when he breathed it in.

'As it is, we're going to have to let the . . . younger performers go now,' said Gabrielle eventually, revolving the ring on her middle finger. 'You can see Cyril about your per diems.' She made an odd gesture in Cyril's direction. 'We're here tomorrow at ten. We've only got the kids for four hours, remember. Adults to stay on, please. Books down if possible.'

Alice and Steve went to collect their coats from the chairs where they'd piled them. Alistair went to do the same but before he'd crossed the room his path was interrupted by Declan, who put an arm over his shoulder and pulled him to one side.

'Listen,' he said, keeping his voice low. 'If I'd had any idea . . . well . . . you know that.' It felt strange to have his adult bulk pressed so close, when Alistair barely knew who he was. There was something flattering about it too, though. 'But this is an amazing opportunity for you. Really.' He gazed at Alistair, his lips tight, nodding his head. 'I want you to seize this. Seize what's just happened. To see this for what it is. I know what you're capable of. I want you to hold the memory of that exercise. Bring those feelings with you. To each rehearsal. To the recording. You do that . . . we'll be with Marcel. With the whole fucking lot of them. Down in that cellar in Cluj. Shut in with their fear. You get it? Remember that feeling, kid. Take it inside. Understand?'

Alistair ran to catch up with Alice and Steve.

'What are per diems?' he said as he joined them.

'Your allowance for food and travel. Come on,' said Steve.

They went and made a line in front of Cyril Davenport. Cyril fumbled with a little pile of small brown envelopes. Each one had a name written on it in pencil. When he handed Alistair his, Cyril said, 'Now are you . . . do you know where you're going?'

'I'm looking after him,' said Steve enthusiastically. 'He'll be OK with me.'

Alistair felt something like pride rising inside him that Steve was so willingly making this connection between them.

'That money's to last all week, don't forget,' said Cyril as they left the room. As soon as they were out of sight down the corridor, Steve shocked Alistair by leaping into the air and banging each of the fluorescent light fittings as they passed under them so they swung and rattled, sending clouds of dust down onto Alistair and Alice.

'Stop it!' Alice protested. Alistair laughed. Somebody shouted for them to 'be quiet out there'. They ran to the lifts, led by a giggling Steve.

# Chapter Four

Alistair sat on a broken bench opposite the Gara de Nord and tried his mobile phone again. He'd walked up and down the Calea Grivitei to kill some time, thinking it better to keep moving than remain stationary. He felt that if he looked like he had some purpose he would be less likely to attract negative attention. It was nearly nine o'clock and Bucharest was coming to life. Still the shock of seeing horse-drawn carriages clopping down the Strada Witing among the buses and parping cars. If he narrowed his eyes the city looked normal, grand even – architecturally equivalent to a Western European capital. But open them wider and the view became more hallucinatory. Moss and vegetation grew out from among tram tracks and between the paving stones, even though they were both in constant use. Crumbling Brancoveanu-style masonry peeked out from between the concrete apartment blocks. An old peasant woman weighed down with a huge sack of produce stumbled along the pavement as dark-suited businessmen walked past her on either side. Alistair looked down at the screen of his mobile. Although the power bars on the right-hand side were fully extended, the signal indicator on the left was completely empty. He'd arranged a roaming facility before he left and the text in the middle of the display now read 'Romtel' but he had yet to get any reception. There was no need to panic. The signal might improve when he was on the train. He turned suddenly, drawn by a commotion. A violent, vicious snarling. Behind him was a wire fence that framed an abandoned-looking construction site. In its middle, scrambling over the chalky ground, a large pack of dogs had appeared. They were fighting fiercely, kicking up white clouds of dust. Momentarily Alistair saw them as being fused together – some fierce multi-limbed yellow mutation joined at the head. His travel agent had warned him that the city had a problem with strays. Alistair turned away before he could see what they were pulling at.

You could just go home now, he thought, an internal voice adding, after a moment: please. He took a deep breath, considering it. A taxi to the airport. Wait there until you find a flight. Four hours in the air. A peaceful train back to Leeds. No need to endure this. No one would know. Not a single person.

I would. He almost spoke the words aloud. He pulled himself upright, adjusting himself beneath his backpack, and made his way towards the station.

The tickets didn't go on sale until an hour before the train's departure. Alistair had already been ahead and located the appropriate ticket office. He'd also rehearsed what he had to say. As the hands of the station clock reached ten past, a small crowd gathered at the window. An old man in a loose-fitting green jacket regarded Alistair with suspicion. He touched his hand to the few strands of hair clinging to his translucent scalp. The queue moved slowly. When Alistair reached the kiosk he spoke as clearly as he could.

'*Un bilet pentru Cluj. Clasa I. Rapid.*'

'*Unde?*' The moustached man only looked up at Alistair when he failed to respond. '*Unde?*' he said again and then, in weary English, 'Where?'

'*Un bilet pentru Cluj.*' He felt shaky. Exposed. Lost in the mapless territory of a language he didn't know.

'Cluj-Napoca? You go to Cluj-Napoca?'

Alistair nodded.

'*Clasa I. Două zeci de mii de lei*. Twen-tee thousand lei.'

Alistair handed over the money. He'd had it ready. He had checked and double-checked the fare. 'Er . . . platform? *De . . . la ce peron pleaca—*'

'*Peronul sapte.* Sev-en.' The man held up seven fingers and gestured impatiently towards the ticket barriers.

Alistair tried to settle himself in the train compartment he'd been allotted. He had been advised to travel first class everywhere. It didn't mean the same as it did in England – there was no level of luxury implied. First class here was akin to standard at home. Despite the fact that seats were allocated, Alistair seemed to be the only passenger abiding by the rule. At least two other passengers had come into his compartment, tried the seats and then left in search of an alternative.

It might even be possible to conjure an illusion of safety. Safety would not be truly experienced for the length of his stay in Romania. But then Alistair never felt safe anywhere. Sometimes not even in his own bed. Wasn't that why he was here? So he might stop feeling frightened *all of the time*.

Maybe for the length of the journey he could entertain some notion of security. Pressed into the corner of this seat, the dark wood rocking around him, he would be transported by other forces to Cluj. For the next seven hours he didn't have to do anything.

The train began to slow. Alistair pressed his face against the glass. A hot oily smell filled the carriage. Alistair wondered if there was something wrong with the train. He looked out of the window. They were pulling into a station. Ploiesti. In the distance, dark against the hazy mountains, stood a huge

71

line of pipe-rendered refineries. Great black columns of vapour rose from them, like ink in water. He sat back in his seat. In his head he began repeating what to say when he got in the taxi at Cluj station: *Vreau sa merg la Hotel Transilvania*. The carriage doors were thrown open. An enormous woman, wearing a voluminous striped skirt and several layers of woollen sweaters, pulled herself into the compartment. She was followed by a younger girl, presumably her daughter. The pair sat down opposite Alistair but neither registered him in any way. He might have been absent or invisible. The woman began unlacing her leather boots. They were like a boxer's, with narrow laces criss-crossing halfway up her ankles. She pulled them off, sighing as she did so, dropping them with evident satisfaction on the floor beneath her. Having done this she rolled down her socks and placed both feet on the arm of Alistair's seat, still making no acknowledgement of his presence. The girl zipped open her bag and withdrew what looked like a dinner plate wrapped in tin foil. She placed it between herself and the older woman, lifting a corner of the covering. She pulled out some of what was beneath and took a bite. It could have been cake or meat.

Alistair found a little alcove in the corridor, between the lavatory and some kind of store cupboard. There was a lone window here covered with a blind. He pulled up the blind and watched the landscape scrolling past. The oil region had been left behind, the industrial panorama had been replaced by thick pine forest. In places, where it was darker, Alistair's reflection became more apparent – his wild hair, thinning on top, the dark loose skin beneath his eyes.

'*Spala huh! Frumoasa!*' A young man had appeared. No older than thirty. He had cropped hair and a scrubby goatee beard. He wore a Chicago Bulls T-shirt. At first glance he could have been a European MTV presenter. Looked at closer, his skin was leathery and pockmarked.

'*Er . . . no vorbesc . . . Romanesteh . . . erm . . .*'

'English?'

'English, yes.'

The man nodded. 'It's cleaner here. Beautiful.' His English seemed fluent. There was an American twang to it. 'Under Ceauşescu . . . even this was all filthy. The trees were black. Things are better now. They are trying to put some things right.' The man pulled out a crumpled pack of cigarettes from his jeans. He offered one to Alistair. 'Tourist?'

Alistair declined the cigarette. They were Chesterfields. Full strength. He pulled his own Silk Cut from his cagoule pocket. 'Kind of . . . yes . . .'

'You're not sure? Why else you come to this crazy country?' The man smiled at him as he placed the cigarette in his mouth. Alistair reached for his lighter but the man had lit his own cigarette before Alistair could.

'My health. For my health.'

'Your health!' The man laughed. 'Well, you go up north. The air is clean. That much is true.'

'My—' Alistair was going to use one word, then swerved, replacing it with another. 'My doctor. He didn't think I should come. Said it would be a mistake.'

The man looked at him. Put down his cigarette, tapping ash on the floor. 'Where you going? Where you heading?'

'Cluj,' said Alistair.

'Cluj . . . Cluj-Napoca?'

Alistair nodded.

'Why there? You have family there?'

'No . . .'

The man nodded once, seemingly satisfied.

'Your English is good,' said Alistair.

'America. Chicago. Been there three years.'

'Studying?'

'*Ce . . .?*'

73

'Er . . . studying . . . college?' said Alistair.

The man exhaled, rubbing his chin. He shook his head. 'I work construction sites. Save up to marry. So come on. Why Cluj? I'm . . . curious. What draws Britanic to Transylvania. You looking for the count?' He bared his teeth vampirically.

Alistair smiled and shook his head.

'What's your name, Englez?' said the man.

'Alistair.'

'Hello, Alleestar. I'm Mihail.' He held out his hand. 'You can call me Mike.'

'Where are you heading?' said Alistair.

Mihail pointed upwards. 'All the way. The end of the line. Suceava. See my fiancée. Haven't been for long time.'

Alistair smiled wanly in sympathy. A silence descended. Alistair turned to look at the trees rushing past, breathed in the heavy smell of the pine. After a moment he said, 'Have you ever heard of Leila Vinteuil?'

'Who?'

'Leila Vinteuil. The Vinteuil family?' Alistair wondered if the man would react to the name.

'They Romanian?'

'Kind of.'

Mihail shrugged. 'Who are they? Not your family?'

'Not family. They lived in Cluj.'

'That's why you go to Cluj? Who are they to you?'

'Something happened to them.' Alistair felt himself tighten. 'It was something that happened during the war.'

'Second World War?'

Alistair nodded.

'Lot a shit happened then. Lot a shit happened in lots of wars. This country always at war. The Turks. The Hungarians. The Germans.' Mihail stared at him expectantly, waiting for the rest of what Alistair was going to say. Uncertainly Alistair looked down. After some thought he reached for the zip of his rucksack. He had to dig around for a bit, moving the bulk of his laptop computer out of the way to get at what he was after. After some moments of this he pulled out an A4-sized jiffy envelope. It was addressed to him at his parents and had a red stamp with the logo of the BBC. The new logo made of square blocks rather than slanted ones. Alistair withdrew the contents – a DVD in a shiny silver case. 'The Best of *Then and Now*' proclaimed the elegantly designed cover. The title dominated the top half, reproduced in the same typeface that had been used on the show – a simple, heavy Helvetica. There were two photos beneath – one melting into the other – a slender-looking boy of nine or ten in seventeenth-century dress banging a drum, and a similar-looking child in seventies school uniform hurling a milk bottle at a policeman. Alistair turned it over. At the top was a quote from the *Daily Telegraph* – 'History is rarely this enlightening.' Beneath this there was a list of the eight episodes and their titles. Four 'Thens' and four 'Nows'. Alistair drew his finger down the list: 'A Brighter Star' and 'The Angry Silence', 'Hope Is a Thing With Feathers' and 'The New World'. His finger paused under 'A Candle In The Darkness'. He ran it further down the cover to a photograph of the cast of that episode. It came to rest under a big-eyed, frightened-looking boy. He showed it to Mihail.

'Me.' Mihail peered at it. He looked from it to Alistair and back again. 'A play. A television play I was in.' He let Mihail read the text on the cover.

'BBC . . .' He eyed it, puzzled. 'This was . . . to do . . . with . . .'

'Leila Vinteuil,' said Alistair.

Mihail squinted closely at the cover. 'This was a long time ago. Why are you here now?' Mihail looked at Alistair intently. Alistair shook his head. 'Come on, Englez. You can tell me. We are nearly buddies. We smoke cigarettes together.' Mihail studied him with his bright blue eyes.

Alistair remained silent for a moment, then spoke. 'There's an exhibition on. In Cluj. They've opened the house up. The Vinteuil house. It's sixty years. I wanted to see it. See it for myself . . .' His voice tailed off. His explanation sounded weak. He began again. 'I'm going down there . . .' *Another* pause, in which Alistair rubbed his forehead, then drew on his cigarette. He found his head empty of words. He had intended to add something else but he couldn't recall what.

'That's all?'

'. . . And then I'm going home,' he said, eventually. Alistair put the DVD back in its envelope and the envelope back in his rucksack. Mihail looked at him, trying to comprehend what Alistair had told him. Then his leathery face broke out into a smile.

'You crazy Britanic. I don't understand you.'

Alistair turned to the window. The trees flicking past the window had grown thicker, the blackness behind them like a cave. They both stared into the silent forest. Then Mihail said, 'The only good thing the communists left us. The trains still run on time.' He turned back to Alistair. 'You know how?' Mihail ground his cigarette beneath his Converse boot. 'They run on time because they run too many of them.' Of course Alistair did know this. He had read about it in one of the many guidebooks he had consumed before he left. 'Is quite possible to get on a train and you are only person on it. Sometimes they even run them empty. You know that?' Mihail put his arm over Alistair's shoulder. 'Let us see if we can find ourselves somewhere quieter to sit.' And with that he led Alistair away from the window and the roaring world outside.

# PART TWO

**Eroul a orbit după ce a fost atacat violent într-un tren de noapte**
**Iată întreaga desfăşurare a faptelor**

Hero blinded in late night train horror attack
Full story inside

From *Monitorul de Cluj*, 17 June 2001

# Chapter Five

'Did the man say what was going on?' said Alice, her hands pushed deep in her overcoat. She exhaled a cloud of steam.

'Just a bomb. Maybe IRA.' Steve sounded almost excited.

Alistair read the chalked sign: 'No trains past Queensway. Bomb explosion.'

'What kind of bomb?' Steve put the question cheerfully to the ill-tempered-looking Indian man in the ticket office.

'An explosion at Marble Arch. I don't know any more.'

'How am I going to get back to the hotel?' said Alistair.

'You're coming home with me. You'll get a taxi later.'

'We can't go into town?' Alistair was relieved.

They walked out onto the platform. Shiny, grey snow smeared the slice of ground not sheltered by the station's roof.

'Well, I'm going to Shepherd's Bush. Get a bus,' said Alice. Alistair watched her brush her hair away from her eyes. She went to sit on one of the narrow benches. Alistair turned to Steve. 'How far to yours?'

'Holland Park. No distance.' Steve had wandered over to the bench and to Alice.

'How often are the trains?' said Alistair.

Steve shrugged.

'Your guess is as good as mine, chief.'

Alice looked up at Alistair. 'Sit,' she said.

Alistair smiled uncertainly. She patted the portion of seat next to her. Alistair perched. Steve was on his knees in front of them. He lowered his head parallel with Alice's chest. Alistair wondered what he was doing.

'Who've we got today?' said Steve. He was examining the badges pinned to her lapel. He read aloud. 'Comsat Angels.' He turned to Alistair and nodded in an exaggerated manner, as if giving his approval. 'PiL – Flowers of Romance.' He moved his head from side to side as if not so sure. 'Girls at our Best.' He pantomimed ignorance.

'And . . .?' said Alice.

'Nothing. Just curious.' Steve sat next to Alice on the bench.

'It's so cold!' Alice banged her rubber-soled feet up and down. 'Where have you got to get to?' She had turned to Alistair. She looked at him intently. This seemed to be her preferred mode of inquiry.

'The hotel. In Shepherd's Bush.'

'You're not from London?' She looked at him quizzically. He shook his head. 'You're here on your own?'

'There's a woman at the hotel—'

'He's all right,' said Steve, interrupting. 'I'm looking after him this afternoon.'

Alice was still facing Alistair. She was chewing the right edge of her bottom lip.

'Don't you mind being on your own?' she asked. Alistair shrugged. 'We've loads of room at our house. There's a spare room. You could stay with us.' There was a moment's silence. Something fluttered in the wind further down the platform. Then, once again, Steve said, 'He's all right.' After a moment he added, 'Why don't you come back with us?'

Alice shook her head. 'Can't. Got to be somewhere.' A train pulled into the station with a penetrating screech.

They all filed inside. Steve waited until Alice had sat down and then sat opposite her. Alistair sat next to Steve.

'You like that stuff, do you?' said Steve, nodding at Alice's badges.

'Stuff?'

'Those bands.'

'*Those* bands?'

'Student stuff.'

'And what do you like?'

'Oh . . . this and that.' Steve grinned at her winningly.

'Girls at our Best are from Leeds,' Alistair heard himself say. He immediately wished that he hadn't.

'Sorry?' said Alice.

He had no choice but to repeat himself. 'Girls at our Best. They're a Leeds band.'

'Do you like them?' She seemed excited that he might.

'Um . . . sort of . . . well . . .'

'Do you like *Pleasure*?'

'Sorry?'

'*Pleasure*. The album.'

'Oh . . .'

'He thought you were asking about something else,' said Steve with a theatrical snicker.

'I don't . . . I haven't heard it. Sorry?' And now she seemed disappointed. 'It's where I'm from. I know they're from Leeds. That's all.'

'You go up to Camden?' said Steve to Alice. He was sitting forward in his seat, blocking Alistair's view of her.

'Sometimes,' she said shrugging.

'*That's* where I've seen you.'

'When?'

'I knew I'd seen you before. That's where it was. Electric Ballroom. Saturday afternoons.'

'You go up to Camden?'

81

'Often.' He pulled out some chewing gum from his leather jacket. 'I remember your face.'

'Really?'

'Sure of it. I remember seeing you.' He handed her a piece, inserting a stick into his mouth at the same time. He put the packet away without offering any to Alistair.

The train had begun to slow. Alice looked out of the window and then at Alistair.

'I'm worried about him,' she said.

'Why?' said Steve. The word came out forcefully, his voice high and loud.

'Being on his own.'

'He's all right.' Steve turned to him and ruffled his hair. 'You're all right, aren't you, sport?' Alice dug in her bag and pulled out a biro. She reached across to Alistair and grabbed his hand. She wrote on its back, hurriedly.

'So you've got someone to ring. If you need someone to talk to.' The train had pulled to a stop. Alice was up and out of her seat, already at the door.

'When do I get your number?' said Steve, grinning again.

Alice just grinned back at him. And then she was gone and the train was on its way again. Alistair looked down at his hand. At the number scrawled there.

'Nice going, sunshine. Top Banana. Get the girl's number, why don't you.' Steve took hold of Alistair's hand. Alistair felt himself blush.

'I don't . . . she was just . . . you know . . .'

'I'm only joking, sport. Out of our league.' Steve stretched his long legs out in front of him, touching the seat opposite. He looked like the kind of boy who could go out with anyone he wanted.

'Have you got a girlfriend then?' he said, turning in his seat to face Alistair.

As he had done earlier when questioned about his acting

experience, Alistair thought about lying but realized, for the same reasons, it would be futile to do so. He shook his head, then said, 'I'm at an all boys' school,' hoping this was explanation enough. 'Have you?' he said.

Steve pulled a face. 'Girlfriends are a no-no. Bad news,' he said.

'Have you had one?'

'Yeah!' Steve thumped Alistair on the side of his arm and laughed loudly. 'Several, my son, several. But they all end up driving you wacko.'

Alistair moved his hand to the side of his arm where Steve had punched him and rubbed it surreptitiously. It hurt.

'I like fucking, though,' said Steve. 'Have you ever fucked anyone?' The question was accompanied by a swift change in his facial expression from lightness to seriousness.

Alistair felt himself blushing again. He'd never heard the word used that way before, not in conversation. It seemed absurd that the question was even being put to him. 'When did you . . . first . . ..' He faltered, still embarrassed.

'Three years ago. With a teacher. Well, she was a student teacher. In a cupboard. In the science lab.' Steve made a thumbs-up sign like Fred Pontin. There were many boys at Alistair's school who would boast about such things but Alistair and Herby would laugh in private at their obvious fictions. The alarming thing about Steve was that Alistair sensed he was speaking the truth. 'You do like girls, don't you?' Steve added after a moment. 'You've been with one? You have *kissed* one?' He looked concerned, as if not to have done so would have been something between an impropriety and a misfortune.

'Yes!' And now Alistair wasn't lying. He had been with a girl. He had French-kissed a girl. Verity Moss. At Chai

Summer School this year. But the experience was brief and the outcome was not as he had hoped.

'Go on then. Who was she?'

'Just a girl.'

The memory of the experience remained raw. He still felt boiled in it.

'You're not dissembling, are you, chief?'

'What?'

'Telling porkies.'

It was as if Steve knew.

'No! It was at Jewish Summer School.'

'Ahhh. Jewish Summer School. I've heard about these places.' 'These places' spoken as if they were brothels.

'How?'

'I know Jews,' said Steve with mock umbrage.


There was something awesome about the wealth on display in Holland Park. There were posh parts of Leeds: Scarcroft where the football players had their houses, some with swimming pools and Greek-pillared front porches. Or Sandmoor Avenue – so-called 'millionaire's row'. But the houses here, even more so with their approaches veiled in snow, had a grandeur and palatial quality of another order altogether. They spoke of a mythical level of prosperity that seemed otherworldy to Alistair. He trod carefully, trying to avoid slipping since the pavements were now glassy with ice. Steve seemed unconcerned, able to navigate the frozen ground without difficulty. He ambled along, swinging his Slazenger bag by the canvas loops of its handles.

'What was she like – this . . . Verity? Did she let you feel her tits?'

Alistair felt that night envelop him. He didn't want to be back there. He'd been surprised to find himself walking along with her. She'd been part of the group of girls they'd all been talking to. And then the kiss had just happened. He couldn't even remember how. Did she lean towards him? She must have done. The shock at feeling the wetness of her tongue in his mouth, wriggling vigorously. A few seconds' repulsion followed by a decision that he liked this very much. His own erection fierce and bone-hard. Sitting down in a hedge and feeling that he was catching on quickly, and fired by this knowledge moving his hand to the region of Verity's chest where he guessed her bra was beneath her sweatshirt. Being aware of a dual motivation – partly driven by the sense that he would be able to tell everyone about how far he had got, and partly by something huge and instinctive, something that felt it knew what it was doing, something much much older than him. In fact, the first thing he thought after he got over the shock of the intimacy of passing saliva back and forth was I remember this, even though he had never done anything like it before in his life. His exploration of Verity's tits ended when she forcibly moved his hand away and said, 'That's enough, Mr Playboy,' a line he remembered proudly. He did recall the feel of her bra, hard and springy, like the packaging round an Easter egg. He couldn't say with any honesty what her tits might have been like. These would be good memories if not tainted by what came after.

'Yes,' he replied, 'I did – a bit.'

'What about her cunt?'

Alistair worked hard not to show any shock at the use of the word. He shook his head.

'I think I am myself, it is fair to say, a cunt man,' said Steve confidently.

Alistair wondered if this was something to do with living in London. Maybe it made you grow up quicker, or gave you access to experiences that didn't come so readily in Leeds. He'd noticed a similar precocity in the boys from London he'd encountered at summer school.

Steve's house was big and grand – more so than Alistair had expected. He'd assumed they were just taking a short-cut past the expensive-looking properties. When they paused in front of the huge ivy-covered townhouse with an immaculate double-doored garage, Alistair was surprised.

'I think we might be in luck,' said Steve, opening the front door and throwing his bag towards a hatstand.

'What do you mean?' Alistair looked around in amaze-ment. The hallway was more like a museum or a shop than a house. It was wood-panelled and there were large framed photographs of various images: a skull fashioned out of ice or crystal, an Inca pyramid, a chalk horse carved into a hill-side.

'Dad's at a meeting and Eleanor's at the hairdresser's,' he said chucking his leather jacket on top of the bag.

'Who's Eleanor?'

'Dad's girlfriend.'

Alistair's immediate reaction was to ask where Steve's mother was but he thought better of it, in case it was a sen-sitive subject. 'Come on – do you want a drink?' Steve headed to the kitchen. Alistair was relieved to see him switch on the kettle, rather than produce anything alco-holic.

'Can I phone for a taxi?'

'You don't need to phone. You'll get one in the street.'

Steve took a bag and coat that were coiled on the huge oblong kitchen table. 'Gonzo's here,' he said, and chucked the items on the floor before sitting down at the table.

'Who's Gonzo?'

'Little brother.' Steve dropped teabags into two mugs.

'Have you done much TV acting?' asked Alistair, wanting

to get the subject of conversation onto something that felt safer than girls and sex. He noted that he wouldn't have thought that if he was talking about it with Herby.

'A little bit in *The Paul Squire Show. Angels. Cowboys* . . . with Colin Welland. *Flame Trees of Thika*. It's good. I like it. Did a film last year.'

'Really!'

'Canadian thing shooting in London. Hasn't come out yet here. Got it on video.'

'Have you got a video player?'

'Yeah! Come on.' He splashed boiling water into the mugs, picked them up and headed through a pair of double doors at the back of the kitchen.

The room beyond was large and spacious. It looked like something in a Sunday magazine. It was L-shaped and split-level, with the foot of the L reached by a set of descending steps. The upper half was filled by a bulky table-football game and a full-sized pinball machine. The bottom half of the room was dominated by an enormous television which was on, chattering away, seemingly to nobody. Alistair must have been gawping because Steve said, 'It's the Den. Dad had it done for him but he's never here so we kind of took it over.' On the wall by the steps was a picture of someone who Alistair took to be Steve's dad because he looked like Steve except he was older and smarter dressed. He was standing in front of Stonehenge. Next to him, with an arm round his shoulder, was Lee Majors from *The Six Million Dollar Man*. Alistair stopped in front of the picture to look at it closely.

'Is that your dad?'

'Yes.'

Alistair thought he could detect a note of weariness in Steve's voice, as if visitors were forever pausing in front of this photo.

'What's he doing with Lee Majors?'

'He presents my dad's programme,' and then Steve changed the tone of his voice and went into a recital mode as if to confirm how tedious he found the topic. 'My dad makes this programme that is based on these books he wrote, which is huge in America, and Lee Majors presents it.' Immediately Alistair wanted to ask more questions but he resisted. They walked down the steps into the television part of the room. A huge white sofa filled one end. Stretched across it was a boy, younger than Alistair. He curled into a ball as they approached. Steve launched himself at the sofa. For a moment Alistair thought Steve was going to dive on the boy, but he didn't. Instead Steve filled the space next to him, immediately turning and pounding the balled-up child with both his fists.

'Gonzo! Gonzo!' he chanted the rhythm to match the pummelling.

''uck off.'

'Gon-zoh! Gon-zoh! Gon-zoh!'

''uck off,' the boy managed again. Alistair didn't know what to do. Since he had no brothers and sisters himself he assumed this was the kind of thing brothers and sisters did. He turned to look at the television, thinking it was best just to let them complete their ritual without getting involved. He recognized Marble Arch on the screen. A reporter was explaining that the bomb that had exploded was probably an accident. It seemed to have been carried by two Iranian terrorists who were on their way to plant it somewhere when it went off inadvertently. Suddenly Alistair found himself thinking of Alice. Hoping that she had managed to get home safely. He risked another glance at the wrestling siblings. Steve was totally on top of his brother now, whose arm was waving in the air as if to signify submission.

'Why isn't Gonzo at school?' said Steve, now sitting upright.

'Let us home early.'

'Bollocks. I'm telling Dad.'

There was something wrong with Steve's brother's voice. As if he couldn't say his words properly. Now he was sitting up Alistair could see something blocky and pink, the colour of an Action Man's body, curled over the boy's ear. It was a hearing aid.

'Then I'm telling Dah abow the aquariah.'

'Are yah?' said Steve, clearly mocking him. 'I doh think sah.' Holding his brother's narrow wrists in one of his hands, Steve reached out to the side of his brother's head and fiddled with the corner of the hearing aid. He played with it until it emitted a piercing screech. The boy started shrieking too. 'You can hear that, can't you?' said Steve. The boy was moving his head from side to side, as if trying to shake the hearing aid free.

'Turn it dow. Turn it dow!' the boy yelled. Steve waited a moment and then did so. The shrill whining feedback ceased. It had been loud even to Alistair and must have been unbearable to the boy, screaming straight in his ear. The boy was weeping softly now and Steve released his wrists.

'Come on,' he said, suddenly turning to Alistair. 'We'll go upstairs.'

Alistair followed Steve up the grand staircase that curved its way round the outside of the entrance hall. There were more framed photos hanging from the oak panelling. One of them was of a very beautiful woman. The picture looked like the front cover of a magazine. Alistair wondered if the woman was Eleanor.

Steve's bedroom was surprisingly small and surprisingly normal. Alistair had expected something more idiosyncratic, something he would be more impressed by. Instead it was like a cliché of a teenage boy's room. There was a poster of Debbie Harry *circa Eat to the Beat*. Next to it was one of last season's Liverpool squad. The floor was messy, clothes strewn everywhere, shirts, trousers and underpants. There was a small bookshelf next to the window. Curious as to what would be on it, without thinking, Alistair went to examine it. There were a number of old annuals: *Tiger*, *Action*, *Roy of the Rovers*. Some standard children's paperbacks too: *Stig of the Dump*, *Heartsease*, *Carrie's War*. Nothing that coincided with the idea of Steve that Alistair had already formed. Steve must have registered him studying the bookshelves. He came over to Alistair's side.

'Don't look at that. Ignore all that.' He moved Alistair over to a white wicker chair on the other side of the room. 'Keep it like that to keep them off the scent.' He pointed downstairs. 'What's it like – an all boys' school? Pretty miserable, I should imagine.' Steve had gone over to his music centre. It was the most impressive thing in the room. Upright and fixed to the wall, its turntable was vertical rather than horizontal.

'It's OK. Don't know. I've been there since I was eight.' Alistair watched intrigued as Steve slid a record from its sleeve. Alistair could read the label. *Casablanca* it read. Steve slid it into the upright receptacle.

'Do you meet up with girls then? Youth club? Anything like that?' The record began – a thumping four-four beat with a heavy guitar chord. At first Alistair thought it was heavy metal. Then a synthesizer melody began and he recognized it. 'Hot Stuff' by Donna Summer. He'd danced to it at the summer school disco with Verity Moss.

'Sometimes. Not really . . . It's hard . . .'

Steve stared at him.

'Don't you feel deprived?'

'No.' Alistair was aware of the belligerent tone in his voice.

'But you don't know anything about girls?'

'I've got a friend. Herby. He . . . we . . . talk about stuff.'

'Really.' Steve had begun dancing around the room. His moves were impressive – adept and fluid – like a stage version of a disco dancer. 'That's the problem with the ladies, though.' He paused to mouth along with the record, repeating 'hot stuff'. 'The real catch-22. They like the guys in the know. But how do you get in the know . . .' He moved his head from side to side in time with the throb of the song. '. . . if you haven't got the know.' And Alistair was back in the summer school disco where he didn't want to be. Standing in the corner. Mustering what courage he could. He'd been thinking about Verity every hour of the twenty-four since she'd kissed him. (He'd dreamed about her when he'd slept so that counted as thought.) Walking over. Trying to ignore the cluster of stripy-T-shirted girls around her. 'Verity.' Hearing the name fall out of his mouth and the laughter it provoked in the female audience. Seeing her laughing too. 'Will you go with me?' It was too late, he knew, even before the words were out. They were all laughing now. Walking away. Walking away.

Quite suddenly, and with striking grace, Steve fell to his knees on to a discarded vest and slid a foot or so across the wooden floor to the bookcase. He pushed it to one side, revealing a small cupboard door, built into the wall. This was pulled open and a large timber trunk – like a dressing-up box – was withdrawn. Steve took a bunch of keys from his pocket and slipped one of them into the trunk's lock. In time to the music he flipped up the heavy lid, which swung easily into an upright position. Alistair tried to peer to see the contents of the trunk but Steve was using his body to block the view. He turned abruptly, throwing something at

Alistair. It was black and heavy. A book. A large, hardbacked picture book. It was entitled, simply, *Horror Films*, in blood-red letters against the black.

'Do you like horror films?' said Steve, sliding the trunk back into its space.

'Yeah.' In truth he hadn't seen that many. Herby's friend Darren Zimmerman had a video machine and they'd gone round there one Sunday afternoon to watch a tape of *Alien*. It was an illegal copy and it had been too fuzzy to follow.

'You can borrow it if you'd like. You might find a picture of your hotel in there,' he said grinning. 'Go on. Take it home. Read it in bed tonight.' Doing as Steve said, Alistair took the book and dropped it into his plastic bag. Steve pushed the shelves back into position. 'You going to be on the phone all night? Stack of two-pences by your side?' he said casually as he turned back to face Alistair.

'What?'

Steve held up his hand and tapped the back of it, whistling as he did so. Alistair self-consciously covered up his own hand.

'There's no shame in it. She's first-division stuff. Nottingham Forest.'

'I . . . she's . . .'

'But you do fancy her, don't you? You do . . .' Steve was looking at him, his serious look again.

'I . . .' Alistair snorted something like a laugh through his nostrils. He looked down at the floor.

'What was that?' said Steve, still scrutinizing him.

'Nothing.'

'Come on . . .'

'Stop it.'

Suddenly Steve was at his side. 'It's all right. I'm just winding you up, chief. Take no notice.' He stood up. 'Just having a bit of a laugh.' He went over to the bed, falling

92

backwards onto it, his hands behind his head. 'But you can dream, my son. We can all dream.'

The Bray Hotel stood stark and black against the darkening sky, no lights in its upper windows. In shape it mirrored the regularity of the other terraced houses in the street, but its red brick had been patched with white plaster. It had iron-work fastened to its walls: great rusted balconies attached beneath windows, and at either side two spiralling fire escapes running from the top floor to the pavement like skeletal helter-skelters.

It was dark in the lobby. What light there was seemed to be coming from the Calgary Bar, off to the left – the door to which was open. Alistair glanced in. The few bottles, hanging sadly from their optics like a sketch of a real pub, were the only things illuminated. The rest of the room fell off into blackness. A movement made Alistair turn back. There was a shape behind the reception desk. A small fluorescent bulb flickered on. And there was Rosalyn Frieze, the pro-prietor, her hair pushed back by a bright red band, staring at Alistair as if he were the Devil. The day before, when Alistair had arrived, she had made him repeat her name until he could pronounce it to her satisfaction. 'I am Rosalyn. Rosa-leen. Say it. Rosa. Leen.' The surface of the reception was covered in a jigsaw. She held a piece in her hand.

'Where have you been?' She didn't look like an old woman because she didn't dress that way. Only when close to her was it possible to discern the lines etched around her eyes and lips. Alistair looked at his watch. It wasn't yet six. *In loco parentis*. You know what it means?'

Her accent was hard to pin down: part French, part American. Alistair put his bag down on the floor and hung his head, trying to look contrite.

93

'I have been doing this for some time. I am trusted to take care.' She lowered her jigsaw piece and moved out from behind the reception desk, still holding her glass. Alistair couldn't help but look down at her shoes. They were gold with high heels that lifted her several inches off the floor. 'Your parents have called. I had a long talk with your mama. She is a charming woman. Quite charming.' Still holding the jigsaw piece she took a swig from a brandy glass at her side. 'Our talk was most revealing. Most . . . perceptive. We are agreed about you.'

Alistair couldn't stop his eyes moving to the jigsaw. There was something wrong with it.

'*Tu est . . . un ingrat. Un ingrat.*'

There was no picture. The surface was completely blank.

'Your poor parents. They await your call. I explained to them. This is how it is with a man-child. They never change.'

The jigsaw was upside down. She was solving it with its picture turned away from her. She followed his stare to the puzzle and laughed. 'I learned this in hospital. Stay long enough and you get to know pictures too well, *mon capricieux*. Much too well. After a while you get to prefer doing them this way.'

Alistair lay on his bed in his pyjamas, stretched out on the orange nylon bedspread. The room was small but long, as if it had been built for some other purpose than housing guests. His bed rested awkwardly against one wall. A brown Formica sink unit stood beyond it. There was a strong smell, not unpleasant, of dust and old library books. He listened to the noise of the hotel around him. Though he had yet to see another guest, the building was not silent. There was a low thudding that followed a regular rhythmic pattern. Occasionally the pipes to the radiator gurgled and rattled.

There were no voices, no other hint of human occupancy. It was quite possible that he and Rosalyn Frieze were alone in the building.

He didn't find it hard to learn lines. There was something enjoyable and comforting about the mechanical nature of the task. It was the same as revising for an exam. There was a part of his brain he was able to access that would hold the information with relative ease. Lying on his back in his pyjamas, holding the script above his head, he found that what he had to say began to penetrate him effortlessly. As if there was a place for it already within. After a while he got bored of looking at the script, sliding down the envelope incrementally to reveal whether he had said each line correctly. He put the script down and shuffled over to his suitcase which was open on the floor, the clothes within already in a state of disarray. He rummaged among the vests and jumpers until he found what he was looking for. He pulled out a small leatherette pouch from inside the sleeve of a cardigan. Dad had forbidden him from bringing his tape recorder. ('It's mine,' Alistair had protested. 'Oh yes? And who paid for it?') He opened the pouch and pulled out the little machine within. Dad's Dictaphone. As he held it in his hand he gave a moment's thought to the consequences of its non-presence at home being discovered. They were horrific. But Dad never used it. It resided permanently in a box behind the bottles of sherry and whisky in the sideboard. Upon his return Alistair would transfer whatever Travulia he had made by holding the machine to his microphone. Then he would erase the tiny silver cassette and replace the machine into its forgotten box.

He held the Dictaphone in his hand, feeling its weight. He pressed the record button.

'What are you doing?' he said. He had found a voice for Marcel Vinteuil. Whether or not it would be the voice he would settle with, he didn't know. It was not unlike his own, slightly higher in register, slightly younger than his. If he was playing the part of his own younger brother, it was the way he would speak.

'Just writing.' That was Alice's line. He'd taken her lines into his head as well. And her voice. Higher still than Marcel's, but with a rolling, confident quality. He tried to make it as he remembered it.

'Why?' he said as Marcel.

'It's just something I do. You've seen me do it before.' He imagined Alice's face as he spoke her dialogue. Let it fill his vision. Already he had an internal sense of her, both visually and sensually. He could recall what it felt like to be close to her. Her holding his hand. He pressed stop on the little tape recorder. Then rewind. He replayed the words – listening to how they sounded in the voice he had recorded. How they felt batted off his version of Alice. He pressed record again.

'What is all this?'

'Henry?' he found himself asking – in his own voice. 'Henry Hudson?'

'Hello. Yes?' The reply was in another voice – Henry's voice. The tension in Alistair's throat, the shape of his mouth, the tautness of the surrounding muscles – these things shifted automatically into the memory of Henry Hudson.

'Tell me where you are.'

'In London. In bloody London.' Despite his youth – Henry was over a year younger than Alistair – he sounded weary, almost comically so, like a little old man.

'What's happening?'

'Got this part. Bloody damned part in a big film. Disney film. *Return of the Black Pirate*. These kids – I'm one of the kids – move into a big old house.'

'What happens?' Alistair stared into the tiny black-mesh circle that covered the microphone, as if that might hold the answer. He didn't know in advance of asking the question. He let Henry tell him.

'Bloody pirate's ghost haunts it. All kinds of stuff goes down. Damn stupid thing. Bloody ghost causes a hell of a rumpus. Steals some experimental car from the scientist next door. My character gets the blame. Real old fool playing the pirate. Bunch of annoying kids. Curious about something,' said Henry, interrupting his own line of thought, 'Who is this *girl*, old boy?' The word 'girl' emphasized disparagingly. There were girls in Travulia. Why should Henry sound so rattled?

'Girl?' said Alistair, innocently.

'The number!' said Henry.

Alistair glanced down at his hand. He'd almost forgotten what was scrawled there. 'She's doing my thing. In my thing.'

'Oh . . . I see.'

Alistair observed the nuanced implication in the voice emanating from his own mouth as if it were another's. An independent thing, with motives, intentions and opinions all of its own. That was how it was with Travulia and all its inhabitants.

'And what are you going to do with the number? Ring it?'

'No!' Alistair protesting to his own character.

'Why not? If the girl gave it to you.'

'It wasn't like that.'

'What's she like, this girl? Pretty? Bloody actresses. All something to look at. Even the ones who aren't do themselves up as if they are.'

'Shut up now, Henry Hudson.' Alistair stopped the tape and dropped the Dictaphone on to the bed. He lay there for a moment, his eyes raised to the patchy ceiling. Once some

97

kind of cornice or moulding had been piped around the room's perimeter like icing. It had been covered over with so many layers of paint it was now as formless as wet dough. His hand reached down over the edge of the bed and found his plastic bag. He reached in and pulled out the book Steve had given him. He had no particular interest in horror films, but he was curious to see what Steve thought he would find so fascinating in it. It was a big paperback, the size of a cookery book or an art book, and the pages were thick and glossy. Alistair drew it closer to his face. The ink smelt sweet and new, even though the book was a few years old. There were large photographs throughout: as much of the space was devoted to pictures as to the text. Some of the more famous images he recognized – various Frankensteins and Draculas. There were other, less familiar illustrations. One photograph showed a line of SS soldiers frozen in ice. Another person was attaching electrodes, clearly trying to revive them. Alistair looked for the name of the film. *The Frozen Dead*. It wasn't one he'd heard of. He flicked through a few more pages. Some of them seemed to be stuck together. Sandwiched between them were other pieces of paper that were thinner and more crinkly – pages torn from a magazine. They must have got wet and been put in the pages of this book to dry. The paper cracked a little as he carefully separated the surfaces, trying not to do any damage. The first page was from a porno mag. There was a pale-looking woman staring out from it, naked apart from a big pair of white knickers. She wasn't particularly glamorous. Alistair noticed that his heart was beating faster. Again without trying to tear any of the paper, he prised apart the next two pages. He really wanted to do so at speed, but he didn't want to harm the book. On the next page the woman from the magazine was sitting on a chair, still wearing the knickers but now with her legs spread. The colours of the picture were faded and mottled – there were random stains spread across the surface of the image, as if it had been found face down in a puddle. The woman's face was unsmiling, her breasts small and droopy. Alistair was aware of a burning thrill in his stomach and a teak-hard erection in his pyjama bottoms. He had seen porno mags before. They'd been passed around school of course, beneath desks in lessons. Herby's brother had a stack which occasionally, if they were feeling brave, they would go and examine, but never for more than three or four minutes at a time. He had never had any pornography in his possession. He wanked of course. He would think about some of the pictures he had seen when he did so, but he had never been in a position to wank while looking at such a picture. Without even really thinking about it, his right hand closed around his cock. He eased the next page apart with his free hand. The woman's knickers were round her ankles. Alistair couldn't help but notice the full-page picture from a film on the opposing page – it was of a disembodied arm in a tank of blue water. He turned his attention to the woman, to her . . . what . . . her cunt, was that the word? Her vagina. Her twat. He knew it from photos as a dark triangle. He was shocked because this woman had red hair and her pubes were red too. They were sparsely spread, making Alistair think momentarily of disease. The next pages turned more easily. This was a close photo of the cunt. She was holding it open. Alistair had never seen such an image. Some of the luridness of the colour had survived. The flesh looked sore and meaty. The next page was all of the woman again. She was holding a spray can – like a deodorant can. The label was foreign. It wasn't a product Alistair recognized. The next image was unexpected. It was another close-up of the cunt. It filled the page like a photo of an operation. The deodorant can was half poking out, the skin stretched tight around it. The burning lusty feeling mingled with nausea now. Alistair was horrified to find he had come, all over the inside of his pyjama bottoms. After a moment he shut the book and stuffed it in its carrier bag. The burning was still there but no arousal, just something like sickness and shame. It wouldn't have been so bad had he not repeated the whole exercise half an hour later and again at five in the morning as the traffic began to announce the dawn of a new day out-side.

# Chapter Six

It was only recently that Alice Zealand had thought of her life as a tree growing wrong. Some kind of focus or panic that had coalesced as she entered her mid-thirties. No plan or expectation of her youth had anticipated the decade spent caring for her father, the slow move from part-time to full-time as his illness had progressed, her stubborn refusal to see him put in a home. Her brothers had helped, of course, but one by one they had married, had families. Alice volunteered quite willingly to do what she had done for Dad. And she didn't regret it, nor even resent it. She knew that she'd worn the experience like armour, voluntarily donning it, grateful for the protection it gave her from aspects of life she was happier avoiding. And had she not taken the path she trod she would not have been alone with him as he died, an experience she would not have given up in exchange for anything. Feeling him pass; the extraordinary peace that had settled silently like a snowfall. But then, within weeks of his death, her unlived life had come pouring in like water from a burst pipe. She had spent the next five years trying to patch the leaks and now, just when she felt that her life might actually be liveable, the water was flooding in again.

Alice was walking down Exmouth Market when she felt someone take hold of her arm. She was shocked to see Ben, because of the firmness of the grip, the hint of harm that she detected in it.

'Ben.' She tried to conceal any fear she felt.

'I was coming to the flat.' He looked straight at her. His face was flushed. 'I thought you might be in.'

'Shopping. I've got no food in.'

He nodded. They both stood for a moment. Pedestrians passed them on both sides. He took a step towards her, lowered his voice.

'Why did . . . why would you have come to the exhibition . . . if you didn't love me?' He was trying to speak slowly and deliberately in order to sound rational. She could smell alcohol on his breath. It was only 1.30.

Now she just wanted to be away from here. Anywhere. She became aware of her bag slung over her shoulder. The book nestling inside: *The Spiritual Exercises of St Ignatius*. Ben placed his other hand on her. She felt pinioned, sensed the beginnings of panic rising. 'We can't talk here.' She was aware of people staring.

'Let's go back.' He inclined his head in the direction of her flat.

'In there. We can go in there.' She pointed towards the café behind them. The seats inside were arranged in little booths. They could have some semblance of privacy.

When she returned with the coffees – an espresso for Ben, ignoring his request for tea – he was slumped in one corner of the booth, staring resentfully at a book. She realized, as she placed the drinks down, it was her copy of Ignatius. He looked up.

'You don't really believe in all this, do you?'

'Please don't go digging through my bag,' she said.

He slid the text across the table towards her. 'But you don't, do you?' It was a hopeful statement. Hopeful, but simultaneously mournful.

'Drink it.' She pushed the little cup towards him.

'You only started it all to stay close to him, didn't you? After he died.'

He was drunk, that was all. Upset and drunk. She understood. As it was, he was only saying what everyone thought when she began the Theology degree, including her.

'His holiness the vicar,' Ben crossed himself theatrically.

'For your information, Dad was agnostic. He was vice-principal of Heythrop College, not the Archbishop of Canterbury.'

'But he ran that course. And he went to church, didn't he? All the time. You told me.'

'He never called himself anything. Catholic, Anglican, Methodist. Not even Christian.' She closed her eyes. She felt defensive. She wanted to hang on to feelings of compassion for Ben. Not intimidation. Certainly not fear.

'And what about you?' Ben wasn't going to stop until she answered. She took a gulp of her coffee.

'What . . . why do you want to know this?' Why couldn't he just go?

'We never talked about it.'

'We did.'

'Not in any detail.'

'Why does it matter now?'

'Because I'm still . . . because I want to *understand* you.' He looked at her pleadingly.

'Dad used to say . . .' she said, as she stirred her coffee, staring into the mini-vortex she created, '"One can study the art of warfare without wanting to go to war."'

'And that's supposed to be an answer?'

Her own agnosticism – if that was the word – had never been questioned by her supervisors. She discovered that it was possible to construct the most complex arguments about God and His intentions without the problem of His existence or otherwise ever coming up. The thing that had really hooked her, that she responded to unreservedly, was biblical Hebrew. She had been surprised at how she had fallen in love with a language so notoriously difficult. Something about the connection it gave her to another time and another world sparked a flame in her heart. Read in its original form, parts of the Old Testament flowered into new and abundant life. And she loved its use of pun and double meaning – the in-built paradox of its method: revelation through riddle. It surprised no one that after completing her degree she immediately followed it up with a Masters in Old Testament Studies.

She looked at Ben. His expectant face. Was he so nervous of coming to visit her that he had to be drunk in order to do it? Did he need to see her so much that it drove him to overcome his fear? She didn't want to contemplate it. She could do with a drink herself. Maybe they could retire to the London Spa on the corner. She dismissed the idea.

All the time she had been with Ben she had sensed something moving within herself. There was part of her, of course, that wanted a partner. But it was only a part. Probably a small part.

Ben MacCawber. His face when she had first seen it. Like a shock. A jolt. A thrill. Being confused and frightened. But warm and right too. The light that came off him. His enthusiasm. Life.

She had never been with anyone like him. He was the first person she'd spent time with where the reasons felt right and good. Not in bed with him because she was drunk or hating herself, but because she wanted to be.

On her second or third night with him she had had a memory. Of being small. In her attic room in Wilberforce Road, lying in bed on a Saturday morning. She had woken up early and it was just beginning to get light outside. She could hear the pigeons in the eaves above her. She felt utterly safe. That was how it was lying with Ben. The first time she had experienced that with a man in her adult life.

That comfort did not last.

The thing that moved within, coiling and uncoiling, would not let her settle. She named it 'the eel'.

All the time she was in Israel she was still unable to find ease. The slithering thing became something smaller, more concentrated, more irritating. It was now like a stone in her shoe. A small but persistent annoyance. Something was being demanded of her. She couldn't decide if the stone was the same as the eel. Or if the stone had been there all along, masked by the eel.

Whatever Alice had expected to find in the Holy Land had not been forthcoming. She had returned after four months, still discomfited but in a different way. The moments of epiphany she had prepared for had not arrived. She had tried to speed them along by visiting as many sacred sites as she could: the Holy Sepulchre, the Wailing Wall, the Haram ash-Sharif. All left her unmoved. She saw nothing but stone, sand or lifeless rock. Felt nothing but the rucksack chafing at her shoulders, the sweat running down her back, the constant thirst brought on by the relentless heat. In the Caro Synagogue in Safed, foolishly, self-consciously, she had tried uttering the only sincere prayer she had ever uttered in her life. Something about the peaceful white-stoned environment had made her take the risk. 'Please. Tell me what I need to do. I know I need to do something. Help me to know what it is and to do it.' No answer had been forthcoming.

Ben had picked up the book again. He read from the back cover: '"As a soldier, Ignatius fought bravely for Spain and dreamed of glory. Seriously wounded, the soldier became a mystic and vowed to fight thereafter *ad majorem*

*Dei glorium.*"' He looked at Alice with something approaching disdain. 'Why are you wasting your time with this shit?'

'Father Pablo recommended it to me.'

'Is he your guru now? Or your surrogate father? Spiritual exercises. What's the relevance of *this* to anything?'

'They're the basis for the training among spiritual directors.'

'Spiritual . . . what the fuck is a spiritual director?'

'Counsellors of others who are in spiritual crisis. Just give the book to me.' She held out her hand for it.

'Alice.' He had closed his eyes and scrunched up his face.

'What?'

'I'm . . . look . . . ignore me. I'm just . . .'

'It doesn't matter.'

'It does matter. We can work it out. I can't . . . just . . .'

'Ben.'

'I won't—'

'Ben.'

'We must work it out . . . this . . . us . . .' He opened his eyes again.

Involuntarily she had taken a deep breath. She heard it leave her body as a sigh.

'You're back in London now. I'm here. You're here. We have to . . . we just need to spend some time together.'

'No, Ben.'

'Please.'

'It's not . . . I can't . . .'

'What? . . .'

'I just . . . I can't . . .'

'You can.'

'I'm not staying here.'

'What?'

'I'm not staying here. I'm leaving London. I'm leaving the country.'

'Where are you going now?'

'I'm – it doesn't matter. I'm just—'

'Stay.'

'Look—'

'I'm asking you to stay.'

'I'm . . . I can't . . .'

'You can. I'm asking you to.'

'No, Ben. I'm going. I'm leaving. No.'

'Then fuck you! Fuck off! You stupid fucking . . .' He couldn't get the words out. He slammed his hands on the table, knocking the espresso cup over. The black coffee spread towards the book. He pushed himself away from the table and out of the café, leaving Alice alone in the booth. An old woman opposite stared, her face set in disapproval, before turning back to her lunch, shaking her head.

Alice looked down at the book on the table surface. The coffee had pooled around its edges. She picked it up and reached for a tissue, wiping what excess she could from its pale cover, then replaced it in her bag. She sat for ten minutes more trying to slow her breathing, then made her way from the café and out into the muggy afternoon.

'You know, Alice,' said Father Pablo, his fingers working the square of paper on the desk in front of him, 'there are people who would think this choice of path quite extraordinary.'

She had been prepared for this. She knew there would be resistance. 'You think it's out of the question. You think it's wildly inappropriate.'

'You have a disconcerting habit of assuming knowledge of what I'm thinking. Neither of these thoughts is in my head.' He picked up what he had made of the paper. It looked like a flower. He offered it on his palm for Alice to inspect. 'It is a gift. For a young boy I write to in Cambodia – Rattanak

Mondol, to be specific. I sent him one for his birthday and now every time I write I feel guilty if I don't enclose another.' He grinned broadly. 'Too effeminate for a boy, you think?'

She examined the carefully folded paper. The care with which he had done it made it beautiful. 'He'll love it.' She handed it back to him.

'An animal would be better. An elephant or bird. But I can only do flowers.' He looked momentarily sad, then took the flower and placed it inside an addressed envelope. 'It would be true to say that you, Alice, are not the traditional candidate to become a spiritual director. You are young. You are female. You are not a Catholic.' He had stood up now, and had found a thread on the sleeve of his jacket. He began to pull at it.

'But you . . . it was you who—'

Father Pablo interrupted her with a raised hand. 'None of these things is necessarily an impediment. The question of what exactly your faith is might be thornier, but again this is not in itself a deciding factor.' He rolled the piece of cotton he had retrieved around the end of his index finger.

'I know what's in my heart. I know what feels right.'

'And your . . . temperament. Do you feel it is ready for the discipline?'

She felt immediately ashamed. As if he knew something about her she never assumed that he could. She blushed. 'You think there's something wrong with me?'

He shook his head. 'The training is rigorous. It starts with the observation of thirty days' silence. And then, over the next three years, things get progressively more demanding.'

'I know . . . I'm aware of the process.' She was prepared to defend her decision. He remained silent, standing in front of the window. It was bright outside. She couldn't see his face.

'Alice,' he said, his voice low. 'I don't sit in judgement on you. I will help you. If I can. That's all.' He moved back to his chair and sat down, bringing his eyes level with hers. 'If this is what is in your heart, if this is the path that has presented itself to you, what business is it of mine to judge it?' He sat back, picking up the envelope with the origami in it. 'I know you're aware of what the training means. And everything you'll be required to leave behind. You've already made these decisions.'

'Yes.' She thought she sounded impertinent. She didn't mean to.

'Then my job is simply to put you in touch with the relevant people. Agreed?'

She nodded.

'Good.' He put the envelope to his mouth and carefully licked the gummed flap. 'Unless . . .' He lowered the letter. 'Unless you came here for something else.'

She looked up at him, momentarily thrown.

'For . . . permission?'

Alice felt her heart beating faster.

'I . . .' She didn't know what to say. Whatever thought she had opened her mouth to express evaporated.

Father Pablo let the silence hold. Then he completed sealing the envelope, placing it on the table in front of him. He stood up again and went over to the oak display case on the opposite side of the room. 'I found something recently. I was going to ask if you would like it.' He slid open the glass on one of the compartments and removed a small cardboard box. 'It was something of your father's.' He walked back to the table and placed the box down. It was made of manilla-coloured card and had a flip-up lid like a cigarette packet. There was a gummed address sticker on the front but the address hadn't been filled in. Alice picked the item up and pulled the lid open. Inside was a cassette tape – an

109

old-fashioned one made of black rather than transparent plastic. A BASF C-120, with a red label. She felt a thrill on seeing Dad's handwriting. She lifted the tape closer to her face. '4.2.82 – Abram's journey.'

'What is it?' she asked, still examining the label, as if it might yield more information.

'Your father used to tape some of his lectures.' Father Pablo had interlaced his fingers, resting them on the edge of the desk. 'He had an occasional correspondent – a blind academic somewhere in Scotland I believe – for whom he would make tapes.'

Alice shrugged. 'I never knew.'

'It was a sporadic communication. You know how he collected such things.'

'Have you listened to it?'

The priest smiled. 'It is your father. As I remember him,' he said.

The anticipation of spending an hour listening to her father speaking filled Alice with joy.

'You miss him?' he asked.

Alice looked up.

'Of course. Forgive me.' He separated his hands and lay them in his lap. 'Maybe it shouldn't be the taboo it has become. Between you and me, I mean.'

'It's not taboo,' said Alice. The word had sounded strange from Father Pablo's mouth.

'He used to speak much of you. Sometimes I thought he was . . . in awe of you.' Father Pablo was not looking at her. His gaze was cast down to his lap. 'Not having children I assumed this was usual between a man and his daughter. Now . . .' his voice tailed off for a moment, '. . . I am not so sure.'

Alice felt uncomfortably self-conscious. The fact that her father had been a colleague of the priest's was seldom

110

referred to and never in this personal way. She didn't know what to say.

'He used to talk much of what you did. Your acting. Your singing. As if he couldn't believe someone he knew could be capable of such things.'

The discomfort was spreading. A tightness in her chest and throat. She didn't want this to show. She smiled. The tightness was reaching for her eyes. The moment stretched on. Alice looked out of the window down into Kensington Square. There were people on the lawn. The closest were a couple. The boy was kissing the side of the girl's neck.

'So. I will contact the monastery at San Castellano,' said Father Pablo abruptly. 'We will see how they feel about taking a young woman. Though you would not have been the first to have trained there. These are progressive Jesuits.' He smiled broadly.

It was as if she had just imagined the conversation about her father. She stood up, slipping the cassette into its box. She stowed the box in her bag, then took the priest's hand. 'Thank you,' she said.

He inclined his head.

She let go of his fingers and moved towards the door.

'Oh, Alice. There was one other thing.' He looked across at her. 'I forgot. When you went to Israel. Just after you left. A young man came calling. He was most perturbed.'

Alice froze. She didn't turn back.

'He was desperate to reach you. Did he find you?'

'I've seen him since,' she said abruptly.

'A good young man, I thought. A good man to have been concerned about you.'

Alice nodded. 'Yes,' she said and opened the door, exiting before she had to say any more.

111

# Chapter Seven

When Alistair arrived at the second rehearsal he found Alice sitting there alone, her back against the radiators, reading a book. He could see she was still wearing her red nail varnish. It stood out against the pale book cover. He felt nervous. He became very aware that he was going to have to remember his lines today, that he would have to act, that he would have to convince. Alice looked up, saw him and closed her book carefully, pushing a bookmark into the pages before laying it on her lap.

'Hello,' she said. 'We're early again.' She stretched her arms over her head yawning. The movement looked deliberate and graceful, like a dancer's.

'Hi.' Alistair put his carrier bag on the next but one seat from her. Then he picked it up and sat down, replacing the bag on his knee. 'Where is everybody?'

'Late again.' She put her book on the floor. 'Cyril Davenport's in there.' She lowered her voice as if conveying a secret. She smiled as she spoke. Alistair felt himself smile too. She pointed towards the open door that led in to the main rehearsal room. The slender figure of Cyril Davenport was visible horizontal on the floor. He was moving around, snake-like across the lino, measuring distances with his outstretched hands. There were lines of coloured sellotape behind him, as if he'd been marking his passage like some outsized mollusc. He looked up, his head twisting uncomfortably over his shoulder, a piece of blue tape emerging from his mouth. Both Alistair and Alice looked away. They laughed. She seemed much more relaxed today. She stretched her legs out in front of her. She was wearing jeans, with black boots. Alistair liked the shape of her legs. He felt it in the base of his stomach. 'I tried to start a conversation with him earlier,' she said, still whispering. 'He just kept talking about biscuits. And the urn.' Alistair laughed again. She started laughing too. She had turned towards him. 'Hey, has anyone ever told you . . .' said Alice. She tailed off, suddenly uncertain of herself.

'What?'

'No. It doesn't matter.'

'What? Told me what?'

She lowered her eyes to the floor.

'Go on.'

'No. It was a stupid thing.'

'Go on. You can say?' What was she going to say?

'All right. But don't take this the wrong way. That you really look like Bob Dylan.' She looked at him searching for a response. His own face must have done something because her smile dropped. 'It's a good thing.' She smiled again. 'Honestly.'

Alistair was confused. Was she taking the piss?

'It's your hair. Like the cover of *Blonde on Blonde*.'

Involuntarily Alistair felt himself run his hand over his head. Her brow furrowed.

'I don't know much about music.' Alistair wanted to help her out.

'What do you mean?'

'I don't really know . . .' He shrugged his shoulders.

'You don't need to *know* anything. Elvis Presley. Bob Dylan. John Lennon. Lou Reed. David Bowie. John Lydon.

113

That's it.' Alistair liked her voice, liked listening to her speaking. Her accent was southern and cultured, giving her, to his ears at least, an air of sophistication, different from the few girls he was used to talking to at home.

'It's good hair. That's all I meant to say.' She smiled again. Little wrinkles formed at the corner of her eyes making her look much older, almost an adult. 'What's Leeds like? I don't know anything about Leeds.'

'Leeds is . . .' What could he say? He wanted to answer her. 'Home. I don't know. I like it.' He did like it. Why did it sound so juvenile?

'The Gang of Four are from Leeds. Do you know them?'

'Heard of them.'

'Do you like them?'

He shrugged his shoulders again.

'What do you like?'

'I haven't got a record player.' He felt stupid and young. He wanted to be able to impress Alice but he couldn't think of anything he might say that would do that. 'Who's your favourite band?' he asked, hoping that would suffice. He didn't want the conversation to dry up.

'Am I only allowed one?' she said. She had moved closer to him, gazing at him, animated by the question.

'You can have five,' Alistair heard himself saying, surprised by a sudden rush of confidence. For a moment he felt like a new person. It occurred to him that because Alice didn't know him he was free to be somebody else.

'OK. At the moment – and it changes week to week I freely admit – PiL; The Associates; Was, not Was; Rip Rig and Panic; Joy Division and The Slits.'

'That's six.'

She laughed.

'The trouble is . . .' said Alistair, intoxicated with a sudden sense of authenticity, 'I don't know what to listen to.

114

There's so much. How do you start? Where do you start?'

'Have you got a tape player?'

'Yes.' Alistair thought about his bulky cassette machine.

'I'll do you a tape. A starter kit.'

'Really?' He felt a rising excitement. It was broken by the entrance of Jack Deal, who blustered in noisily and expansively, swinging his leather briefcase over his shoulder and onto the trestle table.

'Morning, all. Thought I'd be the last, but no, I'm almost the first.' They both said hello. Alistair didn't want his and Alice's conversation to stop. He looked at the book on the floor.

'What are you reading?' It sounded pushy. He was trying too hard. Alice held up the book.

'Voltaire. *Candide*.' It was in French.

'Is it for school?' He was surprised, but then he thought Alice must be in the year above him, which meant first year sixth.

'No. I like to read French.'

Jack had filled a polystyrene cup with black coffee and sat himself down a few seats away from them. 'Coffee's almost as bad as this script,' he said, waving the offending document around with his free hand.

'Don't you like it?' said Alice loudly. Alistair noted her confidence, the ease with which she spoke to Jack – to all the adults. He would have just smiled. It didn't even occur to him to have an opinion on the play.

'Do you?' said Jack peering at her theatrically.

'It's a bit nothingy – a bit obvious. There're two really good scenes.' She flicked through her own copy.

'Yes, dear, but they're not mine.'

'I know,' said Alice, grinning again. 'They're mine.' She turned to Alistair. 'And one of them's yours.'

Alistair wondered which one. He hadn't thought about

115

whether what he had to do was good or not. It was enough to think about remembering his lines and saying them in such a way that they didn't throw him out of the room for his childish incompetence. The thought of the play and what to do made the new person he had touched slip away from him. He felt the idea of it come apart, like paper in water.

The others filed in ones and twos. Steve was the last of the actors. He bounded in panting, although he didn't apologize. Gabrielle looked as if she wanted to say something but she refrained from doing so, possibly because Declan had yet to arrive. He did so five minutes after that.

'I see Barry Sheen's bang on time,' said Jack, and Emese laughed her naughty child's laugh.

After some more wasted moments Gabrielle moved everyone into the large room, the floor of which was now covered with lines of coloured tape. Cyril Davenport was no longer there. The cast hung close to the wall, clutching their polystyrene cups. Alistair guessed that the pieces of tape represented the walls of the set. Declan wandered into the middle of the floor and squatted down on his haunches.

'OK. We're blocking today.' He twirled a strand of his hair round an index finger. 'But we treat it as a full rehearsal. There's precious little time to explore this piece as it is.'

They walked through the opening of the play, everyone holding their scripts in front of them. Declan allowed them to find their own positions as dictated by the action and dialogue. Occasionally he would intervene, placing his hands on their shoulders and manoeuvring them across the room like oversized chess pieces. Chairs were employed to indicate pieces of furniture, as were people's bags and coats. It reminded Alistair of the kind of games he used to play when he was younger. Lunchtime versions of his favourite television programmes reenacted in the playground with benches and trees representing the office in *The Sweeney* or the ranch in *The Virginian*. Nobody was giving a performance as yet, just stumbling through lines. Alistair hoped it would stay that way for the rest of the day.

Eventually it came to his big scene with Alice. This must have been the one she had referred to earlier – one of the good ones. Declan had sidled up to Gabrielle, who was looking at her notebook. They began a muttered conversation. At one point they looked across at him. He looked away, not wanting them to see that he'd noticed. After a short time Declan came to the middle of the room.

'OK,' he announced, 'I just want to do some focused work with Alice and Alistair. Go next door, slip down to the canteen for a smoke, whatever, as long as you're back here by quarter to two – and I mean quarter to – OK?' There was a mumble of agreement and an immediate air of relief, another school echo, as if breaktime had just been called unexpectedly. They filed out of the room, which became unnaturally quiet. Alistair felt himself tense.

'Right.' Declan turned towards them. 'The imagining scene. Are you up to putting books down?'

This was it, thought Alistair. They were going to discover their mistake in giving him the part. Alice nodded to indicate she could.

'Alistair?' said Declan.

'Yeah?'

'Book down?'

'Yes.'

'OK. Don't worry. I'll prompt. From the top of page eight. Leila at the table. Marcel coming from his bed. Take positions and then in your own time.' Declan went back to the side of the room and sat down next to Gabrielle. Alice found her seat and began miming writing. Alistair walked to the other side of the imaginary set, his heart hammering. He

117

could feel the dampness under his arms. He watched Alice mime for a second or two. He observed her grace and naturalness. Even in this artificial set-up she seemed to have become someone else. As he looked at her a memory came to him. Sunshine in his eyes, warming his face. Air on his body. Standing on the edge of a swimming pool in Estepona. Once he had hated jumping in. Then there had been this pool in Spain. On his own, unharassed by Dad, he had contemplated the action. The combination of sunlight and freedom must have kindled some spark of courage. Shocked at the simplicity of it, he had found himself walking up to the tiled edge of the pool. Somehow he walked straight through the wall of fear and discovered it to be no more than a veil. There was no trick to it. You just jumped. He'd spent the rest of the afternoon plunging again and again into the water, enjoying each time the chilly rush and the new-found facility.

He walked over to Alice with his first line in his head. Reaching her, he heard himself say, 'What are you doing?'

'Just writing,' she said without looking up at him.

He struggled for the next word. 'Why?'

'It's just something I do. You've seen me do it before.'

Still the strain for the line – searching in his head. Flatly he said, 'I can't sleep.'

With ease and authenticity Alice responded, 'Neither can I.'

'I get frightened.' He remembered that line. Alice turned to look at him for the first time.

'Shall I tell you a secret?' She stared at him as if it was real, her eyes huge and searching. 'So do I,' she said, her mouth curling into a smile.

Declan stood up and snapped his fingers.

'OK, break it there.' He walked towards them. 'Return to your original positions. We'll run that opening block again.

Alistair. More on your face please. Don't just recite. OK. From the top.' Alistair wasn't surprised at the comment. He knew himself that was all he was doing. It was all he could do. They ran the lines and actions again. Already Alistair felt himself locked into the way he had first done it. It sounded amateurish to his own ears, particularly next to Alice's natural grace. The familiar grind of panic and shame began to spread in his stomach. Declan was close by them, moving around them as they spoke.

'Don't look at me,' he said to Alistair in rebuke. 'Stay focused.' As he reached the point they had stopped at before, Alistair feared that he was going to cry. 'Remember where you are,' said Declan. 'Remember how you feel.' Now Alistair's throat had tightened. The challenge seemed to be just to get the words out, never mind acting them.

'Shall I tell you a secret?' Alice continued. 'So do I.' She seemed unfazed by Declan's closeness or Alistair's incompetence. 'That's one of the reasons I write.'

'But how does it stop you getting frightened?' His voice was high and squeaky now, not even his own.

'I don't know.' She had turned her chair round to face Alistair. She became momentarily lost in thought. Alistair wondered how she knew how to move her face in such a way that it didn't appear she was struggling for her next line. 'I think if I put down the things I'm frightened about it makes them interesting. If they become interesting they feel a little less frightening.'

There was movement at Alistair's side just at the edge of his peripheral vision. He couldn't help but flick his eyes to see what it was. It was Declan, nodding his head up and down in approval. He saw Alistair gazing at him.

'Don't come out of it. Forget I'm here,' he said with surprising volume and firmness. He stood erect and put his hands on the side of Alistair's head, repositioning it so that it was facing Alice. There was a hideous pause. Alistair was unable to remember his next line. They stood there with nothing happening. Alistair felt a physical pressure on his head. Declan was pushing him down towards the floor. '"Marcel has sat down at Leila's feet,"' Declan read from the script. 'And says: "Do you think we'll . . ."'

The line came to Alistair. 'Do you think we'll ever get out of here?'

Alice laughed. Even her laugh was not 'her' yet it still sounded natural and real. 'Of course we will. Sooner than you think, I'm sure. But you know – until that time comes – you can get out of here any time you want.'

'No you can't,' said Alistair half-heartedly. He didn't want to sound half-hearted. He wanted to get it right so that Declan would go and sit down again next to Gabrielle and be satisfied enough that they could get to the end of the scene and the others could come back and join them.

'Oh yes you can.' Alice pretended to put down her imaginary pen. 'Do you want me to teach you?' Alistair nodded stiffly. 'OK.' She jumped to her feet and went to stand behind him. He could smell her perfume again – the patchouli oil that reminded him of the badge shop in the Merrion Superstore. She was standing close to him now. He could feel the warmth of her head on the side of his face.

'Let's go for a walk around Cluj. Where would you like to go?'

What was the word? Alistair could see the shape of the lines on the page.

'The . . .' he began because he wanted the silence filled but he wasn't able to remember what he had to say.

'Apothecary,' said Declan crisply.

'Apothecary,' Alistair said.

'Why do you want to go there?'

Thank God. He knew this one. 'For an ice cream.'

Alice laughed her 'Leila' laugh again. It was sweet and real and it made her next line seem more convincing than it was written down. 'Don't you ever think about anything other than your stomach?'

Alistair tried to pull a face in response to this. It felt like a random scrunching of muscles rather than being of any significance.

'Why don't we go to the synagogue on Strada Horea?'

'Why there?'

'Because it's beautiful. Don't you think it's beautiful?'

These lines were easier, because of the rhythm. 'I suppose.' Alistair shrugged his shoulders.

'Close your eyes.'

He did. He was surprised to feel Alice reaching for his hand. Her fingers gripped his lightly. Her skin was warm against his. There was a reality about it, a presence that seemed unfamiliar and shocking.

'We're going up now – out of the cellar.'

He enjoyed feeling his hand in hers. Again, another pause. Declan at his side shouting now.

'Concentrate!' and then beginning his next line for him. 'But we'll be . . .'

'But we'll be seen.' Alistair remembered it. 'Somebody will see us. They'll see our yellow stars.' Although his eyes were closed, Alistair could feel that Alice had moved round in front of him. She let go of his hand and he experienced a momentary sense of disappointment, which ended when he felt both her hands gently cradling the sides of his head. He could smell her breath. Normally he was squeamish about being so close to somebody else – breath usually smelt eggy and unpleasant like Mum's. Alice's was clean and agreeable, like baking.

'Nobody can see us. We're as light as the air. A wave on

121

the ocean. We've no use for our stars. We can go where we want. Tell me what you can see.'

Alistair tightened again inside. More lines. They were in there. He remembered the images he'd made to try to fasten them into his memory. 'St Michael's church in the square. And the shops around it. And the trees.'

'What do the trees look like?'

'Beautiful. They have blossom on them.' He smiled. It was easy to smile with Alice cupping his head – her unseen face inches from his.

'Good,' muttered Declan. 'Keep going.'

'What colour blossom?' asked Alice.

'White and pink. It's warm. I can feel the sun on my face.' Alistair imagined Alice in front of him. She was around his height, or maybe slightly taller than him. She was older than him. Bigger than him. He imagined her as the sun. He felt a smile spreading across his face.

When the scene was finished and Alistair opened his eyes he was surprised to find Declan was smiling.

'Sorry,' Alistair said.

'It's all right. We'll break it there anyway. That was much better. You just need to relax into it. Is there any chance you two could spend some time running that scene together, this afternoon? After we've finished with you?' He was whispering now. He obviously didn't want Gabrielle to hear him. Alice and Alistair looked at each other.

'I suppose so,' said Alice.

'Have you got anywhere you can go?'

Alistair thought about the Bray Hotel. The smell of dust and disuse.

'We can go to my house – if Alistair doesn't mind,' said Alice. Declan looked at Alistair, hopefully.

'No, that's OK.' He hoped Alice's house wasn't too far away, that it wouldn't be hard to get back.

122

'Terrific!' said Declan, grinning.

The other actors filed back now, including Steve who was walking in with Emese, flirting confidently. They ran the whole thing again, with more ease than before – or so it felt to Alistair. Maybe he had relaxed, knowing that Declan thought he could do it. He felt increasingly comfortable as the end approached and the 'kids', as Declan called them, had to go home.

When they reached the end, Alistair went to retrieve his carrier bag. He was shocked to find himself on the floor. Steve had jumped on him. He locked an arm round Alistair's neck and breathed in his ear in the dramatic tones of a wrestling commentator.

'And Raw delivers the Mick McManus strangle and there's no let-up.'

Everyone else in the room was looking at them in a puzzled manner. Alistair was badly winded. He struggled to his feet.

'Sorry, mate,' said Steve, who helped him up. Alistair tried to blink away the tears that were forming in his eyes so that no one would see them. 'Didn't mean to hurt you.'

'I'm OK.' He forced himself to smile as he turned to find his carrier bag. His arm was shaking as he picked it up.

'Are you coming out to play this after'?'

Alistair wished Steve hadn't asked. He was glad that he had, that Steve still held him in that esteem that he should ask, but he didn't want to have to turn Steve down. 'Er . . .'

'Ah, come on. I thought we could go into Soho.'

Alice had appeared at his side. 'Are you ready then?' she said, buttoning up her big green coat.

'Ready for what?' Steve looked from Alistair to Alice quizzically.

'We're going to do a bit of extra rehearsing,' she explained.

'What!' Steve pantomimed outrage. 'What for?'

'Director's suggestion,' she said and turned to the door.

'Well, I'll come and help.'

Alistair could feel his heart beating again far too fast.

'No need.' Alice had turned but she was looking at Alistair, not Steve.

'Go on,' Steve said, putting a hand on Alistair's shoulder. 'You'll get more done with me looking on.'

'It's OK.' Now she turned to Steve. She smiled fully, opening up her face. 'Thanks Steve. Better just the two of us. Ready?' she said to Alistair again.

Alistair hoped the tube would come before Steve arrived on the platform, and fortunately it did. On the walk down he had glanced over his shoulder a number of times but there was no sign of Steve. Maybe he was dawdling deliberately – or maybe he had gone somewhere else altogether. Alistair didn't like the idea of upsetting him. He didn't want Steve not to like him any more. But a new fear had settled over him too. It was the idea of silence between him and Alice. If there was too much of it, he felt she would get cross with him, or, even worse, want nothing more to do with him. He felt he had to please her with conversation.

'Where do you live?'

'Arsenal. Highbury. Not too far from the stadium.'

Alistair immediately thought of the football ground in Leeds and imagined that they were going to Elland Road. The idea filled him with horror. He saw skinheads, bone-heads, NF graffiti, heard chanting, shouting and sounds of fighting. 'Is it frightening? When there's a match?'

She looked at him quizzically. 'What do you mean?'

Alistair was thrown by her question. Wasn't it obvious? 'All the fans running around. Fighting. Drunk.'

'It's not *frightening*. It's fun. Like going to the fair.'

Alistair nodded as if that settled it. In fact, it settled

nothing. If there was anything more frightening than the idea of going to a football match, it was going to a fair.

On the tube, conversation became easier because Alice was asking him about himself. She wanted to know about his family and his school. Then she started talking about acting. She was surprised when he revealed how little experience he had.

'How did you get the part? Didn't you go to an audition?'

'They came to the school.' He told her about the audition and how Mr Hindmarsh had just about forced him into doing it.

'But why did he force you?'

Should he tell her about Travulia? He never talked to anyone about Travulia. He thought about jumping in the swimming pool again. The heat of the sun. The thrilling rush of the water. 'There's this thing I do. I s'pose it sounds a bit mad.'

'What thing? What do you mean?' She was eating a Cadbury's flake that she'd pulled from her shoulder bag. The yellow wrapper was open in one hand, the chocolate already broken and crumbled. She pushed little pieces into her mouth with her other hand and then offered some to Alistair.

'I make tapes.' He paused, waiting for a flicker of anything that suggested distaste to show on her face. She seemed more interested in the chocolate.

'What do you mean, you make tapes?' Again that directness. It wasn't rudeness. More like a powerful and straightforward curiosity. If there was something she wasn't sure about, she asked for clarification immediately.

'Cassette tapes. I've got this cassette recorder with a microphone. I've made up this place . . .' Alistair felt as if he was taking his clothes off in front of her. But he carried on. 'This town. And I make up everyone who lives there.

And I do tapes of them – on their own, having conversations. I do their voices.' She was looking at him now, not the chocolate.

'Like *Under Milk Wood*.' Alistair knew what *Under Milk Wood* was. They'd listened to a record of it in English once. It had never occurred to him to make the connection before. 'So had this teacher heard these tapes?'

'No.' Alistair was relieved that she didn't seem to think he was mad. But he was also a little disappointed. Maybe he thought she'd react with more wonder. 'He said he just knew from stuff we'd done in English.'

She nodded. 'I'd love to hear one of these tapes. Would you send me one?'

Imagine that. Not just sending a Travulia tape in the post. But someone else hearing it, hearing what he'd done.

'Yes. If you do me a music one.'

'Are you serious?' She was crumbling up the Flake wrapper.

'Yeah.'

'It's a deal.' She brushed the crumbs of chocolate away and held out a hand for Alistair to shake. He looked at its shape, like an asymmetrical diamond. He grasped it, aware this was the second time they'd touched today.

By the time they got out of the tube, the sky was beginning to darken. Alistair didn't like the fact that they had to walk some considerable distance to Alice's house, aware that he was going to have to walk back that way on his own. Eventually they arrived at a large brown-bricked building set back from the others in the road, which were part of a terrace. There was an old wooden gate at the front and a small but eccentrically landscaped garden. Streams of ivy tumbled down the wall above the front porch, parting around the windows and drainpipes. A wooden ramp had been built running from the entrance to the paved driveway.

'It's almost as big as Steve's house,' said Alistair, craning his neck to look up to the green-covered edifice.

'There's a bit of a difference,' Alice said indignantly.

'Have you been to Steve's?' For some reason Alistair hoped that she hadn't been.

'No, but I can imagine. His dad's money. Haven't you ever seen that terrible programme?' She pulled a face as she opened the door, adopting a dramatic American accent. '*In Search of . . . a Load of Old Shit.* You wonder who believes all that crap.'

'We don't have it in Yorkshire, I don't think.'

'Spacemen building the pyramids and UFOs in the Bermuda Triangle.'

'Well, he does . . . probably. Steve's dad, I mean.'

'Bollocks. He's an ad man. They don't believe anything.'

'Ad man?'

'He's *owns* an advertising company, doesn't he? He started those books as a sideline.'

Alistair nodded as if he knew all this already.

The first thing to strike Alistair about Alice's house were the books. Even the entrance hall was lined with shelves that stretched to the ceiling.

'The difference between this and Steve's is that this is a council house,' said Alice as she hung up her coat on a rack already straining under the weight of several dozen others. 'Here . . .' She reached for Alistair's parka and his bag and squashed them on too. 'The biggest council house in Britain.' It didn't look like a council house to Alistair – or at least not like the ones he was used to seeing, the grey and red semis that lined the road in Meanwood and Seacroft. There were voices coming from a room up ahead. Alistair followed Alice, who was heading towards the noise. They entered a huge kitchen, dominated by a massive oak table like one from the dining hall at school. Rather than chairs, there were two long benches on either side. At one end of the table was a drum kit. Behind it sat an older boy, or rather a young man. He had bright red hair tied back in a pony-tail. Sitting near him, balanced on the edge of one of the benches, was another person about a year or two younger. He was thinner, with neat black hair brushed in a severe side-parting. He had the same eyes as Alice, huge and blue.

'The Soviet Union disconnected from the principles of communism after the war,' said the dark-haired one.

'Which is exactly my point,' said the pony-tailed one. 'The principles you're trying to defend are the ones Walesa's fighting for.'

'Don, Alistair, Alistair, Don,' said Alice, gesturing to the red pony-tail, then, 'Marc, Alistair, Alistair, Marc,' to the other. Alistair was amazed when they immediately stopped their argument and turned to acknowledge him.

'Hello, Alistair,' they both said, almost in unison, before turning back to face each other.

'Walesa's in the pocket of the West and you know it. You think there's anything authentic about that rhetoric?' said Marc.

'Come on,' said Alice, with her hand in a biscuit barrel. 'We'll leave them to it. We'll just say hello to Dad.'

Alistair stiffened. He hadn't realized parents would be at home. They went into a sitting room, which was also lined with books from floor to ceiling. There was a corner full of plants in various kinds of pot, some terracotta and some brightly patterned. At the other end was a huge leather-topped desk covered with books and papers. Behind it was a man with steel-grey hair and heavy-framed glasses. He was concentrating intently on a book laid out in front of him. Alistair could see he had written many notes in the margins. 'Dad,' said Alice quietly. There was no response so she tried again, although she didn't raise her voice. Alistair noticed a gentleness in the way she did it.

'Hmmm.' The man looked up and his face broke into a huge grin when he saw her. 'Hello you,' he said, taking off his glasses.

'Dad, this is Alistair – who's in the TV play with me.'

'Really.' He turned to look at Alistair and smiled just as broadly. Then he reached down, moving his arms, and he glided backwards. Alistair apprehended with a jolt that he was in a wheelchair. He rolled around the side of the desk and extended his hand to Alistair. 'I'm really very pleased to meet you,' he said, grasping Alistair's hand firmly. 'Nicholas Zealand.' It took Alistair a moment to realize Alice's dad was telling him his name. 'Has Alice offered you a cup of tea?'

'Er . . .'

'Alice, make the lad some tea, for goodness' sake. And make me some while you're at it.'

She raised her eyes to the ceiling but ran off without complaint. Alistair was to be left alone with her dad. He couldn't help but look for signs of why the man was in a wheelchair. He seemed to have both legs. They looked normal enough – not withered.

'Just up to my eyes in the book of Genesis. Startling stuff. I'm supposed to be giving a lecture on it tomorrow. Haven't done my homework yet.' He grinned as he said it, then began rolling back and forward. Alistair assumed it must be the wheelchair version of stretching your legs. 'Are you at school in London or . . . ?' He reached up and swept his hair from his eyes. Without his glasses he was a handsome man.

'I'm from Leeds. I've come down from Leeds.'

'Leeds. Leeds.' Mr Zealand repeated the word as if there was something mysterious about it. Alistair must have looked uncomfortable because he said, 'Go on, sit down, no need to stand.'

Alistair looked round for a chair and saw one at the edge of the room. He reached for it and pulled it closer to Mr Zealand.

'I had a period teaching in Leeds. At the polytechnic. About twenty years ago.'

'What did you teach?' Alistair wasn't just being polite. He was curious to know what the man did.

'Oh . . . Architecture,' he said dismissively. 'Another life. Still teach now but I changed horses. Beautiful city, Leeds. At least it was then. Expect they've torn it all down and covered it in concrete, haven't they?' Alistair smiled and nodded. 'Town hall's still there though, isn't it? Cuthbert Brodrick. Did the Grand Hotel in Scarborough. That's pretty good too.' He swept his hair back again. It was clearly a nervous habit. 'How's the play going? Is it up to much?'

'It's OK. I don't think I am.' Alistair was surprised to hear himself say this. It sounded like a confession.

'Really.'

Suddenly he felt tears gathering in the corner of his eyes. He squeezed them tightly to make the tears go.

'Why do you say that? Being modest?'

Alistair shook his head. 'No.'

Alice had come back in. Mr Zealand turned towards her smiling. 'Alice – was asking your lad here about the play. Says he's no good. Is it that the case?'

'He's very good,' said Alice. 'Best thing in it. Do you take sugar?' she asked Alistair, as if she'd said nothing at all, rather than the momentous statement she had just made. Alistair shook his head and she went out again.

'There you are. My girl's never wrong about anything. That's the bloody problem. It's pointless arguing with her.' He laughed. Suddenly Alistair started crying. He tried to stop himself but he couldn't. Something had given way.

The tears flowed with their own momentum. It felt like being sick. He just had to go with it.

'Oh, son, come on. You must have been upset. Go on. Have a good cry. Don't worry.' Alistair desperately wanted to stop before Alice saw him. 'It's a scary thing . . . doing what you're doing. Wouldn't fancy it myself.' Mr Zealand reached out and touched Alistair on his arm. Somehow Alistair managed to halt the tears.

'I'm sorry—'

'Goodness,' Mr Zealand interrupted him. 'Never apologize for tears. Certainly not spontaneous ones.' Alice reappeared, carrying a tray of mugs. Alistair made another attempt to disguise the fact he'd been crying for a second time in her presence.

'Come on then,' she said. 'Let's go and do some work on this.'

They went into another high-ceilinged room with a television in one corner and framed charcoal sketches around the walls. Some of them had an unfinished, imperfect appearance but somehow they still looked good in frames.

'How is this a council house?' The question had been bothering Alistair since they'd walked in.

'The council own it but they lease it to the university. Dad works for the University of London.'

'He's not a vicar, is he?' Alistair thought of the big book of Genesis open on the desk. Alice giggled.

'We call him that sometimes. The Vicar. He helps run Heythrop College. Teaches Theology. He's a lay preacher too. Goes on the radio, that kind of thing.'

'Are you religious?'

Alice gave a shrieking laugh 'None of us are. Sometimes we even wonder if Dad is.' She searched the contents of a coffee table. 'He's always getting into trouble for it. Questioning the Virgin Birth. Rubbishing the Resurrection.'

She put her tea on a magazine on the floor and sat down cross-legged next to it.

Alistair sank into one of the saggy armchairs and said, 'I had an idea what we could do. We should do the thing they do – Leila and Marcel, their flying thing – but our version of it.' Alice blew on her tea, keeping her eyes fixed on Alistair. 'Just do it as they do it, to see what it feels like. Then we'll know. Or I'll know. How to make it look real.'

'That's good. That's very good. Do you want to do it now?'

'All right. One of us has to lead the other one.'

'I'll lead you, like Leila does, but I'll be me.'

Alistair was surprised to discover a sudden flash of enthusiasm – the first he'd felt since arriving in London. There was something familiar and pleasant about the feeling, and as Alice moved around the room arranging chairs he made the connection. It was like the feeling he got beginning a new Travulia tape. Having cleared some space, Alice reached for a big cushion lying in one corner of the room and heaved it into the centre. She indicated for Alistair to go and sit on it.

'Close your eyes then.' Alistair obeyed her. He felt unexpectedly comfortable sitting in darkness with Alice stood behind him. 'Take some deep breaths.' He did as she said, feeling himself sink a little into the cushion. 'And just take off. Up out of the room. Then tell me what you see.'

For a while there was nothing, just the fading after-image of Alice's sitting room, or at least the light it contained. Then other images began to form.

'London. I can see London. All the streets below. Cars. Tiny people.'

'And you can go anywhere. Where are you going to go?'

'I can see the station. King's Cross station. I can see the train line that runs to Leeds. I'm going along it.'

'How fast are you going? As fast as a train?'

'Faster than that. Much faster. I can see Leeds already.'

'And where are you going? What do you want to see?'

'I don't know. I thought I was going home. To my house. But I'm somewhere else.'

'Where?'

'All over the place. Flying around. I don't want to go home. I like it up here.'

'What do you like?'

'There's nobody else around. Up here with me, I mean. I can see whatever I want to see. I can go anywhere. It feels safe.'

'Go somewhere then. Go and look at something.'

Alistair hovered, puzzled by something. 'It's night-time. Late at night.'

'Yeah . . .' The temporal shift didn't seem to bother Alice.

Alistair felt the pull of the town centre. He could see the empty streets. There was something delicious about being so safe above them and their darkness and the emptiness below. He wondered where the darkest place would be, the place he would least like to be alone in at that time of night. 'I'm going to look at the Dark Arches.'

'What's the Dark Arches— no. Don't tell me what they are. Just describe what you see.'

'It's tunnels. They go under the station. When I was younger I thought it was something I dreamed about because it seems so unreal, but they are actually there. There's a car park near them—'

'You're telling me *about* them – go there – describe them to me.'

Alistair concentrated and then he was there – at night. It was very clear. 'I can hear the water. It rushes really loud. It's the river Aire. There's about a hundred columns, maybe more, maybe five hundred. And a vaulted ceiling over them all – like a vault in an abbey or a cathedral. Everything's made from red bricks though, not stone. Except you can't see that they're red because it's night-time. You wouldn't think that there could be something so enormous and unreal underneath the place where you live. And the rush of the water. I'm here in the middle of the night and it's still rushing. It doesn't stop roaring ever, even when there's no one there to hear it.' He felt himself move lower, sinking closer to the black water. He sensed a current even though he was above it. He felt the pull of cold lightlessness. And then, unexpectedly, a moment of panic. He opened his eyes abruptly, suddenly aware of the silence in the real world, and of Alice, sitting behind him.

'Pretty good,' she said standing up. She moved round in front of him chewing her lip. 'My turn.' She pushed him off the cushion and took his place.

'Close your eyes then,' said Alistair. 'And imagine your-self flying out of the room.' He watched her face, saw her eyes moving underneath the lids. Her eyelashes were remarkably long. Together with her moulded lips and little nose the prettiness of her face felt like a joke. 'What can you see?' Her brow tightened, causing three small lines to form there.

'I'm going fast, out, down, over London, across the river. I can see it underneath. I'm following the river.'

'What does it look like?' Alistair could feel the breath-lessness in her responses as if she was genuinely rushing through the air. It was as if she was taking some kind of lead from him, copying the path he had laid down but using it to go on a journey of her own.

'Huge and dark. Cold. It doesn't matter. I'm not cold.'

'Where are you going?'

'Down. Over Kent. Dover. The Channel. Over France.' She smiled as she said the word.

'What does France look like?'

'Dark. Darker than England. There are fewer lights. More countryside.'

'Do you know where you're going?'

Again she smiled. 'Right down to the bottom. Down to Provence. I can see Marseille – like a little diamond. Further still. I can see the mountains.'

'Where are you?'

'Massif des Calanques. On the corner – Callelongue. It's night but I can see the rocks. Jagged points. Trees clinging to them. The ocean's black. Even in the moonlight.'

'Go on. Where are you going?'

'Into the sea. I'm in the sea. I'm swimming.' Her face relaxed. The lines on her brow disappeared. The smile flattened into something calmer.

'What can you see now?'

'If I look back over my shoulder I can see the coast. It's rough and huge. Ahead of me is just space. There's a distant shape. It must be the Ile de Jarre. This is my favourite place. In the ocean with nothing around me but the sound of the water. I want to get to the island in the end, but not yet. I want to enjoy being here. Swimming in this space.' She went silent as Alistair had done. And then her expression changed. She looked troubled, as if she had encountered something unexpected.

'What? What have you seen?' But she didn't answer him. She just shook her head slightly. Alistair didn't like the space that had opened up between them or the sense of what might fill it. 'Open your eyes then,' he said firmly after a moment. She did. Neither of them said anything. Alistair suddenly became aware that he was looking directly into Alice's eyes. She was looking into his, too, as if searching for something. Her brow was still furrowed. He noticed the speed of his heartbeat again. 'I'll go and get the script

135

and we can go over the scene,' he said quickly. He went out into the corridor to find it.

When he came back she was sitting on the floor again, sipping her tea. Whatever had been there a minute before seemed to have gone. They ran the lines until they were sure they had them. Alistair was pleased to discover that it felt easy to say the words in a way that sounded realistic. His idea had worked.

It seemed to be enough to go through it three times. When they'd finished, Alice said, 'Do you want to go and listen to some music?'

Alistair looked at his watch. 'Maybe I should be getting back.'

She laughed her Alice laugh. 'It's only six. Come on.' And she did something that felt impossible, wonderful and terrifying all at the same time. She took his hand and led him out of the room.

# Chapter Eight

A sudden shout. The clamour of distant voices yelling in a foreign language. Alistair jerked awake.

A moment's disorientation and panic, then the rock and roll of the train solidified him in his surroundings. He wriggled in his seat, attempting a more upright position while still keeping his semi-open laptop balanced on his knees. The computer was half covered with his cagoule. He didn't want it stolen. Other items were spread around him. Other things he was intending to leave in the Stanescus' cellar.

This carriage – the one Mihail had led him to – was almost empty. It was laid out like an English railway coach with pairs of double seats opposing each other on either side of a narrow aisle. Chrome pipes stretched between the back of each seat and the ceiling. Visible through them on the opposite side of the aisle, but in the seat facing Alistair, was a lone girl. In her mid-twenties, she was dressed in a smart brown jacket with a gold-coloured T-shirt beneath. Her hair was jet black, cut in a stark precise bob. She had a Mediterranean look with dark olive skin. She seemed troubled, perturbed, absorbed in thought. One hand was pressed flat against the glass to her side, the thumb striking the surface at slow but regular intervals. She turned away from the window she'd been staring out of and seemed to look straight at Alistair. He looked down at the collection of things around him.

One of the earlier Travulia books. Phase two or three. The denseness of the writing and the sketches enabled him to date it. In it were listed all the houses on his street and their corresponding Travulian identities. Who lived there in reality and who lived there in Travulia. He hadn't looked at it for a long time. He didn't refer to the books as much any more. The information was in his head. He could pull it down at will and lay it over reality like tracing paper over a photograph. He skipped back through the pages filled with close-spaced handwriting, pausing at the map of the streets around his parents – the Primley Parks. Next to this was another map – a hand-drawn map of Travulia that matched the photocopied real map road for road, building for building. The names were different. Primley Park Close become Alan Francis Gardens. Nursery Lane became the Development. The population – of course – were different. The real people he knew like the McEvoys next door were unwitting actors, cast in other roles. They had become the Capotes – a family on the run who had moved up from London. He knew what happened to the Capotes in the end. The twin daughters were kidnapped and buried alive. The parents later commited suicide together – the garage sealed with damp towels. Across the road were Mum and Dad's friends, the Lipmans. In their Travulian parts they were the Cattermoules – the son a schizophrenic, the father a closet homosexual. The son killed the father in the end. At the bottom of the hill, the young couple whose names he did not know became Janice and Wilhelm. She a dancer and drug addict, he a collector of rare birds' eggs which he kept concealed in a small locked room, hidden in the loft. He died falling from a Scots pine.

Next to the Travulia volume was the Grey Book. The

most recent items had yet to be glued into it. The Grey Book wasn't part of Travulia, although there was a sense that as concepts the two things were connected. He'd been keeping it for five or six years now. It was something he did in bursts. Sometimes weeks would go by and he would almost forget about it. Then something would catch his eye in the *Evening Post* or the *Guardian*, and he would cut it out and stick it in. He looked at a cutting, dated 3 June.

## Freak crane fall horror accident

A 27-year-old father of two was killed on Monday night in a horrific accident in Leeds City Centre. Part of a crane which was servicing the redevelopment of City Square collapsed smashing to the ground below. Richard Allen – a technical manager from Burley – was walking back alone from a night out to his home. He was killed instantly when the crane arm fell directly on to him. A spokesman for Kenton Ford technical contractors who maintained the equipment described the occurrence as 'a one off – an absolute freak of nature'. Police sealed off the site although they have ruled out sabotage. A full inquiry into the incident has begun.

Alistair placed it back in among the pages and pulled out the other piece of paper waiting to be pasted in. This from Dad's *Daily Mail*.

# Couple Assaulted in Burglary Outrage

A young couple were subjected to a horrific four-hour ordeal at the hands of a pair of burglars who broke into their home in the Rusholme district of Manchester last week.

The couple – whose names are being withheld by police – are both students at the university. The men entered the home believing it to be empty for the Easter vacation. Upon discovering the occupants they proceeded to terrorize them until leaving, apparently bored. Detective Inspector John Charnley said: 'This is one of the most disturbing incidents I have had to deal with in a long time involving wilful violence and a serious sexual assault. These men are very dangerous and need to be apprehended without delay.'

The men are both in their mid to late twenties, one white and one black. The white male was between 5'6' and 5'8', the black male over 6'. Both were clean shaven with close-cropped hair. A more detailed description together with e-fit pictures will be issued in the near future.

The Grey Book was full of such items – random assaults, freak accidents, unforeseen disasters. Alistair knew enough to understand the purpose of this compilation. He was looking for a pattern. Something predictable in the unpredictable awfulness. He flicked back through the headlines: 'Terror Pair Kill Teen Victim', 'Unsecured Combine Wreaks Mayhem', 'Hooligan Horror in Snugroom Nightmare', 'Dream of Angels made me cut his throat'. A black-and-white world where horror, terror and nightmare recurred endlessly, like ten divided by three. He read and reread the stories each time another one was

140

pasted in. If he could discern the pattern, he could protect himself.

Recently Travulia itself had been the subject of much analysis. It was meaning Alistair was searching for, and he had settled on the word itself. Searches in foreign-language dictionaries and then the internet had yielded nothing. And yet the word felt like a thing to Alistair. He had the sense that it pre-existed him, and no opposing memory of creating or imagining it. One night, some time after he had moved back to his parents', he found himself in the spare room, up on a chair examining the top shelf with the prayer books, the Haggadot, the Chumash, the books for Rosh Hashanah and Yom Kippur. Books like no other books – not for reading or understanding, but for revering. There were rules governing these books. You kissed them when you closed them. You kissed them if you dropped them. You could never ever throw them away or harm them. As if the paper and binding were flesh and nerve, the letters neural pathways, the whole combining into some form of sentience. You were to behave as if these books could take offence. Straining to stand a little higher, Alistair found what he was searching for. The ancient blue-backed Aleph-Bet that he had learned his Hebrew letters from as a child. Aleph-Bet. The name itself revealing another secret – that the Jews had invented the concept of an alphabet – the Greek word came from the Hebrew. He jumped off the chair and sat on it, holding the slim volume open in his hands, like a preacher. The spine was cracked in places, revealing the thread that held the pages together. There was a line illustration on the front, printed in a darker blue straight on to the cloth cover – a smiling child with a yarmulke and tzitzits sitting on an oversized toadstool in front of a blackboard. Alistair opened the book. The smell. Powdery. Smoky. Being seven years old. He'd turned three pages before

141

remembering Hebrew went from right to left. Back to front. He flipped to the back/front. A whole page taken up with a huge aleph – the first letter of the alphabet. Black and solid. Bent like old wood. He flicked forward. Lamed. A graceful geometry. Like an incomplete S. So much more elegant than Western characters. The horizontal line of differing width to the vertical. The swirl and variance made it intriguing. The letter made an 'l' sound. Remarkable that he remembered – after twenty or more years. It became clear, flicking through the pages, that he knew enough to execute his task – to replicate Travulia in Hebrew letters. In fact, as he reached the back of the book he located a chart which would enable him to complete it.

He took the book into his room and shut the door, as if he was engaged in some highly private task. Finding a clean page in the most recent Travulia notebook, he began carefully to compose his word. He wrote:

ת ָ דּ וּ ל י א

He had made a word in Hebrew. Perhaps that word, written in that language, meant something. Of course he couldn't know this. He had never known what the words meant. He had only ever learnt their sounds. At his Bar Mitzvah, in front of a full congregation, he had read aloud from the Torah for nearly ten minutes. Not just read, but sang, his lips, tongue and throat forming the ancient words as instructed by the text before him (which, so he had been told, was copied by hand from a source that in turn led directly back to the times the words referred to). But Alistair's mind was not connected to those words. He saw only sounds. The infinite potential of the equipment of speech, developed to convey infinite meaning, reduced to a simple sonic instrument. Even now he could remember where his mind had been focused: on the task of reproducing those sounds. That had been the only achievement required. To be less than he was in his normal functioning, not more. Crack a code, make a noise. No need for the path from mind to heart to be connected.

Now he wanted meaning. He wanted the letters to do their job. To join and coalesce into a word that expressed an idea, not a noise.

It was ironic, given that Travulia was a realm without any faith or belief, that it was responsible for bringing Alistair back into a synagogue for the first time in his adult life.

It was two decades since Alistair had sat there and nothing seemed to have changed. The service might have been on a piano roll and the congregation and clergy fixed to some unseen mechanism it controlled. Maybe something in Alistair had hoped to be touched by what happened. Occasionally he was able to locate where they were in the proceedings, and he followed the singing of the chazan, running his finger underneath the Hebrew in the siddur in front of him. When they arrived at a more familiar portion Alistair joined in, trying to connect himself with the others around him. He spoke the words, trying to feel them resonating within him – as if they were some kind of magic spell that might transform him.

After the service Alistair had accompanied Dad to the kiddush. He sipped a glass of sickly sweet wine while the rabbi – Rabbi Gaffni – studied the index card. Dad hovered next to him, perhaps anxious in case Alistair was going to do something mad or say something mad.

'And where did your friend find this word?' The rabbi's voice was soft and high. There was a gentility about him Alistair hadn't expected to encounter. He was probably not much older than Alistair, though his beard was already flecked with silver. He spoke carefully and precisely, his

143

voice thick with a mixture of accents: Polish, Israeli, American.

'He's a designer, he wants to use it on a T-shirt. He wants to know what it means.' He felt certain the lie would be perceived. But the rabbi just smiled.

'I have heard of this phenomenon. In America, Jewish being fashionable. Who would have believed such a thing.'

'He's not Jewish. He found it in an old photograph or a postcard – something he can't identify.' Alistair had hoped this detail would help sell his story.

'Why – forgive me, I don't wish to be confrontational – why does he want this word on a T-shirt if he doesn't know its meaning?' It was as if the rabbi knew this was all deception.

Alistair felt the heat of a blush beginning to rise. 'I think he likes the look of it. I don't know.'

'I don't wish to criticize your friend. I speak merely as one who is careful about the use of words.' He lowered the card, still looking at it in its new position. 'There's a beautiful proverb in the Talmud I always try to keep in mind.' He smiled again. '*Gam tzipor shilachta od tashuv tz'udena, v'davar nimlat mipeeca lo yashuv.* Which means something like: a bird that you set free may be caught again but a word that escapes your lips will not return.'

Dad nodded as if this was something he regularly reminded himself of too.

'I'll confess I don't recognize this word. I would like to consult some texts. Hebrew, particularly biblical Hebrew, is an obscure language and I am a relatively young man. Please telephone me in the week.' He looked apologetic but shook Alistair's hand warmly. 'Good Shabbes, good Shabbes. It's very good to see you, Alistair, very good. Your father tells me you've been ill recently. Please feel welcome here. It will always be a blessing to have you.'

Alistair was fearful of phoning Rabbi Gaffni, even though he had been instructed to do so. But his curiosity was a powerful motivator. And there was the hope of impending revelation – that the word, once translated, would become a key that might unlock many other things.

The hallway was cold and silent. He pressed himself against the radiator hoping for warmth, but it wasn't turned on. He dialled the number.

'Could I speak with Rabbi Gaffni please?'

'Who's calling?' A young woman's voice – more American than the rabbi. Children shrieking in the background. The hum of life.

'It's Mr Black. Alistair Black.'

'I'll see if he's available.' The children on the other end were laughing. He heard a male voice approach, talking in Hebrew. The children quietened.

'Alistair. This is Rabbi Gaffni. How can I help?'

Alistair shrivelled inside. He didn't want to have to precis everything that had gone before. 'I was calling about the word. The word I was trying to get translated.'

'The word. Ahh yes, the word.'

'I wondered if—'

'Do you know, can you remember where this word came from?'

'I – well . . .'

'I'm very curious to know.'

'It was just – I think it was from a photograph . . .'

'The thing is, Alistair. The word – Tr'voolya . . .' The rabbi spoke it differently, with a Hebraic authenticity that made it sound centuries old. 'This word . . . it is all very mysterious.'

The thud of his heartbeat. 'Really.'

'Yes, very mysterious.' Another shout from a nearby child. The rabbi shushed him loudly. 'This word. It doesn't exist.'

145

'Doesn't exist?'

'It is a nonsense word.' Alistair felt himself tighten, felt the hallway reorder itself around him into a different arrangement of planes and shapes. 'It means nothing,' said the rabbi. 'Nothing at all.'

'She's very beautiful,' said Mihail. He was still there, filling the seat next to Alistair, his long legs stretched out ahead of him, ankles crossed in a relaxed manner. Alistair hadn't realized it was so obvious he'd been staring at the girl. He'd watched her fall asleep, lulled there by the darkening sky. 'Many of our women are this beautiful. You noticed that yet, Britanic?'

Alistair nodded.

'They look happier too. Healthier. Americans are all so fat.'

The shouting came again from somewhere down the train. When he'd first heard it Alistair hoped he had imagined it. He looked up, looked around the carriage. The train had emptied out considerably after Alba Iulia, the last station.

'What are you doing with computer?' Mihail pointed at it. Alistair looked back at the girl. Though she was asleep, her hand remained pressed against the glass. 'Well? What is your purpose with it?'

'It doesn't matter,' said Alistair quietly, not wanting to risk disturbing the girl.

'It does matter. It matters to me.'

Alistair turned to look at him, mildly irritated now by Mihail's questioning. 'It's nothing.'

'It's something. You bring heavy thing all this way. You risk theft.' Mihail pointed at it again. 'That would make lots of dollars. What is your purpose?'

Another loud bellow from the further carriages. It could

have been in pain or celebration. His guidebook and map – awkwardly refolded – still rested at his side. Alistair picked them up. He looked at his watch. Tried to ascertain how far before Cluj. Surely not much further. Maybe an hour. The shouting continued. There was a hint of alcohol in it. Something outside the normal codes of behaviour. Alistair looked back at the girl. She had shifted in her seat but slept on. A lock of black hair had fallen across her face.

'I apologize in advance for some of my countrymen,' said Mihail. Alistair swivelled again to face the seat next to him. 'Their behaviour . . . not good. What do they call it? The British Disease? It is not just in your country, my friend. It is getting worse here. Disrespect. Violence. For fun with some of these. For . . . entertainment.' Mihail now had turned to face the window. The lights of a small village flickered past. 'You know, Britanic? It seems that you know everything about me, but I know nothing about you.'

Alistair picked up the guidebook and unfolded the map. He attempted to return it to its original state.

'Tell me something about you.'

'There's nothing to tell.'

'Tell me all about your life.'

'I thought I told you.'

'You've said nothing.'

'I don't work. I've been off work.'

'Unemployed?'

Alistair remained silent.

'Ah yes. You said. You here for your health. Then what's with the computer?'

Alistair had retrieved his rucksack. Hurriedly, inelegantly, he tried to push items inside without opening it fully.

'Where are you going? Cluj is way off. Sit yourself back down.'

'I thought . . . I . . . I should be in my seat. The booked seat. The seat I'm supposed to be in.' Alistair thought about the formidable woman in the voluminous skirt. She may well be still in there, her foil-covered dinner plate on her lap.

'Relax, Britanic. Relax. Take deep breath. You're just fine here.' Mihail looked at him. Stared into his eyes. Studied his face. 'I want to know more about your mission. What you really do here. What you tap away on that thing.'

'Who are they? Why are they shouting?'

'Don't worry about them.'

'I'm going back—'

'Answer me. Why the laptop?'

'I was told . . . somebody told me. If I can write it down – I may still stand a chance—'

'What you talk about?'

'Turn it into something written. It was recommended to me.'

'What you mean?'

'Write it down.'

'Write what down?'

'Everything.'

'What you mean, everything?'

'Why are you asking me this? Why does it matter?'

'It matters to me. What is this everything?'

'You. You. You! Everything imagined. Everything you say.' Alistair had his hand on his face. He looked over at the girl. More hair had fallen in front of her eyes. She couldn't have woken up or she would have brushed it away.

'There are pills, you know,' said Mihail archly. 'You should take some pills. Calm you down.'

Alistair thought of the little brown bottle of Haloperidol. The tiny white tablets with their neatly scored grooves running down the exact centre of each. Emptying them out into the kitchen pedal bin at Mum and Dad's. Covering

148

them with potato peelings and teabags so no one would know he'd dumped them. Scraping the printed label off the bottle, the label that bore his name, the drug having become a label, too, a branding, 'Alistair Black' forever fused with it, identified by it, marked out by the prescription.

Now there came a swell in the volume of shouting from the carriages beyond. Either they were getting louder, or they were getting closer.

'I don't need pills.' He was aware how petulant he sounded. Aware of the professional opinions he was contradicting.

'OK. OK. Keep calm. It was . . . figure of speech.' Mihail smiled. Reached for his cigarettes. 'Have cigarette. Calm down. Better than pills.'

Alistair looked across at the girl again. Her lips relaxed, slightly apart. Her features were strong and full. Clear cheekbones. Definite eyebrows. A model's mouth. But asleep she looked younger than she did awake. Closer to a teenager. Her head moved slightly from side to side with the motion of the train. Somehow she looked very sad.

Alistair reached for his own cigarettes and lit another even though he didn't really want one. He thought of Cluj station. Searching for a taxi. They would be waiting outside. That was common to every city in the world. Even if there was no taxi he could walk to the hotel. Shut the door of his room. Be safe from the world outside. Mihail gestured towards the other carriage. 'You must not give in to these people. You must stay in your seat. Stand firm. Otherwise the hooligans will take over.'

Alistair looked across at him. Mihail's expression had changed. He was now eyeing him with something approaching pity.

'Aleestar. There is something I want to say. Something I want to ask you.'

Alistair brought his cigarette to his mouth. Mihail did the same. They inhaled simultaneously. Exhaled. Their smoke clouds meeting and mingling.

'All of us are worried, Aleestar. All of us in Travulia. We're very worried. We think our days are numbered. That is why I ask questions.' Mihail's face was so vivid. So present. Every line, every bristle, every weather-reddened capillary. 'We think you're trying to do as they say and abandon us.'

No.

You're trying to purge yourself of us. To keep yourself safe.

I'm not.

We know you are, Aleestar. And Travulia will be no more.

I threw out the Haloperidol, remember. That would have done for you.

Alistair had started crying. He needed to stop that if he was going to gain control of himself. He looked back at the girl. Her beauty. Her sadness.

When I think . . . when I think what I might have been . . . what I might have had . . . if it wasn't for the fear.

But Mihail was no longer there. Nobody was there. Apart from the sleeping girl. Alistair sat rocking from side to side, staring at the back of the seat in front of him, trying to tolerate the feeling, the empty void that had opened up deep within his gut. He might have sat like that all the way to Cluj, but eventually his inward attention was broken by an event – a distraction at the far end of the coach. Three shaven heads, potato-thick and waxy-skinned, filling the upper space of the open carriage doorway. Popeyed and red-faced with drink, the young men cheered again as they entered.

'*Haide. Pe-aicea,*' said the tallest of them. '*Să ne distrăm şi noi!*' and they made their way into the carriage.

150

# PART THREE

If you set out on a search or a journey, because you are made to, because you sense something calling from within, some voice which may be still and small but will not let you rest until you pay it heed . . . you will be met. You will be met.

Nicholas Zealand

# Chapter Nine

There were two sets of stairs to climb to Alice's bedroom. She was still holding Alistair's hand, tightly. The warmth from it seemed to spread into him. He had felt it move up his hand and into his body like an injection. It seemed to have given him passage into another world filled with a thick sweetness – a warm, brown hope that he wouldn't even have been able to imagine half an hour before. Something new for him. Was this being an adult?

More charcoal sketches lined the walls, some hanging slightly off-centre. Each one was a drawing of a child. Each child had the same inquiring eyes and slightly pouty expression.

'Who are the pictures of?' Alistair asked. He didn't want to say anything that would cause her to let go of his hand.

'Brothers and sisters. All of us. Mum did them.'

Alistair looked to see if there was one of Alice. There was, on the top landing. 'Is that you?' The girl in the picture looked about ten years old. She had Alice's round cheeks and full lower lip.

'It is.' They both paused before it.

'Is your mum an artist?'

Alice shook her head. She let go of Alistair's hand and reached out to straighten the frame.

'Not professional. She loved to draw. She died three years ago this August.'

'Oh. I'm sorry.' Alistair was shocked. He didn't know what to say.

'It was a car accident.'

'Was your dad . . . ? I mean is that why . . .' He felt unable to even say the words.

'Dad?' She seemed thrown for a moment, in another place. Then she got herself back together. 'No. Dad's got MS. Multiple sclerosis.'

Alistair had wanted to hold her hand again, but now felt selfish for having the thought.

'Come on then . . .' She opened the door to her bedroom.

The smell of patchouli oil combined with something else, something honeyed and powdery. She turned on the light. The room was dark blue. There were paintings stuck directly on to the wallpaper, some larger than others. A number of them looked like album covers. He recognized one of them from a Joy Division album – a little rectangle of thin wavy lines within a plain, darker background. He was sure the album cover was simple white on black. In this home-done version the design was repeated four times, each one rendered in differing primary colours. The room was small and interestingly shaped, tucked as it was into the corner of the house's eaves. As in Alistair's bedroom, there were piles of tapes. These too had home-drawn covers. Some of the names on the spines were done in Letraset. Alice was searching around in a pile of clothes on the floor. There were skirts and shirts and T-shirts all mixed up together.

'I need do to some washing – don't look,' she said. Alistair turned away immediately. It was amazing to him to be in a girl's bedroom. He would do anything she asked of him. He became nervous of a silence descending again and felt the need to fill it.

154

'You know when you're doing Leila,' he said. 'When I read it, read the play, I mean, I thought she was really annoying, a bit of a creep. But when you do her – she's not like that.'

'She wasn't a creep. She was amazing.'

'How do you know?'

Alice left the pile of clothes she'd been tidying and went to a small desk that stood next to her dressing table. It had a lift-up top like an old-fashioned school desk. She dug around and pulled out a sheaf of photocopied paper. She brought it over and handed it to Alistair. They were copies of typed sheets – or, judging by the blurred greyness of some of the words, they were copies of copies.

'What is it?' Alistair asked, scanning the pages for clues.

'Pages of her journal. A translation. Some of it was in French. Some in Romanian. Read it. You'll like it. It's not what you think.' Alistair squinted at the hazy words. 'You'd never believe she was only fourteen when they went down there. It's like she's ten years older than the one in the play. There's stuff about life. Stuff about God.'

'Jewish stuff?' asked Alistair.

'I don't know about that.' Alice looked apologetic. 'It's sort of thoughtful . . . philosophical.'

'Where did you get it from?'

'Dad got it for me. It was a priest who discovered her papers. Do you want to borrow it? You can read it in bed tonight.'

'Does it go up to the end?' he said, after a pause.

'Auschwitz, you mean?' She looked straight at him. 'No. She left this stuff in the cellar – behind a loose brick.'

Alistair scrutinized the pages. The type was very close together. It didn't look very appealing. 'Is there much about Marcel in it?'

''Fraid not. More about Titu. I think she really fancied

155

him.' Alice grinned mischievously. Alistair felt a momentary jolt of what must have been jealousy. He thought about Steve. And it troubled him to hear Alice use a word like 'fancy'. A whole slew of questions seemed to lead off it. Like who she fancied. And whether she had a boyfriend now. Alistair stood awkwardly in the middle of the room clutching the photocopies. Alice was now digging through another pile of clothes. 'Here we are.' She held up a little Phillips mono cassette player, more portable than the one he kept in his own bedroom. This was a squat black oblong covered in stickers and crusts of Liquid Paper upon which Alice had drawn various band names. 'What do you fancy?'

'Sorry?'

'What would you like to listen to?'

'Oh.' Alistair looked around the room as if it might provide an answer.

'Do you like the Velvet Underground?' She looked at him expectantly. There was no malice in her question, as there would be with one of the music weirdos at school. They brandished the names of obscure groups like weapons.

'Erm . . . I don't know them.' He felt awkward but at the same time pleased that he had been able to tell the truth.

'You'll like them. You'll *really* like them.' She seemed excited at the prospect of playing him the tape. She cleared some space on the bed for them to sit down, then jumped on, folding her legs underneath herself. She took off her cardigan and chucked it on the pile with the other discarded clothes. Her arms were bare underneath. The music began and she patted the bed, indicating that Alistair should sit down next to her. There was his heart again, thudding away. There was also the sweetness, the new sweetness that came with it. He didn't know whether he dared think that what was in his own mind might be in Alice's. He perched him-self on the bed in such a way that she could not accuse him of being mistaken about her intentions. Even thinking that thought felt like the most presumptuous, misguided idea in the world.

The tape wasn't what he imagined it would be. He'd assumed there'd be something dangerous or violent or dif-ficult about the music. If it was so obscure that he'd never heard of it, he'd thought that it must be because there was something about it that kept people from listening to it. In fact, the song was beautiful and simple and gentle. Alice was biting her lower lip again. She let it go as she started fol-lowing the words of the song. For a moment there was a tiny depression in the skin where her front teeth had been. It gradually disappeared as she sang. 'Sometimes I feel so happy. Sometimes I feel so sad . . .' She turned to Alistair to observe his reaction. He listened intently. It was good. His stomach had tightened for a moment because he didn't know whether he should be continuing the conversation or not. But then he became interested in listening to the song and watching Alice listen to it too. Sometimes she sang in a gentle breathy way and sometimes just made the appropri-ate motions with her mouth. Although he thought of Alice as being bigger than him, taller and more grown-up, sitting next to her he realized that they were almost the same size. His skin was paler than hers, his hair a storm of brown frizz where hers was neat and straight and precise. His face all wrong in his own eyes with its extended nose and uneven skin, hers so symmetrical and clear.

He looked around the room again, too, at the paintings and the mess. Then he looked back at Alice to find she was looking straight at him again. She seemed sad, as if she had seen something in him that he wasn't aware of, some shadow standing behind him. But when his eyes met hers the sadness left her face. She smiled at him. Without thinking about it, he smiled back. 'Linger on,' said the song. Strange words. Her eyes held his. Everything in the room seemed very bright: the bulb above their heads, the yellow of the curtains. Alice had stopped smiling now. She still held his gaze but her expression was serious. His heart was going faster. An intense moment of panic. He didn't know what to do. He looked away. Sat backward, changing the space between them. When he looked back at Alice her face betrayed some thought he didn't understand, some disappointment or confusion. The song finished and the next track started, faster and scarier. Alice moved to turn it down a touch.

'Where are your albums – or do you just have tapes?' Alistair winced as he asked the question. He didn't know why he had spoken it. He had just wanted the silence filled.

'Downstairs – in the lounge,' she said, looking puzzled. And now Alistair found he had slipped out of the world of just being he had briefly tasted and into one of self-consciousness. He felt awkward on the bed, and couldn't imagine that there would be anything else they could talk about. The feeling that had been there only moments ago had dispersed. It was shocking to discover it had been so insubstantial. Alice looked at her watch. He looked down at his legs, his child's trousers and shoes. The calamitous music continued, but there was no pleasure in listening to it together now. Just a growing awkwardness. Eventually it was Alice who spoke.

'Are you supposed to be back at any time?'

'I'd better be going now,' he said. He reached for his wad of per diem money. 'Can I get a taxi?'

Later, in his elongated bedroom – lying on the bed. Staring at the ceiling. Thinking about her hand in his. He had intended to visit Travulia that night. To find out what had been happening on Henry Hudson's film, maybe hear from some of the other residents. But when he held the Dictaphone to his lips no voice emerged. Instead his thoughts were drawn back to the events of the afternoon. The slight pull that he felt in his arm as she led him up the stairs. Alice's face. Her blue eyes with her straight dark hair. He'd thought her hair was black, but up close it was actually a dark, dark brown. It made him think of a tortoiseshell comb on Mum's dressing table. When you held it up to the light it became a different colour: richer, browner, glowing. Alistair thought that blue eyes went with blonde hair. But the blue with her dark, almost black hair, there was something magical about it. Her face filled his head. Her eyes, her hair. That strange conjunction of blue and black – like the sea against a rock.

Should he have tried to kiss her earlier? Tomorrow he'd see her again. Maybe they could spend another afternoon together. He closed his eyes and imagined what it might be like walking around the West End with her. Maybe finding a coffee bar. Sitting there and talking for hours like he did with Herby on Saturday afternoons. When he got back to Leeds, would he be able to see her? Would she come up to see him? He would be able to ring her and speak to her. There was something delicious about all this imagining. It was like a new game – a better game than anything he'd thought about before. The idea of kissing her felt like something technological – like the idea of having an Atari all of his own to play with, together with a pile of the best games you could get, plus all the time in the world to play those games. But warmer than that. He thought about the shape of her legs in her jeans. How this was something he'd begun to notice in girls two or three years ago. First of all distinguishing between the girls who had yet to hit puberty and those who were getting there or had got there. It was the legs Alistair always looked at first – trying to find that noticeable thickening around the thighs that told him they too were in adolescence and worthy of his attention. Their legs went from being straight like poles, to taking on a conical quality. He never really looked at anything else. He didn't want to see any of them naked or anything like that. It was another feeling – a hugeness that he wanted to be part of, a powerfulness, a himselfness. Somehow being with a girl would bring about an increase in Alistair Blackness. Of course, he would love to be able tell his classmates – or some of them anyway. He would love to join in the lunchtime competition-of-tales that often took place, particularly after a weekend. At the same time he wouldn't want Alice reduced from the solid, soulful thing she felt now to a flimsy boast he could share with classmates in a breaktime conversation. He liked the fact that she felt like his thing. Maybe he would be happy never to tell anyone – if something could just happen between them. 'Oh Alice,' he experimented. 'I love you.' What a strange thing to imagine saying, or even feeling. What did it mean? Was it something like these feelings? There were other voices trying to get in – telling him that she would have an older boyfriend. But then he thought, or another part of him thought: but she'll want to be with me. He turned over to face the wall, gathering some of the peppery orange bedspread in his fist and holding it close to his nose. He brought to mind the smell of patchouli oil, satisfied at the feelings that came with it.

After some time, in which he hoped he might have gone to sleep dreaming of Alice, Alistair gave in to the fact that he wasn't yet tired enough. He padded out to the toilet on the silent corridor outside his room then came back and scrabbled in his Schofields carrier bag for the photocopies of Leila Vinteuil's journal that Alice had given him. He put them on the floor and pulled off his shoes, trousers and jumper, climbing into bed in his vest and pants. He bent down to pick up the loosely bound paper but as he did so he caught a glimpse of the Horror Films book, halfway under the bed where he had pushed it that morning. He bent further and reached for it, twisting awkwardly in order to be able to do so. He pulled it out and lay it on the bed.

After he had come Alistair felt bad. He hurriedly closed the book and threw it as far as he could under the bed. Then he turned over and went to sleep.

'OK people!' Gabrielle clapped her hands together. Everybody had been on time today. In fact Alistair had been the last one to arrive. He'd dawdled on his way up from reception – already nervous about seeing Alice. He tried not to look for her too obviously as he took off his coat. She was there, on the other side of the room. She wore a tight grey jumper over a blue skirt that finished just above her knees. She was holding the sleeves of her jumper over her fisted hands. Her hair was pulled back into an uncomfortable-looking pony-tail. Her pretty face looked startled and tired. She hadn't seen Alistair yet – or if she had, made no attempt to greet him. 'Today is D-Day. We're going to have to blitz it!' said Gabrielle, turning round to take in the whole cast.

'Rather inappropriate imagery,' Jack whispered to Emese, who rather than laughing her usual laugh, pressed her lips together and widened her eyes, nodding slowly as she did.

'We're going into the big room,' said Gabrielle, 'which I have been assured Cyril Davenport has finished taping out. We've got half a day to block this and run it, so I trust that you're all word perfect.' She jerked her head to one side as she spoke, as if trying to click something back into place.

161

'We're at TVC all too soon. So we'd better get going.' They all shuffled into the other room. Alistair hung back to see if Alice would say good morning. But she was already ahead of him. He was pleased when Steve came over and thumped him in the side of his stomach.

'All right, sunshine,' he said. 'Have fun yesterday?'

Alistair nodded. He didn't want Alice to hear them talking about her.

'Get those lines OK?'

Alistair just nodded.

He looked up again to see if he could find Alice, gain her attention in some way so that she might acknowledge him. He needed to see her smile. Declan explained that he wanted to run the play from the top, without scripts, remembering the blocking from the day before. He wasn't going to stop them at any point this time. Gabrielle stared at him as he delivered his instructions – as if she was checking that he was sticking to some plan they'd both agreed to. There was a lot of mumbling and muttering but eventually everyone took their place at one end of the tape-drawn room. Alistair found himself close to Alice. He hoped she would acknowledge him. He wished now he'd read the pages of Leila's diary.

'Hi.' Feeling shaky as he spoke.

'Hello.' She was digging in her bag. Her hand came clutching two hair grips. She reached for a lock of hair that dangled down across her face.

'All right?'

A long pause while she pulled the loose hair back over her scalp. Alistair waited for her to answer him. Couldn't believe that she wouldn't. Eventually she said, 'Uh huh.' She finished the hair-gripping operation. She looked at him blankly.

He didn't understand. He felt desperate, like he'd

suddenly forgotten how to breathe. 'Do you know your lines?' The banality of it. It was all he could think to say. Something burned inside.

'Uh huh.' She was barely looking at him. It must have all been a mistake. Everything he had thought.

'Will you be quiet, Leila. There's nothing to laugh about.' Alistair found himself shocked back into the present moment by the volume and power of Jack's voice. And so the play began, moving slowly across the taped-out parquet like a giant board game. Except a game wasn't the right comparison. There was chance in a game. You threw a dice and obeyed its instructions. Each time you played you didn't know how it was going to come out. This was more like a rail journey, or a ride on a ghost train. You started in one place, you ended up in another and at every point along the way it was decided where you were going to be. The concept of winning or losing required the possibility of different outcomes. Here you knew exactly where you would end up the minute the first word was spoken.

The rails rolled underneath, lulling him back into another place, another time.

'. . . We need to cross the river.' His scene with Alice. Whoever she had been a moment ago was now replaced by Leila Vinteuil. 'I can smell it.' He found his laugh was natural now. The idea of the smelly river was funny. He could giggle for real. 'It stinks.' 'Stinks' was a funny word, too. It allowed him to continue the laugh convincingly. The dialogue continued. He was enjoying what the play allowed him – to be with Alice, close once again. Or was it to be with Leila?

'Keep going, straight and fast.'

'I can see it. I can see the synagogue.' He permitted himself to become excited. He had no idea what the *shul* in Cluj looked like, but he could see Street Lane Gardens, where he had been Bar Mitzvahed, quite clearly behind his closed eyes. The brown brick. The polished wooden doors. His own life now nestling within Marcel's.

'You see. It's not hard, is it?'

'Can we go inside?'

'Of course.' Alice made it sound like the most natural thing anyone should wish.

Alistair floated through the doors, through the lobby with its huge see-through curtains covering the long windows. Through the open doors and into the shul. It was full of people.

'It's busy. Like Rosh Hashanah. People are singing.' And he called to mind the shemah, the prayer you were supposed to say every day, which he actually knew the words to, although, of course, he didn't have a clue what those words meant: *Shemah y'srael, adonai, elohainu, adonai echad* . . .

'Bang!' shouted Declan. This in place of the stage direction which referred to a loud noise coming from above. Alistair flicked his eyes open – the look of fear on his face was authentic. It came easily to him.

'What was that?' he asked in a whisper. Alice's eyes were even wider than usual. She looked over her shoulder.

'I don't know,' she said.

'Bang, crash, bang!' yelled Declan, having leapt around the perimeter of the room to investigate their action from a different viewpoint.

'Is it soldiers?' asked Alistair, still whispering. Now it was easy to imagine them above and the fear they would generate. Jack joined them, listening intently.

'Thieves, I think,' he said. 'Not soldiers.' The three of them stood for a moment, listening to nothing, each of them hearing something different but equivalent in their heads.

'I think they are going. Poor Mr Stanescu is going to have

a shock tomorrow when he arrives at the restaurant.' Alistair knew Alice hated the line, but she said it, as always, as if she meant it.

'These are ugly times,' said Emese who had joined them from the back of the room.

The play ran until the end. Apart from minor fluffs and some moments of vague confusion over who stood where, it had run with remarkable smoothness. At that point Alistair searched nervously for Declan. He and Gabrielle were looking so pleased that Alistair thought however well or otherwise he had done was not an issue for either of them.

Now the run-through was complete he thought of Alice, and the fact that he had yet to speak to her. He turned to face her. She was standing next to Jack – stretching her arms in front of her. He had thought he would ask her what she was doing this afternoon. Now the idea of doing such a thing made him feel stupid and self-conscious. He couldn't begin to imagine how he would raise it with her.

'Fucking excellent!' Declan bounded over towards them, lighting a cigarette. 'Lunch at the Prospect is in order.' He pulled up a chair, swinging it round the wrong way in his habitual manner. 'Let's just take a few moments. Talk about the close.' He reached in his leather bag and withdrew a large black sketchbook. 'We're going quiet and sepulchral.' Alistair looked at Alice. She had her eyes closed. 'Holding on a candle in the foreground.' Declan leafed through the pages in his book. 'Soft on you behind. We won't see what happens. We'll hear.' Alice had a hand on her forehead. 'Bunny doesn't take us right to the end,' said Declan. He picked up his script. 'We are aware of a commotion and raised voices but do not hear the specifics. We see one of the candles flicker and blow out. The other remains lit.' The glass doors behind Alice were closed. The light in the room beyond was switched off. Alistair became aware of the reflections. Steve was looking right at him, seemingly studying Alistair watching Alice. Sharply Alistair looked away from both of them. 'We've drafted some of the "Now" cast to voice Soldiers One and Two but there's no costumes so we're not going to be seeing anything,' Declan continued. 'I want you – cast – to work up the specifics of what we hear from you. It's up to you to create that atmosphere. I'd like to work on that now.' Jack had got his pipe out and started stuffing tobacco into the blackened bowl. 'Don't worry about getting it exactly right,' said Declan. 'Just begin by putting yourself into that situation.'

It didn't take long at all. Jack happily took control of the process. Emese and Alice worked out little screams – 'Not too Fay Wray,' Emese had said. As the session finished Cyril Davenport appeared with a pile of white papers, which he handed out to each of them as they filed past him and made their way to lunch.

Alistair had never been in a pub before. He'd often wondered what might go on behind the mottled glass and high-windowed walls. The air was heavy with smoke. Everything seemed to be dark red or brown. He was worried he wouldn't be allowed inside. He wasn't yet sixteen. He clung close to Jack and Emese, hoping perhaps that he might be taken for their son.

'Jack?' Declan had leaned across – his hand in the air.

'Large brandy, sir.' Jack's pipe was already ignited. He found a seat and withdrew a folded newspaper from his bag.

'Alistair?'

'Get the boy a beer,' said Jack, his eyes already fixed on his newspaper.

'You want a beer?' Declan looked at him, his eyebrows raised. Alistair glanced at Alice, who was taking a seat next to Steve. He looked back at Declan and nodded, feeling grown-up again. He squeezed around the other side of the table to take a seat next to Steve. There was one free next to Alice. He still held on to the possibility of asking what she might have been doing that afternoon, maybe in such a way that it sounded like general conversation.

'All right, sport,' said Steve as Alistair lowered himself onto a stool. 'Declan got you on the booze?'

'Just a half.' As he sat down Alice rose to her feet, as if they were on opposite sides of a seesaw.

'Do you think there's a phone in here?' she said, digging in her pocket. Her face was grave. It felt like she didn't want to be near him. He looked down at the table and picked up a beer mat. Steve gestured to the far wall where a payphone was fixed beneath a grey plastic hood. Alice walked off towards it.

'Oooohhhh,' said Steve, shaking his head as she walked off.

'What?' said Alistair.

'Dunno what you did to her yesterday.'

'What?' he said again, feeling as if something had been injured.

'She's in a foul mood today.'

'I didn't do anything.'

Steve looked at him with exaggerated disbelief. At that point Declan arrived with the drinks. He placed the half pint of beer in front of Alistair.

'That's all you're getting,' he said. 'Not having you going back to the Bray drunk.'

Alistair picked up the glass and took a sip. He felt the bite of the alcohol. Suddenly thought he understood the appeal of getting drunk.

'I'm only joking, chief. Only casing you up.' Steve had a beer too. He gulped at his as if he enjoyed the taste. 'What you up to this avvy?'

Alistair thought about his plan to ask Alice that very

question. He glanced across to the phone booth. She was pushing twopences into the paybox. 'Fancy a doss?' said Steve, wiping his mouth with his hand. Alistair looked back at Alice, now in animated conversation. She could well have been speaking to a boyfriend. He turned to Steve, all thoughts of speaking to Alice released.

'Yeah. That'd be good.'

The entrance to the London Dungeon was advertised by a faded wooden sign. It looked like it had been there a lot longer than it probably had. The logo simulated dripping blood, but sunlight had faded the red to something closer to yellow in places. There were other signs screwed to the dirty brick stating that the queue should stand against the wall. There weren't even any pedestrians walking past, never mind customers.

'What is this place?' Alistair had asked on the journey there but Steve had refused to elaborate.

The doorway was made to look like the entrance of a dungeon. There was a speaker on the wall near the door broadcasting the drone of chanting monks. As they passed inside the chanting became louder, relayed on other speakers around the place. Stepping up to the ticket booth Steve said, 'It's all right – I'll pay,' and he produced a thick roll of bank notes from his pocket. The money glowed bright purple under the ultraviolet striplights. It was more like a school disco than a torture chamber. Alistair glanced at a skull which jutted from the wall on his left. The skull looked real but he noticed that its jawbone was connected to it by loops of plastic.

'Here lies the body of Uncle Ted,' said Steve, reading from a crudely painted gravestone fastened to the wall. 'Once alive, but long since dead.' He laughed a pantomime horror film laugh. Suddenly a huge cowled figure jumped out in front of them. Both Steve and Alistair shrieked. The figure threw back his hood. He was a tall young man in his early twenties. His face was painted white, with grey patches under his eyes. He was supposed to resemble a corpse, but Alistair thought the make-up made him look more like an animal – a panda, or a dog with a patch.

'Good afternoon, gentlemen.' His voice boomed richly – a proper actor's diction. 'Welcome to the dungeon.' He looked at them both keenly, again as if he was giving an authentic performance. 'I wonder' – he leaned towards Alistair – 'does anyone know you're here?' Stupidly, for a moment, Alistair felt like he was in trouble. He shook his head dumbly. 'Good,' said the figure, 'because we're going to kill one of you.' He pulled back into the shadows, laughing insanely.

'Some shit actor,' said Steve as they walked off, 'straight out of Guildhall or Central. Can't get any work.'

The space was huge and cavernous, the air heavy with damp. Alistair kept glancing nervously over his shoulder, eager to retain a sense of the better-lit entrance behind him. But the path led away, descending beneath a low arch. He walked on, trying to stay close to Steve.

The passage opened out into a cavernous chamber. The thin hum of the chanting monks was now accompanied by other sounds, weak and crackly and worn out as if they had been copied too many times: a tolling bell, the crack of a whip, a yelp and a moan. Red and orange lights flickered through the haze of dry ice. The room was arranged into alcoves. In each one was a different tableau. The scenes were built around shop dummies who had been given a new life and identity by being wrapped in costumes and having their features distorted with wax and paint.

'Implements of the Inquisition!' Steve said with relish, reading from a sign. A dummy poked out of a cauldron, like something unwanted thrown in a skip. The repetitive rhythm of the yelps, whips and bell tolls revealed that they were playing on an endless loop.

'What's flagellation?' asked Alistair, trying to make sense of the mixture of straw, soil, hessian and mannequins in front of him.

'Whipping,' explained Steve, moving to another exhibit. 'Look at these.' Lit with more green and red gelled lights were a collection of rusty iron items. Steve began to read again.

'"Jaw ratchet. The implement was placed between the teeth of the heretic. The screw was gradually turned, separating the prongs and hence the jaw."' Steve turned to Alistair and gradually opened his own mouth, baring his teeth in a grimace of agony. Turning back he went on: '"This continued until the crack of dislocation was heard – sometimes even further." Imagine that.' Steve let his jaw loll, waggling his tongue in and out of his open mouth. "Look at this." Alistair ran to catch up with him. '"Choked by the garrotte."' One dummy sat in a chair, another stood up behind him, hands tightening something that looked like a cheese-wire around the other's neck. The wire ate into a groove that had been cut around the neck. Shiny red gloss paint had been applied liberally to the frozen wound. The victim looked out with the sightless eyes of a ventriloquist's doll.

'Look . . . it's moving,' said Alistair. The hands holding the wire were twisting, almost imperceptibly slowly. The head of the victim was creeping from side to side. It looked like it was supposed to move faster but the batteries were running down.

Steve had walked on ahead and disappeared round a corner. Alistair knew that he would be hiding there, somewhere up ahead, readying himself to leap out at him. He thought it best to play along and act shocked when Steve finally sprang. He allowed his attention to wander over the dank, gloomy space. It seemed only half finished. The brickwork was full of gaps and tunnels containing nothing but shadows and draughts. Vaulted arches led off in one direction, disappearing into blackness. They weren't roped off in any way. There was nothing to stop you walking off into the darkness, other than the fear of doing so. He walked over to the tunnel's entrance, hovering for a moment. A sound emerged from the murk, a low deep rumble. The passage looked like it stretched on without end deep into the heart of the city's clay. He thought about Alice suddenly. Being without her. Separated from that feeling of the day before, the warmth and the wholeness. Wham. Alistair fell to ground, Steve on top of him.

'I knew you were going to do that,' said Alistair, brushing himself off. He turned and followed Steve back among the exhibits.

His attention was drawn by a lone metal cube on the far side of the next chamber. He walked over to it, paused there to find out what it was. It was formed out of a grid of rusty iron strips no more than a metre by a metre. It made a cage of sorts, but it didn't look like a cage. It was more like a puzzle or a toy. Crunched into one corner was another howling shop dummy covered in some scraps of old cloth, its limbs twisted into uncustomary positions in order to fit into the confined space.

'"Little Ease",' read Alistair from the small board fastened to the wall next to the rusting exhibit. Steve gave no sign that he was listening but Alistair continued anyway. '"Little Ease was a tiny cell made in a hole under the white tower of the Tower of London. It was situated behind a small door just eighteen inches wide, four feet high and two feet deep. After years spent in this unbelievably cramped space, prisoners would be released into the centre of nearby St Augustus Field. Driven mad by their confinement they would be unable to bear the sudden exposure to open space. Most would drop down dead of fright."' Steve was standing next to him now, listening with interest.

'Fantastic,' he said. Alistair stared at the contorted mannequin. It looked at him through the corroded slats of the cage, peering out through the thick strands of an all-too-artificial wig. 'Do you think this is the actual thing?' asked Steve touching the metal, his grin revealing teeth that glowed in the ultraviolet striplight. Alistair shrugged. Steve gripped a piece of the ironwork as if savouring the feel of it.

'What about Alice, then? Something going on there?'

Alistair was simultaneously struck with the urge to be evasive and the wish to be candid. 'We just went through the scene. Listened to some music.'

'Listened to some music? Sounds promising. Any action?'

'No!' Alistair looked away.

'Tops? Fingers?'

'No!'

'Yeah, but you'd like to, wouldn't you, sport?'

Alistair shrugged his shoulders again.

'Do you want me to ask her for you?'

'Don't you dare.'

'I will. I'll ask her tomorrow for you. In the studio. Just before we're about to start. I'll say, Alistair wants to know if he can feel your little tits.'

'Fuck off, Steve.' But Alistair was giggling. He quite liked it.

'Alistair Black wonders if he can slip his hands down the front of your little white knickers and dip his fingers in your cunny.' Steve waggled his own fingers inside the space of the cage. 'Shall we go to the café?' he said, suddenly abandoning the thought and turning his back on the exhibit. 'They do cheese toasties.'

'Yeah,' said Alistair, happy to follow him.

The café was even more like a youth-club disco. There were fluorescent ghosts and skeletons painted on the walls, along with the suggestion of a library, the spines of books with punning titles. They ordered the food and they sat at the table. Steve fiddled idly with a tin-foil ashtray. Alistair looked around the walls at the ghoulish characters, the famous murderers and drawings of torture implements.

'What's the most scared you've ever been?' he said, hoping to involve Steve, who had fallen into a sullen silence. Alistair didn't want Steve to have gone off the idea of being there with him.

'Why, what's the most you've been scared?' Steve had turned to look at him.

Alistair wasn't ready to have the question thrown back at him. There were too many times. Every day. The woman shouted from behind the counter to let them know that their toasties were ready. 'I'll get them.' He returned to the table, trying to keep the frail paper plates steady. Their undersides, thinned with grease from the hot sandwiches, burned his hands.

'Have you ever been in hospital?' said Steve.

Alistair shook his head.

'I have. When I was seven.'

'What for?'

'Something to do with my stomach. I wasn't digesting things properly.' He was tearing the tin-foil ashtray up now, making a flower of the grubby thing.

'Did you have to have an operation?'

'They slit me open from here to here.' Steve indicated with an extended finger. He thought for a minute, pressing a bit of the contorted foil against the Formica. It rattled like

Morse code. 'That wasn't the bad thing.' The rhythm of his taps repeated their complex pattern. 'I can't really remember that. You know – they put you to sleep.' Steve's normally extravagantly expressive face had gone impassive. 'It was the night before. I was in this side room. On my own. Private ward. Mum was supposed to come and stay.' Alistair picked up his sandwich. It was too hot to hold. 'It was when it was all going down between her and Dad. I didn't know that at the time. I found out later. I think they'd rowed about something. She'd got drunk. I don't know. She used to drink a lot.' Steve pushed the ashtray away. His finger dance continued. 'Anyway – the thing is, she'd said she was going to be there by seven o' clock. Well, it got to five to seven and I thought she'd be there a bit early. And I was sad that she hadn't made it. I can remember. There was this big grey clock on the wall opposite the bed. With a white face and a red second hand.' Alistair tried the sandwich again. He could bear to hold it. 'I watched that second hand going round, dragging the minute hand with it.' Steve used his finger to indicate the passage of time. 'Eventually it got to the top.' He shook his head. 'Still she didn't come. I watched the second hand carry on, taking the long hand to five past, ten past. By the time it got to half past I was more frightened than I'd ever been. I thought she'd forgotten about me. Just forgotten about me. I thought I'd be left in there forever. Forever – on my own.'

'What about your dad?' Alistair tried to imagine Steve as a seven-year-old.

'I didn't even know if he knew I was there. He hadn't been at home. I cried for ages. I can't remember how long. A big black nurse cuddled me. I can remember that. I can remember her smell. But Mum didn't come. And I . . . was . . . so . . . frightened.' The last sentence spoken slowly, as if he couldn't decide on the right words.

Alistair looked at his toastie. 'She came in the end?'

'The next day. With presents. She'd had a row. Been drinking. I don't know.' He waved his hand in the air then turned his attention to the toastie and took a bite. 'Your turn.'

Alistair looked at Steve. He saw how honest he'd been. He thought for a moment. He wanted to do the same. The Ormolu dream swam into his mind. Even thinking about it made him tighten up and go cold inside.

'There was this dream I used to have,' he heard himself saying. 'When I was younger.' He'd never spoken of it aloud before. Never had to form the words to express it.

'What kind of dream? A nightmare?' Steve showed interest, smiling for the first time since he'd told his story.

'I haven't had it for a bit.' Alistair felt himself hesitate. What if just talking about it made it come back? He hadn't dreamt it for years now. But Steve was looking at him expectantly, his appetite for Alistair's fear stimulated. And there was something about sharing these fears that put Steve and him on the same level. In fact, it was the first thing they'd talked about where that had been the case. 'I called it the Ormolu dream.'

'Who's the Ormeloo?'

'Ormolu.' Although Steve's pronunciation was only slightly wrong, Alistair still felt the need to correct him. 'It wasn't a person.'

'Well, what is the Ormolu?' said Steve, irritated at what he felt to be pedantry.

'A place.' Alistair looked at Steve directly, like Alice had looked at him, holding the sharp blue eyes with his own. 'It's a place in the dream.'

'What kind of place? How can a place be so frightening? Is it like this?' Steve gestured around himself. Alistair laughed.

175

'No. Not like this.' He swallowed. Felt a hardness in his throat just talking about it.

'Where is it? Why's it called the Ormolu?'

'I don't know the answer to any of these questions.' He bit at a loose fingernail. 'I can only tell you what it was like.'

'Well?'

'Well . . .' He pushed away the plate with the remains of his food.

'I wake up. In the dream I wake up. Except it's like waking up for real. I really think I'm awake.' He looked around himself with his eyes, as if acting out the dream's action. 'Everything is white. I look up and it's all white. I look down and it's all white. I look to one side and it's all white. I look to the other and it's all white. I look at me . . . you know, look for an arm or something. And there isn't anything. It's like I'm all white too. Part of the white. So I set off. I can move at speed, can feel a rush of moving. But nothing changes. There's only the same continuing whiteness. And I want to get out of there, get away from the blankness. So I make myself rush even faster. The whiteness moves by. But it just opens out onto more blankness, moving on forever and ever, nothing in it. I try to fly upwards, and I can, but it's up into more whiteness, up and up and up and up and it never ends. And I'm trying to force myself out of there but there's nowhere to go because this is all there is. This is all there is. All there is forever and ever. I go down, jump down and sink and sink and sink, the blank white flowing around me. And I want to scream but there is only me. Only me. Just me alone. No one else to hear. No one else to help. And I can't wake up. This is awake. This is as awake as you can be. Just emptiness. Just Ormolu. Alone in the whiteness. Forever. No end.' Alistair paused for a moment. Steve was looking at him but he couldn't tell if he was

176

impressed or otherwise. 'And I used to have this dream all the time.'

They finished their toasties and headed for the exit. They had to pass through a shop first, full of key rings and wind-up toys and jokes in little polythene bags.

'Why is it called the Ormolu?' It was the first thing Steve had said about the dream since Alistair had finished telling it.

'I don't know. I wondered—'

'Haaaaaaahhhhhhhh!' A dark figure leapt out in front of both of the boys, screaming wildly like an animal. Alistair screamed too, even louder. Steve pushed the figure over, making it tumble back into one of the revolving stands which crashed against the till area. 'Fuck off!' the figure shrieked. It was the shit actor from the start. He got to his feet. 'You stupid twat!' he screamed at Steve. But Steve had grabbed Alistair's arm and was already pulling him through the exit door into the cold, London evening.

# Chapter Ten

'So . . . let's go back to the beginning. I mean the very beginning. Where it all started. It's easy to forget sometimes that it had a beginning – or what the beginning was. It's worth looking at in some detail because it answers – I think – many of our questions. More than we might realize. If we look at the text closely, if we apply reason and logic and imagination, it is surprising quite how much it yields.

'Medieval monks used to talk about "chewing" the verses of the Bible. I think that's a marvellous way of putting it. We're accustomed to gulping our texts. If we spend some time holding each verse in our mouth – as it were – line by line everything becomes much juicier.

'The first thing to say is how clearly that beginning is documented for us. Genesis 11:10 through to 12:9. Here's something of note immediately. This is the first part of the Bible that doesn't read like fable. We've had Eden, we've had the Flood, we've had Cain and Abel – powerful fictions discernible as myths – their power derives from their metaphor. And let's not be so arrogant as to assume that their writers thought any different. But now we are presented with twenty-two verses of names and ages – the line of Terah. It's like a list of English kings. Does it strike you that this might be an attempt to record something actual? That this reads more like history than fable? I'm not arguing for its accuracy or historicity, I'm searching for its meaning.

'It strikes me that this is an attempt to get down some nugget of something that actually happened. Something extraordinary. Some extraordinary act that was remembered down the generations.

'We're given this list of descendants because they culminate in one man – Abram. And here's the next thing that strikes. This is an ordinary man. He's not spoken of as a king of kings or a prophet or a saint. Quite the reverse. In his first chapter he's revealed to be a very human individual – happy to pimp his own wife to a pharaoh in order to assure his survival . . . but I'm getting ahead of myself. Forgive me.

'Now, what can we glean from the opening of this man's story? Abram lived in the city of Ur with his father Terah. But the family leaves Ur and travels north-west to Haran. Archaeological research tells us that this was a sane and reasonable decision, given that at this time their hometown was in a state of permanent decline, the harbour clogged with silt and the city too poor to dredge new channels. Ur had been one of the cultural capitals of Mesopotamia and Haran was not a dissimilar place – an analogy that has been used is San Francisco to the other's New York, and both were dedicated to the moon god Sin.

'The family prospered, and their business flourished (according to Jewish lore they manufactured idols). But there was a second part to this migration, a subsequent voyage that does not seem so sane and reasonable. After Terah's death, Abram – a man well into middle age, a prosperous man with a barren wife Sarai, also middle-aged, therefore with no children to care for, no hope of a future for their line – decides to leave his wealthy, comfortable life and set off into the wilderness, literally with no idea where he is going.

'What was this act? An affluent, middle-aged man leaves his thriving family business and takes his family and "all the gain that he had gained" and sets off into the desert on an indeterminate journey with no definite destination. Why would somebody do such an insane thing? Particularly this man, this ordinary man. From what we can glean from the rest of his story and from related legends, Abram had been a fearful man all his life – had built up wealth, yes, but had always stayed rooted in the place of his birth, surrounded by the same people. So to get up and go in this manner must have taken some kind of courage, some notable amount of effort and energy. What made him get up and go, implement this radical change?

'Genesis tells us. He heard a voice.

'The voice said, "Go forth from your native land and from your father's house to the land that I will show you." And, "I will make of you a great people, and I will bless you . . . And the families of the earth shall bless themselves by you."

'Now, let's just return for a moment to my original proposition – that what we are reading here is an attempt at history, at getting down something that actually happened. I want us to look at this as atheists – or at least as agnostics. In measurable, human terms, what might this act mean? How might we understand it?

'If Abram had lived, he would have been a man, subject to the same laws of the Universe as you and I and everyone else. Therefore, God's voice would not have boomed from the heavens with a cavernous echo. I think that people four thousand years ago lived in the same physical universe that we inhabit. In fact . . . I'm bloody sure of it. So, if we assume that we are reading an account of something that actually happened – at least in some form – what *did* happen? How did this voice – that made this man behave in this irrational

180

way – manifest itself? What would it have meant then to have heard this voice? To Abram it must have been nothing more than a hunch or a feeling, maybe articulated as a recurring thought. A thought that things might be different. That there might be another way. A thought that grew out of a dissatisfaction with what he saw around him. A dissatisfaction with the culture he was steeped in – a culture of cruelty, a culture which denied all possibility of change, a culture based on fear and determinism.

'And yet this thought was more than an idle fancy. However quiet the voice, it compelled Abram to act. Though the thought was counterintuitive, Abram followed it anyway. In the face of his habitual anxiety, he showed great courage.

'And make no mistake – this was not a sane understandable act that Abram undertook. People did not do things like this. People did not uproot themselves on a whim. These were people who lived in a world governed by fates dictated by the stars, the cycle of the seasons, the great, unchanging, ever-turning circle. You did what you always had done and what you always would do. What must Abram's relatives, Lot, Nahor, Milcah and the rest, not to mention the servants, made of it? What must his poor barren wife Sarai have made of it? They would have thought him mad. And yet his conviction and weird self-belief must have been considerable to overcome their doubts, not to mention his own. Think of the context. There was no God to appeal to in explanation. Today, four millennia later, in this supposedly secular age, you could explain such a decision by invoking His name. People might look at you oddly, but they would understand the source of your actions. But poor Abram, standing on the banks of the Euphrates, only had gods to invoke. Little 'g'. Gods with names – like Lugalbanda and Dumuzi – gods whose statues you anointed or whose amulets you carried. Good-luck charms. The transaction between you and these deities was quite different to the one we're accustomed to. If you wanted success you satisfied the duties of your cult through sacrifice or orgy. You did things for them. They didn't do things for you. They didn't suggest change. Mankind was locked via his gods into an unchanging cycle – the Great Wheel of Life and Death. What would Abram's peers have said about his pilgrimage? They would have shaken their heads at his folly: "It is written in the stars, man cannot escape his destiny." As they would have done on every other continent around the globe two thousand years BCE. Nevertheless, Abram went.

'And thus the next chapter of civilization was begun. The whole circus we still inhabit. Seven-day weeks broken up with a sabbath. An egalitarian legal system and, behind all of this, the curious concept that every man is equal, made in God's image, et cetera et cetera – what extraordinary ideas. And they all started with this one man taking this irrational journey out into the desert because he sensed – deeply, profoundly – that there was a better place to live than the crude, deterministic world of magic, cruelty and iniquity within which he resided.

'I think this account has another message – something that resonates even deeper with me. It's not as explicit but it's definitely there. It's something like this: if you set out on a search or a journey, because you are made to, because you sense something calling from within, some voice which may be still and small but will not let you rest until you pay it heed, something that tells you you are in fact free to act in a different manner however impossible it might seem, well . . . if you set out on such a journey . . . you will be met. You will be met.'

*

182

Alice switched off her Walkman. She was weeping. Caught up in his argument, his mind as she remembered it before the years of incoherence and dementia, she found herself transported to another time. The yearning to return there was overwhelming. It was a time before the knowledge of death, of hurt, of loss, of disappointment, of fear. But it could not be accessed, though the feel of it could be remembered. It hung in the room like a scent, pungent and vivid. But of course it was gone. As Dad was gone. Never to be seen again.

Alice sat for some while, staring through the open windows of her flat, watching the sky darken. She saw Abram and his family, packing their possessions in silence, strapping them to mules and oxen, aiming themselves at the wilderness with no sense of a destination.

The thought that followed this vision was surely too ridiculous. It was terrifying and impossible. She knew the source of this notion. It was the stone in the shoe. It had become grit in the oyster. And now it had brought forth a ludicrous pearl. The idea that she was to go and see Ben again. Now. This minute. Never mind how humiliating this might be. Never mind how much he might hate her. Never mind how terrified she might be.

Every component of reason told her she mustn't go, mustn't think about going. What would he think of her? What would she say to him? The negatives flowed without end. And her preferred path was to heed them. Never mind preferred. That was the only possible path. Staying where she was.

And then, without looking at her watch, without really thinking what she was doing any more, she put on her coat. She sat down again, unsure of herself. She pulled out her address book, flicking to the page with Ben's details on it. It was written in his hand. Next to it was a sketch of her face, her hair falling over her eyes. Alice stared at the drawing, remembering him doing it in a café on the Old Kent Road, capturing his sense of her in a few deft lines.

Then, closing the book, she stood up, retrieved her keys from the bedside table and left the flat, slamming the door behind her.

# Chapter Eleven

It was dark in the dining room at the Bray Hotel. Most of the tables were visible in the gloom, chairs stacked up-ended on the surfaces, like the end of a school day. Alistair and Rosalyn Frieze sat in a circle of light, lit by a dim bulb above. There was one other table down, a single place laid. Alistair had been glancing at it throughout the meal, wondering if its occupant would be joining them. He must have glanced at it too many times, because Rosalyn said, 'Mr Balasco is no longer with us, my dear.' Had he left or had he died? Alistair didn't want to ask. 'He was far too fond of the third channel,' said Rosalyn. 'We don't like the third channel on at any time.' Rosalyn pushed back her plate, pouring out yet more wine for herself from the carafe. 'How old are you, my darling?' she asked, studying him over the cut glass. Her eyes were half closed, as if weighed down by the heavy mascara she wore. Together with the rouge and eyeshadow, she looked as if she was about to step on stage.

'Fifteen.'

'You are so young. A young angel.' Rosalyn flicked the column of ash that was dangling from the end of her cigarette into her own cupped hand. 'Have you been studying your script . . . hmmm?'

'I . . . um . . . I started to.'

'You should be studying. Study, study, study.' She banged

185

her fist on to the table, releasing some of the ash in a small cloud. 'Study is the key. The absolute key. I would consume a script. Digest a script. Absorb it into my bloodstream. Let it course through me.' She pushed herself back in her chair. 'We will go through it together. We will dissect it and scrutinize it. I will teach you how to prepare.' Her hand reached for the open folder of photographs that lay in the centre of the table, where the food had been. She flicked through a few more. 'Of course, I was very young to play the Countess. Such a difficult part. Such a difficult play, *All's Well*. A sad play.' Alistair stared at the picture she had paused at, trying to find Rosalyn's face beneath the white make-up and lavish wig. His script lay on the table next to him. Its cover was now scattered in breadcrumbs, and a wet ring where Rosalyn had laid down her glass of red wine for a moment. 'It is behind me now, *perdu, perdu . . . tout perdu*. And I mourn now. Like the Countess . . . my husband has gone. I played it. I am become it.' Her eyes flickered closed for a moment.

Alistair wondered if she was going to sleep. She remained there, her eyes shut, her head poised delicately, looking as if it was about to fall forward onto her chest. Alistair could see the wrinkles in her face, the sag in her cheeks. She looked even older than she had done the previous day. Maybe he should wake her. He touched her gently. 'Rosalyn.'

Her eyes snapped open and she sat upright. 'Non! No. You must call me Mrs Frieze. Mrs Frieze.' Her eyes closed again.

Alistair looked around the rest of the room. The empty dining places receded into the darkness. Alistair glanced back at the folder. Next to the picture of Rosalyn as the Countess was a newspaper cutting. The front-page banner of the *Montreal Times* had been preserved, neatly cut out and reattached to the text of the story, which must have appeared on the inside pages. The paper looked yellow and brittle, despite being preserved in the transparent plastic of the folder. Alistair tried to read it upside down. He picked out several words:

Leading Canadian stage actress Rosa Baptiste has announced her retirement aged only 44. Miss Baptiste, who won the Toronto Critics' Circle Award twice, has declared

The book of photographs slammed shut. Rosalyn – Mrs Frieze – was awake again. He noticed his heart was beating faster.

'Mrs Frieze. Why did you give up acting?'

She stared at him, her eyes beady and alert now. The stare became a squint. 'My husband gave me this hotel. How kind of him. How *kind*.' She snarled the last word as she repeated it.

'But that wasn't why you gave up acting. Was it?'

She refilled her glass, nearly to the brim, and took several gulps. Then she closed her eyes. They sat together in silence for a time. Alistair thought she must be asleep. Quietly, as silently as he could, he began to rise from the table. Her eyes snapped open.

'A call came for you. Another call.' She was staring straight at him, suddenly alert. He'd spoken to his mother earlier. Surely she hadn't rung again. 'A girl. A young woman,' said Rosalyn, as if answering his thought. 'She wanted to speak to you. He is not here, I said.' Who? Alistair felt a lightness in his chest, a rapid fluttering, a small bird in a cage. '"Give him this message. Tell him I'm sorry about earlier. This morning. My father was ill. But everything is OK now. I will see you tomorrow. Alice." Alice – a nice name. One letter away from Alive.' Abruptly Rosalyn gripped Alistair's hand. 'The work.' He felt his fingers pressed together. 'It was the work.' Her hand clenched around them. '*Le travail. Comprends.* Understand?' Her grip relaxed. 'No more,' she said. 'No more.'

What did it mean that she'd rung him like that? He found it difficult to keep still. He moved around on the bed epileptically, trying to hold an image of her in his mind. The fact of this telephone call seemed to change everything, re-arranging his memory of the last twelve hours. The despair he had felt out with Steve evaporated, turning even his time at the dungeon into an ecstatic reminiscence – a period in which she may have been thinking about him, holding him in her head. He wished he had a photograph of her, something to look at, some image to study and feel within. He turned on his front and reached under the bed. He brought out the sheaf of photocopied papers – the pages of Leila Vinteuil's journal that Alice had given him. He sat upright and spread them on the bed, excited by the connection that they gave him to her.

*Sept. 6th, 1940*
*We came down here today. I know I've never been good at keeping diaries so I'm going to pretend this isn't a diary. It's going to be my place to come, this jotter. I'm not doing it because I have to. I'm doing it because it might do me good.*

*Father wasn't going to bring his violin. He said we all had to be careful that we brought as little as possible, to think about what was essential. I couldn't believe he would leave it. I think he was more*

*worried about making too much noise – that we might be heard by
Stanescu's people. I said it would be awful to be down here without the
chance of music, of his music (I know I pretend I don't like it but I do).
It feels like we're leaving so much behind. I don't want to leave
anything that we might have a chance of keeping.*

*God help us, I think. Be brave, says Father. Mother doesn't say
anything, as always. He grabbed me by my shoulders last night and
said, 'It is an adventure, Leila – life is adventure. People mistake
adventure for play. Adventure is nothing to do with play and
everything to do with releasing expectations. Think of Amundsen.' I just
smiled. He was whispering so as not to wake Marcel. I lay on the bed
staring at the ceiling. I do not want to leave Passedat, certainly not for
the Stanescus' smelly cellar. I fear if we go down those steps I will never
see the garden again, or sit in the bath or hear Father at the piano.*

*Sept. 12th, 1940*
*Father has made bedrooms by hanging towels and sheets from the
ceiling. It was Titu who spotted the possibility: a series of pipes running
the length of the roof, with enough space around them to throw things
over. This means we've all got our own 'rooms'. There are only two
bedsteads, however. Two of us will have to sleep on the floor (Milea has
made 'mattresses' out of old blankets). It was easy to persuade Titu. I
just looked at him when we were discussing it. (Why did Father include
him? He smells of sweat and socks. Imagine him in a month). Marcel
was not going to let me have the bed. He is scared of spiders and did not
want to sleep close to the ground. He started crying. I said it would be
just for a bit and we all could swap over, but since I'd been ill last week
it was only right it should be me. Doctor Kogalmiceanu said I had to be
in the bed. I'm hoping he will forget the arrangement after a few nights
and get used to being on the ground. I am the end furthest away from
Titu. Father was not subtle about insisting on this arrangement. I
couldn't help but smile as I made the bed. The idea!*

*Every day Jews are being thrown out of railway carriages, said
Milea last week. The Government tells the newspapers to tell people not*

189

to molest minorities but it makes no difference. So we stay down here.
Father knows it will pass. He explained how three years ago the
Guardists introduced a law to expel the Jews from the country and
what happened? The lei collapsed because no one could imagine the
economy running without the Jews – the very opposite of what the
stupid Guardists were arguing. And in Bukovina when they forced the
frommers to keep the shops open on Shabbes they only succeeded in
making the Christian shopkeepers angry because up until then they'd
enjoyed competition-free Saturdays.

### Sept. 14th

News from Milea this morning when she brought the bread. King Carol
has fled Romania (I know we are Hungarian now, but Mother refuses
to accept this and insists on 'news from home'). This means the son
takes the throne. He is only three years older than me!

Imagine being a queen. Imagine being warm at night. No one has
said anything but what are we going to do if we are still here in the
winter? Father will not light the stove after 10.30 or when the
restaurant is closed.

### Nov. 11/12th

I'm less sure about exact days when we are midweek. Tuesdays or
Wednesdays anyway. I can feel Fridays and Saturdays, and on
Sundays the restaurant is closed, of course.

Milea brought Father's paper from home yesterday. I couldn't
understand why he wouldn't let us read it. Having watched where he'd
hidden it I sneaked a look before supper. I found the report about the
Legionnaire gangs armed with guns and staves, hunting Jews on the
street. There was a paragraph about some of the bodies of the murdered
being hung on hooks in a slaughterhouse with placards around them
saying 'Kosher Meat'. This was the first time in four months that this
smelly, damp, cold cellar felt like a friend.

I don't really understand this. Why any of it's happening. I mean, I
understand, of course, the events that have brought us here. Why Father

*didn't take us back to Paris. The war in Europe. Herr Hitler's part in it all. But deeper than that. The Jewish thing. I look at Milea every time she comes now to see if I can see a difference. If there is something about the way Milea is put together that means she is free to walk around above ground while we crouch down here. Five fingers on each hand. Arms and legs in the same proportions. Face. Feet. I prayed for an answer to that question. Really. I know I never do anything like that normally but I lay on the bed and squeezed my eyes shut and asked. And I got an answer. It was the strangest thing. In a specific tone of voice, almost cross (although not in a cruel way). 'Of course not.' It was very definite.*

*Feb. 9th, 1941*
*I know I haven't written for a bit but I've been lost in fear. It seems like weeks of it. I wake in the morning (if I've slept at all) and the first thought of the day greets me like a slap. 'They are going to find us today.' It feels like that's the truth as well. Father is always there, brewing tea. Marcel still asleep. Titu doing his stupid carving. No Titu. Sorry. You're not stupid. You're doing it for the same reason I'm writing this. And that's the thing. Nobody says anything about it. Nobody ever mentions the word 'fear', or being frightened, or thinking that today's the day we might be taken. It seems instead that we've hit upon a little routine that we try and repeat day after day. Mother peeling potatoes or carrots meticulously. Marcel cleaning every inch of the cellar floor as if his life depended upon it. (I know! Marcel cleaning.) Father composing in one of the little black books he's ruled with staves, or reading and re-reading the week's paper as it might give him some information he's somehow missed. And we carry on as if all is well and all is fine and it's the most natural thing in the world to be buried down here beneath Stanescu's restaurant, as if we just happened to choose to do this like a strange vacation.*

*Only once was there a time when we all revealed our fear – or it escaped like a rat from a box. There were noises above that woke us in the middle of the night. Loud, like someone breaking into the restaurant,* someone who didn't care if they would be heard or not. Father lit a candle and we huddled together in the middle of the room, all looking at each other, keeping as silent as we could. It felt like an hour or more but judging by the candle it couldn't have been more than ten minutes.

Why can't we own up to it? Would it be so terrible to say, 'I'm frightened'? What else are we supposed to feel? I think maybe it's because it would be like admitting defeat. That something else has won. Or is it just that even admitting to being frightened – never mind feeling the fear itself – feels dangerous?

*April*

I miss the sun. Oh God what I would give to cycle out to Turda. To lie in a meadow. To hear crickets. Is it all still out there? Or has it been rolled up and put away till all this is over – if it will ever be over.

It seems hard to imagine something beautiful existing when I feel like this. I don't mean I am unable to imagine it. I mean, why does it have a right to exist when I feel like I feel?

*June*

Titu has finished his carving. It is a little house. I think it is the most beautiful thing I have ever seen. It is not so because of his craftsmanship, but for the opposite reason. You would not buy it in a shop. Titu cannot carve. He likes to think he is an academic, not an artisan. But Father suggested that he take this up. And he did. And he worked out his own way into the wood. The house has little gables and a front that opens on a kind of hinge. There are windows on all sides. A chimney. A fireplace. I told him how fine I thought it was. He thought at first I was laughing at it. I explained I was in earnest and that he must make more. I've asked Milea to find some good wood. She laughed because wood is so scarce. But I know she will bring some.

*August*

I wondered about all the poems I've been writing and tearing up. I suddenly thought, what if Titu had set fire to his petit chateau (which is

192

what I call it) rather than keeping it on the recess above the basin where it gives us all pleasure each day? So I resolved to put up a poem on the wall near by and let everybody read it. Even if they have wobbly feet they still deserve a chance to try to stand. I can remember the cat one.

Maiorescu. I miss you.
I once spent an entire afternoon
looking at your face, when you slept
so I can bring it to mind with ease.

What is this thing called 'cat'?
I think you may know more about life
than I ever will.

When you mew and tumble over
for a tickle and a stroke
we call it 'loving'.
'Ah, he wants a love.'

But do you love?
Or are you something other?
After all our language is a gas
You do not breathe.

We share the same house, Maiorescu.
We are in the same world.
But if I saw it through your eyes,
for just a second
the difference would destroy me.

I know it's hardly Marina Tsvetaeva. But I'm copying it out anyway and pinning it up.

*November*

*Something wonderful happened tonight. There was a big wedding party at the restaurant. Milea had been going on about it for weeks. You mean they're still having such things, I thought.*

*So there we were listening to this raucous din above getting louder and louder and drunker and drunker. Sitting as quiet as we always do when the restaurant is busy. Suddenly this huge grin breaks out across Father's face. What? I asked. He didn't say anything. He just got up from his crate and began digging under his bed. There was a familiar 'plink' and when he turned round he was holding his violin. 'You can't,' Mother mouthed. 'They're not going to hear,' he said. 'It's OK.' Quietly at first he started playing. Oh, it was wonderful. The most wonderful sound, like light pouring into the room. All our favourites: The Hall of the Mountain King, The Nutcracker, Mozart – all played out on one violin although you'd swear you were hearing a whole string section at times. But best of all was when he played his own Sonata in A Major, which is my favourite (and he knows). No piano of course but still the most glorious melody. The delightful thing was that he played it better than he has ever played it. And I am not exaggerating because of where we are. He really did. I'm glad I was there to hear it.*

# Chapter Twelve

*'Cred că e cineva aicea!'*

Alistair felt his stomach clench. Three men stood in the doorway, jostling each other slightly with the movement of the train. They had positioned themselves eccentrically, heads held close together as if for some non-existent audience. Their close-cropped hair looked at odds with their evening clothes. They looked like a Ska group from 1980, lined up for a photo shoot. Nutty boys.

As suddenly as they had appeared, the faces withdrew. And then the three heads appeared again one by one around the doorway. They looked worse than Alistair had imagined. Streamlined and evil.

One of them, the tallest, oldest-looking, stood upright. He pressed a finger to his lips, shushing the others theatrically. Alistair turned around in his seat and faced towards the dark window, thinking himself out of the carriage. As if by an act of will he could blend into the upholstery. The thing was to imagine having disappeared, to become temporarily absent, to visualize the air around himself as a prophylactic bubble. The thing was to look straight ahead and to breathe calmly, to silently assure the antagonists that you were not going to get in their way in any way whatsoever, to will the transmission of that thought from within you to inside them, without drawing attention to yourself. In fact, the worst thing you could do would be to draw attention to yourself. And so Alistair pressed himself into his seat, kept his hands at his side and focused on the Grey Book in front of him as if he were reading it, though his mind could barely form the letters into words.

He knew what it felt like, this behaviour. He had been struck by the irony before in similar situations. It felt like being a child and being good. Being good in order to avoid a beating from an angry dad. Violence and Dad. He could feel it in his chest, hot and salty like impending tears. I'll be good, just leave me alone. He knew if these lads were to do something to one another that was intended to be funny, he would most probably smile, as if to indicate his willing supplication before them.

They were fully in the carriage now, the three of them, still standing close together as if they were involved in some kind of performance. They had their backs to Alistair – none of them were wearing coats or jackets. Maybe they'd left them with their seats. Maybe they were going to go back there when they'd finished whatever it was they were up to. One of them, the nearest, with the head closest to being clean-shaven, was wearing a shiny satin shirt, only adding to the feeling they had all just walked off a nearby stage, some loutish Romanian boy band. The one at the front raised his fingers to his lips again and they all moved suddenly, like spiders, settling into the group of seats nearest Alistair. So far there was no indication that they'd noticed him in any way. He risked the slightest glance to his left to better determine what they were doing. The tallest one with the blond hair, who looked like a football player, had placed a bottle of spirits on the table. They were whispering to each other.

'*Cred că e cineva aicea!*' Said again in a sing-song hiss.

Alistair's heart was thudding now. He refused to look at them. He would not risk any engagement.

He looked again at the Grey Book. Perhaps the thing was to pretend to be involved in some activity. He reached into the pocket of the computer bag at his feet and pulled out a biro, keeping his movements as minimal as possible. Placing the end of the pen on the page he moved it slowly along, jerking it slowly from one word to the next. He wasn't reading. This was a mere simulation to give the appearance of unconcerned activity. There was a tightness in his head, a hot muddledness that seemed to block his powers of concentration. It felt like a fever.

The girl.

Had they seen her yet?

He strained to see her for himself. Her hand was visible, nails elegantly painted, drumming rhythmically against the side of her seat. She was untroubled, but then her eyes were closed, fingers jiggling to some imaginary beat, unaware of any change in her environment. She had no idea of what was going on.

The lads were whispering to each other. Alistair could hear their mutter without being able to understand what they were saying. He didn't want to look at them. The muttering continued. He would have to look. Slowly he twisted his head to the right. The rest of the glance was completed by eye movement alone. His eyeballs were swivelled so far to the right his sockets ached.

'*Ia uite*,' said the lad in the satin shirt, suddenly and loudly. They were all up on their knees, chins resting on the headrests of the seats in front of them. They were looking at the girl.

Alistair turned his attention back to the Grey Book. He began writing over one of the pasted news reports, writing something, pretending it was a word. It wasn't a word. He was just moving the pen about the paper, making random shapes. He was cold now, rather than hot, the coldness spreading like anaesthetic from his solar plexus into his chest and arms.

'*O cunoaştem?*' The football lad spoke forcefully and loudly now, the pretence of whispering gone. The one next to him, who had yet to say anything, shook his head.

'*E Lilli Gaspar,*' Football-player said. Alistair could detect, even through the veil of an unfamiliar language, a theatricality in the voice, as if a performance was being given for another's benefit.

'*Cred că doarme.*'

'*Nu, se face.*'

'*Las-o-n pace.*'

They sat down again in their seats. Alistair returned his eyes to the scribbled-on page of his book.

'*Hai că nu mă faci să râd. Nu mă faci să râd deloc.*'

'*Hai s-o trezim.*'

The girl's hand was gone altogether from his field of vision. The only evidence of her presence was a bit of bare leg and shoe. Now what were they doing? Satin Shirt had taken a folded newspaper that was stuck between the seats they were kneeling on. He removed the front pages and crushed it up into a ball. He tossed it into the air and headed it with alarming force across the carriage.

Could he get off at the next station? Leave the girl to them. She'd be all right. What could they do to her?

He pushed his face against the glass. It was just black outside. Were they actually moving? He could make out a pole of some kind inching past. There was no sign of any station, or any light. He could gather his things. Go and stand in the space between carriages as if he was readying himself to get off. These were legitimate actions. The relief this possible escape promised was enormous.

'*Scoǎla-te, Lilli. Scoǎla-te, Lilli Gaspar.*' They bawled the words as if at a football match. There was no way she could get away from them. Football-player had got up from his seat, clambered over the other two and was standing in the middle of the aisle. He still had the newspaper in his hands and was making himself another ball. The third one, the squat short one, got up off his knees and stood upright on the seat for a moment before jumping down to join the other in the middle of the aisle. They walked slowly down the carriage, chucking another ball of paper as they went. Satin Shirt followed them, taking a swig from his bottle. They were now no longer parallel with Alistair. In fact, they were much closer to where the girl was sitting than they were to him. Slowly Alistair stood. His limbs felt light and weak, twigs in a gale. He stuffed his useless mobile into his trouser pocket and moved backwards out of the carriage, each second running as a minute. Yet he made it unnoticed through the open door into the dark space beyond.

He'd left his computer. He needed his computer. You can't just get off the train, Alistair, without your computer. The computer cost £800. You cannot just leave an £800 computer behind as if it was a newpaper. His father's voice.

Alistair moved round the little corner where the toilet met the wall. The calamitous noise of the train filled his head, which he was grateful for because he couldn't hear anything else. Was there any way of rationalizing leaving his computer on the train? No. Stop it. Just run in and grab it and then stand here and get off as soon as possible. Shut up.

He moved his head round the corner, looking towards the light, through the open door. They were no longer standing in the aisle. They were in the set of seats directly behind hers, again on their knees, peering over the head-rests, looking right at her. It was OK. They wouldn't see him, and she wouldn't see him. Thank God he'd been sitting in the seat nearest the door. Almost with his eyes closed Alistair leant into the carriage, angling himself towards where he'd been sitting and reached for the folded black plastic case in the luggage rack. Just as quickly he was back out in the dark rocking passage, standing with his things, bunched against the door.

'And this is what you're going to do, Britanic? Get off the train? You don't even know where you are.' Mihail was standing there, staring at Alistair, the blue of his eyes vivid and real. Alistair didn't answer him. He could wait in the station. Get on the next train. Mihail himself had said how frequent they were.

'Alistair Black. Alistair Black!'

'What?' Alistair hadn't wanted to answer him. But Mihail was insistent.

'You cannot do nothing. Doing nothing is not an option for you.' Alistair stood upright, then held his hands out, palms facing the door. He allowed himself to fall against it until his splayed hands hit the glass of the window and he held himself there, staring into the invisible darkness beyond it. And then, with some resolve, he pushed himself back again and turned to his right, and the other carriage, the carriage the men had emerged from. He was aware of Mihail following him, several paces behind.

This carriage was only marginally more populated than his own. A pair of Turkish-looking women, not quite far enough apart in age to be mother and daughter, sat next to each other two seats in. Further back, three or four rows away, was a fat middle-aged man, seemingly sleeping, his chin propped on the heel of his hand, fingers over one eye. Alistair walked to the end, expecting that there might have been some guard's post beyond the carriage. There wasn't anything, just a blank locked door that must have led to the driver. What about knocking on that? He turned round and went back the way he had come until he reached the rattling, clattering space between.

He peered back round the corner into his own carriage. The men were standing with their backs to him. One of them – Football-player – said quite loudly:

'*Fac pariu că n-are chiloţi pe ea.*'

Alistair withdrew.

Mihail stared at him. Then he dropped his head, his eyes.

Maybe the thing to do now was to go back into the other carriage and speak to somebody there and see if they could help. One of them might speak English. Or at least understand it.

The train seemed to be moving with a new fierceness now. Standing in this nameless conjunction of two rocking carriages the noise was so loud and calamitous that the whole thing seemed to be completely out of control.

He went back into the other carriage, the safer carriage, again sensing Mihail's persistent attendance. It wasn't going to be possible. He wasn't going to be able to do anything to stop them. You are useless, Mihail, he thought. You are imagined and thus useless. He sat down in the first seat past the door and then shifted himself next to the window. Suddenly Alistair stood up again. He approached the Turkish women. One of them was in the process of peeling an apple. She used a small pocket knife. The peel hung down in one piece like a ribbon. Would he be able even to speak, to put it into words?

'English . . . *Vorbesk Engleksi.*' The woman nearest him looked up, startled by his presence. She reached for her ticket, maybe thinking Alistair was a guard.

'No. No.' He stood rigid for a moment, unsure how to

proceed. 'There's a girl . . . a girl in the other carriage . . .' He
spoke slowly, gesticulating, hoping somehow through some
process of natural telepathy she might understand him. 'I
think she might be in some kind of trouble.' The women
looked at him blankly. There was a pause. Alistair tried again.

'I don't know if you saw – there was a group of young
men.' He mimed three shapes, taller than himself. 'I think
they're . . . I think they might be harassing this girl and
maybe we should . . .' Alistair felt like a ghost. He knew
very well what was happening in that carriage, thirty metres
away. He did not have the willpower, the energy, the ability
or even the language to express it. The women were still
looking at him. The one further from him said something he
couldn't hear or understand.

Maybe the man would understand.

Alistair left the women and walked, with great expendi-
ture of effort, towards the fat man, who was still sleeping.
He kneeled down next to him. The man had a white
doughy face. His mouth was slightly open and Alistair could
smell alcohol, warm and sweet. He gently reached out and
touched the man on his shoulder, immediately regretting it.
The man jerked, pulling himself upright. He, too, reached
for his ticket. For a moment Alistair wondered if he should
go along with the man's mistake, pretend to have that
authority and demand that the man accompany him into
the other carriage. This wasn't going to happen either. He
spoke quietly.

'*Engleski*. Please. Speak English.' The man looked at him
puzzled, then scratched his head. He looked like Oliver
Hardy. 'Please,' said Alistair. 'The other carriage. A girl.
Trouble.' He waved his arms and grimaced. The man stared
at him, his mouth open, his jaw slack. Alistair attempted to
touch him, to encourage the man to accompany him. The
man jerked his arm away.

'*Lasă-mă-n pace!*' he shouted. '*Lasă-mă-n pace!*' The man sat back with force into his seat. He closed his eyes and splayed his fat fingers across one side of his face.

Now what. What about pulling the communication cord? The communication cord. What did he think this was? A comedy sketch. There was a handle, a rectangular lever with a red sticker that you could pull down in the event of an emergency. Well, what was he doing? It wasn't his emergency. Surely the girl could pull the handle. What if they were sitting on her arms and she couldn't reach. He stood there swaying foolishly in the middle of the aisle. Ahead of him was the door to the driver, sealed and impenetrable. He turned and faced the other way and went back to stand with his things.

As he stood rocking in the darkness, head pressed against the cold glass, hoping the shriek of the train would drown out anything else he might hear, another option presented itself to him.

It was so ludicrous that he almost laughed. But the thought had caught immediately in his mind, like a midge in a cobweb. It was there, unavoidable.

It wasn't possible. It simply wasn't possible.

Nevertheless, the thought remained. It flashed again and again, as hard to ignore as a crackling neon sign.

It would have been easier to open the door he was leaning against and hurl himself out into the night.

Mihail was there, hanging back now, merging with the shadows. Alistair heard what he had to say clearly enough.

'You will have to go in there, Alistair Black. You will have to go in there. You will have to stop them yourself.'

# PART FOUR

History adds that before or after dying Shakespeare found himself in the presence of God and told him: 'I who have been so many men in vain want to be one and myself.' The voice of the Lord answered from a whirl-wind: 'Neither am I anyone; I have dreamt the world as you dreamt your work, my Shakespeare, and among the forms in my dream are you, who like myself are many and no one.'

Jorge Luis Borges, *Labyrinths*

# Chapter Thirteen

'Have you seen the set yet?' said Alice. She was clearly upset.

'What's wrong with it?' said Alistair, putting his bag down in the pile with everyone else's. They were in a cramped coffee bar that clung to the curve of the BBC building. The air was thick with bacon grease and burnt coffee.

'I thought we weren't allowed in,' said Emese.

'We aren't,' said Jack, who was concentrating on the segments of his pipe which lay unscrewed on a paper serviette in front of him. 'They're *lighting*.' He raised his eyebrows and pronounced the last word as if it had great and mysterious significance.

'I just wanted to look at it, so I did,' said Alice. ' And it's ludicrous.' She wasn't quite crying but her voice quavered with emotion.

'Why?' said Alistair.

'Have you read those pages I gave you – Leila's diary?'

In that moment, he was very glad that he had.

'Yes.'

'I won't say any more then. I want you to see for yourself.'

She sat down as Cyril brought a tray of drinks over. He handed them out trying not to spill anything. His exaggerated care seemed to have the opposite effect and each saucer filled with an amount of liquid as they were placed down.

'Can I offer some advice, my dear, which may or may not be of help,' said Jack, clearing the bowl of his pipe with a tissue-covered finger.

Alice looked at him and tried not to glower.

'I have worked on many sets – some marvellous examples of the designer's craft, some woeful atrocities that would shame a fringe production in East Acton, but in all cases if they – I mean the audience – has a chance to notice, then *we*' – he circled his finger around the table – 'I mean the actors, are doing something wrong.'

'That's not the point,' said Alice. She looked like she was going to stamp her feet.

'Well, what is the matter with it?' asked Alistair, interrupting her before she got into an argument with Jack. He was keen to appear as sympathetic as possible, even if no one else was going to.

'It doesn't matter. You'll see.'

'How's your dad? Is he all right?' Since he'd got Alice's message from Rosalyn, Alistair had been concerned – for Alice, but for Mr Zealand too. He had warmed to him very much. Alice's face softened. Her lips regained some of their fullness. Alistair felt something liquefy inside. Just looking at her face. Her face relaxing as it took him in.

'He's fine now. He has these . . . mini-seizures. "Turns" he calls them.' She paused, taking a sip of coffee. 'They're more than that. He had one yesterday morning. If something upsets him, it can bring it on. He's OK.'

Alistair picked up his hot chocolate and held it to his lips, taking a small mouthful. He suddenly became aware of everything in the moment and the fact he was enjoying the unusualness of it – the combination of early morning and hot cardboard and hot chocolate and Alice and being sat at the BBC in London.

'He liked you,' Alice continued after a moment. 'I'm not

208

sure what you said to him.' The way she said this, the soft smile on her face, maintained the glow of hope in his chest.

'Good morning, kiddies.' Steve arrived, dumping his bag down with a confident thump. He sat next to Alistair, shoving him to the side of the plastic chair. 'All set for TV stardom?' he said to Alistair, turning towards him. He smelt strongly of aftershave.

The first thing Alistair was aware of as they moved into the studio was curtains. Big heavy black curtains, like the ones that hung at the back of the school hall. Then he noticed the fat cables that snaked and coiled across the floor in front of them. A man in a blue sweatshirt and jeans who looked like a builder pushed in front of him, grabbing Alistair by the shoulders without looking at him then moving him sharply to one side so he could get past. It was dim and the walls were lined with plugs and more cables. There was an acrid smell in the air like burning dust. Eventually they reached a gap in the heavy drapes and Cyril led them through. Directly in front of them was a huge construction of wooden panels strutted with paler beams. Near the top a hole was cut for a window.

'Declan's in the gallery with Gabrielle. He asked if you'd wait here for him.'

'Why all the big mystery?' asked Emese, who was holding her shoes in her hands.

'Ours is not to reason why,' said Cyril, who seemed uncharacteristically jolly. He wandered off round the corner, leaving them huddled as a group behind the back of the set.

'Look how big it is,' said Alice, gazing up at the top of the wood. Her voice was full of scorn. 'The Stanescus' cellar was no more than ten foot square.'

'It's not a documentary, dear. It's a drama. They're allowed some licence.' Jack smiled at Alice like a primary-school teacher. Alistair thought she was going to hit him.

Steve pulled at the side of Alistair's jumper. 'What's up with the girlfriend?'

Alistair chose not to react to the taunt. 'She sneaked in earlier to look at the set. She thinks they've got it all wrong.'

'Since when has she been the expert?' Mischief flickered across Steve's face. He moved closer to Alice and bent down to her ear. 'Looks good, doesn't it?' he whispered, loud enough for Alistair to hear.

'Got X-ray eyes now,' she said, without turning towards him.

'Sorry?'

'You haven't seen it from the front. Or are you commenting on the quality of the chipboard?' She still avoided looking at him.

'I meant the size of it. Very dramatic.'

Before either of them got any further, Declan and Gabrielle appeared. Declan looked extremely tired, with dark marks round his eyes. Gabrielle's face was fixed into a frown. It seemed clear that they'd been arguing about something. They both started talking almost at the same time. Gabrielle stopped, held up her hands and, her eyes suddenly wide, gestured that Declan should now continue.

'Good morning, cast,' said Declan, turning towards them.

'Good morning, Declan,' everyone said in unison like a group of schoolchildren, then they laughed at their own joke.

'I just wanted to walk you through some aspects of the set before we began rehearsing. We were going to do so in costumes.' He stressed the 'were' a little too heavily. 'However, there's been a slight change in plan. It does mean we won't have costumes until we tape, which means I want to compensate by achieving perfection this morning. OK?'

'Perfection's easy,' said Jack, raising his eyebrows before adding in a theatrical whisper and after a perfectly timed pause, 'comedy is hard.' Declan didn't smile. He gestured that everyone should follow him round the side of the set.

'Now there are a number of camera traps I want you all to be aware of from the start. I don't want shots obscured because someone's forgotten where they are.' They squeezed past a huge television screen in a wooden box – the screen of which displayed an old picture of some roses – coming to rest in front of the set.

'Scooby dooby doo!' said Steve immediately as if it was an involuntary response. Alistair stared up and down then slowly moved his head from side to side, taking in the expanse of the set. Dark wooden beams stood out against the stone of the wall, others hung suspended on cables making a ceiling where there was none. At the back a flight of steps, made from planks and struts canted at odd angles, wound crazily down to the floor. There must have been lights concealed in odd places because the walls were covered with huge distorted shadows. There were tables and chairs fashioned from thick chunks of timber like Geppetto's furniture in *Pinocchio*.

'Some set,' said Emese, leaning towards Jack.

'Where're the pipes with the blankets hanging down?' Alistair asked Alice.

'You did read it.' She sounded surprised. Then she looked genuinely pleased.

'Yes.'

'What did you think of it?'

'I wished there was more of it—'

Before Alistair could continue Declan began to address them. 'The expressionism is intentional. A nightmare brought to life. But remember the work we've done. I want performances to remain on the scale we've rehearsed.' He glanced at Jack. 'I want you to imagine real space around you. Be driven by what's in here.' He tapped his temple. 'At

211

points the cameras are going to be very close to you – closer than you may be accustomed to.' He looked at Alistair, maybe forgetting that Alistair wasn't accustomed to any cameras at all. 'Sometimes at odd angles' – he gestured above him – 'sometimes we're going to be shooting into a mirror. Ignore it all. It's complex but that's not your problem.' Gabrielle looked at Declan. She didn't seem very pleased, thought Alistair. 'And one other thing – we begin on an empty set. You all descend from there.' He pointed to an area at the back of the set. 'The stairs are practical, but tricky. I'd like to begin with your just familiarizing yourselves with the space. Then I want a technical walk through, for lighting and camera. OK?'

Everyone nodded. They were still looking at the set. Alice spoke, 'But it's nothing like it.'

There was no answer at first. Declan had not assumed she was speaking to him. After a short pause he realized she was.

'Hmm?'

'It's nothing like the Stanescus' cellar. That was tiny and poky and stuffy. She says so.'

'Who says, where?'

'In her journal.' Alice stared at Declan, clearly expecting an answer.

Declan was preoccupied, examining something attached to one of the walls. 'Hmm?' Then he turned back round to face her. 'Don't you trust me?'

'You're making it into a Hammer film,' she said, looking more sad than angry now.

Declan smiled. '*You're* playing Leila. It's more in your hands than mine. Don't you think?'

'Good point,' said Steve to Alistair. 'Anyway, I think it looks pretty smart, don't you, chief?'

Alistair didn't know whether he liked it or not. Alice

212

didn't and that was more important. He looked at her face. The voice within was little but persistent. Say something. Ask her. Do it.

They were shown to their dressing rooms so they could leave their bags and coats there. Alistair was sharing with Steve. They had a few minutes before Declan wanted them back on set. Alistair contemplated raising with Steve the subject of asking Alice out. Maybe even asking Steve if he'd do it for him. Certainly Steve would be able to give him good advice. And then there was the pleasure to be had just from talking about it. Steve was lying stretched out on the floor, his hands behind his neck.

'I keep forgetting this is your first time.' He looked up at Alistair, who was sitting on one of the orange plastic chairs.

'What?'

'Your first telly.'

Alistair nodded. 'What are camera traps?'

'What? Oh. Bits in the wall of the set that open up so they can shoot through them.'

Alistair nodded again.

'Nothing to be nervous about, this, you know.' Steve had sat up on his elbows. 'Easier than theatre. Lots of stopping. Paddy Murphy's not going to go straight through without stopping.'

Alistair was reluctant to remind Steve that he'd barely been on stage either. But the truth was he wasn't that concerned about his performance anyway. He had to say something to Alice before he went home. How could he put it to her? He looked at Steve, wondering whether it was safe to take him into his confidence.

'When was the last time you asked a girl out?' he heard himself say. He thought there was something about the question and the way he had put it that made him sound quite unlike himself.

213

'Whoah. That came from nowhere, chief. Why do you ask?'

'I was talking to a friend of mine, Herby, last night – back in Leeds,' said Alistair, making it up as he spoke. 'His sister's best friend – Christine – he doesn't know how to ask her out. And I don't either.'

Steve looked at him sceptically. There was a long moment of silence. Steve held Alistair in his gaze. As it became uncomfortable, Alistair spoke again.

'I said I'd ask you for some tips.'

Steve nodded slowly. He leapt to his feet. 'How old is this mate?' The edges of Steve's mouth tipped upwards into the slightest of smiles.

'Herby – he's nearly sixteen, about four months older than me.' Alistair delivered the line as confidently as he could.

'Has he been out with girls before?'

Alistair quickly worked to make the scenario real in his head by drawing on truth, calling to mind something Herby had once told him.

'He's snogged people at parties – he's never really had a girlfriend.'

'Does this . . . Christine?' Steve tilted his head and waited for confirmation of the name from Alistair.

Alistair nodded.

'Does this Christine fancy him?'

'He's not sure how you tell.'

Steve laughed. The laugh seemed good-natured. 'Don't you know how you tell?'

Alistair widened his eyes. He wanted to communicate how absurd it was to think that he might.

'Number one – does it laugh at his jokes?'

Alistair's mind raced. Had he made any jokes in front of Alice? He couldn't really remember. She'd laughed a lot when he'd been with her though. When he thought of her face it was easy to picture it smiling. Though it was possible she was like that all the time.

Steve continued.

'Number two – does it touch him?'

'Touch him?'

'Casually, when they're talking.'

Alistair thought of Alice taking his hand and leading him up the stairs, thought of her touching his leg on the tube. Each moment of contact was seared into his mind.

'Then number three, most important – are her pupils dilated when they're together?'

'What?' Alistair was incredulous. 'Where does that come from?'

Steve flicked his eyebrows up and down. 'Science, my friend. Simple biology. The eye sees something it *really* likes. The pupil widens to let in more light.'

Alistair absorbed this information. He couldn't remember anything about the state of Alice's pupils.

'Is that true?'

'Gospel. Trust me. Now tell Herby this.' He looked straight at Alistair as he spoke the name. 'It's a law of diminishing returns. If none of these apply – forget it. One of them – it's a gamble. Two of them – a safe bet. All three – an absolute cert. He has to ask himself – what does he really think it is in his case? Really. Honestly.' The trace of a smile had left Steve's face.

'And then what do you do? I mean, how would he ask her out?' Herby, Herby, remember it's Herby.

'Do you want to know a secret?' Steve sat down on the chair next to him and pulled it closer, shuffling it forward with his feet. Alistair's heart began thumping fast. 'It doesn't matter. That's the beautiful thing. If it fancies you, it wants you – like you want it. You can say anything as long as you give it a chance to say yes.'

'What do you mean, anything?'

'Anything. Do you want to see a film? Do you want to go skating? Do you want to go for a pizza? It doesn't matter which. Because if it wants to, it will.'

Alistair imagined forming the words in his head.

'The only thing he has to do is decide what he's going to say and stick to it.' Steve looked at him, beaming. 'Simple. That's gold dust I've given him – and you, chief, don't forget it. Let me know how he gets on.' Steve stood up from the chair then lay back on the floor and closed his eyes, his hands pillowed behind his head. Alistair sat back in the plastic chair. Suddenly, though his eyes remained closed, Steve's face broke out into a grin. He lifted his head slightly, releasing one of his arms, and he reached across and gripped one of Alistair's ankles.

'The only downside is this. He only gets one chance. One chance only. Tell him that. Tell him to make sure he doesn't blow it.'

The knock came from Cyril Davenport a few minutes later. Alistair flicked through the script again and put it under his arm, without taking in any of the words. Steve was pissing loudly into the toilet with the door open. Cyril knocked again and came in.

'Come on . . . about to begin, I mean. Technical run.'

'On our way,' called Steve, who came out of the toilet still holding his cock, pushing it back into his trousers with one hand as he reached for his jacket with the other. If he'd wanted to provoke a reaction from Cyril he didn't succeed.

After the rehearsal the painfully bright studio lights were dimmed. The huge room became marginally cooler. The set stood black and monumental in the flatter light of the fluorescent strips. There were men behind the cameras now – ordinary-looking men in jumpers and brown trousers or

216

jeans. They moved around experimentally, pushing their charges back and forth with smooth, balletic movements. Alistair saw Alice on her own, perched on a high stool near the black cloth at the back. He walked slowly towards her trying to forget everything Steve had just said, or at least trying to keep it from the front of his mind. She was flicking through the pages of the *Sun* that had been left on the stool next to her. She smiled when she saw him approach.

'I'm shutting up now,' she said. 'Declan's right. I hate prima-donnary actresses.' She chewed on her bottom lip, the pink whitening around her teeth. 'It just felt all wrong, that's all.'

Alistair stood next to her, looking at the set. It seemed to have even less connection to the images he had in his head when he was reading Leila's journal. He noticed that the high window, the one Steve and Jack had to cover up at the start of the play, was not a square or rectangle, but had rather been cut into the wood as an eccentric jagged shape with irregular angles.

'Anyway, how are you?' said Alice, who had swivelled round on her chair to face Alistair.

'All right . . .' He frowned and shrugged his shoulders. He looked across at the newspaper. The headline read: 'Horror of the Hell Camps. Thousands of Polish rebels herded into barbed-wire camps.'

'You know you don't have anything to worry about.'

'Hmm?'

They were alone. She was looking at him. He tried glancing at her pupils but at that moment a number of studio lights came on and she blinked in the new brightness, the black circle in the middle of each ocean-blue iris shrinking down to a dot. Alistair felt the intention to speak slipping away from him. It had almost been there.

'I know. Just say the lines.' And then, in a moment of

boldness, 'I must get your address from you, before we finish, I mean. So I can send you that tape.'

'You've got my address,' she said, slipping off her chair.

'What?'

'I mean you've been to my house.'

'I know, I meant your postcode and everything.' But she was walking over to Emese now. Alistair felt sick. Exposed and tiny. He watched Alice at Emese's side. Emese was talking in the speeded-up way she adopted when she was excited. She pulled a script from her shoulder bag and Alice riffled the pages then pointed at something. Emese nodded enthusiastically. After a few moments Alice wandered back.

'Sorry. I just needed to ask Emese something.'

He was confused. If Alice wanted to avoid him, or avoid the moment – why had she come back? But now Cyril Davenport had appeared.

'Make up . . . Costume. Costume first. Need you immediately. Come on.'

Penny the costume lady was as jolly as she had been on Monday. She had an assistant with her this time, an older woman who sat in the corner, sewing. She had pins jutting out of her mouth.

'Are we all set?' said Penny, pulling Alistair's anorak off.

'I think so,' he said, unbuttoning the top of his shirt in case Penny was about to do it for him.

'Put your togs on there.' She indicated one of the chairs at the back of the room.

He took off his trousers and folded them neatly in half. Penny was gathering his costume together from the confusion of clothes on the metal rail in front of her. He sat down on one of the chairs, hugging his knees to his chest. Penny arranged the items of Alistair's wardrobe on a wooden hanger and placed it over a hook on the back of the door. One by one she took the items down and carefully dressed him in them. The rough shirt was itchy but the woollen trousers now fitted him perfectly. She pulled the hat around his ears.

'Over to Grace then,' she said, patting him on the head and gesturing to the older woman. Alistair did as he was told. Grace asked him if he'd kneel down in front of her, which he did. Reaching to the table at her side, she picked up a yellow star from a small pile and moved it round the front of the coat. Settling on a particular position, she fixed it with a pin, then sewed it into place with fast, confident movements.

Next Alistair was told to go to make-up, three doors down. The door was already open. It looked like a make-up room from a film, each mirror framed with glowing light-bulbs. In front of one of the mirrors was an ill-looking woman he didn't recognize. She had her eyes closed and a white towel over her shoulders. Her grey hair was tied back into a bun. Upon hearing Alistair enter she opened her eyes.

'My son,' she said, an anguished expression on her face, her voice thick with accent. 'It's good to see you.' Alistair realized with a shock that he was looking at Emese. Seeing his puzzled expression she grinned broadly and added, in a cod northern accent, 'Eh up, chuck, it's only me.' Alistair smiled back and took the seat next to her. 'I don't want you thinking this is my natural colour,' she said, patting the grey hair.

A make-up lady approached Alistair. She was tall and blonde and extravagantly dressed in a white blouse with a ruffed collar. She leant over him and looked at his reflection in the brightly lit mirror. 'Now then – who are you?' she asked, talking to his face in the mirror.

'Alistair. Alistair Black,' he said. The make-up lady looked down at her call sheet.

'I can't see an Alistair – there's a Titu, and a Marcel—'

'Marcel – that's me. You mean, who I'm playing?' asked Alistair, twisting his head to look over his shoulder at her. The make-up lady turned his head back so it was facing the mirror. She stared at the reflection again.

'So you're what? Thirteen years old? Undernourished, pale from lack of sunlight?' she said, reaching for various pots and brushes.

'And grubby,' said Emese, in her Mrs Vinteuil voice. 'The boy is grubby. He will not wash. He will not bathe.'

'Grubby little thing, are you?' said the make-up lady, dabbing Alistair's face with a small cold sponge which smelled powdery and sweet. He watched as she evened out the colour of his face. Gradually he changed into someone else, layer by layer. His hair was smoothed down with thick white cream and parted in the centre. He had dark rings applied beneath his eyes. His normally red lips were whitened with a crayon of grease-paint.

'Now we belong together,' said Emese, who had stood up from her chair and leaned over Alistair with her chin on his shoulder.

Alistair paced along the curving corridor towards the studio. You couldn't get lost in this building. It was shaped like a ring or a doughnut. If you missed the door you were heading for, you could just keep going and eventually you would pass it again. As he walked, Alistair reached a decision. He was going to ask Alice out that night. He was going to do it now.

It was the most unusual sensation, to walk on the set and see a group of people he just didn't recognize. Presumably that was Jack with his hair pulled back and Brylcreemed down and a small goatee beard. And the girl. Who was the girl? Even though Alistair knew it must be Alice, there was an odd moment where he was looking at a stranger. Her hair was curled into elegant waves, her face looked narrower, her eyes darker. As he neared her he recognized their colour, but her eyebrows had been shaded, which had the effect of altering the shape of her forehead. Only Steve still resembled his natural self. Smiling broadly, he just looked like he was wearing a different set of clothes.

'It's Bugsy Malone,' he said as Alistair approached.

'Oh it's depressing,' said Jack. 'It takes me back to my youth.'

'What was so depressing about your youth?' asked Emese.

'It was so long ago.' Jack pantomimed tears and Emese cooperated by taking his head upon her shoulder.

'You look . . . like Leila,' said Alistair, edging towards Alice.

'Like her, or like you imagine her?' she asked. It was weird to hear Alice's voice coming out of somebody who seemed so alien to her.

'What's the difference?' Alistair said, wondering if she was being funny with him.

'I mean, do I look like the person whose journals you read – or like a photograph you've seen?' He stared at her, trying to marry up her voice with what he saw.

'I've never seen a photograph of her. Have you?'

'I looked. I couldn't find one.'

'You look good,' she said

'I look terrible.'

'That's what I mean.'

There was a short pause. Like a vacuum waiting to be filled. Alice studied Alistair's face. He felt the urge to speak, caught like a bubble in his chest.

'Well, well, well. I'm impressed. You go with the furniture.' It was Declan, who emerged from behind the staircase in the cellar. He gestured towards the set with his big black sketchbook. 'This is the only time you are going to see me this afternoon. Gabrielle has banished me from the studio floor.' He looked at his watch. 'I will bark my instructions to you through Duncan over there.' He pointed to a bald man in a jumper. 'Final checks please,' Declan announced to the side of the room. The make-up ladies emerged from the darkness, followed by Penny. Alistair searched his head for his first line. He felt it slip away from him like a rubber brick in a swimming pool. He began to panic, like he was drowning. All he could do was turn to Alice.

'What's my first line?' he said, trying to speak as quietly as possible. She laughed when she saw the expression on his face.

'"Is that why we had to leave the house so early, Papa?" Relax. You *are* Marcel.' Alistair looked at her quizzically. 'I mean it. I'm Leila Vinteuil and you're my brother.'

She leant across and kissed him on the cheek.

Now.

Do it now.

And as he was about to speak, as he felt the words gathering like a line at the back of his throat, something stopped him. A memory arose, lucid and bleak. Standing in the common room at Chai Summer School, Verity Moss before him, smirking with her friends. The feeling lived in him, malign and bitter, alive again, searing him as mercilessly as it had in its first incarnation.

'OK?'

Alistair nodded. He searched for Alice but now could only see Leila. But she was in there, beneath the sculpted hair and whitened skin. He would try again.

'Righto, chaps! Attention.' Duncan the floor manager had clapped his hands, placing himself in among the cast. 'I'm to take you up now. Orders from on high.' He raised his hands above his head and indicated that they should move after him.

They filed off, leaving the carefully designed madness and crossed over into the unintended chaos at the back of the set. Duncan paused before a temporary staircase fashioned from pine-boards and scaffold pipes.

'Attention please! Not the most stable bit of construction. To be mounted with care.'

'If there's anything dangerous I want my stunt double present,' said Jack. His unease seemed genuine.

'If you could just file up singly and wait at the platform,' said Duncan firmly. Alice was in front of Alistair. Emese was behind, with Steve behind her. Now was the time to speak, as they were climbing. She was just ahead of him, but he could bring himself closer. He only had to say a few words. I was thinking . . . What you doing after . . . ? Tonight, would you like to . . . ? She climbed with careful and deliberate steps just ahead of him. And just as he was about to speak, another idea presented itself to Alistair. A notion that intervened between the thought of what he had to do, and necessity of doing it. What would it be like to take Alice into Travulia? To make an Alice that lived there – alongside Henry Hudson, and Reverend Evans and Mr Drevel and Jacquie Shoulder. An Alice that might flower and bloom with all the beauty and vivacity of the one climbing ahead of him now but with none of the attendant uncertainty and unpredictability. An Alice he could conjure, could know whenever he pleased. He held the idea in his mind, tasting it to see what it might be like. Easier than this. No need to carry the pain of doing. There was a rising sense of relief, of solution, of ease. Alice rose ahead of him, reaching the platform, elegantly pulling herself onto it. The need to speak to her had sunk inside. She vanished above him.

'Come on, get a move on,' said Steve, shouting in mock impatience from below.

The platform was edged with a set of safety railings, fashioned from pieces of scaffolding. Alistair glanced down at the studio floor. They were twenty feet or so off the ground. The fake stone flags of the cellar looked more solid and real from this height. The others peered over the edge as they arrived.

'No room for a camera up here then,' said Jack, gripping the rails tightly.

'The camera's going to be down there, looking up at you as you climb down.' The floor manager pointed with his finger. He strode around the perimeter of the platform, unfazed by its height off the ground. 'That's why we've hung a portion of ceiling around it.'

'Oh look.' Emese was pointing in the other direction. 'You can see into the gallery.' Alistair followed her gaze towards the glass windows that ran along the wall opposite at ceiling level. 'There's Gabrielle, look. Oohhooh!' Emese waved enthusiastically at her. Alistair peered to make out the smudgy figure. It waved back limply then made a big show of looking at its watch and tapping.

'OK,' said Duncan, 'order of descent.' He pointed at them in the desired sequence. Jack now peered over the edge of the platform, gripping Emese as he did so.

'Well, little ones. Over the top we go.' Steve had hooked an arm over both Alice and Alistair's shoulder, drawing them together. His aftershave smelt stronger, as if he'd reapplied it. 'I've been thinking . . .' He lowered his voice. 'Dad's taking my brother away for the weekend. House to myself. I can feel a do coming on.' He looked from Alice to Alistair and back. 'A little goodbye do. What do you say?'

Alice looked at Alistair – or Leila did. He still had to work to find her in the make-up.

'Sounds good to me.' There was a hint of a question in her response, as if waiting to hear what Alistair might have

224

to say. Alistair felt the last shred of the idea of an evening alone with her slip silently away, floating down into the darkness beneath the platform.

'Yeah. Sounds great.' He smiled.

And then Duncan clapped his hands. He pointed at each of them sequentially, indicating that they should approach the edge of the rostrum. Alice made her way to the brink of the steps that led down to the set, followed by Emese. Jack hovered in the middle of the platform. Alistair waited near the other side with Steve. They were the last ones to descend. He gazed up at the mad inverted forest of lights and cables above him. When he looked down again the others had gone. Duncan waved at him with some urgency. He ran carefully across and knelt down on the rough wood and felt for the first step with his right foot. Slowly he began to descend. Somehow, as he left the unfinished chaos of scaffolding and fixtures and cables and wires, and passed into the artificial order of the cellar set, he felt as if he was slipping down into a subterranean world. It was a world that he didn't think of as being his, and yet one that was somehow a part of him – some kind of huge secret companion that hid behind or beneath him every second of the day, whether he was aware of it or not. He thought that this sensation would leave him as he reached the ground but, as his feet made contact with the artificially distressed floor, the feeling became more solid and tangible instead.

Alistair abruptly became aware of Marcel's life within him like a dark fog. With the blinding glare of the lights it was hard to see most of the cameras. He could focus on the details of the set. The space of the Stanescus' cellar was as simple to get to as anywhere in Travulia. What it felt like to be there came just as easily. He began breathing different air. Old and fetid, like the air beneath the restaurant. It filled his lungs. It entered his bloodstream.

As the first scene ended the studio lights dimmed. The others moved around him silently, the only noise coming from their clothes brushing past one another. In the dimness Alistair saw Leila taking her place at the table, setting her diary out in front of her. And he was scared. Then, when he saw the pool of light the candle made as she lit it, it warmed him up, made him think that Leila perhaps knew something he didn't, something that might help him. He walked slowly towards her, not wanting to disturb her. He stood looking over her shoulder, watching her scratch black ink onto the paper. He didn't want to give her a shock.

'What are you doing?' he asked.

She didn't look up immediately but carried on writing, attempting to finish the sentence she was on. 'Just writing.' She made a definite full stop then turned round and smiled.

'Why?' What did she have to write about, he wondered. It wouldn't be a very interesting diary. Got up. Cleaned cellar. Spent day in state of terror at possibility of discovery.

'It's just something I do. You must have seen me do it before.'

If he had, he hadn't really registered it. And he'd certainly never woken in the night to see her doing it. He knelt down at her side. 'I can't sleep.' He wanted to put his head on her knee, but she wasn't really the kind of sister that let you do that. She'd cuddle you when it pleased her but she wasn't affectionate to the extent that you could walk up to her at any time and expect it.

'Neither can I,' she said.

He really wanted to confide in her. Maybe that would help. 'I get frightened,' he said. He felt that he'd owned up to the most shameful thing in the world. She twisted round in her seat and looked him in the eyes. She was smiling. It was a long time since he'd seen her smile, a few days at least.

'Shall I tell you something?' She looked right into his eyes. 'So do I.'

He felt a great relief flood through him. Just to hear someone else admit to it. That it was frightening, being where they were, with the world around them threatening to stamp them out at any minute. Of course it was frightening. What else could it be?

Once she had admitted this to him they played a game, something she had invented where you could fly just by imagining it. You flew wherever you wanted to. What a fantastic thing to be able to do. The fact that it was so easy to imagine made him wonder if it was something you were meant to do, something that nature or God had put in you. He asked Leila if you could play the game to go somewhere you'd never been. Of course, she said, that was the best game of all. If, somehow, everything went right, or people learnt how to live well enough, that was where all the world would get to, being that free.

The days passed quickly. He forgot how long they'd been down there. Sometimes there was a sense of hope, that each day was one closer to getting out; sometimes it was like being in a tunnel that went on and on and refused to end. There were mornings when he awoke and felt overwhelmed by panic, reconnecting abruptly with the truth of where he was, rudely evicted from the freedom of whatever dream he'd been dreaming. But Leila was there. There was always Leila. He would watch her from the other side of the cellar, writing in her exercise book, sewing, playing kalukie with Titu. Somehow she just carried on living, as she would have done if they were back in Passedat, or anywhere.

And then it was the day of his birthday. He knew it was his birthday. It was one of the things he'd tried to hang on to. Birthdays had been special in his life before. A pillowcase full of toys. Singing songs with all the family. He thought they'd forgotten. Nobody had said anything this morning. Here he was playing Old Maid with Titu and Titu wasn't even letting him win.

'You two,' called Mother. 'Finish your game and get ready for dinner.'

'Come on. It's a special night,' said Leila reaching for the candlesticks.

'Because it's Shabbat? It's Shabbat every week,' he said sulkily.

Leila was saying the Shabbat prayer. Mother and Father and Titu had gathered round too. They wished each other good Shabbat.

'No,' continued Leila, 'it's a special day because it's your birthday.'

He beamed at them. 'I thought you'd forgotten,' was all he could say as they handed him small parcels, mostly wrapped in newspaper that Leila and Titu had decorated in black and purple ink.

'No chance of forgetting a date with our walking diary here,' said Mother, touching Leila on the arm. They all hugged him. As he began to tear carefully at the newspaper he turned to look at Leila and said, 'I wanted you to forget. I didn't want it to be my birthday.'

'Why?' She looked hurt.

'Because you said to me it would be over by my birthday.' He looked down at the half-opened gifts. Leila squeezed his shoulder.

'Maybe by my birthday instead,' she said. She looked directly at him. He was aware now in a way he hadn't been when younger of the closeness that they shared. The others in the family didn't know it.

'That's only two months away,' he said.

'I know.' She smiled in her reassuring way.

228

Father approached them, his hands on both their shoulders.

'Come on then. Let's have some music. You haven't forgotten how to sing, have you?' He was unusually cheerful as he dug out his violin. Titu looked surprised.

'I thought you said no music at this hour. That it was too dangerous,' he said.

Father was still grinning. 'There are times when it is appropriate to take risks.' He cradled the violin under his chin. There was a sense of expectancy. It was a long time since any of them had seen him do his. He began to play the first few notes. Marcel felt the inside of his chest warm with joy. It was 'Shalom Aleichem' – his favourite. Father started playing quietly and gradually allowed the music to get louder. His movements became jerkier and more expressive. Everyone began to clap, looking at each other, as if for permission to continue. Soon they had all abandoned themselves to it and were circling round the cellar, linking arms and throwing each other around. Titu began stamping on the floor with his foot in time to the music. Then he began to thump the wall behind him. The thumping and the music got louder and louder, and the dancing more vigorous. There was a point when the thumping became louder than the violin. It seemed to be coming from all around them, certainly from above them. Marcel was sure he heard a voice calling out. There. He definitely had then. It was muffled but still horribly loud. The thumping had lost its rhythm. It came from the ceiling.

'Open up now!' It was a heavy, loud voice – a military voice. The singing and dancing ceased abruptly.

'Listen,' said Leila.

'We will force our way in unless you open up,' the voice yelled.

'Stay where you are. Don't make a sound,' Father whispered to them. But almost before he had got his words out there was a tremendous crash from above. Marcel watched Father's face contort with shock, then looked up himself. Shards of wood fell to the ground. A huge pair of boots appeared at the top of the steps. A uniformed soldier emerged through the ragged remains of the trapdoor. He ran down the steps, followed by two more.

'You are all under arrest!' the first soldier screamed. The other two ran behind them. Alistair felt himself grabbed roughly by the soldiers. This wasn't what they'd rehearsed. This wasn't in the script. Alistair struggled in the man's thick arms, which held him in a firm and horrible grip. He heard Alice screaming behind him. He twisted his head to look and see what was happening. He saw Emese held by another soldier in an olive-green uniform. Alistair was shocked to see her thrown over the soldier's shoulder. One of her shoes came off. The soldier headed towards the stairs. Suddenly he became frightened. He pushed against the grip of the man holding him, only to feel that grip tighten.

'Get off me. Let go,' he shouted. But the man only held him firmer, moving him towards the stairs. Panic rushed up from his stomach like vomit. 'Fuck off. Let go.' Now the man moved him, under his arm, carrying Alistair like a bag. Alistair kicked out, but the man was big, built like a wrestler, and he was able to reach out with one hand and restrain Alistair's feet. They were at the stairs now. Emese was ahead of him, screaming now.

'How dare you,' she was crying. 'How dare you.' The worst thing was that Alistair was crying. He found he was crying with great wracking sobs. Crying like a child. Crying like a baby. Crying in rage and fear and impotence. And much as he didn't want it recorded on camera and broadcast

230

to the nation, and even more didn't want Alice to see him reduced to such a level, he was unable to make himself cease. But then something worse. Alice struggling. Alice struggling to free herself from the thick hands that gripped her. And him held tight, unable to stop it.

# Chapter Fourteen

Alice was beginning to panic. It was pouring with rain, she had almost reached the end of Roman Road and she hadn't found the door. She wished now that she could phone Ben. But she didn't have a mobile. She was the only person of her age she knew of who didn't possess a mobile phone.

The rain had stopped now. She pulled the hood of her anorak down and rested for a moment. There was a café open on the other side of the road. It sold fried chicken. Two men stood close to one another in the doorway. They each held a bag of chips. She didn't recognize the place but it could have opened since she'd been away. Was it possible that Ben had moved? Yes, it was possible. She was just assuming that because he had bought this place after falling in love with it, it was unlikely that he would have abandoned it already. It was a maisonette, above a hardware store – its window full of handpainted special-offer signs. Ben had the top three floors. The place had been a sweat shop, probably, since it was built in the mid-1800s. When Ben found it the rooms had been gutted. There was nothing but brickwork and timber. There were great gashes in the structure revealing pipes and ancient wiring.

The first thing he did was to knock out two more holes to make way for extra windows. He loved the atmosphere –

the sense of all the work that had been done there. The decades of stitching and cutting and making. She understood what he meant.

Last time she'd been here the front door had been red. Ben's door was white now. But there was no relief on finding it. Because she had to face him again, risk incurring whatever she was going to incur. Alice found it unbearable that she was going to be causing yet more pain. But maybe this would release him. Grateful pain. Finally set him free, clearly, unambiguously free. Let him find someone who deserved him. His kindness, his warmth, his wit, his love.

The buzzer with the lopsided sticker confirmed this was the right place. MacCawber. She always thought of a brightly coloured bird. Plumes of beautiful feathers. She didn't want to look at her watch. Mad Alice living by her own rules, ringing doorbells uninvited at midnight.

She could turn round and run now, back to the minicab office, back to Exmouth Market in an old Datsun, safe in the back, all this nonsense done with. She rang the buzzer again and held the discomfort inside her, tolerating it in this moment alone, sensing this was all she had to do.

A crackle.

'Yes?' Tiredness in the voice. But music audible in the background behind it.

'Ben.'

'Yes?'

She paused. 'Ben. It's Alice. I'm sorry.'

'Alice? Is that you?'

'Can I come in?' Another moment, in which she heard a can blowing along the street a thousand miles away. The buzzer went. She pushed the door and it gave.

He was bare-chested above blue tracksuit bottoms. There was a daub of red paint on his stomach.

'I'm sorry.' It was all she could think of to say. He looked

233

at her. He wasn't smiling. Often his face would take on this aspect. Not a frown – more of a neutral space in between the expression of an emotion, a space in which he was working things out.

'Come upstairs.' He turned and she followed him.

Everything was as bare as when she had last seen it. There were more bricks missing, exposing copper pipes and older, darker parts of the structure. In the centre of the room were four uneven piles of books, all leaning against themselves in a self-supporting arrangement.

'Your legs are all wet.' He was over by the kettle, filling it from a tap that jutted out from between two pieces of timber. 'Your trousers are soaking.' He pointed with the spout of the kettle. She looked down at them.

'It's all right.'

'Take them off. Come on.' He had put the kettle down and moved towards her.

'I'll roll them up.'

'Alice. For God's sake.' She stepped backwards and fell onto the couch. 'Come on.' He disappeared into the bathroom and came out holding a big towelling dressing gown. He stood aside, held the door open and gestured that she enter. 'I'll put them in the drier. Go on.'

She sat on the couch, holding a mug of Earl Grey tea, her legs curled under her. He sat opposite on a wooden stool. He had put a white T-shirt on and sipped at his own mug, looking at her over the steam.

'So? What's . . . going on?'

She winced at the weariness in the question. 'I'm sorry about . . . I wanted to speak to you. After you left. I didn't want you to go like that.'

'Alice, it's quarter past twelve. A phone call would have sufficed.'

'No.' She almost shouted it. 'No, it wouldn't.'

234

'Yes it would, Alice, because there's nothing more to say. Is there?' He got up from his stool and began walking around the room, circling it still nursing his mug of tea.

'You're still angry.'

'I'm as happy as a fucking sandboy.' He found another chair, in the far corner by the door.

'I needed to see you once more. To try . . . to say what I tried to say on Monday. I'm going to go away again. I wanted to say it before I went.'

'You see, once more this is all about you, isn't it? What you want to do.'

Was he right? Was she thinking about herself only? Was that all this was? 'I want both of us to feel better.' She risked a look up at him. He was rocking back and forth in his chair.

'The thing about you, Alice, is . . . my perception of you . . . at your heart is this shining diamond . . . this . . . this sun . . . that warmed me up, like nothing has ever warmed me . . .'

She didn't want to cry. Not yet. It would be useless.

He stopped rocking. He was staring straight at her. 'But it's buried, under sixteen hundred layers of shit.' He took a gulp of tea. 'I used to think it was worth digging through the shit to get to the diamond. But I've realized now . . . better to let it go. I might find something somewhere else, without having to wade through all that shit.'

And now she felt as if she was falling, dropping down some great hole she'd been teetering on the edge of for days. He was staring at her coldly. She knew something had passed. She knew something had finished. This was why she had to come. These were the very feelings she had been avoiding. She imagined a future alone. An elderly woman dying alone. Lots of booze. She could do with a drink now.

'Where are you going again?' His question pulled her back.

235

'To a Jesuit monastery. In Spain. To take training for spiritual direction.'

He looked sad now. The coldness gone. She expected sarcasm but he said nothing. Silence settled and then unexpectedly he said, 'I made you a present. Not recently. Ages ago. Months ago. Just after you went.'

She wondered what he meant.

'I started it as a joke. Then I decided I liked it.'

'A painting?'

He stood up and beckoned to her.

They went upstairs to his studio. He reached down to a plug on the floor and clicked it into a wall-socket. An old theatre light came on with an electrical crack. Ben and Alice's silhouettes were thrown against the far wall. He walked over to the stack of canvases that filled one of the shadow-covered corners of the room. He pulled through them, flicking each in turn into his waiting hand. Eventually he found what he was searching for near the back. With one athletic movement he hauled it over his head and placed it onto an empty easel. The back of the canvas faced her. Painted on it in large, neat red letters was the title. 'Genesis 32:25 for Alice Zealand.' Seeing that she had registered this text, Ben picked the canvas up again and swooped it round so it was displayed correctly.

The painting was divided into equal quarters. It reminded Alice of one she'd done herself when she was a girl – a version of the Joy Division album cover repeated four times like a Warhol print. Ben's subject was figurative – two men wrestling on rocky ground. The men were chunky and rounded – not quite cartoons, but equally not as naturalistic as his more usual work. These were more like Chagall figures, but they were shaded and solid in a background that had been rendered with correct perspective. Unlike a Warhol sequence, the images were not simply repeated. Each one differed from the last like consecutive frames in a comic book. Sometimes one of the men was on top, sometimes the other. The background went from day to night and back to day again – the sun setting in the first frame and rising in the last.

'Jacob and the Angel,' said Alice. She had stepped closer to the easel and was examining Ben's work in all its beautiful detail. She heard a rustling from behind. She turned to see Ben searching among a pile of papers on the dresser at the far end of the room. He found what he was looking for and moved into the brighter part of the room in front of the lamp. He held the paper closer to his face and started reading aloud.

'Jacob was left alone. And an angel wrestled with him until the break of dawn. When he saw that he had not prevailed against him, he wrenched Jacob's hip at its socket, so that the socket of the hip was strained as he wrestled with him.' Alice turned back to face the canvas, searching for the story in the image. Ben continued: 'Then he said, "Let me go, for dawn is breaking." But Jacob answered, "I will not let you go, unless you bless me." And the angel did so, saying, "You are blessed because you have struggled with beings divine and human and you have prevailed."' He put the paper down, folding it unconsciously into quarters, like the painting.

'Why did you choose that passage? Why did you paint it?'

'It was supposed to be a joke. Halfway through I realized it was serious.'

They both stared at it for a moment.

'The angel looks like a man,' said Alice, bending closer to the image in order to try to see its face.

'I don't believe in angels. There are only men.'

Alice reached out and touched the canvas. The paint had been applied thickly in places, more like clay.

237

'It's yours if you want it,' he said sullenly.

'Of course I want it.' She stood upright and looked at him.

'Then I'd better sign it for you.' He walked over to his paints and found a brush. Wiping the turps off it with a piece of rag, he put it behind his ear while he searched for some paint. Finding a tube he squeezed some onto the wood at the bottom of the easel. Carefully, delicately, he added his signature to the canvas, speaking it aloud as he did so. 'Ben MacCawber, 16.6.01.' He looked at his watch. 'It's gone midnight,' he said, and then carefully changed the date from '16' to '17'. Alice pulled the dressing gown round herself and looked for somewhere to sit. There was a bench at the side of the room, in front of one of the windows that Ben had put in.

'It's a beautiful painting. I don't deserve it.'

'Correct,' said Ben. He screwed the cap back on the tube of paint and returned it to the workbench. The brush went back in the jar of turps. He went over to the hi-fi and ejected whatever he'd been listening to before she arrived. Then he began searching through a pile of CDs. He turned back to face her. 'It's too late for music now,' he said simply and sat on the wooden unit, beneath one of the speakers. 'You know I was remembering various things, various times.' He fiddled with a dial on the front of the hi-fi, spinning it all the way to its end point and then spinning back again. 'Remember the day we went to Brighton? Freezing cold. Daring you to go in the sea and you did. I thought – she's really brave – how can she do that?'

She felt the need to dismiss this quickly. 'I'm good with discomfort. That's all. It's not bravery if it comes easy.'

'Or the day you told me you loved me.' He was still looking at the dial, twisting it back and forth in smaller, staccato movements.

'What about the days I didn't love you?'

'Why did you come here? Why the fuck did you come here? In my life. Out of my life. Like the fucking hokey cokey.' Staring at her, his eyes wide and livid. 'If you're going to go away . . . just do it . . . don't keep coming back to . . . to reprise it . . . again and again and again.'

'Can I have my trousers, please.' She was on her feet.

'Why *did* you come here?'

'I don't know. Can I get my trousers, please?'

'You must know.'

Now she was in that dark, cold sea. She could feel the pull of a current – fierce and pitiless. It was drawing her towards a black, breathless place. 'I'm going.'

'You must have come here for something.'

She was trembling, feverish, clammy with sweat. 'When I was sixteen . . .' The words were a shock in her mouth. Her instinct was to try and stop them because it made her feel wrong, suddenly inverted – inside out – liver, guts, heart everything exposed to the air. 'No . . .' she said. Could she start somewhere else?

'When you were sixteen? What? What when you were sixteen?'

'My relationships . . . have always . . . been catastrophes.' Surely this bald statement of fact would be enough. She sat down again. Something was stuck in her throat. She wanted a glass of water.

'We know that much, Alice. When you were sixteen . . . what?'

'I made a vow . . . when I was sixteen.' She was shocked again. She saw an image of herself as a cartoon, wide-eyed, with her hand clamped over her mouth.

'What vow . . . why?'

There was concern in his eyes. She was suspicious. Sometimes she saw nothing but a devil in him. Even in

239

him. In dear sweet loving Ben MacCawber. Sometimes she hated him.

'That I would never get married.' The vow spoken aloud? This had never been done.

'Why? What happened to you, Alice? Why?'

She could see his concern, suddenly there, a change in the weather. She knew he could feel what was in the room. The dark currents swirling around.

'I would not . . . could not marry . . . I would not have a . . . I would not have another child. Never.' She felt breathless as if the water had pulled her under for a moment and threatened not to release her.

'Another child? You had a child?'

'No.' It was as if her blood was burning, super-heated like lava in her veins. A searing ancient magma. 'I was going to have a child. I . . . terminated it. I had it terminated.'

'Whose child? When?'

So mundane the memory of it. But it was there every day. Literally, every single day. 'I was raped.' More mundanity. More melodrama. But the words were just labels applied to experiences. For her the word didn't describe the experience. Didn't account for it. It was a shorthand for something else.

'Who by?'

'I was raped. OK. I was raped.'

He looked at her differently now, as though she was suddenly something different, something that he was fearful of breaking.

'What happened?'

'I'm not telling you what happened. You don't need to know what happened.'

'Did they catch him? Was he imprisoned?'

'No one knew.'

'No one knew whether they caught him?'

'No one knew I was raped.'

240

A pause while he took this in. 'I'm not the first person to hear this?' He looked appalled.

'No. Later. Years later. I had counselling. At the time . . . I never told anyone.'

'Alice, I—'

'My father was ill. I thought I could deal with it myself. I didn't call it rape. It was kids messing about.' She found she had sat down, back on the bench by the window. She could tell Ben wanted to speak, to ask question after question as they were piling into his mind. She could see him working to resist the urge. 'But I was pregnant. So I went to Marie Stopes. I was sixteen. I was a good actress . . .' Her voice trailed off. 'The vow was . . . a price.'

'Why did you have to pay a price?'

'Because it was a baby.' She shouted this, heard it reverberate around the beams. 'It would have been a baby.'

'Alice . . .' He got up. Came across the room towards her. His arms went round her. She remained limp. Her arms hanging down at her sides, receiving his hug without response. He was kneeling on the floor, holding her.

'I can't be with you, Ben.' She knew that converted into mere words it must have all sounded so small. She knew also the difference in scale of the things the words expressed.

'Alice, you can get help. Not . . . not to be with me. But anyway.'

'Been there, done that.' She thought she might try and smile. She felt the corners of her mouth curl.

'I . . . I don't know what . . . I'm sorry.' Ben's voice trailed off. She nodded her head. He carried on holding her. He didn't say anything else for a while.

Later he led her downstairs. He pulled her jeans from the drier and laid them over the back of a chair. Then he disappeared into his bedroom and returned with blankets and sheets in his arms.

241

'What are you doing?'

'Making you a bed . . . on the sofa.'

'I don't need to stay.'

'I won't let you go home tonight.'

'Ben. I'm not—'

'Alice, you're staying here . . . on this sofa tonight. I'm not going to argue about it.' He had already begun tucking the sheets in. She sat, perched on the end of one of the arms, looking around the room at all the paintings. Many of them, most of them, were Ben's own fictitious portraits.

'Where do they come from?'

'What?'

'All those faces you paint. Where do they come from?'

He glanced up from his bed-making at her and then at the paintings. 'I once had this thought,' he said, pushing at the edge of the sheet so it went beneath the sofa cushions. 'There are no "yous" in the world. Only "I". In our heads we populate the world with "yous" and "hes" and "theys". But these concepts only exist in our heads. They're something we layer over reality.' He paused in his bed arranging and looked up at her. 'If you were to sit quietly and sense yourself, that thing you feel, that buzz of consciousness, that's the thing you call "I". Well, that's all there really is in the world. Six billion "I" buzzes.'

'Ehyer Asher Ehyer,' said Alice.

'What?'

'Ehyer Asher Ehyer. Exodus 3:14. When Moses asks God his name, God says "Ehyer Asher Ehyer. I am that I am."'

'The paintings are all "yous",' said Ben, clearly not wanting religion brought into it. The bed was finished. He folded back the blanket.

'Do you understand, Ben? Why I can't marry you? Because of what happened. Why I have to go away? You do understand.'

He looked at her, his face suddenly sad again. 'I understand, Alice.'

After she had brushed her teeth – there was an old toothbrush of hers in the bathroom cabinet – she got under the blankets. Ben came down the stairs again from his bedroom to use the bathroom. On his way back up, without saying anything, he turned off the light.

# Chapter Fifteen

There was much indignation in the green room afterwards.

'It was nothing more than a cunt's trick, excuse me, ladies,' said Jack, who was unable to sit down, moving with quick nervous paces from one side of the floor to the other. 'I'm an actor,' he continued, ' I do not need to be tricked into giving a performance.' When Declan finally appeared, Jack repeated this statement several times, adding, 'If you'd wanted me to scream, then you could have just asked and I would have screamed. Or do you not think that I have acquired that ability in thirty-five years of professional engagements?'

Declan remained calm. He held up his hands in a gesture of reasonableness.

'I know it felt unforgiveable – and I'm sorry. But I think you'll agree it was worth it.' He was looking very pleased.

Emese obviously disagreed. 'For heaven's sake.' Her words were mild but there was a greater anger burning underneath. 'What were you thinking of? What were you thinking of?' she said again.

Jack had stood up again, having only just sat down. 'And the boy . . .' he hissed, pointing at Alistair. 'He's only a child. For God's sake.'

'But it packs a punch.' Declan was grinning now. 'It packs a real punch.' He walked into the middle of the room. 'What an energy. Wait till you see it.'

'I don't want to see it,' said Alice. 'You fucking idiot.'
She pushed past him and left the room. Declan looked as if
he was going to say something. He changed his mind, raised
both his hands again, and then, shaking his head, reached
into his pockets and produced his cigarettes.

Alistair sat in the far corner of the room. It seemed
nobody had seen him crying in all the fuss and clamour.
His tears had dried sufficiently for him to conceal his upset.
Alice had been too busy screaming at Declan to notice herself. Surprisingly it was only Steve who seemed to have
registered Alistair's genuine distress. While the others were
still gathered around Declan, he came and sat next to
Alistair.

'Are you all right, chief?' he asked. 'Bit of shock – being
dragged around like that?' Alistair nodded. Steve ruffled
his hair. Alistair was warmed by the motion. 'Don't you
worry. We'll have a laugh tonight. That'll make up for it.
And the girlfriend's coming.'

'She's not my girlfriend.'

'She likes you.'

'That doesn't make her my girlfriend.'

'But you like her, don't you?'

'I like her as a friend.'

'But wouldn't you like it if she was your girlfriend?'

'Steve!' said Alistair, protesting. He didn't know how to
respond to this interrogation. Part of him wanted to give
into the vanity of thinking that that is what Alice would
be – and another part didn't want Steve to know the turbu-
lence he now experienced inside simply when he heard her
name. And then there was the part that wanted to please
Steve, that wanted Steve to like him and accept him and
approve of him. And then there was the part of him that was
still in the cellar, still with the heavy-set, unknown man's
arm around him, hauling him up the stairs to an undefined

fate. For a moment he hadn't known where he was, powerless and lost, gripped tight by the huge stranger.

'The stupid idiotic pathetic lunatic. Thoughtless and stupid and awful.' Alice had come over to join them, saving Alistair from having to continue his fruitless conversation with Steve. She put her arm around him. He felt her warmth. She seemed fragile after the big man in the Nazi costume. There was no sign of any of the Nazis in the green room. He couldn't enjoy her closeness with Steve standing there grinning like an old man. 'Are you all right?' she asked, squeezing him against her. He was even more conscious of her frailty.

'Yes.' There was a moment's uncomfortable pause. 'I don't really understand. Why they did it that way.'

'For dramatic effect,' said Alice, with contempt.

'Are you up for it? Party, party,' said Steve as if he hadn't been listening.

'What?' She looked like he'd spoken to her in a foreign language.

'Still on for my house?'

'Oh, I don't know. I feel sick now.'

'You're still coming, aren't you, sport?' he said turning to Alistair. Steve nodded slightly, covertly gesturing back to Alice with his eyes. 'It won't be the same if it's not the three of us.'

Alistair wished it was just him and Alice – going to the pictures. He didn't know if he had the energy to spend a whole evening with Steve. And now Alice seemed like she didn't want to come at all. 'Aren't you going? It won't be much fun if it's just me.'

'Oh cheers,' said Steve pretending to be offended.

'I'll come. As long as he lets me sort out the music,' said Alice.

'You can be Annie Nightingale all night if it makes you

246

happy.' Steve put his arm round both of them. 'I'll expect you at eight.'

And so, four hours later, having packed his suitcase and avoided Rosalyn Frieze who was weeping because he was leaving her the next day, Alistair found himself standing in Steve's front porch. He'd rung the doorbell twice. The chime was very elaborate. He pressed his nose against the ridged glass that stretched the length of the front door, turning the hallway beyond into luminous abstract lines. One of the lines darkened, lengthening vertically. Then it became two lines. Then four. Alistair pulled his head back then the door opened. Steve was wearing a blue blazer with the sleeves rolled up and new-looking jeans. They made his legs look thick and heavy, like a grown man's.

'All right, chief. Still getting ready.' His shirt was half unbuttoned, revealing a chest covered in light blond hair. 'Follow me.'

'Am I early?' Alistair felt uncomfortable, as if he'd made a mistake. Loud music filled a room upstairs. 'Roxanne' by The Police. He thought of Steve's deaf brother.

'Uh uh. I said eight. I told your missus to come later.' He was heading back towards the stairs. Alistair followed. 'Thought we could have a laugh first.' The upstairs was huge. There was a kind of gallery that stretched around the hall with a rail made of black wrought iron. Steve turned left, slapping the wooden banister that topped it as he went. Alistair chased him, struggling to keep up.

'Do you want the tour?'

'Sorry?'

But as he turned the corner Steve was already opening doors. 'Her dressing room.' He exaggerated the enunciation, his voice full of disdain. The room smelt dusty and little used. Steve flicked on the light. There were white wardrobes with gold edges round the mirrors. 'Hey – do

247

you want a drink?' He opened one of the wardrobes. Alistair was surprised to see it was full of drink bottles. A light came on like a fridge. Steve reached for a new bottle of Jameson's whiskey.

'It's OK.' But Steve had already pulled open a can of Coke from a pack at the back of the cupboard. He emptied some away in a nearby sink and poured a measure of the whiskey in, then swirling the liquid he handed it to Alistair. Brown fizz swelled through the triangular hole.

'I only put a bit in. You'll like it.' Steve turned the light off before Alistair was out of the door. They'd passed into a narrower hallway with doors on both sides. One of them had a joke sign on with a cartoon of a shark. It said: 'Trespassers will be Eaten.' 'This is Gonzo's stink palace,' said Steve as he put his hand on the handle. Alistair hesitated.

'Won't he mind? Your brother, I mean.'

'Ain't here. Not that it matters. Dad and Eleanor have taken him to Paris. Christmas shopping.'

The first thing to hit Alistair was the smell. Time fled backwards and he was seven years old, lying in a bed he had wet in the night. Actually this smell was stronger. It was so strong it made him want to retch. Steve looked at him, grinning.

'Told you it stinks.'

It was strange. Alistair thought Steve almost seemed proud. He looked round the room. It seemed ordinary enough. A poster of *Diamonds are Forever*. A TCR racing set, the track disconnected, spread out across the floor. An aquarium surrounded by a mess of books and battered-looking board games. It was illuminated but there didn't seem to be any fish in it. The stench of old piss was violent and overpowering. Sometimes such a smell was tolerable – say in a phone box or in the toilets at school. But this. This was just wrong. You wouldn't expect to smell a smell like this inside a house. Sometimes, passing a doorway in town, or on the steps of Schofields car park, Alistair had been assailed by a urine smell so strong it caught in his throat. This was worse than that. It smelt damp and rotten and filthy – a bright, livid decay that was sharp and bitter and filled his nose and his gullet. Alistair couldn't imagine being able to bear staying in the room for more than a few minutes. Steve was laughing. He was standing in a corner next to a small wooden bookshelf. He beckoned with his head that Alistair should join him. His hand pointed to a green-tinged patch in the beige carpet that bled from the skirting board towards the centre of the room.

'The dirty cunt. He pisses there. In the night when he needs the bog. He just pisses there.' Grinning, Steve reached for Alistair's can. 'He's been doing it for years.'

'Why doesn't—'

Steve didn't let Alistair complete the question. 'Oh they tried. They tried everything. But then Dad decided one day, fine, let him. Let him live in his own stink. When he gets sick of it he'll stop.' Steve was laughing hard now. Alistair felt that he should be laughing too but he couldn't see anything funny in the awful smell or the dreadful, crawling stain. 'But he hasn't stopped. He just keeps pissing and pissing and pissing.' Steve handed the can back, still giggling. Alistair forced himself to smile. He took a swig of the whiskeyed Coke – just to take the taste of the room out of his throat.

They left the piss room and headed back the way they'd come towards Steve's bedroom.

'Is he all right – your brother?' Steve didn't answer him and Alistair wondered if he'd said something wrong. He changed the question hoping that might help. 'Has he always been deaf or—'

249

'He's not mental, if that's what you mean.' Steve cut him off. 'Though I think he'd like it if he was.'

Alistair didn't quite understand what Steve meant. He didn't want to ask for any qualification. The music had stopped now, but the click of the needle filled the hallway.

Steve's room was as untidy and plain as it had been when Alistair was last there. Steve was over at the music centre putting on the B-side of the single. There was an open bottle of whiskey on the nearby bookcase. Steve took a swig directly from the bottle. He began self-consciously dancing around the room, like he had done the other day, except now he was singing along.

'"Don't want to hear about the drugs you're taking, don't want to hear about the love you're making—" Hey, that reminds me.'

'What?' Alistair wondered if Alice was still coming.

'Do you want a laugh?'

Alistair shrugged his shoulders. He felt very cold and shivery, as if he was coming down with a bug. Steve had buttoned up his shirt and was spraying aftershave on the side of his neck.

'Come on.'

Steve left the room at speed. His body moved like his mind, suddenly darting off in an unanticipated direction. Once again, Alistair followed. Steve had opened another door and stood in the dark frame waiting for Alistair.

'Wait here,' he said with exaggerated secrecy. He disappeared into the room and turned on the light. There was a large bed reflected in a wall of mirrors beyond. Alistair could see Steve bending down on the floor with his bottom in the air, reaching for something under the bed. He pulled it out. It was a big grey machine about the size of a grocery box. Steve moved it to one side and returned to his original position. After a moment he withdrew, and turned towards

Alistair still on his knees. He was holding some black wires in his left hand and in his right some small rectangular boxes. They were video cassettes. He stood up, disappearing around the side of the door frame then the light was flicked off again. Steve emerged from the black room, clearly struggling with the weight of the machine.

'Dad's Betamax. Claimed he got rid of it. I found it under the bed. After I found the tapes hidden under her shoeboxes. Come on.'

'What tapes?' But Alistair had already guessed what tapes. And he was excited. It was a dangerous, unfamiliar, new kind of excitement, fuelled by the fact that there was nobody around to stop them.

'You'll see. Grab the lead, would you.' The plug had got away from him and was trailing through his legs like a shiny tail.

They managed to get to the Den without Steve tripping and falling.

'I make sure everything goes back exactly where it came from. I make a little map in my head.' Alistair was surprised at Steve's caution. It sounded like something he himself would do. Steve fiddled behind the back of the giant TV, pulling out leads from the smaller video player that sat at one side on a smoked glass coffee table. He pushed it out of the way and lifted the older recorder next to it. 'Here we go . . .'

'Alice will be here in a minute,' said Alistair. He couldn't imagine what she would make of a dirty film. Well, that wasn't true. He knew enough to realize that she wouldn't like it.

'So.' Steve clearly wasn't bothered.

'We can't have it on when she's here.'

'Why not?'

'She'd hate it, wouldn't she?'

'Some of them love it.' An image had come on the screen. The picture looked washed out and flickery. The colours were muted like an American programme, *Soap* or *Sesame Street*. A woman was on all fours, her tits hanging down like bags. They swung back and forth as the man did it to her from behind. Alistair stared at it transfixed. He was aware he was getting an erection. He felt uncomfortable being aroused with Steve in the room. He started the conversation again in order to try and distract Steve from the fact.

'What do you mean, some of them love it.'

'Some women like dirty stuff. There was this girl I went out with. She made me buy her a Knave. And Eleanor. She loves it. Obviously.'

'Your dad's girlfriend? How do you know she knows about it? Your dad might just hide the stuff in her cupboards.' Steve let out an exaggerated laugh.

'Well – he might.' Steve pressed the stop button on the machine. The rectangle in the centre sprang up with a clunk and he pulled out the tape. He looked at the small pile behind him and found another, inserting it into the open video player and pushing it down with pointed force. 'But that hardly explains this.' He pressed the play button and a different kind of image came on the screen. The picture was brighter and clearer than the one before. There was a woman with her back to the camera. She was sitting on something and moving up and down. The image flickered. The camera hadn't moved but the woman had jumped round like a cheap special effect and was now facing the camera. There was a man behind her. He was thrusting backwards and forwards with great energy. Alistair was shocked at the force. It looked like violence. He'd seen the man before. For a moment he'd thought it was Steve, until he registered the greying hair. It was Steve's dad. The woman looked up into the camera and smiled. Her eyes stared emptily ahead and then closed. 'Go on, Dad,' shouted Steve, baring his teeth. 'You fuck her. You fuck the arse off her.' The elaborate doorbell rang.

'That'll be Alice,' said Alistair. 'You've got to turn it off.' He was aware of the pleading tone in his voice. Steve had jumped to his feet.

'She won't mind. It'll put her in the mood.' He grinned his broad grin and ran his fingers through his hair, then turned and bounded out of the room. Alistair crawled over to the machine. The woman was crying out now. It seemed terribly loud. He searched desperately for the stop button. The symbols were the same as on his tape recorder at home. There was a fast forward and a rewind. The red round one must be 'record'. There, next to it, was a black square. He pressed down with two fingers and there was a clunk from the machine. The screen went black just as he heard Alice's voice.

'I brought some wine. I sneaked it out of the kitchen inside my coat.' Alistair was still kneeling on the floor when she came in. 'Hello there.' He scrambled to his feet.

'We've just been watching video tapes,' said Steve, taking the wine off Alice. 'Alistair had asked if he could have a look at some.'

'Oh really. What of?' She was asking Alistair directly.

'Er . . .' He didn't dare appeal to Steve. He was too unpredictable. 'It was a film that Steve was in. A Canadian thing.'

'Really. Can I have a look?' She grinned at the idea of it. Steve was pulling the cork from the wine bottle.

'Shall we show her, chief?' He winked at Alistair. 'I tell you what. I'll leave it up to you. I'm going to find some glasses.' He left the room again, leaving Alistair standing uneasily by the television. Alice walked over to him, slipping off her big green coat. She'd spiked her hair up and put more make-up on than usual. There were heavy black lines beneath her eyes that made them look even bigger. She had a tight grey jumper on over her long black skirt. The only colour on her was her lips, which were bright red.

'What are you two up to? Why's he acting so suspiciously?' She put her coat down on the sofa.

Alistair was sure that he was blushing. 'He's just being Steve, isn't he,' he said, hoping that that would be enough to satisfy her.

'What's this film then?' She had sat down next to her coat, pulling up her skirt around her knees. Alistair shook his head.

'It's nothing. Have you got over today yet?'

'I just wish there was something we could do about it. Someone to complain to. I was going to tell my dad but he'd not been good again. When he gets angry it can trigger an attack. I don't want Declan Shitface killing him.'

'I'm sorry. Should you have stayed in with him tonight?'

'Oh, he made me come. Anyway, I didn't want you to disappear without seeing you properly.' Alistair felt the thrill spreading through him. It was like lying in a field feeling the sun as it comes out from behind a cloud. 'It's been really nice meeting you.'

'It's been the best thing that's happened to me for ages. Or ever.'

Alice laughed. 'Well, you need to get out more.'

'No, I mean . . . well, I just really like you, that's all.'

Steve came back in with three expensive-looking glasses balanced between his hands. Each one was filled to the top. 'Right, get these down you. Does anyone want a fag?' He managed to get the glasses onto the coffee table without spilling anything, and reached for a large wooden box decorated with African carvings. He opened it – it was packed with cigarettes. Alistair was surprised to see Alice reach out and take one.

'I didn't know you smoked,' he said, realizing that he sounded disapproving.

She looked up at him as Steve reached out and lit the fag for her. 'Sometimes.'

Steve took one for himself and grinned at Alistair as he lifted the big marble lighter to his face. 'Sure you don't want one, chief?'

'No, thanks.'

Steve and Alice both sucked at their cigarettes, extravagantly blowing out smoke for a few moments while Alistair looked on. Alice pulled a cassette box from her bag and waved it around with her free hand.

'I brought some music. I thought you'd only have shit stuff,' said Alice, grinning.

'Oh bugger that, darling. We're not having any of your whirr music killing the party atmosphere.'

'Piss off.' Alice sounded offended but she was grinning. She made her way over to the hi-fi which filled one corner of the den. 'What's "whirr music"?'

'Oh you know. All that dreadful stuff that goes "werrrrr".' Steve made a droning noise as he pulled an exaggerated gloomy expression and nodded his head up and down.

'How do you turn this thing on?' The massive speakers on either side of the windows banged like cannons.

'Alice!'

'Sorry.' She pulled a sheepish face then turned back to the tape player. The clicking thump of a bass guitar filled the room. She turned the volume up and a drum cracked in.

'Oh for God's sake – what's this?'

'Good music,' she snapped at him.

'All right – keep your knick-knacks on. Come on. Have

another drink.' He poured some wine into Alice's glass, which was still half full. 'Hey, does anyone fancy a cocktail?' Before anyone could answer he'd put the wine bottle down and made for the drinks cabinet at the back of the room.

'Where did you learn to mix cocktails?' It seemed that everything Steve said Alice was determined to challenge. And yet she was doing it with a smile. There was something about this sparring that Alistair felt excluded from, or, at least, didn't understand.

'I'm very creative when it comes to drinks. The glass is my canvas.'

Alice laughed, taking a swig of her wine. 'Go on then. Impress me.'

Alistair felt awkward standing in the middle of the room, and wandered over to where Alice was sitting. He tried to do so at a speed that wouldn't draw attention to what he was doing. Then he slumped down on the seat next to her, as if he was suddenly tired and it was a matter of little consequence whether she was there or not. He took a mouthful of wine, like she had. It was hot in his throat, unfamiliar and adult.

'Hello,' she said, laughing.

'Hello,' said Alistair.

'Hey – do you want to dance?' She smiled broadly, and her eyes widened, as if there was something magical about the idea.

'I'm not a very good dancer.'

'I didn't say do you want to dance *well*. A shit dance will do.'

Alistair wasn't to be allowed the option of refusing. Uncertainly he got to his feet. Alice grabbed his hands and pulled him into the middle of the room. The heat from the wine seemed to spread from his throat into the rest of his body. She lifted his hands into the air and began to move with a quirky grace that at once seemed expert and uniquely her own. He bobbed up and down, trying not to do anything too ridiculous – however, that fear was soon replaced by the sense of something wonderful. Of Alice's fingers gripping his, warm and small and tight. Of the shape of her body beneath her dress and jumper. Of the music, which like the wine was unfamiliar and yet thrilling. 'Heart and soul,' she sang, following the lyrics, 'One will burn.' The song came to an end and Alistair was disappointed, but Alice didn't let go. It was followed by another with a mournful bass guitar intro which didn't promise much in the way of inspiring movement. But then the drums began to surge and the guitar soared with a magnificent desperation and Alice was off. She moved her head from side to side, her hair swinging wildly around her face, her hands rising into the air, taking Alistair's with them. She looked up and into Alistair's eyes. He smiled back. She didn't return the smile, but she held his gaze, the deep blue of her irises almost swallowed by the black of her dilated pupils. Alistair couldn't remember ever standing before a stare of such intensity before – except maybe Dad, when he lost his temper. But this wasn't anger.

'There you go, then.' Steve had returned with a tray, laden with three glass tumblers. Each was full with an ugly-looking liquid coloured somewhere between yellow and black. 'I call it a Raw Nog.'

'What's in it?'

'Best not to ask. Just drink it down.' He handed out the tumblers with reverence as if they were something valuable or very delicate. Alistair had to let go of Alice in order to take his. They moved apart and went back to the sofa. Steve turned the volume down on the hi-fi. Alistair sniffed at his drink. It smelt somewhere between medicine and jelly.

257

'Go on. Get it down you.' He took a mouthful. It wasn't like the wine. It was vile and sickening and corrosive. Yet he swallowed the mouthful because its sweetness – like melted penny chews – made it surprisingly easy to do so. Besides, the alcohol he had already consumed was beginning to have an effect – and it had established a craving within him that recognized more alcohol and wanted it, regardless of the flavour.

Alice let out a shriek of laughter when she sampled her drink. 'That's quite the most disgusting thing I've ever tasted.' She took another sip then said, 'Mix me another.'

As they all sat with the glasses in their hands it occurred to Alistair that Steve might have mixed each drink differently, tailoring it to each of them individually. Why he might have done this or what effect each one would have Alistair didn't really know.

For a while they sat listening to the music, swigging their drinks and talking about TV programmes and music. Then Steve got somewhat unsteadily to his feet.

'Listen, listen – I've got an idea. Why don't we play a game?'

'What kind of game?' Alice looked dubious. 'If you're going to suggest strip poker, you can forget it. I've no desire to see either of you with your clothes off.'

Alistair laughed, but he also noted – was embarrassed to note – that he felt something like disappointment at the statement. Steve was shaking his head and holding up his hand.

'Nah, nah, nah. Don't be stupid.' He moved over to where Alistair and Alice were sitting. Looking up at him Alistair thought he looked very tall, again that feeling that this was a man in front of him, reminding him that he was still a boy. He looked across at Alice. He felt shut inside his own head, fuzzy and thick. He would have liked to kiss her.

'I think we should play the truth game.'

'What's the truth game?' Alistair found his own voice sounded distant and thin.

'Everybody knows the truth game. It's the easiest game in the world.' He was smiling now. Looking down at Alistair and Alice and smiling. 'The only rule is that you have to tell the truth.'

'Where's the fun in that?' Alice reached for another cigarette from the African box.

'Well, obviously,' said Steve, making exaggerated gestures as if he were a quiz master or a comedian, 'it's the *questions* that make the game. It's the fact that if you agree to play – you *have* to answer them.'

'What if you don't want to answer them?' Alice looked uncertain.

'You still have to answer. Once you start it's like being on a roller-coaster. You can't get off until it's over.'

'And when's it over?' asked Alistair. The room felt more like a tunnel now with him at one end, and everything else at the other.

'When everybody's answered all the questions.' Steve didn't seem drunk at all.

'All right,' said Alice waving her cigarette about extravagantly, 'but I get to ask the first question.'

Steve thought for a moment and then nodded. Alistair looked on as if this was all nothing to do with him.

'Let's sit on the floor then.' Steve had gone over to the hi-fi and turned the tape off.

'Why do we have to sit on the floor?' said Alice, slightly indignant.

'So we can see in each other's eyes and tell if anybody's lying.'

'And leave the tape on. It's The Slits.' But Steve shook his head.

'We need my music on.' He opened a drawer at the bottom of the hi-fi unit and pulled out a tape.

'Well, what is it?' She was clearly suspicious.

'Just my stuff.'

'What stuff?'

'You'll see.'

'You mean, "you'll hear",' said Alistair, but nobody responded to him. Steve put the tape in the machine and pressed the play button. The speakers hissed for a moment and then came a rotten old crackling noise. The tape was a recording of an old record. It sounded so old and broken that Alistair found it easy to imagine the act of playing the record alone would have done irreparable damage to the needle. In fact, it was quite possible that by just playing this record, whatever it was, the needle would never work again.

'What the fuck is this?' Alice was indignant that her tape should have been taken out and replaced with this.

'My favourite song,' said Steve. Somewhere distant, behind the crackles, there were voices. Two thin reedy voices. Two old men singing softly, accompanied by an accordion and a piano.

'Well, what is it?' Alice looked at Alistair, who shrugged his shoulders. He listened closely, straining to make sense of the voices beneath the clicks, pops and hisses.

'I found it. At my grandpa's. This is real music.' Steve grinned at them both. Alistair wasn't even sure that the men were singing in English. 'Right, first question to Alice – what colour are your pubes?'

'Oh fuck off, Steve.'

Alistair laughed at the predictable nature of Steve's question. Also, he was relieved at its innocent stupidity. He must have been expecting something worse. The record troubled him. It made him think of a place. Or rather a non-place. An emptiness. A vast aloneness. No one to turn to.

He listened closely, trying to concentrate on the soft, aged voices. The men must have been very old when they made the record.

'Oh my Lou,' one of them seemed to be singing, followed by the other who replied with 'Oh my darlin'. 'Oh my Lou. Oh my Lou.' The foreign accent made it sound like all one word. 'Ormolu, Ormolu.'

'I'm not going to tell you – you stupid baby.' Alice was laughing.

'Ormolu.' Of course the man couldn't be singing Ormolu. That was impossible. Alistair now knew he was drunk.

'But you're not playing the game.' Now Steve was indignant.

'I don't see why I should do something just because you say so.'

'You have to because that's the rules and you've agreed to it.'

Alistair was trying to laugh along with Steve and Alice, but he couldn't bring himself to. He was worrying about the record on the tape.

'All right. They're green.'

'Ha, ha. Answer the question.'

'I have answered the question. My pubes are green. Now it's my turn to ask you a question. Why are you such a twat?'

'Can we put on another tape please? This is driving me mad,' said Alistair. He'd gone very cold.

'Well, I'm afraid I can't answer that question. Not until you answer your question.'

'But I have answered my question.'

'No you haven't, Alice.' Steve had gone uncharacteristically quiet.

'Yes I have, Steve.' She mimicked his intonation.

'Well, not truthfully.'

'Well, you don't know that.'

'Yes I do.'

'No you don't.' She was smirking at him now, letting him know that she had won.

'Can't we play another game? This is boring.' Alistair had stood up, shakily. He wanted to turn the tape off, to put Alice's tape back on.

'Not until we've settled this.'

'Oh, and how are you – how are we – going to settle this?'

Alistair could tell, even with his thick head, that Alice was drunk.

'By you showing us your green pubes.'

'Oh, I think you'll just have to trust me on that one.'

Through the mud in his head, which felt like the melted penny chews he had tasted earlier, Alistair registered shock at how Steve was talking to Alice. Was this still part of the game?

'Can I ask a question?' he said, hoping this would divert the troubling course of Steve and Alice's dialogue.

'Yes,' said Alice, turning away from Steve, 'that's a good idea. Let sweetie ask a question. He hasn't got a foul mouth like yours.'

'Sweetie? Is that what you call him?'

'He is a sweetie,' said Alice. She seemed to be swaying now. Was it good that she was calling him sweetie? The 'Ormolu' song had finished now but the crackles continued. Steve strode over to Alistair. He was steadier on his feet than either Alistair or Alice. He ruffled Alistair's hair as if he were a small dog.

'Ahhh.'

'Ignore him, Alistair – ask your question.'

'No,' said Steve, reaching for the jug of foul brown liquid. 'I'm going to ask another question. Alistair,' he said, turning round swiftly, making the liquid slosh horribly in the glass jug, 'is it true you're in love with Alice Zealand?'

Was it possible to blush when you were drunk? Steve started giggling. It must have been because Alistair felt his skin burning.

'Shut up, Steve,' said Alice. She had flopped backwards onto the sofa.

'Come on, Sweetie,' said Steve, pouring out more drink into Alistair and Alice's glasses. 'Answer the bloody question.'

'Steve,' said Alistair, 'don't . . .' Alistair attempted to pull an imploring face.

'Don't what? You told me you were in love with her.'

'What's he saying?' Alice had lain back on the sofa completely now. Her eyes were fluttering.

'You told me you wanted to sleep with her. Don't you remember?'

'I did not, Steve. You know I didn't.'

'Huhhh?' Alice was making an odd noise. It sounded as if she started to speak but then couldn't be bothered to finish the word. It ended as a gurgle in her throat.

'You told me you wanted to see her tits and fuck her hard.'

'Shut up, Steve, shut up, shut up. Alice, I never said anything.' Alice made a noise like a child's impersonation of a pig. One of her legs was on the floor, the other was on the sofa, knee bent upwards. Her arm was thrown lazily over her forehead. 'Alice.' There was no response. 'Alice, are you all right?'

'Hmmm . . .' She shifted slightly, allowing her leg to fall over until it hit the back of the sofa.

'Steve – is she all right?' Steve was at the tape recorder, rewinding the cassette. 'Steve. I don't know if Alice is all right.' Alistair stood up with the intention of moving towards her to see if he could wake her up. However, the room lurched alarmingly. Alistair turned one way and the room moved in the opposite direction. It was like trying to make the needle on a compass line up. The horrible crackle rumbled from the speakers.

'Listen to it when it belts out.' The gentle singing started, quiet and distant and seemingly no louder than before. Only the scratch of the vinyl was magnified. Like someone crunching an apple into a microphone. Alistair felt sick. He stumbled towards Alice. He was cold all over. A sudden clamminess crept over him like a shadow. Steve was ahead of him, reaching down and shaking her.

'All right, Mrs. Are you awake?' She snorted again – then gave a little moan. Steve turned to Alistair with a satisfied expression on his face. 'She's still with us, chief. But only just.'

'Should we get a doctor?'

Steve started laughing. 'Why? She's only pissed.'

But she seemed more than pissed to Alistair. The way she had flopped back so suddenly. And why wasn't he like that? He felt horrible and drunk and sick but he hadn't passed out.

'Don't you be worrying yourself. The missus will be just fine in the morning.'

'She can't stay here. Her dad'll worry.'

'Blah, blah, blah, blah. Don't be so bloody boring, chief. Worry worry worry. Hey, you know what?' The scratchy, shrunken song had got to the 'Ormolu' bit. Alistair wanted to think he had made a mistake about it, that it was just being drunk that had made him hear that word. But now it sounded even less ambiguous. 'We can see if she was cheating.'

'Huhh . . .'

'We can see if she was cheating. She's never going to know.' Alistair wasn't sure what Steve meant. He clutched his stomach because he felt sick. Then he realized what Steve meant. Of course, Steve was joking.

264

'There's nothing worse than a cheat. Come on.' At that moment Alistair felt like there was somebody else in the room with them, someone who hadn't been there before. Steve sat down next to Alice's spread body; her limbs now rested at odd angles, like a dead cat in a cartoon.

'Do you want to look first?'

'Steve – what are you doing?' Steve had reached for the bottom of Alice's long black skirt. This was still a joke. Steve wouldn't actually do what he was pretending he was going to do because people didn't actually behave like that.

'Come on, chief. Don't leave me out in the cold here.' One of Alice's legs shifted slightly. Steve pulled at the hem of the skirt and flapped it up and down as if he was trying to create a breeze. Alice stirred a little and muttered. Alistair could see the line of her woolly tights leading up the inside of her thighs.

'Steve. Leave her.' He was feeling really sick now. He swallowed hard, trying to repress the urge to vomit.

'Whahey.' Steve pulled the skirt right up and then quickly down again. Alistair reached out for Steve's arm, trying to grab hold of it. 'Whahey.' Steve repeated the action, waiting for Alistair's hand to reach him before moving suddenly to avoid it. The skirt came up over Alice's stomach. Alistair registered the lightness of her knickers beneath the black tights.

'Come on, mate. I don't think she's well.' Alistair heard himself using the word 'mate', aware that it was in a conscious attempt to win Steve over.

'She's only sleeping. Sleeping like a baby.' Steve reached for her stomach now, as if he was going to tickle it. As well as his nausea, Alistair was terribly cold inside. Is this what an accident feels like? he wondered. You can see it coming and the world thickens around you as the unalterable path reveals itself ahead – hidden railway tracks that have always been there, suddenly becoming visible beneath you and before you. Is this what it feels like when you know death is finally coming? Unavoidable and terrible and sickening – something old, so old, so familiar, so black. An inversion of every single thing that has gone before. Steve carefully rolled up the skirt around Alice's waist. He slipped his fingers into the waistband of her tights. That action alone revealed a smile of creamy white skin.

'Stop it now, Steve.' The other hand was beneath the stretchy material. Steve looked over his shoulder and grinned at Alistair.

'Catch a look at this baby.'

Alistair moved towards him now and grabbed hold of one of Steve's arms. He pulled at it. 'Stop it. Please stop it. Please leave her.'

'*Please leave her.*' Steve mimicked Alistair's plea, reproducing his northern accent with cold skill. 'You've been dreaming about this, mate, haven't you?' He began to yank at the tights, pulling the knickers with them, taking Alistair's arm with his. In turn, Alistair tried to jerk it away. Steve removed his hand from Alice's clothes and struck out at Alistair without even looking where he was aiming. His knuckles caught Alistair's eye with force. The inside of Alistair's head went bright as he fell back onto the floor. His heart was thumping now, thudding away in that familiar way, beating the repetitive rhythm of fear, the inner dance he knew so well. Except always, when he had felt this before, beneath the terror was a subtle comfort that really he was safe, that this was a game, a trial, a practice, a fantasy designed with the single purpose of fighting off the real danger. If he experienced the imagined danger again and again, he would never have to face the real one. That was the bargain he had struck with the Universe and he assumed it was a price worth paying. But now the Universe

266

was reneging on its deal. He wasn't strong enough to fight Steve, who was twice his size and knew how to hurt people. Alistair had never had a fight in his life. He pulled himself uncertainly to his feet, wondering what to do next. Steve was back at the sofa, bending over Alice like Dracula. Maybe it would be better if she woke up. If there was one person who could stand up to Steve, it was Alice. But she seemed even less conscious than before, her head lolling back, her mouth slightly open. There was only Alistair there to stop him, alone in the stupidly opulent room. Steve went down on to his knees as he pulled the clothes down, baring Alice's lower half.

'Ta da!' he said triumphantly. Her legs were like a man's below the knees. But her thighs were full and fleshy. There was her cunt. The first Alistair had ever seen in real life. He stood, fixed to the floor, staring at the white leather sofa, hoping she wouldn't wake up – that she'd sleep through it like an operation. 'No green pubes. I win.' Steve had found one of the tumblers on the floor and raised it, taking a triumphant swig. There was something else rising within Alistair, fighting for his attention beneath the nausea and the fear. He really didn't want to have to label it, he hoped all this would be over before he did.

'Come on, fellah,' said Steve, grinning at him and waving the glass in front of him, 'come and have a feel.'

Alistair didn't speak. He stared ahead, trying to keep his eyes away from the flesh, trying to fight the pull of the muscles in the orbits of his eyes that wanted to swivel the balls down and to the right. He thought if he said something he might draw attention to himself and Steve would make him do something.

'No?' Steve pulled an exaggerated sad face. 'I doubt you'll get another chance.' Alistair remained where he was, as if he was playing musical statues and trying very hard to win. 'Oh well. Please yourself.' Steve turned back round towards Alice. And that was the point that Alistair ran from the room.

He went and sat in the hall, staring at the extravagantly framed photos on the wall – the crystal skull, the illuminated pyramid, the squat standing stones. Then he heard something that he didn't want to hear from the other room, so he opened the front door and sat on the steps beneath the porch light, which made everything beyond look absent. Perhaps a policeman would walk past, but then the policeman would ask what he was doing there and why wasn't he in there saving her. Perhaps he could go back in. Perhaps Steve would have finished now. Finished what? Yes, I'll go back in, he thought. But somehow he couldn't make himself stand up. And then there was a movement behind him and he turned round. And there was Alice, her skirt on wrong, her chin shiny and wet, holding her coat. Her face was shockingly pale. That was probably what a corpse looked like. Alistair stood up and went towards her, holding out his hand.

'Are you al—' But before he could even complete the question she had pushed him away with almost as much force as Steve had struck him. She made a noise, a terrible low growling noise like an injured animal. Alistair felt completely hollow as if his insides had been eroded. It seemed to him that he would feel like that forever more. Alice stumbled forward, into the cone of brightness cast by the porch light. She tripped and her shoe came off. She turned slowly and jerkily and squeezed her eyes shut. Her mouth opened and closed and opened again. A sound came out. She was trying to speak and it was apparent to Alistair that a great effort was evolved.

'D . . .'

He stood rigid, his hands clawed.

'Don't – ever – say.' But it was too much for her and then she was gone from the light, taken by the absence beyond. Only her shoe remained, like Cinderella's. For a moment, a second, he was relieved she was gone, but the relief didn't last and he was swallowed by a wave of dreadful coldness and fear which felt like drowning. Finally he vomited, the violent spasms shaking him out of his immobility.

And he did as he was told. In the taxi home he never said. To Rosalyn Frieze he never said. To Mum and Dad and Herby he never said. To God he never said.

But Alice. Oh, Alice . . .

# Chapter Sixteen

Alistair stood swaying with the motion of the train, aware of the pulse thumping in the side of his neck. He risked another glance at the three men grouped around the girl, then pulled himself sharply away from the carriage entrance.

People did such things. Intervened in such situations.

'Come on, Britanic. Remember what I told you. These people must be resisted.'

The shape of Mihail's face in the darkness, flickering as the light cast on him flickered.

The Grey Book was full of such stories. People who got involved.

Something else entered his consciousness. The thought of the girl. Her face. Her hair. Their hands on her.

'That's right. Think of the girl,' said the voice in the shadows.

It drew something up from within. The thought of them hurting her. Her beautiful face. Her dark, dark hair.

All right. I'm going to go in there.

(YES, BRITANIC. YOU'RE GOING IN THERE.)

The very idea.

The cacophony of motion, white noise in his ears.

I'm going to move one leg in front of the other and keep moving them until I arrive at the other end of the carriage, to the seat where she's sitting and they're standing over her and forcing her to do whatever it is they're forcing her to do.

Maybe they've stopped. Maybe they're just sitting there now. Chatting. Having a laugh.

No. One leg in front of the other. Me standing there will be enough to make them stop. They won't want to be watched.

Alistair moved some way towards the exit of the carriage. And then he sat down again.

He noticed himself trembling, his hand actually shaking like an alcoholic's. The girl's beauty. She had been so beautiful. He had felt it inside – in his stomach. What if they were doing something to her face?

Who was this? Making him move. But there was a rightness about it. Or if not a rightness a flow, like a current in water, or a marble in a groove.

Wasn't there always somewhere deep in his mind the thought – what would I do? What would I do if they knocked on my door in the middle of the night to drag me away? What would I do if I was standing naked in the dark somewhere, shivering and freezing, knowing they were going to kill my sister or my mother or my wife? (I have no wife – it's easier not to have a wife than to face up to that – to think I might have to fight to save her. Or worse, watch myself do nothing as they take her.) Is this that? Is what I'm doing a version of that? Am I running towards it because I can't bear to wait for it to run towards me? They can kill you. Did you know that, Alistair? They're allowed to kill you. Nobody stops them. The Universe tolerates such actions.

I'm going to keep moving towards them. I have to because of the girl.

Imagine someone stabbing you. Imagine someone sticking a knife into you. Imagine cancer. (He often did imagine cancer. There were days when he knew he had cancer.)

271

Imagine that pain. Imagine what it must be like to die. What must it be like to die? Imagine being destroyed by somebody else – another human being, watching as they do it. Imagine being a piece of worthless shit. Imagine looking on and doing nothing as another human being is hurt in front of you. And why are you doing nothing? Because I'm scared. Because I'm scared. Because I don't want to be hurt, because I don't want to be destroyed. Because I want to be here more than anything else. Because it's all I know.

Imagine being so worthless and weak that the world might do all these things to you. That other people, who are worth more than you, might do these things to you. You worthless, valueless, weak, soft piece of shit. That's all you are. That's all you are. Flimsy. Paper thin. Airy but brittle. Who are you kidding? Nothing. No thing.

Keep the legs moving. Keep the feet moving. Moving yes, but he only got as far as the pile of things – the coat, the computer, the phone, the bags. He picked up the computer and held it under his arm, gripping it against his chest with his bicep. Bicep. No biceps. Weak and thin and weedy. Useless and weak and . . .

He reached down, bending his knees, and picked up the phone in the other hand. He stuffed it into his back pocket.

(WHAT ARE YOU THINKING, ALISTAIR?)

Shut up. I'm thinking. It was dreamlike now. Unreal. Because surely, he shouldn't be doing this – couldn't be doing this.

The world changed. The mien of the world changed. It looked brighter. More metallic. Projected on steel. The brightness of the carriage beyond like a cheap plasma screen, almost painful to look at.

(GO NOW, ALISTAIR. GO NOW OR YOU NEVER WILL.)

Alistair wanted to laugh. I can do this. Keep moving the

legs. I don't know what's going to come. I have absolutely
no idea what's going to happen. But I can do this. I can
keep moving my legs. One foot in front of the other. Bare
linoleum floor passing. There they were. Huddled over her
like foxes round roadkill.

'*Lilli, Lilli, arată-ne chiloţii, arată-ne chiloţii, arată-ne chiloţii.
Lilli, Lilli arată-ne chiloţii. Arată-ne, arată-ne arată-ne chiloţii!*'

The seats passed, one by one. Again the urge to laugh. I
don't know what's going to happen. Something enormous
ahead and not caring. Sensing it doesn't matter. Fuck you.
Fuck you. Fuck you. Fuck every one of you ever. Fuck
every one of you who's ever thought bad. Fuck every one of
you who's hurt. Fuck every one of you who's done evil.
How restricted the language of hate was. Fuck fuck fuck.
You won't do this. I won't let you do this.

There was the girl. There were the men. The glee of
abandon. His abandon. Alistair's abandon. Not theirs.

'*Lilli—*'

Wham. Into his face with the bottom of the laptop. Into
his stupid Football-player's face. It made a loud noise.
Louder than you'd think. Somewhere between a crack and
a bang. And there was blood. He fell down and Alistair swivelled and thumped the one next to him with the heavy
plastic. Less of a crack this noise, more of a dull thump.

'*Băga-mi-aş,*' said the third one, the smallest one. The girl
was screaming. Alistair didn't want to look at her in case
they'd done something to her. He got ready to smash the
third one, but before he could move he'd been leapt on. He
whirled his arms madly in an attempt to throw his attacker
off.

'*Ce faci mă, ce faci mă, ce faci mă?*'

The computer had been pulled from his hands. He
reached for his phone from his back pocket. He wasn't
thinking now. It was like wanking, like looking at porn and

273

wanking, do this, do this, do this. Thought didn't belong here. The phone was in his hands. He smashed it into the face of Satin Shirt who was still in front of him, aiming the stubby antenna straight at him. Something soft gave way. Satin Shirt screamed. Imagine that. He'd made one of them scream. He could hurt too. Is that all there was to it?

BANNN—! Comic-book bright. A sudden whiteness. Nuclear bright. Nothing but white. Dizzy, dizzy, dizzy. Blackness below. A vacuum pull. Don't give in, don't give in. Don't take the world away. BANNN! again. Do I still want to be here? Stay here. Stay here. Stay here.

Alistair's head throbbed. He'd been hit by the computer too.

More screaming in his ear this time. Who was screaming in his ear?

'*Ce faci mă, ce faci mă, ce faci mă?*' It was the girl. The girl was on his back. The girl was trying to stop him. The girl pulled his arms behind his back and sat on him. Satin Shirt was sobbing. There was blood on his face. He was reaching for a phone. The girl was pulling Alistair's hair. It really hurt. 'What are you doing?' she said, in between her screams. Alistair thought he might say 'I'm saving you' but he couldn't get the words out. Even with his head pressed against the floor, Alistair could see Satin Shirt holding a mobile – not Alistair's bloodied and useless mobile – pressing his teeth together to try to stop screaming. He held the phone to the other side of his face, the unwounded side.

'*Pune-ţi uniforma*,' he screamed into the phone. '*Pune-ţi uniforma până-n gara Cluj. Pune-ţi uniforma imediat.*'

'Britanic,' Alistair heard himself say aloud, in Mihail's voice. 'I . . . me . . . Britanic.'

'*Ce faci mă?*' said the girl. 'What have you done?' Now sitting on Alistair's arms, pressing them painfully into his back. 'What the fuck have you done?'

274

# PART FIVE

*Die gantze velt iz a cholem – nor beser a gute cholem aider a sclechte.*

The whole world is a dream – better a good dream than a bad one.

Yiddish proverb

# Chapter Seventeen

The cell door thumping closed, like something heavy falling to earth from the sky. And with it the feeling – the terrible enveloping feeling, like being swallowed alive.

Each phase of the beginning of it – if that was the beginning of it – was clear and bright and alive in his memory. The arrival of the police. Their uniforms more like English postmen than officers of the law. Until he saw the guns. The bursts of incomprehensible language – presumably questions, fired out relentlessly.

'*Eşti răspunzător de fapte?*' Alistair looking at them blankly. '*Eşti răspunzător pentru rănile astea?*' The one asking the questions was young – and, strangely, bearded. He certainly looked too young for his beard. Alistair could barely speak. He felt as if he was going to wake up, at any moment. He tried to talk.

'Britanic,' he said. In his own voice now. Just him. 'Britanic. Britanic. Britanic.'

Within moments of being pulled from the train he felt something cold and hard on his wrists and it brought things into focus. Handcuffs. The night air in the station was cold. His breath clouded in the dim light.

And then the cliché of the arrest undercut by a confusing mixture of friendliness and aggression.

'*Cum te cheamă, mă?* . . . What's your name?' This from an

older officer. His English was spoken with an American intonation like Mihail's. He seemed friendly, his voice softer and more sympathetic.

'*Tu eşti ăsta?*' The bearded one had pulled the passport from Alistair's coat pocket. He opened it to the photo page and showed it to the older one. 'Alistair Black? *Tu eşti Alistair Black?*' The man sounded incredulous, as if Alistair's name was well known in Cluj and he was somehow a disappointment in actuality. At the end of the platform was a huge billboard filled with the words '*Sar Transilvania*' and an image of a baby's head. The baby seemed to look at him with infinite sadness.

'Alistair Black – *te arestez pentru vătămare corporală cu scopul de a provoca răni grave şi de a instaura frica . . .*'

'Be good, be good,' said the desperate voice in his head. Just be good, just show them how good you can be. Look at the floor. Look sad. Look guilty. Agree to everything. Call them sir. In the back of the van – just a transit van, like an English transit van, painted in a special way, he noticed himself thinking – with three other officers. One of them young, younger than him, shouting, '*Un tip de-ăla tare. Asta eşti? Un tip de-ăla tare?*'

Alistair looking at the floor, holding his breath. And then, within minutes, seconds even of the van driving off it had stopped and he was pulled out and dragged inside and now they were being almost polite again.

He was bundled straight from the van into what looked like a changing room. There were benches with coathooks on. His head hurt.

'*Ai băut, Alistair?* Drinking? You drink?' The older policeman mimed the action, lifting an imaginary bottle to his lips.

'No.' Speak it. Don't just shake your head. Show them how compliant you are. You're no trouble at all.

278

'*N-ai băut nimic toată noaptea?* Not one drink?'

Would it help if he said yes? No. Just tell the truth. 'No.'

'*Ai luat droguri?* Drugs?' There was no action to accompany this question. Instead the policeman just raised his hand, holding something invisible between his thumb and forefinger.

'No.' He tried to look guilty and apologetic, as if ashamed that he had no chemical excuse for . . . no, don't think about it yet.

'*Eşti sigur că n-ai luat droguri?* No drugs?' The arresting officer looked on, almost concerned.

'Yes. I mean I haven't'.

'Do you want to see doctor, Alistair?'

Be good, be good. 'No.'

'You sure, Alistair? You not injured?' He spoke haltingly. There was care on his face.

Be good. His head really ached. 'No. I'm fine. OK.'

The officer looked at him then nodded. Then he withdrew and shut the door. A key twisted in the lock. The room was bright and quite large, the brickwork painted white. A poster on the wall with the word '*Remedium!*' repeated in a line from the top downwards. Don't think. Don't think for a minute. The brightness of the room. A striplight buzz.

After some time – minutes or hours – the door opened again. Another policeman came in, accompanied by a short man in a dark suit. His tie was fat, with a big knot, like a mid-seventies schoolboy's. The short man was bald, with dark clumps of hair on either side of his head. His pate shone in the fluorescent lights. The policeman was holding a big plastic bag. It was see-through, but the plastic was thick like you might find round a new electrical appliance. Inside, shiny still with blood, which smeared and bubbled against the polythene, was Alistair's laptop. In a smaller bag was Alistair's phone. There was blood on that too.

'Are these yours?' the bald man said. His English was more fluent. Alistair thought about saying 'yes, sir' but instead he just nodded. Be good. Be good. He was taken out of the changing room into some kind of reception. The room was cramped and smelt of stale tobacco, like a betting shop. The bald man undid Alistair's handcuffs and positioned him in front of a high counter where another policeman sat. Slowly, carefully and calmly the bald man asked for all his details. Certain of them he translated back into Romanian. The policeman behind the counter took them down. Recently Alistair had renewed his car insurance on the phone. Apart from the language gap, the process was identical – the patient questioning and recording of information, the double checking and reading back. Everything else was taken from him. The change in his pocket, his keys, tissues, a tube of Lockets. They had his rucksack. He signed a form. It was a strange moment of calm in which he gathered himself, or thought that he did, held and supported by the neutral business of bureaucracy.

'Is there anyone you want to let know where you are?'

'The hotel. The hotel where I was staying.' He knew it was absurd before he'd even finished saying it.

'Any family?' the bald man clarified.

Family? Alistair shook his head.

'Do you have an attorney you'd like to contact?'

An attorney? Once more he shook his head. Again the unexpected reasonableness. It seemed to have passed from one to the other like a whistled tune.

'We will arrange for you to see a consulate. It will probably be a few hours before he arrives. How are you feeling?' The man sounded like he was genuinely concerned, a friend now all that nonsense was over, as if it had been a football match Alistair had lost.

'My head hurts a bit.'

'We will get a doctor to look at it.'

And he was being led along a long low-ceilinged corridor, alive with working detail of its own that made it seem real and alien. A hospitally smell and institutional echo. On his left conventional-looking doors – no different to English doors. They were all closed, quiet for the night. Presumably they led into offices, interview rooms or cupboards. On his right, however, were bulky metal cell doors. This wasn't a prison, was it? No. Only the cells at the police station surely, but the corridor seemed to extend far further than it should, the regularly spaced doors receding into the darkness. Flashes of brightness ahead in that gloom. Were they in the gloom or in his head? Eventually they stopped and the policeman, still holding Alistair's arm with one hand, produced a rattling circle of keys with the other. He opened the door they had paused before, pressing a light switch outside. Be good. Be good.

'*Te rog să îţi scoţi cureaua*. Your belt?'

It took a moment for him to realize he was being asked to hand it over. He had to look down. He couldn't remember if he was wearing one. He wasn't. 'No.' He shook his head.

'OK. Shoes off, please.'

Without thinking to ask why – of course he wasn't going to ask why – Alistair removed his shoes.

'*Ai nevoie să bei ceva?* A drink . . . water?'

Alistair shook his head. Whether he did or he didn't, he wasn't going to say yes. There was gentle pressure on his shoulder, which Alistair had to work hard not to resist. Then he was inside the cell. The policeman was framed in the door.

'When the consulate arrives, we'll come and get you.'

281

And then he shut the door.

Worst of all was the noise. The huge, resonant, calamitous slam, followed by the tumbling of some heavy mechanism within. Almost immediately came the shocking realization that he couldn't get out. That nothing he could do would get him out. Over and above the obvious fact that the door was locked, there was no action he could take that would make them let him out. He could scream and kick and cry and wail and bang his head against the metal or the brick or the painted concrete floor and they still wouldn't let him out. Something that he didn't even know he owned had been taken away from him as easily as they had taken his shoes.

He could see his hands shaking. His shoulder hurt from where the girl had pulled his arms back and sat on him. He reached up and felt the side of his head. There was a huge, sore lump. Tentatively he pressed it. The room went white. Bright white. He pulled his hand away sharply.

He thought about the men on the train. Wondered where they were. The girl had known them, hadn't she? They'd known her. The policemen seemed to have known them all. The sense of trouble – of being caught in it like quicksand – rose around him to join the terror of being locked up. You can't send me to prison – I get claustrophobic. Mum, Dad – don't let them. He was firm with himself. You're not going to prison. They'll send you back to England. He repeated the phrase several times and looked around the cell to try and anchor himself while he was doing it. There was a raised plinth against the wall to his side, with something like a mattress propped up against the tiles. Alistair touched it. It made him think of school and gym lessons – an oblong of foam rubber covered in grey vinyl. Someone had drawn on the vinyl in biro – an elaborate picture of a werewolf that resembled a tattoo, the words 'I am the wolf man'

282

beneath. Alistair lay the mattress down and sat on it, tapping his foot on the floor. It's only waiting. You're just waiting.

He flashed back, with alarming clarity, to the train. Striding down the aisle with the intention of striking first. It was all he could imagine. The only way out of that train. The force he used – the physical movement of the plastic and metal through the air – was like a sentence. A question maybe – or a statement of introduction. In that moment he knew he'd felt a thrill. For a moment he'd felt freer than he had ever felt before. He felt powerful. He felt strong. And he was saving the girl. He felt that she was the way out. Her acknowledgement of his action – of what he was doing for her – was the door he'd been heading for.

Now there was no door at all.

The fear began to rise. Panic like water running into the tiny space. When it was full to the top he would drown.

More flashes of white, even without pressing the lump.

I'm tired. Tired of this life of constant fear. The fridge-hum of it.

Enough fear now. Enough.

White. More white. The white seemed to be coming into the cell. Like a light being shone.

He wished it would shine into the fear. The fear that had been there since the earliest age, like something bad approaching – an unexpected turn in the road; a sudden powercut; being hopelessly lost in a dark, dark forest. Something with teeth, somewhere up ahead. Calling out and no one coming.

A cry that had started when he'd started. It never stopped; he just got used to it, so it faded out, or seemed to fade out.

Underneath the cry, underpinning it and every related idea was a thought: a blanket resistance to his own mortality. A refusal to comprehend the fact that he was capable of ceasing. A magnetic repulsion to the idea that brought too much pain. This was the place where all his fear came from. The big black sun belting out darkness. He was going to cease. His inevitable nothingness an oceanic panic too huge to even risk a glance at. In this moment, in the coldness of the foreign police cell, he saw the treachery of his mind, turning a vacuum into a thing. But there was also the flicker of something else glimmering in the certainty of his cessation. The cessation wasn't empty after all. It contained some information. Information about everything that preceded it, that made a nonsense of Alistair's daily interpretation of his life.

His understanding of life – the meaning he had structured – was based upon a mistaken assumption: namely that he, Alistair Black, would go on forever. The assumed infinity of his own existence: this was the light background against which he defined the dark outline of the concept of his non-existence. But that original assumption was false. He acted as if he would go on forever. He judged as if he would go on forever. He assessed as if he would go on forever. But of course, inevitably, a day would come when he would stop. It was true that this fact was slippery – a fish coated in oil, that he attempted to grasp with wet hands. But in those moments, those brief moments where it made cold contact with his fingers, as it did for Alistair then in the prison cell, it afforded a certain insight. And Alistair realized his error. He had mistaken fear for death. But fear was a liar. Fear was something else entirely. Fear was the crackle of being alive. The physical product of synapses and nerve endings and respiration and sensation. The business of being. Death, whatever it might be, was another matter.

It was as if he had found a plug and pulled it, and the panic left. The cell was filling with clean, clear air. Purer than air. Purer than oxygen.

Other thoughts came with the clarity. Or rather left him. Things seemed to peel away. Layers of identity. I am this. I am that. It seemed so flimsy. It was what other people thought about him. Or even what he thought they thought. You are mad. You are Jewish. You are ugly. You are a failure. You are a disappointment. You are ill. They floated off into the whiteness. There was just him, breathing – in and out. Respiring. Nerves firing. Heart beating. Being.

Next to go was his name. As if he had forgotten it. He had never had it. It was given to him. He was just this. Sitting. Breathing. Waiting. How could he have been that name?

He couldn't have been because it had gone and he was still here. He tried to call it to mind but there was nothing to grab hold of.

The fear was gone. There was another sensation, like sunshine, warm and welcoming like being hugged.

Fear? Even that seemed like it had never really been. Not solid. Not like the solid core he was now. The irreducible thing. He must have dreamt it all.

He wanted to laugh. Laugh at his own foolishness.

It had all been nothing.

Nothing at all.

No thing

# Chapter Eighteen

Alice lay on the bed Ben had made for her, hoping that sleep would come. The blankets were rough against her bare arms. In the dimness the faces in the paintings stared down at her. She imagined that each had an opinion of her, useless and helpless and finished. She closed her eyes to avoid their non-existent gaze.

At one point she must have nearly dropped off. Her arm jerked in spasm and she was awake again. She could have got up and made herself some tea, but she didn't want to make any noise.

Some indeterminate time later, sleep came, and with it a dream.

Alice was lost. She felt like she'd been walking in a fog, but the fog was underground. Can you have a fog underground, she wondered.

How did she know she was underground? Something about the earth beneath her feet. The way it crunched. The sound of it echoing around her.

But she was walking around in a circle, surely. Trailing her hand around the edge of a curved wall. Now she knew where she was. The ground still crunched. Gritty and damp.

This was a cellar. A cellar made to live in, or to hide in until life was safe again. A table and chairs. A black iron stove. Makeshift beds. There must be a door. She continued walking around, her fingers running along the earthy wall, searching for some crack that she might lever open. Or stairs. There might be stairs ahead. A ladder. A way out.

There was no way out. Above her there was nothing but darkness. No ceiling even. Just a black space with no sense of anything beyond it.

She was lying on one of the beds. It was made of canvas. She looked over at the bed next to her. It was occupied. There was a shape beneath the ragged cloth.

'Hello,' she said. There was no response. She reached out and pushed the cloth. The thing beneath felt light, like it was made of twigs and string. She pulled back the cloth. It was a body. It had been human. The clothes were human. But the thing beneath them was no longer. The skin was drawn around the bone, the eye sockets were dark holes. The teeth were exposed beneath a lipless mouth. The head turned, slowly, imperceptibly, but it still moved. It was still, somehow, animate. She didn't know if it had seen her. She feared that it had.

She wanted to scream, to be out of there, but nothing happened. She remained resolutely on the bed. The other beds had shapes on them too, shapes under fabric. Parts of them crept beneath the cloth.

There was a rustling beneath the earth emanating from the centre of the room where the stinking black stove was. She could just make out an undulation beneath the compacted ground, loosening the soil and clay. It snaked towards her, unseen, burrowing beneath the dirt, moving closer, gathering speed, disappearing out of sight, blocked from vision by the end of her camp bed. And then it rose, looming over her, a wet black tentacle, squirming through the air, inches from her face. It steamed in the cold like something newly born. It extended over her, disappearing behind her. Then it sprouted a series of wriggling ribs, each one slamming down into the ground, fusing with it, weaving a cage around her.

Something seemed to seep from this enclosure, spreading into her, breaking her down. She could feel the flesh falling from the tips of her fingers. Her teeth crumbling in her mouth.

She was to become one of them. A desiccated, barely moving thing. She didn't want to look at her own hands for fear of what she would see. She could feel the rough thin cloth over her knuckles. She could feel her movements slowing down. This was where she was to remain. This is what it was to be no more.

She tried to wake. It was a question of moving. Of crying out. Of making sound and motion. But it was impossible. Like pushing the heaviest weight imaginable with all her power and seeing no movement whatsoever. She channelled all her will into it. She would force herself awake. But she was rigid. Cast in black iron, like the ancient reeking stove. And panic descended. For now she couldn't even scream.

She would die down here.

She would die down here.

# Chapter Nineteen

# Noaptea de sărbătoare a eroului sfarşeşte cu violenţă

Aseară un soldat decorat din Gherla a fost supus intervenţiei chirurgicale pentru a i se salva ochiul drept, după ce a suferit multiple lovituri în faţă într-un atac violent din gara Cluj Napoca.

Sergentul Gheorghe Vasile, de 25 de ani, sărbătorea primirea decoraţiei Crucea Mare, împreună cu doi colegi ofiţeri şi logodnica sa, Felicia Kallos, de 24 de ani. Vasile primise medalia Crucea Mare, ordinul clasa I, pentru curaj la datorie, în urma misiunii de apărare a unui spital de campanie din Republica Centrafricană. El a servit într-o misiune a Naţiunilor Unite de menţinere a păcii.

Atacul s-a petrecut în trenul inter-city Bucureşti, când acesta se apropia de Cluj Napoca. Vasile şi prietenii lui se întorceau de la Alba Iulia, unde fuseseră în permisie. În jur de 22:30, de grup s-a apropiat un individ străin, de peste 30 de ani, care a pornit să îi lovească in mod feroce şi neprovocat.

Dra. Kallos a reuşit să reducă individul la tăcere, în timp ce caporalul Miron Sălcudean, de 25 de ani, a solicitat ajutor.

Ochiul sergentului Vasile a fost vătămat când atacatorul l-a lovit în mod repetat cu un telefon celular. Doctorii speră să îi recupereze parţial vederea. Caporalul Sălcudean şi colegul acestuia sergent Tiberiu Mlesnilă au fost trataţi pentru răni uşoare la cap. Un cetaţean de 35 de ani a fost arestat.

# Hero's night of celebration ends in violence

A decorated soldier from Gherla underwent emergency surgery to save his left eye after he had been repeatedly struck in the face in a violent attack at Cluj-Napoca railway station last night.

Sergeant Gheorghe Vasile, 25, was celebrating being awarded the Grand Cross with two fellow officers and his fiancée Felicia Kallos, 24. Vasile had received the medal – the Grand Cross of the first order – for dutiful bravery in peacetime service while defending a Field Hospital in the Central African Republic. He was serving on a United Nations peace-keeping mission.

The attack happened on the cross-country train from Bucharest as it was approaching Cluj-Napoca.

Vasile and his friends were returning from Alba Iulia where they had been on leave. Sometime before 10.30 pm the group were approached by a foreign man in his early thirties who launched into a ferocious and unprovoked physical assault.

Miss Kallos finally brought the man under control while Corporal Miron Salcudean, 25, called for assistance.

Sergeant Vasile's eye sustained the injury when the attacker struck it repeatedly with a cell phone. Doctors are hopeful that partial sight will be restored. Corporal Salcudean and his colleague Sergeant Tiberiu Mlesnila were also treated for minor head injuries. A 35-year-old man has been arrested.

From *Monitorul de Cluj*, 17 June 2001

*Extract from the medical report on Corporal Miron Salcudean, prepared by Mr Mircea Trestian, Consultant Neurosurgeon, Clujana Hospital, upon the instruction of the State Prosecution Service and the Ministry of the Interior.*

The patient was admitted to the Emergency department at 12.00 hrs, having been transferred to hospital by paramedics following an alleged assault some 20 minutes earlier. During his transit to hospital, his level of consciousness had deteriorated, having initially been alert, but disorientated, and in pain. He had been administered oxygen via a facial mask and placed in the recovery position in order to prevent aspiration of his stomach contents. He had vomited several times.

Upon admission he was found to be in a confused and drowsy state and was unable to answer questions in a coherent manner. His coma score was 9/15 (suggestive of moderate brain injury). There were obvious contusions to his face and head (outlined below). Initial examination showed two obvious injuries to the left temple and to the right cheekbone (zygoma) with marked pain and swelling (see attached photographs). There was a laceration of approximately 6 centimetres extending across the left temple, which extended to the level of the bone of the cranium, with no obvious signs of compound fracture or leakage of the cerebrospinal fluid. These injuries were consistent with having been struck with a blunt instrument more than twice, using heavy to severe force. During the course of the next hour, whilst waiting for a skull X-ray (to exclude undetected fracture) and for repair of his laceration, his level of consciousness rapidly deteriorated (Glasgow coma score 6/15). Resuscitation was instituted – Emergency intravenous infusion commenced and intubation and hyperventilation initiated. A neurosurgical opinion and anaesthetic assistance were quickly sought. Further neurological examination revealed a fixed and dilated left pupil. Emergency X-ray revealed a depressed fracture of the left temporal/occipital bones and a fracture of the right zygomatic arch. Emergency CT scan revealed a space-

291

occupying lesion over the left cerebral hemisphere, consistent with an extra-dural haematoma of recent onset.

The patient was quickly transferred to the operating theatre where craniotomy was performed. Two small burr holes were formed over the left cranium, and the collected blood was evacuated with ease. An electrical manometer was placed and left in-situ to monitor intra-cranial pressure in the postoperative period.

Whilst under anaesthesia, the fractured right zygomatic arch was repaired by myself, using wire and clips to restore the original position.

The patient obtained a good cosmetic result following the repair of his fractured zygoma, with no facial asymmetry. He has residual surgical scars over his right cheek (5 centimetres) and left temple (7 centimetres) – see attached photos.

*Extract from the medical report on Sergeant Gheorghe Vasile, prepared by Mr Mircea Trestian, Consultant Neurosurgeon, Clujana Hospital, upon the instruction of the State Prosecution Service and the Ministry of the Interior.*

Upon admission the patient was alert and orientated and in pain, with obvious localized pain and swelling over his left eye. Following analgesia and a skull X-ray initiated by the casualty officer, an ophthalmological opinion was sought. The patient had marked oedema (swelling) and erythema (reddening) of the peri-orbital soft tissues, with reddening and haemorrhage of the entire conjunctiva (see attached photographs). There was marked loss of visual acuity in the left eye (6/36), with normal acuity in the right (6/6). Ophthalmoscopic examination showed a marked intra-ocular haemorrhage over the anterior and posterior chambers of the eye, and it was not possible to visualize the retina. These injuries were consistent with a blunt, non-penetrating injury of the eye.

Visual acuity improved slowly over the next two weeks, but there has been residual pigmented scarring of the retina, and a persistent loss of visual acuity (6/24). At six months following the injury, the patient cannot expect any further improvement in vision. The residual loss of acuity is therefore permanent and is not of the type that can be improved with corrective refractive glasses.

The patient complained of persistent memory problems from the hours immediately following his injury, but was able to give a good account of the alleged assault. He also complains of persistent psychological symptoms (low mood and reliving the assault) and I would recommend an expert opinion be sought to establish the longer-term psychological sequelae.

*Report of post-mortem examination on Mr Alistair Black.
Prepared by Dr Rajindah Bibi MD ASCPath, Consultant
Pathologist and Senior Lecturer in Pathology, Alexandru Doja
Institute, Clujana Hospital, Piata Cipariu, Cluj-Napoca.*

This report has been prepared at the request of Mr Ionel Costin,
State Coroner, Cluj-Napoca, Cluj County

**Demographic details**
Name: Mr Alistair Black
Sex: Male
DoB: 1966
Address: 24 Primley Park Garth, Leeds, United Kingdom, LS17 8TP

Date of death: 17 June 2001
Approximate time of death: 12.35 hrs
Place of death: Cluj-Napoca Central Police Station

Date of post-mortem: 18 June 2001
Time of post-mortem examination: 09.30 hrs
Place of post-mortem examination: Hospital Mortuary, Clujana
Hospital, Cluj-Napoca

Persons present at post-mortem examination: Dr Bibi
Mihai Nedezki – mortuary assistant
Sgt Bitai Karoly – coroner's officer

Authority for post-mortem: by order of State Coroner and Ministry of
the Interior following death in police custody
Identification of body: hospital tag pending identification by next of kin
(Mr Neville Black) in presence of State Coroner's officer (Sgt Karoly)

Type of post-mortem: Complete, including neuro-pathologial examination

## History

Mr Black was a fit and well man in his mid-30s with no apparent previous medical history. Evidence of a sedentary lifestyle and a positive smoking history.

Approximately four hours before death, Mr Black was allegedly attacked by an assailant and sustained a minor head injury, having been beaten about the head by a blunt instrument (a laptop-style computer).

Witnesses report that Mr Black was visibly shaken and upset by this assault, and that he complained of a headache. There are no reports of loss or impairment of consciousness in the immediate aftermath of this attack.

I understand that Mr Black was taken into police custody in the hour following the attack and had complained of a headache. The police desk sergeant reports that there were no signs of external bleeding at the time and Mr Black was taken to a cell following his reception at the police station. A request was made for the police surgeon to visit in the next six hours.

Mr Black was found to be collapsed in his cell at 12.00 hours and attempts to revive him by a sergeant with knowledge of first aid were instituted – basic CPR (cardio-respiratory resuscitation). Mr Black was transferred immediately to the Emergency Department at Clujana Hospital and was pronounced dead on arrival by Mr Mihail Festus, consultant in emergency medicine.

## Summary of findings

A fit and well 35-year-old male who died rapidly following a blow to the head, with a brief period of time elapsing between injury and death and no reported loss of consciousness. Post-mortem findings show a linear fracture of the left temporal bone of the skull and damage to the underlying middle meningeal artery and consequent extra-dural haemorrhage. Evidence of consequent herniation of the cranial contents with brain stem compression.

**Cause of death**

Respiratory arrest secondary to extra-dural haemorrhage sustained following a head injury.

**Commentary and initial conclusions**

Mr Black sustained a blow to the head of moderate force, but was unfortunate enough to suffer a fracture and immediate damage to a small blood vessel (the middle meningeal artery). The blood loss over the next few hours caused a gradual build-up of pressure within the skull. The victim would typically have complained of headache and visual disturbance, but would not have been aware of the serious nature of the developing injury.

Rising intra-cranial pressure over a period of four hours eventually resulted in herniation of the brain through the foramen magnum and pressure to be applied over the brain stem. This pressure and herniation would have caused few symptoms in the early stages, but would have eventually resulted in compression of the parts of the brain responsible for breathing.

Death would have been rapid, following a respiratory arrest and loss of consciousness. Unless the person was within a hospital and under the care of a neuro-surgeon at the time of loss of consciousness, there would have been little real prospect of survival.

*Extract from the transcript of the State preliminary inquiry into the death of Alistair Black*

Colonel Graur: Sergeant Vasile, I'm Colonel Graur, this is Lieutenant Colonel Ciceo. Thank you for coming in to speak to us today. We understand that you're still undergoing treatment for the injuries you sustained on the night of June 16th this year. As you're no doubt aware, this is an internal inquiry into the events of that night which resulted in the death of Alistair Black, a 35-year-old man from the United Kingdom.

Sergeant Vasile: Yes, sir.

Graur: We've already spoken to your fellow officers, Mlesnila and Salcudean, but we'd like you to give us as clear an account as you can of your view of the events of that night.

Vasile: Yes, sir.

Lieutenant Colonel Ciceo: You're not on trial here, Sergeant Vasile, but it is vital that we build up an accurate picture of what happened that evening. You understand this?

Vasile: Yes, sir.

Ciceo: Good. We'd like to begin by asking you to give us an account of your activities from when you boarded the train up until the beginning of the attack.

Vasile: Myself and the others, that is Mlesnila, Salcudean and Miss Kallos, had been on leave together. We'd been staying in Alba Iulia.

Ciceo: Had you been drinking?

Vasile: Yes, sir. I suppose I was celebrating. I'd just been awarded the Grand Cross. Also myself and Miss Kallos were about to announce our engagement.

Graur: How much would you say that you'd had to drink?

Vasile: I wouldn't be able to say exactly, sir.

Graur: You don't have to be spot-on. But roughly? Say . . .

Vasile: It would be hard to be definite.

Ciceo: Had you drunk more than would be normal for you, say, on an average weekend?

Vasile: No, sir, not really. We were drunk. I wouldn't say we were incapacitated.

Graur: And did you carry on drinking when you were on the train?

Vasile: We weren't on duty, sir.

Graur: I'm well aware of that fact, Sergeant Vasile. As Lieutenant Colonel Ciceo explained, we're merely trying to build a clear picture of the events running up to this man's death.

Vasile: Yes, sir. We had a bottle with us.

Ciceo: Would you say that you were being noticeably loud or raucous in any way?

Vasile: Not particularly, sir. We might have been laughing and joking.

Graur: Do you think it's possible that someone may have found your behaviour objectionable?

Vasile: We weren't threatening anyone. I accept we may have been loud, sir.

Graur: So nothing you could have been saying or doing could have caused anybody any offence?

Vasile: We weren't intending to cause anybody offence, sir. We didn't have any contact with any other people. We were just having a good time.

Ciceo: Sergeant Vasile, when you were in the train, did all your party remain together for the duration of the journey?

Vasile: Not for all of it, no, sir.

Ciceo: What caused your party to separate?

Vasile: Miss Kallos left at one point – to go and sit in the other carriage.

Ciceo: And why did she leave you?

Vasile: I think she was feeling tired, sir. Maybe a little ill.

Graur: And was there any other reason that contributed to her departure?

Vasile: Another reason besides how she was feeling?

Graur: We want you to speak as frankly as possible. As we've encouraged the others to do.

Vasile: Yes, sir. Miss Kallos sometimes reacts against Mac, I mean Mlesnila, when we're all together.

Graur: How do you mean, reacts against him?

Vasile: She finds him a bit much to take, sir. His sense of humour.

Graur: What about his sense of humour?

Vasile: She thinks he's a bit sick, sir. In poor taste.

Graur: Could there be any other reason why she left the carriage?

Vasile: Not that I'm aware, sir.

Graur: It's not possible that she would have left because she found all your behaviour in general to be objectionable?

Vasile: Miss Kallos often comes out with us. She likes being thought of as one of the boys.

Ciceo: And how did you feel about Miss Kallos leaving your company?

Vasile: Feel, sir?

Ciceo: Were you angry with her? Did you feel she'd snubbed you in some way?

Vasile: I don't remember it being a problem, sir. It didn't spoil anything.

Graur: And can you tell us what happened after this? Were you happy that your fiancée had left you to go and sit in a different carriage?

Vasile: I wasn't happy or unhappy. It wasn't a remarkable thing. She'd just gone off.

Graur: But you didn't leave her to make the rest of her journey on her own?

Vasile: After some time I wanted to go and see if she was all right.

Ciceo: All right?

Vasile: I didn't like the idea that she might think I was ignoring her - favouring the others.

Ciceo: So you went alone to find her?

Vasile: I was going to. And then when I'd got up to go, the others asked where I was going. They said they wanted to come with me.

Ciceo: Why did they do that?

Vasile: They were just being playful - messing about.

Graur: Can you tell us about what happened when you entered the carriage where Miss Kallos was? Can you remember what you saw?

300

Ciceo: What can you tell us about this man, Alistair Black?

Vasile: Sir, this is the strange thing – the thing I keep going over .... I know I was drunk, but I have a really strong memory of the carriage being empty – apart from Miss Kallos.

Ciceo: But the carriage wasn't empty. Someone was sitting in it.

Graur: We have witness statements that support this fact.

Ciceo: Can you explain why this memory should be so clear?

Vasile: Sir?

Graur: By your own admission you were quite drunk. Why should you have such a distinct memory of not seeing Mr Black?

Vasile: Because I can remember the fact – the fact that the carriage was empty – apart from Miss Kallos – influencing how we behaved.

Graur: In what way?

Vasile: I don't believe we'd have been so loud, messed about like we did, if there'd been other people there.

Graur: Is that really the case, Sergeant Vasile?

Vasile: I'm sorry, sir.

Graur: Are you quite sure that's how it seemed?

Vasile: I know how it sounds, sir, in the light of what happened. But I've returned to the memory many times, like you do with anything where you wished it hadn't happened – to see if there was a way it might have been avoided. Stupid really. I've been in the army enough to know it's a waste of time to think

301

like that. But I have this memory, sir, of making that calculation. Like a feeling of freedom that we could have some fun, sir. That's what it was, sir, I promise you. We were just . . . having fun . . . I know Miss Kallos feels the same, sir, because we've spoken about it . . . and . . .

Ciceo: So you entered the carriage and saw Miss Kallos. What happened then?

Vasile: She was sitting at the far end. She was listening to music through headphones.

Ciceo: Did she respond to you at all, when you came in?

Vasile: No, sir. It's like she was already playing the game herself, sir.

Ciceo: Playing the game?

Vasile: As if by pretending that she hadn't noticed us that she was . . . giving us the go-ahead.

Ciceo: The go-ahead to do what?

Vasile: To mess about . . . to carry on with the Lilli Gaspar thing.

Ciceo: Lilli Gaspar?

Vasile: It's just a thing. A benign thing. A game we have. Something we tease her about.

Graur: Sergeant Vasile, you said that you'd originally intended to go and check on Miss Kallos, to let her know that you weren't favouring the others over her. Now you're telling us that your intention has shifted to playing a game.

Vasile: I admit I was drunk enough to be changing my mind, or maybe to be swayed by the others.

Ciceo: And what happened next?

302

Vasile: We stopped a few seats down from her. We were trying to get a reaction out of her. That was the game.

Ciceo: So what kind of thing were you doing?

Vasile: At first we were just making a show of ourselves. Like we were an act. Like the Three Stooges. Which is what she calls us a lot of the time. Curly, Mo and the other one.

Ciceo: And how did she react to this act?

Vasile: She didn't react at all. I guess that fired us up even more.

Ciceo: So what was the next stage?

Vasile: I think Mlesnila started throwing newspaper at her. He'd found a newspaper and was rolling it into balls then throwing it at her.

Ciceo: And did this get a reaction?

Vasile: She was still deadpanning us.

Graur: And did you notice anything else go on around you, anyone coming into the carriage or leaving the carriage?

Vasile: No, sir. That's why we started singing, to see if we could make her crack. It's a game we've played before.

Graur: And what did you start singing?

Vasile: A song. A stupid song, like a child would sing. Not crude. Just childish. About Lilli Gaspar.

Ciceo: Who is Lilli Gaspar?

PAUSE

Vasile: It's like a pet name, sir. An affectionate name I have for her.

303

Graur: Did Miss Kallos react to this in any way?

Vasile: She almost went at one point, although she was still trying to pretend that we weren't there. It was when we saw that she was about to laugh that we decided to . . . decided to keep going.

Graur: And what happened after this?

NO RESPONSE

Graur: Can you remember the next thing that happened?

Vasile: I saw a shadow, sir. It appeared almost from nowhere. Covering Miss Kallos. It's really weird. I just remember thinking, where's that come from? I started to turn round . . . and then this . . . like an explosion. Falling down. I only really remember the hospital after that.

Graur: I know this is a difficult question, Sergeant Vasile, but if you'd been in that carriage yourself, as an observer, what conclusion would you have drawn, what might you have done?

NO RESPONSE

Graur: If it makes it easier, Sergeant Vasile, please think of this question as being off the record. I'm asking you merely to try and build as clear a picture in my own mind of the state of mind of the late Mr Black.

Vasile: Maybe he didn't like being disturbed. Maybe we were being loud and it made him angry. He just lost his temper. He might have thought we were louts. He was sick of louts on trains. But he must have been some kind of psycho. To take the three of us on. Maybe he wanted the ruck. I don't know, sir.

Graur: You think there was something wilful in this man's actions? That he was looking for trouble?

PAUSE

Vasile: I've known it before. People seeing soldiers off duty. Recognizing they're soldiers. Thinking, let's have a go. Psychos.

Graur: I see.

Ciceo: There is another version, isn't there?

Vasile: Sir . . .

Ciceo: It's possible to construct another version of what happened.

Vasile: I'm not sure, sir.

Ciceo: That Mr Black – a stranger in a strange land after all – misinterpreted what was going on. Misunderstood what he saw.

Vasile: Misunderstood how?

Ciceo: That he thought Miss Kallos was in some kind of danger. That he was doing his civic duty. There are witness testaments that could support this interpretation.

Vasile: I don't know, sir. Don't people have a nous for these things?

Ciceo: A nous – for what kind of things?

Vasile: I know what trouble feels like. Something nasty. There was nothing nasty in what we were doing. I don't know, sir. If he did get the wrong end of the stick, then he was bloody brave. I'll give him that. I wouldn't have been able to do it. Take on three of us. I don't know, sir. I really don't.

Graur: Sergeant Vasile, I've received your letter expressing your intention to resign from the regiment. I understand that this is because of your injury and the consequences of your injury.

Vasile: Yes, sir.

Graur: If I could make a recommendation to you, it would be to defer any decision about your career. You're a gifted and able soldier and you may feel differently with some time between you and this incident.

Vasile: With respect, sir, I've made my decision.

Graur: If that's the case then there's nothing more to say. But once again, informally, I'd like to suggest to you to let some time pass. You'd be surprised what a difference it can make.

# Chapter Twenty

Alice lay ossified on the canvas bed. Still aware. Rigid and deadened as if encased in black iron. If this had ever been just a dream, then she had forgotten that fact. The panic was indescribable.

There was a crack from above – a huge, explosive bang. Shards of wood fell on her. She wanted to move, to get out of the way, but what was left of her body would not respond. Another report from above. She could hear the dry old wood shattering. More fragments showered down. She used all her effort in order to move her head, to see what was happening. Her head barely responded. With even greater exertion, as if lifting a London bus, she swivelled her eyes. They moved fractionally.

There was light. Light was streaming into the cellar. The wooden square of a trapdoor was being kicked in. Dust was pouring onto her face. She could see shapes silhouetted against the patch of light that had been torn above her. A foot. A hand. The oval of a face. More light flooding in. She felt she was drowning in dust. She couldn't move to get out of its way.

A hand had stretched down. It reached for hers. She wanted to grab it but all her energy was gone. The hand found hers nevertheless. It pulled her. Such strength. Such vigour. The energy seemed to run into her. Flying towards the light. Through the broken trapdoor and out into the light. Such warmth. Like being a child, naked on an August afternoon.

She knew the person stood in front of her. It was the boy. That boy. He looked older now. Or maybe not older. Maybe fuller. More life about him. Alistair. Alistair Black. What a curious thing. She remembered his face. She remembered what it was like to look at his face. A spark inside her. An ember. He was still holding her hand.

She smiled at him. He smiled back. And then suddenly, without expecting it, she reached for him with both her arms and, simultaneously, he did the same. They held each other very, very tightly. As if they both knew something. As if they both knew each other, better than anyone else. Now he was holding her, she didn't want him to let her go. An action that had been interrupted a long, long time ago.

'I want you to stay with me, Alistair,' she said. 'I want you to stay with me.' They separated, standing slightly apart from each other. Alistair nodded. Then he stepped back, moving apart from her.

He was moving back into the burning light.

'Where are you going?' Now she felt bereft. This reunion was too brief. She didn't want to be alone again, or for him to be alone. She wanted to cry. But it was all right. Alistair was smiling. The last thing she saw was his smile.

She woke up. She was aware of the softness of Ben's sofa. She was definitely awake. She could feel the blanket on her wrists and forearms. But it was as if she was still in the dream. The extraordinary atmosphere of the dream. Alistair Black. Vividly she remembered feeling him close to her that night at the end of 1981. Dancing with him in the back room at Steve Raw's house. Half drunk. Looking into Alistair's face. Feeling such tenderness for this strange, beautiful boy. Far stronger than she'd felt about anyone she'd known before. I think I'd like to spend more time with him. I think I'd like to know him. I think I'd like to show myself to him. And such an attraction. A strong deep attraction. She'd wanted him to kiss her. It had been a simple feeling. Pure and powerful. This memory had been obliterated by the apocalypse that followed it. That fragile beginning had been swept away, broken by dull, lazy evil.

It had been such a simple feeling. When she'd first met Ben, it had been the same. She hadn't classified it that way at the time. Simple hadn't felt simple. It had made her uneasy.

She sat up in the sofa, allowing the blanket to fall off her. It had got a little lighter outside. The sky was visible through a crack in the curtains – a deep, lucid blue. She got out of the bed completely. She stood up, letting the blanket fall away.

Feeling the cold air on her legs she climbed the steps to his room. Up through the studio, past the painting of Jacob and the Angel, a portion of their battle caught in a shaft of pale light. Up the final set of banisterless steps which emerged through the floor at the bottom of his bed. He was stretched out, diagonally, his arms over his head. Without thinking about it she lifted the side of the duvet and slid in next to him. He was naked. His skin was hot. She pressed herself to him and found the curve of his back with her bare stomach. Ben stirred. He turned over. His dark hair covered his eyes. Sleepily he lifted his hand and brushed it away.

'Alice? Are you all right?' His voice was cracked with sleep. He reached for her. They held each other.

'I love you. My darling boy.' She breathed in his smell. Felt her heart pumping. Her mouth found his. She wanted him so much. She knew it so clearly.

This time it would be different. This time she would make a difference.

# Acknowledgements

I am grateful to the following who helped with various elements of research along the way: Jemma Rodgers, Justin Crossley, Alex Agbamu, Lucy Dibdin and Marie-Elsa Bragg. I would like to thank Simona Fulgeanu for the Romanian translations. I am indebted to Dr Simon Gilbody both in friendship and for crafting the medical reports and post-mortem at the end of the book. I would also like to thank Jan Roldanus, Steve Cook and Simon Rosenberg for reading early versions of the manuscript and Joby Talbot and Claire Burbridge for casting their eyes over a later one. Finally I would like to express gratitude to my agent Simon Trewin for his wisdom and patience and to my editor Antonia Hodgson for her faith, enthusiasm and skilful shepherding.

# NEVER TRUST A RABBIT

## Jeremy Dyson

With a new introduction by the author

In *Never Trust a Rabbit*, set throughout the world from Leeds to the Far East, we meet a flatmate born to save all mankind, an eighteenth-century automaton so beautiful that men have killed to posses her, a Cornish resort where the tide goes out, never to return, and a curious old man who discloses the dark secret of the London Underground.

Unsettling premonitions, fortune-telling cashpoints and disappearing mazes all converge in a collection of short stories that demonstrate Jeremy Dyson's formidable talents as a storyteller.

'A striking debut. His stories nestle in the little vacant chink between Roald Dahl and Borges'
*Observer*

'With the intelligent, surreal humour we might expect from a member of BBC2's *The League of Gentlemen*, *Never Trust a Rabbit* breathes new life into the drama of the ordinary urban thirtysomething, in a series of modern morality tales about enchantment in everyday life'
*The Times*

## Now you can order superb titles directly from Abacus

☐ Never Trust a Rabbit         Jeremy Dyson         £7.99

*The prices shown above are correct at time of going to press. However, the publishers reserve the right to increase prices on covers from those previously advertised, without further notice.*

──────────────── ⟨ABACUS⟩ ────────────────

Please allow for postage and packing: **Free UK delivery.**
Europe: add 25% of retail price; Rest of World: 45% of retail price.

To order any of the above or any other Abacus titles, please call our credit card orderline or fill in this coupon and send/fax it to:

**Abacus, PO Box 121, Kettering, Northants NN14 4ZQ**
Fax: 01832 733076    Tel: 01832 737527
Email: aspenhouse@FSBDial.co.uk

☐ I enclose a UK bank cheque made payable to Abacus for £ . . . . . . . .
☐ Please charge £ . . . . . . to my Visa/Delta/Maestro

| | | | | | | | | | | | | | | | | | |
|─|─|─|─|─|─|─|─|─|─|─|─|─|─|─|─|─|─|─|
| | | | | | | | | | | | | | | | | | |

Expiry Date ☐☐☐☐      Maestro Issue No. ☐☐

NAME (BLOCK LETTERS please) . . . . . . . . . . . . . . . . . . . . . . . . . . . . . . . .

ADDRESS . . . . . . . . . . . . . . . . . . . . . . . . . . . . . . . . . . . . . . . . . . . . . .

. . . . . . . . . . . . . . . . . . . . . . . . . . . . . . . . . . . . . . . . . . . . . . . . . . . . .

. . . . . . . . . . . . . . . . . . . . . . . . . . . . . . . . . . . . . . . . . . . . . . . . . . . . .

Postcode . . . . . . . . . . . . . . . Telephone . . . . . . . . . . . . . . . . . . . . . . . . .

Signature . . . . . . . . . . . . . . . . . . . . . . . . . . . . . . . . . . . . . . . . . . . . . . .

Please allow 28 days for delivery within the UK. Offer subject to price and availability.

Please do not send any further mailings from companies carefully selected by Abacus ☐